A New Leaf

Samm Wilde

Author's Note

Themes in this book include grief and loss, which may be distressing and triggering to some readers. My FMC has lost both her parents unexpectedly. Not all grief journeys are the same; everyone handles grief and loss differently. Throughout the story, my FMC is learning how to navigate her grief journey and cope with the loss of her parents. Please take care of yourself while reading. Your mental and emotional health is a top priority.

—SW

Content Warnings:

- Off-page parental deaths (car accident in the past, not described)
- Grieving process and themes of loss
- Strong language/profanity
- Descriptive sex scenes

- FMC has anxiety
- The dogs don't die

A New Leaf

SAMM WILDE

Chapter One

CHARLIE

WILL THERE EVER COME a time when I stop being tired?

Honestly, there must come a point when I won't want to just flip the sign to "Closed," crawl under this table, and sleep until I wake up in a different year.

Or a different decade.

I let out a giant yawn, shaking my head awake as I continue pruning this monstrosity of a pothos. Dark green vines trail to the floor as I begin clipping away stems slower than a grandma walking into Bingo.

Perseverance is the word of the day while I try to push through the fatigue and down my second Diet Coke before noon.

I run on three major sources of fuel: Diet Coke, social anxiety, and the optimism of retirement in thirty-something years. As the relatively new owner of A New Leaf, a quaint plant store in Hemlock, Oregon, I get to be around plants all day. Which is great. Mainly because plants don't talk, and I'm not the biggest fan of conversation.

A match made in botany.

Although plants and I have had a rocky relationship in the past, they're starting to grow on me . . . sort of.

The store has immaculate vibes, all thanks to my parents.

When customers walk in, they're instantly greeted by a jungle of lush, green, indoor houseplants. The space is airy, with white walls, wooden floors, and skylights. Colorful plant displays are set up all around the shop, showcasing various plants such as cacti, philodendrons, calatheas, and more. Plants in hanging pots cascade down from the ceiling, making it feel like you're being completely enveloped in a big, green hug.

It's a plant lover's paradise.

When my parents passed away, just under a year ago, I made the choice to move back home from Portland. This store was their baby and it only felt right to take it over in an effort to keep their memory alive. My younger sister travels too much to manage the store, and my older brother already has his own business. That left me, and my anti-social self, to take over A New Leaf.

Uprooted is the best way to describe the last year of my life. Since starting over from scratch, every day is now filled with unpredictability.

I wish life had a self-help manual. That way, whenever I hit an obstacle, I could thumb through the pages that provide guidance on how to handle said situation.

Shaking my head to myself, I regret not paying attention to that one business course I took during my undergrad. Instead, my e-reader is currently filled with books on how to run a business, soup recipes for one, and shirtless men wearing kilts.

I like what I like and I won't apologize for it.

Still clipping away at the plant before me, I fixate on how deeply I miss my mom and dad. I went from speaking to them almost daily to . . . nothing.

It feels weirdly silent.

And that's because it is.

I still don't have it in me to delete their text messages on my phone. A delusional part of me hopes they'll send me a message, even though I know that's impossible.

Since they died, there's been a constant ache in my chest that stays with me every day. This store feels like the last living, breathing piece I have left of them, and I'm determined not to let it fail. Just the thought of closing the store for good makes me physically sick to my stomach. This plant shop was them, right down to the creaky floorboards, chipped green paint, and dirt-covered countertops. People in Hemlock have such a deep love for this store. When my parents were still alive, residents and tourists alike would regularly hang around the shop every Saturday afternoon. The whole town was in mourning when word got out about their unexpected deaths.

Tears burn behind my eyes as a lump begins to grow in my throat. I quickly blink away the unshed tears and tell myself that I can cry later since I have a store to run.

There's one, eerily quiet customer in the store, and the *last* thing I need in this small town is everyone knowing I was crying.

Everyone knows it's the quiet ones you have to keep your eyes on.

Myself included.

Still laser-focused on the pothos in front of me, I hear the bell chime from above the door, and a rush of autumn leaves drifts inside with the breeze.

A booming, frantic voice fills the small space of my parent's store.

Well, I guess it's *my* store now.

"Oh my god, Charlie!" the individual screeches. It doesn't take a detective to know that the screech is coming from Mrs. Jenkins, the town busybody who can't go more than an hour without gossiping to someone about *something*.

Closing my eyes, I mumble, "Fuck me, not again," as I hear the scuffle of her too-expensive shoes reach the counter that I'm standing behind.

Her eyebrows raise. "I'm sorry, what did you say?"

I drop the pruning shears on the wooden counter and wipe my hands on my apron, "Oh, I said duck confit is for dinner again. Anywho, how can I help you?" I place my hands on the counter and give her my best, phony, customer service smile.

Her eyes narrow. "That's an interesting meal choice."

"Well, what can I say? I'm an interesting woman," I reply, my tone dripping with sarcasm.

"Right. Well, Charlie, I was hoping you could help me with something." As she speaks, I glance down at my comically lazy golden retriever. Vera, the dog I also inherited from my parents, perks her head up, gives a dramatic groan, and promptly falls back asleep—doing what I only wish I could do right now. Inspired by Vera, I make the mistake of letting out another slow yawn.

"—and I was hoping you could show him around," Mrs. Jenkins finishes, staring blankly at me. "You weren't paying attention to anything I was saying, were you?"

My tired eyes glance back over to her. I give a sheepish smile and slowly shake my head. "No. I wasn't."

Mrs. Jenkins gives me her famous disappointed sigh.

And I couldn't care less if I tried.

Since my parents died, the people in town have gone easier on me and my Oscar the Grouch attitude. Granted, I've always been a little curmudgeonly, but my crankiness really escalated after they died because of all the added responsibilities. Even though I'm a grown, thirty-four-year-old adult woman, I'll always need my parents. And having them missing from my and my siblings' lives is a wound that I don't believe will ever heal.

Mrs. Jenkins clears her throat. "As I was saying, my nephew is new to town and is opening a coffee shop down the road." Her tone is a touch too happy and exuberant this early in the day. "I was hoping you could show him around town since I'm leaving on vacation," she finishes. Mrs. Jenkins looks at me with such optimism, and all I can do is stare back at her with my brows furrowed.

She's stumbling over her words now. "It's just . . . you seem like you could use a friend."

I don't need one.

She's still rambling. "You've been holed up in this shop with your dog forever!"

That's how I like it.

Vera's head perks up again, giving Mrs. Jenkins the side eye while making a loud, disapproving groan that turns a nearby customer's head. Sometimes, I truly believe this dog is a sassy old lady reincarnated.

Closing my eyes in frustration, I pinch my eyebrows together and give a weighty sigh. "Isn't there anyone else available to help? I have a lot on my plate right now, as you can see." Mrs. Jenkins looks around my store with only one customer, then glances over at the drooping pothos in front of me, and finally down at Vera. The dog groans again and immediately flops down, having zero capacity for this nonsense. Mrs. Jenkins slowly locks eyes with me, giving me a quizzical look.

I'm a people pleaser to my core, and even though I dislike 92 percent of the population, saying "no" to anyone is still difficult for me. I'd rather not spend the next few weeks helping some random man. He's got a phone, which has a map, which presumably can show him around. I'm sure he's a big boy and can figure it out.

With a slow shake of her head, she says, "No, hun, I've asked, and everyone else has said no." Mrs. Jenkins and I have a brief stare-down until I notice her lips start to twitch in an unsettling way that makes everyone in town feel uneasy.

She knows my people-pleasing weakness. If I had a dollar for every time I said yes to a favor, I'd finally be retired on a beach somewhere, drinking margaritas while watching shirtless men play volleyball.

Looking up at the ceiling, I let out a groan so loud that the lone customer jolts with surprise and hastily leaves. My head drops to see Mrs. Jenkins looking at me with such hopefulness, while I'm giving her a blank stare.

The exasperation is heavy when I'm the first to give in. "Fine." I throw my hands up. "But I won't be charming or nice. I'm getting in there, doing the mission, and getting out quickly." My finger is now pointed directly at her.

Better to be honest than to set false expectations.

"I wouldn't expect anything else, dear," she says before promptly turning to leave.

"Good-almost-afternoon, my grumpy little Gremlin!" sings my coworker Marnie, my only employee at the store. Extroverted to the heavens, covered in tattoos with long, jet-black hair, and fierce as they come—she's a force to be reckoned with. She usually comes in to work a bit later since she teaches art classes at the community center some evenings and needs the mornings to prep.

"I thought I fired you this week?" I say without looking up from my laptop at the counter. I'm researching common houseplant pests and am quickly regretting it. Photos of these tiny bugs are making me itch.

"You did. Three times, actually! And it's only Tuesday. Quite impressive if you ask me." She shrugs, inspecting a few plants.

I let out a small laugh, shaking my head. You know how there's always an extrovert who adopts an introvert by accident? That's Marnie and I. She saw me, sunk her talons in, and we've been stuck together ever since. I close my laptop, shove it under the counter, and rub my tired eyes.

"I saw Mrs. Jenkins prowling around out there. She didn't stop by, did she?" Marnie asks, eyeing me suspiciously as she puts her apron on.

Letting out a sigh that radiates deep in my chest, I round the corner of the counter with a spray bottle in hand to begin misting some of the tropical plants. "Unfortunately, yes. She wants me to show her nephew around Hemlock," I reply, mildly irritated.

"Is that a euphemism for something?" she says, wiggling her eyebrows.

I'm definitely ignoring that comment.

"Apparently, he bought the building a couple of doors down and is opening a coffee shop there. Did you even know that building was for sale?" I ask, misting a monster of a Monstera. They don't name them "monsters" because they're tiny. I'm waiting for the day that it takes over the entire store and swallows me whole. Which, at this point, sounds like a dream.

Marnie walks behind me, organizing the succulent table. She glances over at me from the corner of her eye. "Yes, I did, because unlike you, I pay attention to my surroundings. The world could end, and you'd be too hyper-focused on a new plant fertilizer or propagation technique to notice."

I stop what I'm doing and look at her. "Okay, first of all, you're fired." She nods knowingly. "And second, it's been almost nine months since I took over the shop, and I still have no clue what I'm doing." A thought about my situation hits me. "Then again, maybe this guy has useful insights on running a small business, since he's opening one here." I sigh wearily. "I was a software engineer. Programming? Easy. Designing distributed systems? A breeze. Keeping overgrown weeds alive? I'm clueless."

Marnie chuckles, adjusting her glasses on her nose. "Fair point. But, you could look up and around sometimes. I'm sure you can only read so much about . . . prop—whatever that word is." She waves her hand.

Setting one hand on my hip, I point the spray bottle I'm holding at her. "Propagation. And, listen, one day, knowing the difference between soil and water propagation will come in handy." I pause, getting an idea. "Oh! Maybe you could tell your next date about propagation? But you have to get the word right first." I shrug nonchalantly, continuing to mist the plants.

Marnie hums. "Yes, because nothing says 'take me to bed and rearrange my insides' like walking a man through the finer points of plant propagation." She dreamily sighs. "You know, I do have some seeds that could use fertilizing."

The water bottle almost slips from my grasp as I look at her in disbelief.

Marnie waves her hand, dismissing me. "Hush. Don't get your overalls in a twist. Also, you didn't explain why Mrs. Jenkins wants you to hang out with her nephew?"

"Well, she's going out of town when he's opening his café. I guess she needs someone to be a 'friendly face' for him. Or emotional support. Neither of which I'm great at, as you already know." I set the mister down and grab a cloth to wipe down some of the larger leaves of this plant.

Her head tips back with a laugh. "Oh, I know. Remember that time I came crying to you because that guy I was dating in our math class was flirting with the TA, and you told me to 'grow a pair of ovaries and get the fuck over him.' Ruthless."

There's nothing wrong with tough love.

Especially when it comes to steering your best friend away from mediocre men.

"Let me guess, you felt too awkward to say no to her face because she does that weird lip thing that makes you uncomfortable?" Marnie snickers. "You know, it never ceases to amaze me how someone so crotchety like you can be so nice and accommodating."

"Oh fuck off. But yes . . . I could see the beginnings of that weird lip thing when I zoned out." I shiver. That lip thing she does is so disconcerting.

"Ahh, my people-pleasing, petulant little Gremlin is getting a new friend! How sweet." She claps. "Do we know how old he is? Is he hot? Is he single? What's his zodiac sign? Can I ask him to fertilize my seeds?" she says too excitedly, wiggling her eyebrows once again.

I groan, refusing to make eye contact with her as I wipe down more leaves. "You know I'm bad at asking follow-up questions."

"Yes, I do know. That's how you ended up in city jail that one time and your dad had to bail you out. Your dad *literally* went to the grave with that secret because he refused to tell your mom for the sake of her blood pressure." She chuckles.

My chest tightens at the mention of my parents. My dad and I had a special bond—an unspoken bond, I'd like to think —where we said so much in comfortable silence, and knew exactly what each other was thinking with just a simple look. Thinking back to that time when I was in our tiny town's jail (it was for only two hours), my dad may or may not have given the deputy a couple of hundred dollar bills to keep his mouth shut—which is also illegal, right?

I shake off the memory and look back at Marnie. "Either way, I'm helping this dude and then ignoring his existence. This is my one and only good deed for the year. No more." My tone is unconvincingly assertive.

Marnie erupts in laughter, tapping my head gently as she says, "You keep telling yourself that, Gremlin."

Chapter Two

FINN

"FRANK! FRANK NO—"

THUD.

My shoes pound the pavement as I run to rescue my dog.

Poor guy, he ran into the door . . . again.

Frank is my three year-old, blind, Australian Shepherd. He's an incredibly good-looking dog, but he's unfortunately a bit obtuse. Sometimes, I wonder how a dog like him evolved from his wolf ancestors because in no universe could he survive on his own.

Frank shakes off the collision as if nothing happened. Trotting over to me with his tongue flopping out, I crouch down to give his soft head a reassuring scratch. "Bud, we've talked about this before. Some of your parts aren't working properly, and you have to be more careful."

Obviously, he can't talk back, but his eyebrows pull together in the classic, puppy dog look.

This dog lays the guilt on thick whenever he runs into doors, knocks over tables, or steals something he's not supposed to.

Frank's nose twitches as he sniffs the air at my closeness to him, and his fluffy ears are pinned back to his head like he did something wrong. I'll be the first to admit that Frank's recall is not great. The dog just refuses to listen. I was worried he might be deaf, so I took him to the vet—but they said his ears were in pristine condition. Their exact words were that he suffers from *selective hearing.*

Don't we all suffer from that?

After securing Frank's leash, I rise to my feet, adjust my glasses, and turn toward my new shop. Settling my hands on my hips as I approach the charming, old brick building, memories flood my mind.

Just a few short months ago, my life looked vastly different.

I was living in New York, working on Wall Street, slowly climbing the corporate ladder one step at a time, and completely unhappy with my life. At thirty-five years old, it felt as though all my friends and colleagues had their lives together, whereas I was adrift. From changing jobs to living in new cities, I've always felt unsettled, with nothing to ground me.

I felt restless.

Even though I was surrounded by thousands of friendly faces and exciting opportunities, I still felt that something was missing from my life. I felt lonely. Physically, I knew I wasn't alone. But mentally? That's where I felt the loneliness the most.

There was an ever-present heaviness residing in my chest, and no amount of travel, job changes, or fleeting relationships could reduce that feeling. Which led me to really reflect on where I wanted my future to be and, more importantly, *who* I wanted to be.

They call it a third-life crisis.

First, you have your quarter-life crisis, when, in your twenties, you're worried about where you'll go in life.

Then there's the infamous midlife crisis, when, in your fifties, you look back and reflect on what you've done with your life.

In the middle of those two? You're in your thirties—a time when you begin to wonder what the fuck you're *actually doing* with your life.

Society tells you that your thirties should be your prime.

Society can keep their opinions to themselves.

That self-discovery led me here, in front of an almost-finished coffee shop. For years, I've wanted to own my own business, but I never had the courage to take the leap. And there's always been a small flicker of a dream of owning a coffee shop—a relaxing place where people can come to enjoy great company and even better coffee.

One day, I started pulling on that thread of an idea, and soon, that idea kept unraveling day after day. During my time at my finance job, I found myself using company time to put together a plan.

After hours of assessing my finances, many late-night spreadsheets, and countless business strategies later, I decided to take the plunge. I'd had enough of being unhappy and burnt out while working for someone else.

It feels weird starting over at this age—a little uncomfortable and a lot terrifying. You think that you'll have it all figured out once you're in your thirties. In reality, you're just putting on a mask every day, making people believe you have your shit together.

I close my eyes as a sharp pang of worry hits me in my chest. Friends around me are settling down with successful careers and beautiful families, and a part of me feels like I'm getting left behind and can't catch up.

Uncertainties run through my mind at a rapid pace. Should I be married by now? Maybe on kid number two? Should I be a CFO somewhere? Or a fancy supervisor? Was it irresponsible of me to quit my old job and start all over again? Will people think I'm being reckless and impulsive? My family and friends were the most supportive of my decision. They could see the dark circles under my eyes, hear the fatigue in my voice, and feel the exhaustion almost three thousand miles away.

Deep down, I knew this was the right choice because life is way too short to feel unfulfilled all the time. But even though I know in my heart I made the right choice, those thoughts full of doubt creep into the back of my mind every so often.

The daily grind of my old job was knocking me down faster than I could get up. Toxic leadership, unethical workplace practices, and gossipy coworkers had me wanting to quit daily. I would come home, look in the mirror, and see a shell of a man. Burnout was a constant feeling that I could never seem to beat. After one heated meeting with my boss about ethics, I hit my breaking point. I decided I was done.

It was time to put myself and my passions first.

And I *may* have given them the finger when I walked out on my last day. So there was no going back.

My heart was craving a new challenge and, ultimately, a purpose. Because isn't that what we all want in life? A feeling of purpose? Whether that purpose is to help others, care for the environment, or save animals. Whatever your dreams may be, there will always be a small part of all of us who want to make a big difference in this world.

Now, I'm standing on the sidewalk in front of Dark Side Brews, in an unfamiliar town. It sounds edgier than it is, considering that a Star Wars-loving, glasses-wearing, former finance geek is running the place.

Oregon is my home state, and I figured opening a business in a place I'm most familiar with was a solid plan. So I did what any wannabe business owner would do—I printed out a map of Oregon and threw a dart at it one night after a couple of beers. Wherever it landed, I had to open the shop. Thus, Hemlock was chosen.

Foolproof business move if you ask me.

I'm absolutely positive that the business moguls will soon be lining up at my door to discuss this carefully executed location scouting strategy in more detail.

Maybe I'm just getting older, but the big cities and millions of people were grating on me, so I was happy to have landed in this small coastal town, waking up every morning to the fresh sea breeze coming off of the Pacific. My parents were overjoyed when they heard I was coming back to Oregon. They were quickly let down when I said I was moving to Hemlock, since they live a couple hours away in Eugene. Still, it's the perfect distance for me to make it home for Sunday dinner.

In a stroke of wild good luck, I bought a small house in a neighborhood just off Main Street. And it has a fenced-in backyard, which is perfect for Frank.

Apartment living in NYC is a nightmare for a blind dog, so I'm grateful he has a nice, safe space that he feels comfortable in. Despite the panicked thoughts that crossed my mind earlier, I can't ignore the sense of relief that has washed over me since moving to Hemlock—like I can finally take a full breath of air after being underwater for so long.

Looking around the town, it's easy to see why Hemlock is every small town lover's dream. It's got one road, lined with old brick buildings, dark cobblestone sidewalks, lush trees wrapped in twinkling lights, vintage lamp posts, and friendly faces at every corner.

It's also coincidentally where my crazy aunt now lives with her new husband. *I think she's on husband number four now?* I lost track about three wedding invitations ago.

I can confidently say that I never imagined living in a town with a slower pace. Especially since I'm used to the hustle and bustle of the big city, where everyone is always in a hurry. People even walk slower here, and with my above average long legs, I'll need to practice my stride so that I don't look like I'm sprinting to the finish line while doing my grocery shopping.

The cool autumn breeze rustles a few leaves on the sidewalk, which Frank attempts to chase, and for a moment, I briefly lose sight of him.

It's the end of September and Hemlock got a head start on setting up Halloween decorations. Main Street is filled with decor in front of almost every shop. The building next to mine is a Halloween emporium, complete with cobwebs, skeletons, and spiders all over its facade. I whistle for Frank as I'm about to head into my shop, and I look down to see my dog, who finally comes back to my side.

The damn dog has a skeleton arm in his mouth. Glancing over to the neighboring store, I notice that the life-size skeleton standing near the door appears to be missing a limb. I swipe my hand down my face, and start to chuckle. Along with being blind and having selective hearing, Frank loves to steal things because he thinks no one can see him. He's just standing there, wagging his nub of a tail like he did the best job ever.

Little does he know, *everyone* can see him.

Out of the corner of my eye, I notice a curvy brunette a couple stores down from me rearranging a sign in the front of a store. Her long, dark hair is pulled back as she concentrates writing on the chalkboard. After she's finished, she stands up and takes a couple of steps back. Her head tilts as she reads the sign and nods to herself, seemingly impressed with her work. A smile tugs at my lips. She appears to be in her own world, completely oblivious to everyone and everything around her.

The pretty brunette slips the chalk into the front pocket of her burgundy overalls before wiping her chalk-dusted hands on her pant legs. I let out a small chuckle to myself—she's cute with her magnetic mannerisms and chalk-covered clothes. As if she senses someone staring, she looks up and our eyes lock. I give a small smile and wave to her. Overalls girl knits her brows together, scowls at me, and swiftly walks back inside the store.

Well, that was a nice, warm welcome.

Shaking off the awkward interaction, I unlock the door to my shop, and Frank heads right in as I follow. I'd done some minor renovations to the building to make it more my style. Brick walls, exposed ceilings, and pendant lights give the space an industrial yet warm atmosphere. Pair that with dark hardwood flooring, a large gallery wall to the right of the front door, an open counter with leather bar stools to the left, and mismatched furniture—the space feels like an elevated version of a cozy night in. I want my customers to feel relaxed in this space, like it's their home away from home. A place where they can enjoy a coffee, maybe a pastry, and just take a breather.

Because Frank and I are a package deal, I was very particular about the layout of my coffee shop. Blind dogs are special edition pups and need some extra love and care. Before Frank ever set a paw into this place, I placed scent markers on pieces of furniture throughout the shop, which is helpful because it trains Frank to identify any obstacles before he runs into them. It allows him to navigate the café using his other senses, ultimately reducing any problems he may encounter. However, no plan is foolproof, and my sweet boy still runs headfirst into a stool as soon as he enters the building.

I blow out a breath. He's a handsome devil with a smooth brain.

Rubbing my hand against the smooth, wooden counter, I realize that the interaction with the overalls girl reminded me that I'm truly alone here. The unfortunate part of moving to a new city is not knowing anyone. The only person I do know is crazy Aunt Donna, and the woman has a reputation here that I'd rather not be associated with. She has a way of inserting herself into everyone's business and persuading people to do ridiculous tasks for her.

One summer, when I was seventeen, she even convinced me to attend her book club. And now, I have three boxes of historical romance books with half-naked men on the cover in my attic. There's no way in hell I can show my face at a local library and donate them. So, for now, they stay hidden.

Sitting at the coffee counter, I run a hand through my hair. I love my family, but I also need breathing room, and I'm hoping that Donna won't muddle in my business too much. However, my aunt has already mentioned that a local guy could help me during my first month here while she was off on a cruise with her husband. She gave me his number and told me his name was Charlie. I'll probably send him a quick text over the weekend, since it can't hurt to know at least one other person in town. According to Donna, this guy is a bit unique, with only one friend and a dog. She also mentioned something about them and plants. Maybe he's a gardener? Who knows.

Either way, I'm looking forward to meeting the guy. One of the reasons I wanted to open a coffee shop is that I enjoy the opportunity for socializing. I hope to develop relationships, hear people's stories, learn about the small town community, and bring people together in the name of coffee—something that will keep this dream alive for me.

I've spent too many years hiding behind computer screens and buried in paperwork. Now it's my turn to go after what I want.

Chapter Three

Charlie

THERE IS ABSOLUTELY nothing I despise more than socializing and developing relationships. Even though I conversed regularly with people at my previous job, it doesn't mean that I was necessarily good at it. The stereotype of engineers being awkward does have some truth to it, and I'm living proof. I've perfected the fake laugh, the faux smile, and the feigned pleasantries. Basically, I have enough tricks up my sleeve to ensure that I don't come off as a rabid, snarling, wiener dog to customers.

I'm content with the circle of people in my life. I have my lovingly-annoying siblings, my lazy dog, and my unhinged Marnie. What more could I want? Nurturing meaningful relationships to enrich my life?

That's not me.

My fingers are white-knuckling the wedding invitation that arrived in the mail today. In this town, people love to invite everyone to their weddings. And since I've moved back to Hemlock, I'm officially on every wedding guest list.

Kill. Me. Now.

Deep down, like most introverts, I don't want to go. Everyone will want to talk to me—it's like I have a magnet on me at all times that attracts all the social butterflies. I know that after three martinis, feral Susan will need "help" walking by the town's hunky pharmacist, creepy Dale will try to touch my ass, and melodramatic Mark will rip his shirt off during an intense lip syncing session.

It'll be like the town's annual Christmas party, except with fancier clothes, more alcohol, and fewer inhibitions.

My own personal hell.

Slumping down in my worn leather chair, I have a million questions running through my mind about the December wedding invitation. What am I going to wear? Where will I park? How many pieces of cake is it socially acceptable to eat? Do I have to wear heels? A plus one is strictly out of the question after the two mediocre relationships in my life. One didn't work out because I was too cranky and anti-social, and I broke up with another guy because he ate his cheeseburgers with a knife and fork. Other than that, I've been on a handful of failed dates that have only confirmed the fact that I'd rather be happily single than miserably coupled.

A cheer interrupts my thoughts. "Oh my god, this is PERFECT!" I hear Marnie yell and clap at the same time. There's a brief silence before I hear muffled, furious voices coming from the front of the store. With a groan, I stuff the invite into my office desk drawer and take a few deep breaths before I go to mediate the situation out front.

Typically, I try to minimize my interactions with

customers. I answer questions, smile, and hurriedly send them on their way.

Sometimes, Marnie has other plans, including, but not limited to, pissing off customers.

"Where is your manager? I want to speak to them NOW!" a new voice booms. Reluctantly leaving the back office, I navigate through the indoor forest that is my store, scuffling my feet loudly to get to the voices. I stop and look at our new display of succulents and tiny cacti, with a chalkboard sign saying, *"Fucc-you-lents—Was your ex a prick? Grab one of these fellas and tell them to succ it!"*

Huh. That's pretty clever and creative.

Marnie sees me and bites a smile back. She makes a big gesture by opening her arms upon my arrival. "Oh, here's the manager of our store! Charlie, this woman has some concerns about our new display. I think it's perfect; she thinks it's inappropriate. We were hoping you could help resolve this little conflict." Marnie clasps her hands together in front of her, rocking back and forth on her heels.

I take an exasperated breath, stuff my hands into my apron's pocket, and kick out one hip with annoyance. I don't get paid enough for this shit, and I'm the one that sets my own wages. Every muscle in my face tenses, and my eyebrows pinch together, producing a single, unimpressed vertical wrinkle between them. Before I can get a single word out, the customer, a woman who clearly has too much time on her hands, begins babbling.

"I don't think this sign is appropriate. What if young eyes see it? Especially in a professional place of business. Now, I implore you to take that sign down and create a new one right this instant. It's so unpalatable! I want to see you make a new sign. Right. Now!" she screeches.

Marnie slowly spins to me with wide eyes and a slack jaw. She knows I don't take orders very well.

Will I lose a customer today? Yes.

Will I regret it? No.

Will my business receive a bad review online? Oh yeah.

My mom and dad would've taken the "kill them with kindness" approach—which I respect. But I'm in my thirties, with a lot of rage, and I'm too tired for this bullshit.

Relaxing the tension in my face, I take a steadying breath. "One, no one said this business was professional. Two, thank you for reminding me to put a *Parental Advisory* sign on the storefront," I answer, my tone thick with sarcasm. "And three, if you're so offended by this sign, then I *implore you* to leave. No one asked you to come in here, and certainly, no one asked for your opinion on how I run my business. Comments? Questions? Concerns?" The woman stands there, mouth gaping like a fish. Before she says anything, I end my monologue by answering for her. "No? Didn't think so. Good. Now leave."

She stands there, wide-eyed and unmoving, so I do what I do best—I stare and blink at her, like one of those creepy, haunted dolls. Out of the corner of my eye, I see Marnie's eyes dart back and forth between us, waiting for the customer to make the next move.

The customer scoffs. "Well, if that's how you feel, I'm going to write a review online about what a deplorable business you run!"

Christ. Does this woman consume SAT words every morning for breakfast? Rubbing my fingers on my temples, I start walking to the front door, hoping she'll follow. Spinning around to face her, I give her a pointed glare and reply, "By all means, if writing a bad review about a silly sign will help you get a good sleep tonight, then please do. Be sure to add a few of those ten-dollar words you love to use in your *contemptuous* review of our *deplorable* business." I smile as I open the door. The chime of the bell echoes through the store and I wave my hand, motioning for her to exit.

She walks through the door before making a disgruntled sound and leaves. The woman takes a few steps onto the sidewalk and slowly turns her body to me. Despite her attempt to speak, I cut her off in a second. "You aren't winning this game, ma'am. Collect your losses and leave." Defeat washes over her face as she spins around in her too-expensive heels and finally walks away.

"I need some sage to cleanse the store after that encounter," I tell Marnie, readjusting my apron.

"I actually think your parents have some in here somewhere," she muses.

The smallest laugh escapes through my nose. "Of course they did. That's just like them."

My parents prided themselves on owning a "good vibes" store, which I guess included sage.

When Marnie heads to the back to look for the sage, my eyes fixate on the custom sign that my parents had made and which now sits on the back wall behind the shop's counter.

Plants Thrive with Good Vibes

EXHAUSTION HITS me after the long day I've had. Between the customer from hell, the wedding invitation, and a crowd of kids knocking over one of my displays, I need to decompress.

I usually stay late at the store to bask in the calm and clean up—it gives me a chance to unwind from the day's events, so I can head home with a clear mind and enjoy cake for dinner.

Since I've been here for a few hours after closing time, the streetlights have turned on, casting an eerie glow over the street. I kick open the front door to get some cool, fresh autumn air in the store. Inhaling deeply, it smells like it's about to rain as a light breeze fans over my face. Sadly, my moment enjoying the outdoors is cut short by my phone ringing.

I kick the rubber door stopper at the bottom of the door and walk to the back of the shop. Just as my phone stops ringing, a message pops up on the screen. Shaking my head, I look down at the text from my sister.

JOEY

Sorry! I needed to know what temperature to cook chicken at.

NEVER MIND! Figured it out.

I love my siblings. I really do. But they text me some of the silliest shit. Releasing a weary groan, I place my phone in my apron pocket and make my way back to the front. As I grab my broom, a large crash and a whimper stop me in my tracks. Thinking Vera got hurt, I immediately look around for her, only to find that she's sound asleep behind the cash register.

Again.

This dog. Sometimes, I have to check to make sure she's breathing.

With another shake of my head, I glance around the store, and spot my rookie mistake.

I left the front door wide open. "What a nice night to be murdered," I mutter to myself.

Naturally, as any perpetually anxious, single female, alone at night in a store would do, I grab my "intruder golf club" that I keep in the back. Some people have bats, some have tasers, hell, I know someone who has a sword in their store. However, I have a golf club—a nice, hefty 5-iron. It's got a good grip and a long shaft.

I never realized how erotic golf was as a sport.

Pushing the random thought aside, I grip the club tight in my hand. At a careful, slow pace, I begin walking to the front of the store. My head whips around, peering around every frilly fern, prickly cactus, and vining philodendron in an attempt to spot the whimpering intruder.

A whimpering intruder. What a weakling.

After combing over every corner of the store, I find no one and drop my club. As I walk towards the front door to close it, my foot comes down on something. A piercing yelp screeching in my ears.

I look down and see a sheepish dog whose paw I accidentally stepped on.

"Oh my god, I'm so sorry! Are you okay?" I crouch down, cradling this pup's furry face in my hands. "Wait. Where the hell did you come from? Why are you here? Where is your owner? Do you even have an owner?" I stop, wondering if the universe dropped this dog in my lap for a reason. "I don't know if I'm ready to be a single mom to two kids. I can barely handle one." Continuing to stroke the dog's face with my thumbs, I take a closer look at the unlikely intruder.

He's a cute Australian Shepherd with the fluffiest ears and the bluest eyes. His long coat is multicolored with black, brown, and white, and has added specks of green from a few leaves hanging out of his mouth and ears. I pull out the stray leaves from his coat and make sure he isn't injured by checking his paws.

Vera, my reliable guard dog, finally comes around the

corner to see what the fuss is about. Her big stretch is accompanied by a yawn. I guess we're being an inconvenience to her nap time. Furrowing my brows, I look over at her. "*So* sorry to wake you up, princess."

A deep sigh escapes from my lungs. How I ended up here, talking to two dogs who don't understand what I'm saying, is a mystery to me. "Maybe I should listen to Marnie and get out more since I'm talking to dogs as if I'm Snow White," I mutter to myself. When I stop the one-sided conversation, I realize how ridiculous I must sound, especially if anyone is listening. "I also need to stop talking to myself aloud or else people will think I've totally lost it." I continue petting the sweet dog until he finally calms down. "There you go, big guy. It's all going to be okay," I say softly.

A deep, velvety voice interrupts the quiet moment between this dog and me.

"Interrupting your own conversations is considered insane. However, talking to yourself is perfectly normal," the voice says, chuckling. "In fact, it's actually encouraged since it helps increase emotional regulation."

Fantastic. Now, there's an *actual* intruder.

With a quick glance at Vera, my suspicions are confirmed about what type of dog she is. She's happily wagging her tail at the person in my store.

I look at her, dumbfounded, and whisper, "You're going to get us both killed!"

"I heard that," the deep voice replies, clearly amused. "I'm not going to kill you. In fact, I actually don't think I would survive prison. I know my limits."

"That's what they all say!" I screech, hiding behind one of the plant displays, desperately searching for that golf club. When my eyes find the club, I rapidly snatch it off the ground.

Between the hanging plants, I see a tall, lean, human silhouette standing near the door. The store is dim, casting shadows all over this person. I can't make out any describable features, but this person is freakishly tall. Tall enough that I'll probably have to tilt my head all the way back if I want to get a better look at him.

Gumby—that's what I'm now calling him—slowly walks towards me with his hands up in a gesture of surrender. However, everyone is deemed a threat until proven otherwise.

"If you don't back the fuck up now, Gumby, I will break your kneecaps!" I yell. But there's not a single ounce of confidence in my voice to back up that threat.

The man's shoulders shake as I hear him laugh. "Gumby? That's a new one. What's your handicap, by the way?" He motions to the club in my hand. "You'd have better luck with a putter fighting off an intruder. It has a little more weight at the bottom, for force."

This man is just full of random information. I didn't know criminals could double as encyclopedias.

The balls on this guy though. Gumby is spewing fun facts while I have one scared dog who ran into a plant display, and another dog who has an affinity for possible killers.

Great.

I keep backing up until I hit the counter, and he keeps inching forward. Finally, this overconfident man walks into the light, and I stop dead in my tracks, completely forgetting about my golf club as it crashes to the floor.

Chapter Four

Finn

"Ugh." Flopping into my office chair in the backroom of the shop, I tip my head back and blow out an exhausted breath. It's been a ridiculously long day. I've been here since dawn and now night has fallen.

Everything hurts. My body. My mind. My soul.

Even a bit of my ego.

All of it hurts.

After taking my glasses off and setting them aside, I press my palms into my eyes, hoping to relieve the tension headache that's been building for the last week.

These last few days preparing for the opening have been relentlessly brutal. Being a one-man show and opening this coffee shop has kicked my ass. And, because I love self-destruction, I keep forging ahead like I know exactly what I'm doing.

Me? Struggling? Never.

My parents called last night, asking if I needed their help with anything. They said they'd be more than happy to drive down and stay for a few days to help with the opening next week. Being the stubborn man that I am, I said, "It's fine! I have everything under control. I know exactly what I'm doing over here!"

I have no fucking clue what I'm doing.

Then again, does anyone really know what they're doing? I don't trust people who have their lives all figured out. Those are the people you have to watch out for.

Every morning since I decided to open a business, my breakfast has consisted of two ibuprofen, a shot of espresso, and a silent prayer to the universe that I won't spontaneously combust. Although working for myself is exhausting, it's also freeing.

My phone buzzes in my pocket and I see that it's my younger sister on FaceTime. Ellie recently moved to Hawaii with her husband, Evan, who's in the Navy, and their newborn.

"Hey, Finnster!" she says with a beaming smile. Her excitement is infectious.

Ellie is holding my nephew, Owen, in the crook of her arm. He's sleeping so peacefully and looks so content that my heart brims with happiness. The sun hasn't set yet over there, casting a warm evening glow over the two of them.

"Ellie! And baby Owen! How are you guys? How's Evan?"

"We're doing great." She smiles, her face sunburnt, making her cheeks rosier than usual. "Owen is finally sleeping through the night. Evan is working his ass off as usual, but he's doing great as well."

I smile. "Good, good. But how are *you* doing?" I pointedly ask, raising one eyebrow at her.

A soft smile spreads across her face. "I'm doing a lot better. I think I finally found a routine for me and Owen, and I'm really getting to know our new neighborhood. Plus, I don't need GPS to get around anymore!"

"See, now that you said that, you'll need the GPS tomorrow," I say, laughing. "You've always been exceptionally horrible with directions."

Her unamused stare pierces through me from the screen. "First, fuck off. Second, I'm a landmark person. Tell me what corner the nearest McDonald's is on and I'll be there in no time. But tell me to get off at exit thirty-seven? No. I don't know what that means."

I roll my eyes, chuckling at her.

"Anywho," she continues. "How's the coffee shop? I'm so glad you got out of your old job." Her face drops the slightest bit. "That corporate world was sucking the life out of you."

I'm a guy who doesn't hide his emotions—a quality I appreciate about myself. I fearlessly expose my heart for the world to see, embracing my vulnerabilities. So, it was obvious to everyone that my life in New York had been wearing me down to the point of complete exhaustion.

Owen's cooing interrupts my thoughts as Ellie glances at him with a gentle smile. A warm swell of joy settles in my chest at the sight of their bond.

"It's going pretty good. There's still a lot to do before I open in a few days. I just hired a couple of employees, actually. They seem promising, so I'm cautiously optimistic," I answer.

"Oh, good! That's amazing to hear. I can't wait to come back and visit when you've officially opened!" Owen begins to stir and fuss. "Shit. Sorry, Finn, I have to cut this call short. I'll call tomorrow?"

I smile. "Of course, of course. Have a good night, and tell Evan I said hi."

"You got it! Night, Finnster."

Relief floods through me when I hear how much better she's doing. Ellie's move to Hawaii took a toll on her in the beginning, especially since she was so far away from home. Anytime she called, morning or night, I would pick up her call. During her husband's deployment, I would stay on the phone with her during those quiet nights, just so she wouldn't feel so alone.

I slump back in my chair, blowing out a breath. It's just Frank and I in my quiet, empty coffee shop. My sister looks so happy with her family and her life in Hawaii; I can't help but feel a pang of jealousy. Will I ever have that? All her life, she's always known exactly what she's wanted. A steady career by twenty-six? Done. A doting husband by twenty-eight? Secured. Have a child by thirty? No problem. Ellie had a plan, and she stuck to it.

The same can't be said for me.

Still, I can't help but feel the nagging pull at the back of my mind that tells me I'm running behind. Logically, I know that life isn't an hourglass; there are no judgmental grains of sand scolding you for not checking off each life milestone.

Yet, I still feel the proverbial weight on my chest—the societal pressure of being in my thirties, without a wife or kids, and starting a completely new career.

I was able to find my way once.

Now? I'm on a mission to find it again.

Running my hands through my hair in frustration, I think

I'm officially calling it a night. The sun has completely set, and my deep exhaustion is about to take me down. Between training new hires, checking inventory, managing finances, and talking to suppliers—I'm ready to turn my mind off. All I want to do is fall into bed with a good fantasy book until sleep takes over.

I whistle for Frank, but he doesn't come.

Huh. That's weird.

I whistle again, but don't hear the pitter-pattering of his paws on the floor. Trying to keep calm, I look around the café, but panic when I don't see him.

Where is that damn dog?

My head whips around and . . . shit. I accidentally left the door open to air out the fresh paint fumes. Thankfully, I have an AirTag on his collar and can quickly spot where he is. Frank tends to wander and, because he relies on his other senses, he can sometimes get a bit carried away by his overactive snout.

His location on my phone shows that he's just down the street, and I'm relieved to find out that he didn't get too far. When I lock up behind me, I zoom in on his location.

Perfect, only two buildings away.

I quickly jog down the street in the cool autumn air and notice another shop with its door open. This must be where Frank is hiding.

As my pace slows, I peer into the dim store. A soft, feminine voice flows over me.

". . . where the hell did you come from? Why are you here? Where is your owner? Do you even have an owner? I don't know if I'm ready to be a single mom to two kids."

I make my way inside the store, but the woman doesn't

notice me. She's too focused on comforting Frank. Behind her, I notice a lazy golden retriever slowly walking towards the chaos, and the hushed voice mentions that the dog is a terrible guard dog.

Judging by that dog's nonchalant pace surveying the scene . . . she's right, that dog is a *terrible* guard dog.

The woman continues speaking. ". . . need to stop talking to myself aloud or else people will think I've totally lost it."

I have to make my presence known, but an uneasy feeling sits deep within my gut, aware that I'll spook her. Because what person wouldn't be scared by a random stranger, alone, in a store at night?

I'm mentally preparing myself to grab Frank and make a run for it, just in case this person decides they want to kick my ass.

"Interrupting your own conversations is considered insane. However, talking to yourself is perfectly normal. In fact, it's actually encouraged since it helps increase emotional regulation," I comment as I slowly approach my dog, who is surrounded by a mess of dirt.

Everything unfolds in front of me so quickly. She jolts, grabs a golf club, and threatens me.

Yep. That went as well as I thought it would.

I should've stuck with a one-syllable word to let her know I was in her store. In one smooth motion, I hold up my hands in surrender to show that I'm not a threat. Trying to break the tension, I tell her that a putter might be a better weapon.

She doesn't laugh.

Definitely not surprised.

Now she's backing up, and I'm carefully walking forward with my hands up to get into a more well-lit part of the store, to show her I'm not dangerous. I'm wearing a sweater vest and glasses, for Christ's sake. All she'd have to do is knock my glasses off—the easiest way to get this man down and disarmed in less than three seconds.

When I reach the better-lit area of the store, my stomach drops faster than her golf club drops to the floor.

She is so . . . beautiful.

I know I shouldn't be thinking about her looks under these distressing circumstances, but I can't help it. Her curious, wide, brown eyes pair perfectly with her fair skin and deep mahogany hair. She's wearing an oversized gray sweatshirt with a green apron and jeans. Her flushed pink cheeks are the same color as her soft lips, which are slightly parted in shock. There's a swipe of dirt on her forehead, which, under different conditions, I would tell her about.

However, I'm not risking a 5-iron to the balls tonight.

She's breathing heavily as her eyes search me, probably deducing that I'm not a threat. Being an unusually tall guy at around six-foot-eight on a good day, my worst fear is scaring other people. I know my height can be intimidating, and it's actually an insecurity of mine.

Noticing her fear, I take a few steps back and accidentally bump into a table behind me. The table, full of potted plants, begins to tip over, sending them crashing to the floor.

A *stupendous* first impression.

It takes me a moment to realize I'm in a plant store and that my dog also created a mess before I walked in here.

Like father, like son, I suppose.

I can feel my face heat with embarrassment. This is not how I wanted my first impression to be with a pretty girl. I'm usually much more charming than this, but the universe seems to be working against me today. I open my mouth to speak, then quickly close it. I'm so flustered that I need a moment to collect my thoughts. The brunette looks at me with raised eyebrows, waiting for me to say something—anything at all.

As luck would have it, my brain forgot everything I learned in school.

Words? What are those?

Finally, after moments of awkward silence, I compose myself. A barely coherent string of words escapes me so fast that even I can't keep up with what I'm saying. "F-first, I'm so sorry. Frank is blind. Second—"

Before I can get another word out, she speaks. "Your dog is blind?" Her eyebrows shoot up again. Those big eyes of hers are swimming with questions. Mumbling softly to herself, she continues. "Hmm. Well, that explains why he was so frightened after crashing into the display." She stands up on her tiptoes to peek over at Frank, who is hiding under a table with his tail between his legs.

For some reason, her, standing on her tiptoes, looking over at Frank to check on him, absolutely enchants me.

I roll my lips, biting back a smile because I don't want to seem like a creep. She looks back over at me as I tell her, "Yes. He's a special edition pup . . . on many levels."

This pretty girl is flustering me as her dark brown eyes bore into mine. I feel like we are the only two people in the world right now. My thoughts become muddled, and I have to get my act together. Closing my eyes, I take a deep breath and attempt to continue. "B-before I lose my train of thought again, I'm also sorry for following Frank's lead and crashing into another display. Where's your broom? I'll clean this all up." The words spill out rapidly while I search the store for a broom and dustpan.

"Oh. Don't worry about it." She waves me off. "You don't need to clean up. I can take care of this." Her voice is quiet, and shaky with nerves. I catch her gaze with mine and she sharply inhales before hastily heading into the backroom.

I look down at what I assume is her dog, with shining brown eyes and a bright pink tongue lolling out of its mouth. Crouching down next to the dopey golden retriever who, in fact, is not a good guard dog, I glance at its name tag.

Vera.

I wonder if that's a play on words? This must be her store, and I think I knocked over an Aloe Vera plant back there.

Mystery woman is clever.

I think I'm going to like her.

The owner finally emerges from the backroom after what feels like forever with a broom and dustpan in hand. She stops dead in her tracks, and her eyes widen. "Oh. You're still here? You can leave, you know."

I try to stifle a laugh because she winces at the delivery of her comment—instantly recognizing she wasn't using her "customer service" voice. I quickly pull myself together because I don't want her to think I'm laughing at her. The rosy color on her cheeks deepens, and I gather she isn't the best in awkward situations like this one.

A tall dude and a blind dog crash into a plant store sounds like the beginning of a bad joke, so it's understandable for her to react this way.

"Uh, yes, I'm still here. I made the mess, and I'll clean it up. How much do I owe you? I didn't break the plants, techni-cally." I shrug. "But they also seem like they've seen better days." Reaching for my wallet, I pull it out of my back pocket. "Actually, here, take my wallet, I'll buy them from you and put them to good use." I go to hand it to her, and she just . . . stares.

Treating this situation as if she's a scared, wounded animal, I slowly walk around her so as to not spook her and gently place my wallet on the counter.

"May I?" I softly motion for her to hand me the broom and dustpan. She furrows her brows, and her delicate throat moves as she swallows. After a moment, she quickly nods and hands me the broom. Our fingers slightly brush, her cool fingers contrasting with the warmth of mine feels electric.

She rolls her lips and nods. "I forgot something back there." She hitches her thumb over her shoulder, then disappears into the backroom.

Again.

I look down at Vera, who is now looking at me and wagging her tail, getting even more dirt all over the place.

That tail is a broom in itself—it's impressive.

I give Frank, the panicked pup, and Vera, the slothful pooch, a quick command to sit and stay while I clean. Thankfully, I don't have to worry about Vera going anywhere, seeing as she moves at a snail's pace, but I have to keep my eye on Frank.

I think he gave me five extra gray hairs tonight.

Once the dogs are settled, I begin working on cleaning up her shop and notice I haven't heard a single sound from the backroom. Is she even still in the building?

Like her, I'm not ready to be a single parent to two dogs.

Although, one thing I can't get out of my mind is how stunningly beautiful this woman is. She appears to be a foot shorter than me and, even though she had an oversized sweatshirt on, I could tell she has generous curves that would make any man drop to his knees in worship. Her deep, dark eyes were the first features that captivated me, though. They have purplish shadows settling beneath them. She looked bone-deep exhausted, and my heart aches a bit in my chest for her.

Even though she hasn't spoken more than a few short sentences to me, or even told me her name, I wonder if she was okay.

Chapter Five

ANY OTHER SELF-RESPECTING human who finds another human attractive would typically have a polite conversation. Possibly even flirt. But me? That gene got lost in my DNA somewhere, somehow.

Gumby is a very classically handsome man. It wouldn't surprise me if he had been pulled straight from an old Hollywood film and dropped directly into this decade. He's the kind of handsome that is unabashedly my type, from his tortoise-shell glasses and boyish smile, to his black sweater vest and long, denim-clad legs.

I'm in big trouble.

He stands at least a foot above my five foot seven frame, and his medium brown hair looks soft with waves that border on curls. Unkempt but polished. It's exceptionally good hair with a couple of curlier pieces flopping over his forehead in the most perfectly imperfect way. My fingers itch to reach out and push them away from his face. The stranger also has a strong, sharp jawline paired with panty-dropping dimples. Either I'm ovulating, or all my systems are short-circuiting because I feel the sweat start to bead around my hairline. This man has that hot, nerdy, "intellect in the streets and freak in the sheets" vibe emanating from him.

I need to check myself before I start looking like a rabid animal that's foaming at the mouth.

Softly clearing my throat, I hitch my thumb over my shoulder. "I forgot something back there." My feet spin around so fast that my hair fans around my face as I scurry to the backroom.

I need a quick moment to collect myself.

It's been a while since I found anyone even remotely attractive. Between the grieving process, taking over the store, dealing with my siblings and their lives, my life, and Vera, I had assumed my libido was another unsolved mystery waiting for its own documentary on Netflix. Much to my surprise, the mystery of the missing libido has seemingly been solved by a certain long-limbed man and his special edition dog.

Logically, I need to come out of the backroom at some point. Illogically, I'm hoping if I hide in here long enough, maybe he'll leave. I could try to talk to him, but I hate small talk. The last time I made small talk was on a date. I ended up talking about the top five most prolific serial killers in the United States and why they were all amateurs.

To no surprise at all, the guy didn't want a second date.

Blowing out a breath, I close my eyes and lean my head back on the wall. Maybe I can clean up here and stall for some time. Surely he'll get weirded out by being alone in an unfamiliar store with two dogs. Plus, I don't hear anything out front. Hopefully he left.

Carefully, I peer around the door . . . nope, he's still here. I jolt back inside behind the door, dropping my face into my hands and cringe at my ridiculously immature behavior.

"I just saw you, you know." Amusement evident in his tone. "No offense, but that wasn't very subtle."

I groan, knocking my head back on the wall behind me a few times.

So embarrassing.

I'm wondering what the probability is that lightning will strike me down.

Probably not great since I'm indoors.

Attempting to be more subtle, I look out to the front again. He's sweeping up the store, and I feel horrible. I should be out there, but I can't bring myself to face him. What the actual fuck is wrong with me? It's not like I haven't ever been touched by a man.

Then again, I haven't been touched by one who looks like a hot professor. Why is this guy having such an effect on me? I'm putting the blame on my exhaustion and crazy long day. I've been so discombobulated since my parents died that I may have forgotten how to act around new people. While I see new people come into the store, I'm usually in my work mindset and have no time to pay attention to faces or names.

Wait. I don't even know his name.

I peek out once more; he's still there but this time our eyes lock and it feels like we're both frozen in the moment.

My heart flutters at the playful glint in his eyes.

That deep voice that could narrate all my dirty historical novels calls out to me while our gazes are still on one another. "I promise I'm not dangerous. If it'll make you feel better, I can call my sister and mom for references? They can vouch for my behavior. Here, I'll pull up their contact info and set my phone on the counter. You can call them." He laughs again —one of those deep, hearty laughs that makes my stomach feel like I'm on a rollercoaster.

The sound of his phone unlocking fills the store as he sets it on the counter.

Holy shit. He wasn't joking.

I'd be lying if I said that didn't make me feel a bit better.

Maybe this is when I should mention, "*It's not you, it's me. I'm like an unsocialized dog who forgets how to act around humans. By the way, I'm Charlie!*" Being caught off guard is when I'm at my weakest, and this man completely threw me off balance by simply existing.

Deciding to put on my big girl overalls, I take a calming breath and head out to the front of the store, but stop at the sight before me. Both dogs are lying next to each other under a table. Vera and Frank look like two furry donuts touching one another, sleeping peacefully.

Gumby is so intently focused on cleaning up every speck of dirt on the ground that you'd think he was entering a clean floor competition. I'm debating whether to tell him that this is a plant store, and dirt on the ground is par for the course, but I admire how meticulous and serious he's taking his task.

Finally, my feet decide to forge ahead, and I sheepishly walk out to him, giving him a small wave. "Hi. I, uh . . . I'm sorry about that. You just startled me," I say, anxiously wiping my sweaty hands on my apron and flashing him a tight-lipped smile.

He abruptly stops what he's doing, looks at me over the rims of his glasses, and arches a single brow.

Fuck that's hot.

With the dustpan firmly gripped in his hand, he stands up to his full height and cocks his head. "Huh. You don't say?" A wide, amused smile takes over his face, and I feel my cheeks start to heat. "You know, I've never had that kind of reaction before to people seeing me."

He places the dustpan down and sets his hands on his narrow hips. It looks like he has more to say as he rolls his lips with a contemplative look. "Well, except for that one Halloween party back in 2008. But I was also dressed up as a Ninja Turtle . . . and very illegally drunk—they had every right to be scared." He shakes off the memory and resumes cleaning, carefully sweeping up the spilled dirt and placing the plants back in their respective pots. Then, he places those plants all together on one table. "I'm putting these all here together because I'm buying them." The look on his face is stern in a way that tells me that if I said no to his offer, he'd end up throwing his credit card at me and running away.

Instinctively, my head shakes. "That's not necessary. Seriously, I'll repot them tomorrow and they'll be ready for whoever wants them."

His head whips so fast toward me that I jolt. "And make even more work for you? Because of a clumsy dog and his owner? No, absolutely not. My wallet is on the counter, and the credit card is inside." He nods toward his brown leather wallet near the cash register. "Go ahead and ring them up. I don't care about the cost."

To say I'm startled is an understatement. I've only known this man for less than thirty minutes, and he's concerned about my workload?

People are strange. But I won't argue with him.

Standing there, I stare at him, still utterly confused. I slowly nod and walk over to his plant hoard on the table. My eyes catch on a cardboard box nearby to set them in, and I head to the counter to cash him out. As a store owner, who am I to fight with a customer who wants to buy thirteen plants?

Once I scan all of them, I say, "All right, the total is going to be . . . $263.76. You said credit, right?" I sneak a glance at him to find he's petting Vera and cooing sweet nothings in her ear. Of course Vera loves him. I can practically see hearts bulging out of her large brown eyes.

I narrow my eyes at her and I swear she smirks at me.

Traitor.

"I'm sorry, I missed what you said," he says, standing up. I'm temporarily mesmerized by him taking off his glasses and cleaning them on his sweater. Slowly, Gumby makes his way to the counter as he surveys the store. With a wide, curious gaze, he takes it all in.

"The total is $263.76 for your plant casualties. You said credit?" I ask, rolling my lips. Seeing that I'm not making a move for his wallet, he reaches for it on the counter and pulls out his credit card. I try not to stare at his face for too long but notice that his eyes are a deep blue with little brown specks— like a rocky ocean shore. Clearing my throat, I snatch his card, swipe it and hand it back to him with a curt nod. Part of me wants to talk to him longer because I'm a little interested in this guy.

But as fast as that initial thought comes into my mind, I shove it right back out into the universe. I've never seen him around here. Maybe he's passing by for the night, or in town visiting family.

With the store looking almost as good as new, thanks to Gumby, I can officially head home. I pull my apron over my head and hang it on the hook before heading into the back-room to grab my bag and keys.

Then, the realization that Gumby is still here hits me, and I feel like an asshole for ignoring him. I place my hand on my forehead, embarrassed at my forgetfulness. So I head back out to the front, ready to tell him that he doesn't have to hang around. When he sees me, though, he starts laughing.

Is he laughing at me?

Okay, now I'm a bit irritated, or maybe I'm just sensitive.

Probably both.

Most likely both.

"Laughing to yourself like that could be a sign of a psychiatric issue, you know. I'd get that checked out," I huff, crossing my arms over my chest, glaring at him.

Spinning on my heel, ready to stomp off, his deep voice stops me.

"Your sweatshirt. I'm laughing at your sweatshirt. It says 'Plant Mama,' and I was wondering if having"—he counts the plants in the box—"thirteen plants makes me a 'Plant Daddy'?"

My head whips in his direction just as his fucking eyebrow quirks like he said something clever.

Which he did.

Frozen, I stare and blink a few times, still processing what he said. I'm semi-annoyed at Marnie for getting me this ridiculous sweatshirt. I make a quick mental note to fire her . . . again. Even more, I'm very annoyed at myself for not doing laundry since this was all I had to wear.

I'm not entirely sure how to react, so I try to coax him out of the store. "Okay, well, this has been fun. You're very clever with that little one-liner," I say, clasping my hands in front of my chest. "Thank you for retrieving your dog, cleaning up my store, and adding to my 401k with your large purchase. It's truly been a pleasure. Here, let me walk you out." I wave my hand, motioning for him to follow me to the front door.

His body doesn't move as he cocks his head to one side. "I'm not letting you walk out of here alone, especially at night. My mom raised me better than that, so grab your things, Plant Mama. I want to head home as much as you do."

Exasperated, I rub my hands down my face. I don't know if I should laugh, be annoyed, or be aroused. I'll need to discuss these feelings with my therapist during my next session.

A headache is forming behind my eyes due to feeling worn out from today's never-ending events. "Okay, that's a very kind offer—very gentlemanly of you—but my mom taught me not to walk with strangers. So it seems like we are at a bit of an impasse here." I shrug. "I guess you'll just have to leave now."

I need this man to leave my store because my bed is calling to me. Even though I appreciate the eye candy, he's becoming an impossibly attractive thorn in my side.

My brain is so flustered with this man that I almost forgot about my dog. I move my head in all directions of the store, looking for her. Carefully, I walk around the dimly lit store, feeling a set of deep blue eyes on me as I search for Vera. Lo-and-behold, Vera and Frank are cuddled under another table, looking as cute as can be.

"Damn. That's really cute," his deep voice mutters close enough behind me that his breath brushes the wisps of my hair in the back. It causes me to jolt and yelp in surprise.

"Sorry, I thought you heard me walking behind you," he says apologetically.

At this point, I'm so exhausted that I want to go home and have my scheduled 8 p.m. cry session.

I decide not to fight it and walk out with him.

Apparently, I never listened to my parents' "stranger danger" talks.

Although a tall, lanky stranger who owns a blind dog can't be much of a threat, right? Plus, he wears glasses. If push came to shove, I could knock off his glasses and make a break for my car. He wouldn't be able to see, making it the perfect escape plan.

Confident with my hypothetical scheme, I smile and grab my keys off the hook by the office door.

"Do I want to know what you were smiling about just now?" he questions with another charismatic eyebrow quirk.

I clear my throat. "Nope. Let's head out the back. I park behind the building." I walk ahead of him, but his footfalls stop.

"Whoa, hold up. Are you taking me into a dark alley, Plant Mama? Should I be concerned?"

Oh my god.

I abruptly stop, roll my shoulders back, and turn to march up to him, pointing my finger into his lean chest. "If you call me 'Plant Mama' one more time, I'll knock off your glasses and steal your dog."

Gumby tries to hold back a smile now; the wheels are turning in his head for a comeback.

"Before we leave, I have two questions," he inquires.

Here we go.

I fold my arms over my chest and wait for him to continue. Irritation must be radiating off of me because he rolls his lips again, this time trying not to smile.

"One, have you ever . . . I'm not sure what the correct term is, but made a new plant out of an existing plant?"

I have no idea where this is going, and frankly, I'm terrified. "You mean propagate? If so, then yes, I have. A few times."

He nods, and I see his cheek twitch. "Perfect. My second question is, what's your name? Because if your plant babies had babies, then you're technically a 'Plant Granny,' and I'm not sure which name you'd prefer to be called?"

I'm going to kill him.

Chapter Six

Finn

She's going to kill me.

I can see that spark in her eyes as they bore into mine. I try my luck (again) at breaking the tension, hoping it doesn't go as poorly as my previous attempts.

My voice is serious when I say, "How many ways are you thinking about killing me right now?"

That gets a cute smirk, and I can feel her guard come down ever so slightly. Briefly, her shoulders drop the tiniest bit and her head tilts softly.

"About seven ways, Griffin. And my name is Charlie." Her soft voice fills the silent room. I slowly nod as I take in her face. She really has the prettiest face now that I can see her in the light.

She looks strong, yet vulnerable. Tired, yet ready for battle at a moment's notice.

I give her a tender smile before I register what she just said. "How the hell do you know my name?"

Now she's laughing. "My dad always taught me to be aware of my surroundings. I checked your name on your credit card."

Pretty and perceptive? She's way out of my league.

A laugh rumbles out of my chest, and I rub the back of my neck. "Touché, Charlie. Touché. But you can just call me Finn."

She gives the tiniest smirk back at me, and I notice she has a single dimple on her left cheek that has me smitten. For the rest of my night, I'll now be thinking of all the ways I can make that single dimple appear again.

We stand there in silence, looking at one another. It feels like we're both assessing the other, trying to figure out the other person just by their body language and facial expressions.

At the same time, we realize we're about to walk out of the building without our two furry children. Are they still canoodling under the table? Frank always did have a thing for blondes, so his infatuation with Vera isn't shocking to me.

Personally, I've always had a thing for brunettes.

Side by side, Charlie and I both begin searching for the dogs in her store. It really is like a forest here. My head keeps smacking on various hanging plants with every other step I take. Out of the corner of my eye, I notice Charlie holding back a smile. At least someone is getting amusement out of me being assaulted by these green monstrosities.

We walk back to the table we last saw them sleeping under, and find both pups still snuggled next to each other. They must be in a deep sleep since their eyes are twitching, and Frank is making soft whimpering sounds.

Once we wake them up, we hook their respective leashes on their collars; Charlie grabs her things, I grab my box of plants, and we head out into the alley.

We stroll in silence for the short walk to her car. She turns to me, looking even more beautiful in the moonlight. "This is me. Thanks for walking Vera and I back here and for not murdering us."

I chuckle, hoping my glasses don't fog up just by looking at her. "I should be thanking you for not robbing me and my plant babies in this dark alley." I lift the box of plants and give it a shimmy.

Charlie rolls her eyes while she opens the door to the backseat and coaxes Vera inside. As she opens the driver's side door, she hesitates before sliding onto the front seat. Her expression shows there's something on her mind, but she struggles to say it aloud, with her lips parting and closing.

"Thank you, you know, for cleaning up tonight. I really appreciate it," she finally breathes out, her eyes showing deep appreciation.

The look of relief in her exhausted expression cuts deep through my chest. "O-of course," I stammer out.

I should've stopped there, but I love self-sabotaging by setting myself up for rejection by a pretty woman, so I continue. "If you ever need help with anything, and I mean anything at all, I'm about to open a new café a few shops down. I'm not that difficult to find . . . unless you're Frank." She closes her eyes and shakes her head at my joke.

One day, she'll think I'm cute, funny, and charming.

However, today's not that day. I pick and choose my battles wisely.

"Ahh. So you're new here," she says. "I thought you were either passing by or visiting someone."

Before Charlie closes the door of her green SUV, I find myself speaking again. This poor woman probably wants to go home, but my mouth can't seem to stop rambling.

"Get home safe, okay? I'm sure I'll see you around. I also can't promise that Frank won't wander into your store again, so I apologize ahead of time for that."

She flashes me another tiny smile. An almost dimple smile. "Frank can come keep Vera company anytime. She mostly just sleeps anyway, so she could use a new friend." Before she closes the door, her eyes roam over me from head to toe, and I can feel my ears heating up. "Well, have a good night, Finn," she adds.

Gripping my box of plants tighter, I dip my chin. "You too, Charlie."

Standing there, in the cold, dark alley with Frank snug against my leg, I watch her pull out of the parking lot and onto the road. I can't explain it, but I wanted to see her off and ensure she was safe. Even though, once she left my line of sight, I wouldn't know where she went. But that didn't matter. Something in me felt the need to keep an eye on her.

Once her car is out of sight, I whistle for Frank to follow me back to the coffee shop so we can pack up and head home for the night. On the walk back with Frank, my thoughts drift back to Charlie. Our exchange while walking to her car was simple and brief but, despite our rocky introduction, I have a feeling that I'll be seeing her a lot more.

AFTER THE QUICK drive out of town, Frank and I finally pull up to our small, craftsman-style home. The house is a deep, slate blue with large, white-trimmed windows, but the porch is my favorite part. It's large, with two cobblestone columns bookending each side of the wood-plank patio. There's a built-in swing where Frank and I enjoy our evenings peacefully—rocking and listening to music after a long day.

Just as I'm about to unlock the front door, my eighty-two-year-old neighbor, Angie, calls for me.

"Finn! Oh Finn, I'm so glad you're home," she calls out.

Setting the box of plants down on my front porch, Frank and I make our way over to Angie's garage. She's in a long, pink nightgown with curlers in her hair, and her slippers scuff against the cement floor of the garage. Her eyes are frantic as she looks around at the boxes that are too high for her on the shelves.

"Hey, Miss Angie, everything okay?" I ask her, looking around the cluttered space.

"No, it's not. My son put these damn boxes too high up, and I can't reach them. Can you get them down for me? I need a tall man." She waggles her eyebrows and her innuendo isn't lost on me. Deciding to pretend I didn't hear what she said, I grab the boxes from the shelf.

"Oh, thank you so much, Finn. You're a true hero." She beams up at me.

"Not a hero. Just a guy that was blessed with good genes," I reply, smiling down at her.

"They are good jeans indeed." She peers around to look at my ass. "You know, you remind me of my late husband, Andrew."

Ah. There it is. I clear my throat, needing to remove myself from the situation. "Well, if you don't need anything else, I'm going to head in for the night." I give her a polite smile.

"That's all, dear, thank you. Also, don't forget about the

ladies' book club! We're always looking for some male perspective." Her eyebrows waggle again. She's been trying to recruit me to her erotica book club since Frank and I moved in.

I've dodged the question just as long.

"Sure thing, Miss Angie. Have a good night!" I sprint to my front door with Frank close behind me.

After we're both safely inside, Frank drops something at my feet and runs straight for his food bowl. I kept the layout of the house uncomplicated for Frank's sake. The living room has a simple, off-white couch with an oversized leather chair adjacent to it. There's a large wooden coffee table on top of a soft beige rug that Frank loves to sleep on. In front of the seating area is the fireplace, complete with a TV mounted above it and built-in bookshelves on either side. I look around my house, and since I don't have many tables, I'm left with the question of the decade: *Where the fuck am I going to put all of these plants?*

Choosing to ignore that question temporarily, I bend down to pick up what Frank dropped off at my feet.

Fuck. Me.

Frank stole an adult magazine. I assume it was from Angie's late husband's collection, since this magazine is *very clearly* from the seventies. There's a lot . . . happening on the cover.

"Frank! For fuck's sake. Out of all the things you could've stolen, you stole this?"

The dog couldn't care less, and over my dead body am I returning this to Angie.

Sighing, I look at the scantily clad woman on the cover once more, wondering where I can discreetly dispose of it before Frank's boisterous bark startles me. Even though Frank can't see what I'm doing, a flush of embarrassment creeps up my neck. I swear he can sense what I'm looking at. Deciding to shove the magazine in the junk drawer of my entryway table, I slam the drawer shut in an attempt to pretend this whole situation never happened.

Frank's firmly planted by his food bowl and is whimpering as if he hasn't eaten all day, and even though he can't see it, I shake my head at him. I usually keep a bag of treats in my pocket because Frank stays close to me if there's a scent of bacon radiating from my body. Which means he usually gets a small meal of treats throughout the day.

Frank's living his absolute best life.

I step into the pantry, reaching for Frank's dog food and scoop some into his bowl. I fill his other bowl with fresh water from the sink before setting both on the kitchen floor. As my special edition pup devours his dinner, I give him a quick scratch behind his furry ears before heading upstairs to change into my pajamas.

With each step, the wooden stairs creak under my weight as I make my way back down after changing. The coldness of the hardwood floors sends a shiver up my spine but reminds me that I need to gather all of my socks that Frank has been stashing away. As I shuffle my way back into the kitchen, I decide on cereal for dinner since it's late and I'm too tired to make anything else. Plus, I haven't gone grocery shopping with all the chaos of opening this coffee shop.

While I'm eating at the kitchen island, I can't help but think of my encounter with Charlie. Granted, I barely know her, but there's just something about her that I can't get out of my mind.

I peer over to the living room and see Frank is already on the couch for our nightly ritual. He doesn't understand the concept of personal space. Instead of lying next to me like a normal dog, Frank lies on top of me.

Every. Single. Night.

Sometimes it's cute, sometimes it's hard to breathe.

After I put my dishes in the dishwasher, I make my way over to where Frank is on the couch. When I sink into the cushion, he places his head in my lap and I soothingly stroke his back. As I'm watching the football highlights, I begin zoning out and my mind begins drifting back to Charlie.

This feeling with her reminds me of when you have a crush on someone in high school. You don't know them all that well because you see them in the hallway or a classroom. There's just something about this person that you can't shake from your mind—that makes your stomach flutter with excitement. Your thoughts are consumed by when you'll see them next, how you'll act when they notice you, and what you'll say when they do. So until then, you push your desk a little closer to them, linger outside their classroom for a few more minutes, and maybe "forget" your pencil just for a chance to talk to them and be near them for a little longer. Then, finally, when you lie down at night, you replay that previous exchange with them over and over again until your eyes close, and drift off to sleep, hoping to dream about them.

And tonight, I know I'll dream of her. My eyelids are heavy as I think about the guarded girl with the doe eyes and a single dimple in her left cheek that appears when she smiles ever so slightly.

Chapter Seven

C‍HARLIE

T‍HIS HAS TO BE A JOKE. My face pales as I stare at my phone. I must've blocked this out in my memory somehow.

Despite that text message, I'm determined not to let it interrupt my and Marnie's Saturday ritual of pizza and *Guess Who?*—Hemlock Edition. In this game, we find photos of the various town locals and tape them to the face cards on the game and voila, you have the perfect game of *Guess Who?* Hemlock Edition. Then, we take turns describing people using the most random, obscure descriptions you can come up with.

For example, who streaked during the Fourth of July parade while waving around two popsicles?

Easy. Jerry from the bank.

With my eyes glued to my phone, I can feel Marnie's stare burning into me.

"What the fuck is that face? Why is your forehead extra scrunched? I mean, it's usually always scrunched, but it's more scrunched than usual." She's sitting on the ground with a sleeping Vera in her lap, absentmindedly petting the snoring dog.

I shoot her my famous, unimpressed look. "I hate you."

"That's a lie if I've ever heard one." She winks.

We both smile at each other. From an outsider's perspective, you'd think we'd have the oddest relationship. Which we do, but it works for us. It's blunt, it's brash, but it's us. She's been my lifeline during this whole chapter of losing my parents, and I'm not sure where I'd be without her.

We're both sitting on the floor with the coffee table between us. The TV is playing some random true crime documentary, and our board game is half-finished.

I get up for a glass of water before I call out, "I got an odd text message, and you're absolutely going to lose your mind. Not that you haven't lost it already, but you know what I mean."

"You know, I take that as a compliment!" she yells out from the living room.

My slippers drag across the floor as I walk back into the living room and sit down in front of the coffee table.

"Remember that guy I told you about that came in a couple days ago with his blind dog?"

"Gumby? The hot professor?"

"Finn, but yes."

Her eyes widen. "Did you cure your dry spell? Thank fuck, Charlie. I was ready to take out an ad to find someone to break your back six ways to Sunday. I was thinking of a billboard that says, '*Looking for someone to break backs, not hearts.*'"

I sit back and blink at her in shock. "You need a damn muzzle for that mouth. But no, I didn't. I think Finn is Mrs. Jenkins's nephew."

She pauses, biting her lip and cocking her head at me. I can almost see her putting it all together in that demented brain of hers.

Awareness settles across her features. "Oh my god, do you think—"

Running my hands through my hair, I release a deep breath. "It has to be. There's no way it can't be him."

I hand over my phone so she can read the message, her brows furrowing as she rereads the words on the screen for a second time. "Wait. Did Jenkins tell him who you are? It kinda sounds like he thinks you're a dude."

"That's why I'm saying it's weird! Part of me wants to tell him who I am." I look over at Marnie, and it's as if she's reading my mind.

"But . . . part of you wants to be a shit disturber and play a prank." Her mischievous grin lights up her face.

I press my lips together and try not to laugh. Yes, I'm old enough to know better, but also, it's been a rough fucking year and dammit, I deserve to have fun.

Marnie pipes up. "Okay, you shit disturbing gremlin. You're only allowed this juvenile prank if you tell him who you are at the end of the night. We're mature bitches, after all."

"Deal. Now, what do I say to him?"

IT'S A COLD, rainy, Saturday night. Frank and I are watching football and eating popcorn. Well, I'm watching football and eating popcorn, while Frank is listening to football and gnawing on a bone. Both of us are sprawled out on my over-sized couch. We haven't moved from our spots for most of the day, and I'm sure there are human and dog imprints on these cushions by now.

With nothing else happening, I decide to text the guy my aunt had mentioned to me a few weeks ago. I'm about to shove another handful of popcorn in my mouth when my phone chimes. He replied to me, which is surprising because I wasn't expecting a response so soon.

CHARLIE

Hello, Finn. Sure, I would be happy to meet up with you for a drink. Perhaps we could get to know each other a bit beforehand?

I hum loud enough that Frank perks his ears up at me. Interesting response. Usually, I'm not much of a texter; I prefer phone or video calls over texting. Too much can get lost in translation when you text.

But here I am. Alone on a Saturday night with my dog, texting a stranger to cure some boredom.

I shove the handful of popcorn in my mouth and chew as I type out a short reply.

That sounds fine to me.

CHARLIE

I stop mid-chew as I read the message again. What in the *Nightmare on Elm Street* is happening here? And what kind of people is my aunt associating herself with? Deep down, I know this guy is fucking with me, but that being the first question right out of the gate? He could've warmed me up by asking about literally anything not related to murder.

CHARLIE

Munching on another handful of popcorn, I pause and my brows drop, reading the message. *What is "redrum"? Is it some kind of drink?* I do a quick search . . . this guy is definitely fucking with me.

CHARLIE

Huh? *Good boy?* Strange.

My head shakes in disbelief. This whole text exchange is bizarre and I'm wondering how many horror movie references are up his sleeve.

Pretty ambivalent.

Interesting. Do you like saws?

No.

Thought so. You seem more like a knife guy
anyway. Final question: You're driving to
your life's final destination, do you think you
could cheat death?

Setting aside my phone, I take my glasses off and press my palms into my eyes.

What the hell have I gotten myself into?

CHARLIE

I HAVEN'T LAUGHED this hard in almost a year. Tears are streaming out of my eyes, and Marnie and I are wheezing like seals on the living room floor—sniffling and crying because we are laughing so hard. Sweet sweater vest-wearing Finn must be terrified or confused.

Probably both. Which is understandable.

I'm shocked he hasn't blocked my number.

Laughing like this feels freeing. My chest feels lighter than it has in a long time, and just for a moment, I feel like I can take a deep breath.

Tonight, I feel glimmers of happiness that haven't been there in a long time. It feels so good to have fun and laugh so hard that my stomach muscles are spasming.

I can just imagine Finn's face, those blue eyes narrowing as he runs his hands through his hair in confusion—it's great. He either knows someone is messing with him, or is on the phone with the sheriff's department right now. Marnie looks at me, and I know it's time to confess my real identity since he hasn't replied to my last text.

> Hey, Finn. So, funny story, this is Charlie. Plant shop girl. I didn't know Mrs. Jenkins was your aunt. What a small world! I guess I'm showing you around Hemlock?

Ten minutes pass with no reply, so I decide to send a follow-up text with Marnie looking directly over my shoulder.

> The girl with the golf club? Your dog knocked over some of my plants?

"Such an odd choice of weapon," Marnie remarks as she sips her margarita.

"You have no room to talk. You keep an icepick next to your bed," I scoff.

"Yeah? Your point?" Her blue eyes roll before finishing off her margarita in three gulps.

Our conversation is interrupted by a notification from Finn.

FINN

> Sorry, I don't know anyone named Charlie. I think you may have your Finns mixed up?

My stomach plummets, and I feel the back of my neck begin to sweat.

Is this not Finn? The guy who walked into my store?

I look over, and Marnie's eyes are as wide as saucers as she pets Vera.

"Oof. That's embarrassing," she says, giving a sorry grimace.

"You think?" I deadpan, my voice heavy with sarcasm.

Leave it to me to prank a poor, unsuspecting guy on his first week in a new town. Even I know better than that.

Feeling like a certified asshole, I hastily come up with a plan to help extract my foot from my mouth. A quick apology and offer to meet up with him—short and sweet.

> I'm so, so sorry. I should've known better than to play a silly prank, I thought you were someone else. But yes, I would be happy to meet up next week. What day and time work for you?

FINN

How about Monday, 7:30 p.m. at Freddie's?

> Perfect. See you then.

I throw my phone across the floor as my face burns with embarrassment. How am I going to face this guy on Monday?

Vera strolls over to me and flops over, belly up. She clearly senses my embarrassment and is providing her only available emotional support—belly rubs. While I rub Vera's belly, Marnie is snickering, and I feel like crawling into a hole. I just need to get Monday over with since I'm ninety-nine percent sure Finn 2.0 already hates me.

Even though I dislike the majority of the population, I hate when people hate *me*.

THERE'S an excited flutter in my stomach as I read the last message Charlie sent.

Who knew that shy, soft-spoken Charlie was a trouble-maker? That little spark of fire she showed tonight only makes me more intrigued by her.

The mature thing to do would have been to tell her she had the right person, but after those horror movie, murder-esque questions, I had to play her game.

She's clever, I'll give her that.

I can't ignore the nervous excitement coursing through my body at the thought of seeing her on Monday. I've been tired all day today, but suddenly, after this text exchange, I've found more energy than I know what to do with this late.

That's when an idea hits me. I sit up on the couch and glance at my table full of plants—the plants that I have yet to find homes for because I have thirteen of them. Frank is sound asleep at my feet, and I carefully slip out of the blanket I was under. After I tuck the blanket around Frank to keep him warm, I make my way over to the table. Each pot is labeled with the plant's name and comes with corresponding care instructions that I'll file away.

I take my Plant Daddy duties *very* seriously.

About an hour later, I'm able to water them all and give them new homes in various places in my living room and kitchen. The majority live on my built-in bookshelves, next to my books, and the miscellaneous trinkets that my mom and sister have gifted me over the years. Even though I have to sacrifice some space for books to make room for the plants, it's worth it.

As I pad around the house, feeling calmer and less ener-
gized, I turn off all the lights and double-check that the doors
are locked (especially after that murderous conversation.
Yikes.). Frank's still asleep on the couch, and I give him a
quick whistle so he knows to follow me upstairs.

After brushing my teeth, I find Frank patiently sitting at
the foot of my king-sized bed. The poor guy had one too
many falls trying to jump onto the bed, so he knows that if he
waits, I'll help him. Gently, I pick him up and place him on
the soft, blue blanket that's just for him. With a few sniffs and
a couple of twirls, he curls into himself like a furry donut and
lets out a content groan.

When I crawl under the covers and turn my bedside lamp
off, I roll over onto my back and stare up at the ceiling in
complete darkness. My mind drifts to Charlie and my heart
races as I think about what will happen come Monday.

There's excitement with a sprinkle of apprehension.

I can't wait to see her . . . even if she finds seven more
ways to kill me.

Chapter Eight

I'M ABSOLUTELY DREADING meeting Finn 2.0 tonight. I don't even know what this guy looks like or how old he is.

Maybe tonight is the night I end up on an episode of *Dateline*.

If I die tonight and end up wherever souls go to rest, my parents are going to be pissed. I'll be in deep shit with them in the afterlife.

Plus, who is going to look after my siblings?

My older brother, Jack, is a reserved guy with a heart of gold. He has full custody of his daughter, Lucy, ever since his ex-wife left him a few years ago for another guy. After his ex-wife cheated on him, I went online and bought one thousand live maggots and had them delivered to her lover's apartment that she was occupying. I planned to deliver five hundred maggots, but shipping was free for orders over twenty-five dollars.

I'm never one to pass up free shipping.

Joey, my younger sister, is a modern day flower child who travels around in a VW van and is only home a few times a month. Needless to say, we are an eclectic group and my parents had a great time raising us.

I'm huddled in A New Leaf's backroom prepping a few propagation plants in test tubes when I hear an unmistakable deep voice.

"Hey, Char!"

Speak of the devil. It's as if my brother knows I was thinking about him.

Dropping my plant shears, I stroll out to the front.

"What?" I sigh, completely exasperated. My hands make their way to my hips as I stare at my brother with mock annoyance.

He runs a hand through his disheveled, wavy, brown hair, laughing. "Is that how you greet all your customers? You say, 'What?' when they walk in? Not even a full sentence?"

My eyes narrow. "You're right, that was rude of me. I meant to say, *What do you want?*" I tilt my head to the side, raising my eyebrows at him.

Jack shakes his head, still laughing. Mimicking my stance, he places his hands on his hips and exhales. "I wanted to discuss a few ideas about the house." My heart aches all over again.

Jack took it upon himself to renovate our parent's home. Luckily, he works in construction and is familiar with home renovations.

My brother looks around the shop, taking everything in. "You've done real good with the place, Char. I know it wasn't easy for you since you didn't know the first thing about running a business, but it looks great."

"I still don't know the first thing about running a business. Or plants," I mumble.

"Well, you're good with the plants, even if you have to Google everything. With people, though? You leave a lot to be desired." He jokingly winces.

I roll my eyes. "I'm pleasant enough to get by, and that's all that matters."

He raises his hands in surrender. "Hey, whatever helps you sleep at night."

Stepping around Jack, I head to the front of the store and flip the sign to "Closed," and I pull out my phone to video call Joey so we can all have input on the design choices for the home. When my parents passed, we all agreed to keep their house in the family because those walls hold too many good memories.

Joey's bright face pops up on the screen, the sun shining on her auburn hair. "Hey, orphans!"

Jack and I both let out a deep sigh, dropping our heads as laughter from our sister fills the space.

Leave it to Joey to make dead parent jokes.

"Hey, Joey." I lean in closer to the phone screen, squinting my eyes. "What part of the country are you in, by the way?" Judging by her surroundings in the background, she is definitely not in Oregon anymore.

"Eh. Maybe in Arizona. Maybe in New Mexico. Who can say?" she replies, glancing around as the wind tosses her auburn hair in every direction.

"Christ. If you need bail money, call your sister," Jack murmurs.

My head rears back, my eyes snapping in his direction. "No fucking way. You're in charge of bailing her out."

"I love when you two fight over me," Joey quips. "It makes me feel loved."

<hr />

A COUPLE OF HOURS LATER, we've exhausted ourselves with home renovation choices and Jack packs up the blueprints and material swatches he brought. Before he reaches the door, I call out to him. "Wait! Before you go, I have a question."

Jack turns to me, eyebrows pinched together in confusion.

"I like your red and black flannel. Has anyone told you recently that you're a walking, talking, lumberjack cliché? Where's your emotional support ax?" I roll my lips, fighting off a smile.

He narrows his dark brown eyes at me as he tries not to smirk.

I'm waiting for him to give me a comeback that'll equally hurt my feelings and make me laugh.

Jack looks me dead in the eye, a serious expression matching his tone. "I didn't want to tell you this news like this, but you've left me no choice. I have proof that a pack of weasels raised you . . ." Jack dramatically shakes his head, pretending to get choked up. "Which explains so many things about your prickly personality, distaste for human interaction, and"—he looks me up and down, grimacing—"your stubby limbs. Must've inherited that from your ancestors." He winks, then walks out the door laughing to himself. I flip the sign back to "Open" and begin checking the moisture levels of the plants.

A few moments after Jack leaves, Marnie comes blazing in. Tiny specks of paint dot her face and hands, meaning she just came from the community center where she was most likely prepping for her next art class.

A mischievous grin takes over her face. Usually, I love them. Today I don't because it's directed at me. "Today's the day, Gremlin! Want me to dress up in a disguise when you meet this new Finn? I'll sit in the back and—"

I interrupt her before she continues. "Marnie, no. I don't need you there." If you don't interrupt this woman at some point during her absurd monologues, she won't stop.

She huffs. "What if you get kidnapped?"

"No one, and I mean no one, wants to kidnap this." I make a motion, gesturing to the entirety of my body. "Plus, I'll have a knife on me."

She nods, a smile spreading across her face as she points her finger at me. "And there it is. Never mess with the Gremlin when she has a pocket knife."

We turn our heads at the sounds of an unimpressed groan from my dog interrupting our conversation.

I glance at Marnie. "I know you just got here, but could you watch the shop while I take Vera out? She's making her old lady noises again."

"She really is a grumbly old lady, isn't she? Must take after her sister," Marnie snickers, sending a wink my way. Before I can reply, she puts her hand up to stop me. "Don't say it. I know, I'm fired. Have a nice walk with Vera! Make sure you both bark at anyone who tries to come near you."

Choosing to ignore her, I clip on Vera's harness, put a hat on my head, and step outside. The cool, misting rain surrounds us while the gray skies above block out any sun as we begin our walk. There's a small, quiet park around the corner from my shop that Vera and I visit often to get away from the chaos of Main Street.

As my boots hit the wet pavement, I think about tonight. I don't enjoy meeting new people, especially in a one-on-one setting—the mere thought of it makes my chest constrict. I can admit that my people skills need some fine tuning. Yet, here I am, forcing customer service smiles every day from open until close.

Vera and I make it to the small park, bypassing the sign that says, "Keep Dogs on Leash," which I always ignore. I unclip her leash and wander over to the bench to keep a close eye on her. Looking up at the sky, I notice the clouds have become darker, making it seem much later in the day than it is. When my eyes land back on the park, I see Vera rolling in the park's only muddy spot.

I take my eyes off of her for five seconds and now my golden retriever isn't golden anymore.

"You've got to be fucking kidding me," I mutter. "Vera, no!" I yell.

She doesn't listen to me.

Since I'm new to this whole dog ownership thing, I've discovered there are two types of golden retrievers in the world. The first type are the smart and easily trainable ones who listen. Then you have ones, like Vera, where the lights are on, but nobody's home.

When I march over to Vera, something bumps into my legs, causing me to slip and fall on a patch of wet grass with a sloshing thud.

"FRANK, NO!" someone bellows.

I hear heavy, wet footsteps come up behind me.

Just my luck.

It's Frank and Frank's hot owner who has a perfect view of my muddy dog and soon to be muddy ass.

"Shit, are you okay? I'm so sorry. Frank is blind and

doesn't know any better." He crouches down next to me, and I turn my head away from him, hoping he doesn't recognize me. "Wait, Charlie?"

I'm still on the ground, not moving a single muscle. I'm a dead fish in this park. My fear and embarrassment have frozen me and I've lost all ability to move.

Finn puts a large hand on my shoulder, attempting to get my attention. "Hey, are you okay? Are you hurt? You're not moving. Can I help you up?" The man's so close to me now that I can smell his cologne—slightly woodsy, with a hint of coffee and a touch of lavender.

My intrusive thoughts tell me to bury my nose in his neck like a drug-sniffing dog, but I resist.

Closing my eyes, I swallow my embarrassment. "Hi! Yes, I'm fine. A little disoriented, but totally fine." When I try to stand up, my body betrays me and I fall *again.*

Seriously. At this point, *someone please* put me out of my misery.

"Whoa, whoa. Easy there. Here, let me help." Finn's deep voice rumbles into my ear and it annoyingly gives me goosebumps.

I'm abundantly aware of his close proximity, with his minty breath ghosting over my cheek as he speaks. Finn ever so gently grasps my upper arm to help steady me. For a tall, lithe man, he handles my clumsy, sturdy body with ease. Swallowing, my eyes swiftly shift upward to look at him. He's watching my body so intently, making sure that I don't fall for a third time.

Once I'm safely upright, I straighten my coat and my hat. "Well, that was embarrassing," I say casually, giving a small shrug.

My external demeanor says I'm too cool to be embarrassed, but my internal demeanor is screaming to leave Vera to fend for herself so I can run far away. He quietly laughs, a deep throaty chuckle that could liquify my insides if I allowed it to.

"Yeah, you took quite the tumble, twice. I'm sorry about Frank for the first fall, and I'm sorry about your unsteady coordination for the second fall." An amused smile crosses his face as he looks down at me.

Scoffing at him, I attempt to wipe the dirt off my ass and look over my shoulder to see if my clothes have mud on them, but my neck only bends so far and I'm clearly struggling. I can sense Finn's eyes glued to me and it's making me feel warm all over. When I turn to look back at him, a smirk plays on his lips as he cocks an eyebrow, his amusement clear in the crinkles around his eyes.

He clears his throat. "Do you want me to check for any dirt on your back?

I stare at him with a blank expression and blink. I want to say something sarcastic, but he did just help me up.

"Yes, please." Before I turn around, I stare right into his dark sapphire eyes. "You touch my ass and I'll cut you." I poke a scolding finger at him.

He bellows out a laugh and simply nods. "Noted."

I turn around and can feel the heat of his large hands wipe my upper back through my three layers of clothes. My pulse picks up at his touch, even though it's utterly harmless.

His hands inch lower and lower, right above my belt line. I clear my throat. "You're teetering on forbidden territory, big guy."

He laughs again, making my stomach flip. It's the kind of laugh that gives you a sense of accomplishment.

"You know, for someone so quiet, you sure have a little spark in you," he says.

I smile at that because that's what my parents always used to tell me. *Charlie's a little quiet but has a fire inside that just needs some stoking to get her aflame.* My smile widens even more at the memory.

"I've been told that before. It's a character flaw." As I turn around to face him, I'm met with a hard to read expression. "What's that look for?"

"Nothing. I don't think it's a character flaw. More like a character strength, if you ask me." He gives me that charming, boyish smile that makes me forget everything.

Flustered, I anxiously shove my hands in my coat pockets, unsure how to respond to him. His gaze on me is intense, which quickens my pulse. It's as if he's trying to decipher my thoughts by looking deep into my eyes. Strangely enough, this would make me uncomfortable, but with Finn, it feels *different.*

When I say nothing, he clears his throat and whistles for Frank. "Uh, sorry about Frank. Again. He seems to have taken a strong liking to Vera."

We both look over at the dogs, who are frolicking in the disgustingly damp grass, only getting wetter and muddier.

Upon a closer look, I notice Frank has something in his mouth.

"Does Frank have a baguette in his mouth?" I ask, my eyes on both dogs.

"About that, Frank has a tendency to steal anything and everything he can get his paws on. Because he thinks no one can see him, he believes he can get away with it."

I look up at him, noticing he looks a touch embarrassed as he pushes his glasses up on his nose.

"That being said, Frank is indeed carrying a baguette that he stole from the corner market."

He has a kleptomaniac dog.

This poor dog is blind and steals.

An unladylike snort slips out of me as I giggle. "What else has he stolen?"

Finn blows out a breath. "Well, socks are his favorite, which is why mine are always mismatched." He pulls up his pant legs to show me his mismatched green and blue socks. "Aside from socks and food, he's stolen phones, wallets, and a few pairs of underwear. Oh! And one time he stole a rat."

"I'm sorry, what?"

"Yeah, back in New York. One night I took Frank out, and I wasn't paying attention because I got home at midnight from work. Didn't find out until the next morning when the rat was on my counter eating cereal." He chuckles, running his hands through his now wet hair. It's started raining heavier since we began talking.

"Wow." I shake my head in disbelief.

Glancing away to look at our muddy dogs, I say something I'd never thought would escape my antisocial lips. "I'd love to hear you tell me more stories about Frank's kleptomania sometime."

Chapter Nine

FINN

THE PRETTY PLANT girl with large brown eyes wants to know more about Frank and possibly about me as well.

Which could be a delusion on my part.

My heart skips a beat. Heat spreads from my cheeks to the tips of my ears. Internally, I'm hoping she just thinks my flushed face is from the cool air. It's taking every bone in my body not to smile because if I smile too big, Charlie may run away. She seems like the type of person who doesn't like to make a big deal out of things and keeps it pretty low-key. Instead of screaming, "*Yes! Absolutely. Are you free now? I'll buy lunch. Do you like sandwiches? How about coffee? I know a place . . .*" I simply say, "Sure, I'd like that," while giving her a small, reassuring smile.

She turns to grin at me, and that single dimple makes its appearance. "Well, Vera and I should get back to work. It's cold out here, and my ass is caked in mud." She laughs. "Also, your glasses are a little fogged up." She motions to her face like she's wearing a pair of invisible glasses.

And she said *she* was embarrassed.

More heat crawls up my neck that'll make my glasses even foggier. I casually shrug. "It happens sometimes. Perks of wearing glasses." *And being around a beautiful girl.* But I kept that an inside thought. "I'll let you get back. I'll see you around, Charlie. Hopefully soon." That last part was barely audible, but I'm assuming she still heard it by how her eyes lit up for just a moment.

Charlie walks over to Vera, clips her leash on, and walks away from Frank and I. As I watch her, she glances over her shoulder, back at us, and gives a shy wave. A sudden wave of guilt washes over me as I think about seeing her tonight. I should've said something, but I was so caught off guard by her sudden warmth that my brain was misfiring.

Now, I'm knee-deep in two emotions—anticipation and anxiety. I'm excited to see her, but scared about how she'll react.

FINANCE-GEEK-TURNED-BUSINESS-OWNER is a new territory for me. Today is the grand opening of Dark Side Brews and my stomach is twisting with anxiety as I wait and think about all the strangers who may pop into my shop. Thankfully, I'll see at least one familiar face today.

My grandpa, Arty.

Growing up, I've always been close to my grandpa. He taught me how to swing a golf club and talk my way out of speeding tickets, and was there for me whenever I needed advice.

Arty is also a smooth talker, and guilt trips me into smuggling mini liquor bottles in my coat whenever I visit him at his retirement home.

Today, he and a few of his friends are visiting my coffee shop as their "daycation," which is a weekly program offered by their retirement home.

My arms are crossed as I lean up against the shop counter, watching the large white van pull up in front of Dark Side Brews. I smile to myself, knowing my grandpa and his friends will be my first customers.

Arty and four of his buddies get out and slowly walk inside the shop with their walkers.

"My favorite grandson!" Arty yells, shuffling over to me to give me a hug. I bend down, wrapping his frail body in my arms.

"I'm your *only* grandson, old man." I laugh.

He waves me off. "Nonsense. I got around back in my day. It wouldn't shock me to learn that I had a few other grandchildren running around somewhere. Woodstock was *life changing*." He gives me a mischievous wink and I try to hide my visible cringe.

The last image I want today is my grandpa seducing some woman at a music festival in the sixties.

"Well." I clap my hands, laughing. "I'm going to pretend I didn't hear that. What can I get you guys to drink?"

The five men give me their orders and my barista gets to work. While their drinks are being prepared, Arty pushes his walker around the coffee shop, admiring the space. As he shuffles around, his blue eyes are bright and crinkled at the corners with happiness. A smile tugs at the corner of his lips and it's infectious. While his four friends are chatting at a nearby table, my grandpa continues to look around.

I walk up to him and lean my hip on an unoccupied table. "All right, tell me your thoughts. I know you have them." My tone is humorous and light because my grandpa *always* has thoughts.

"You did good, son. I'm real proud of you," he says. "I know you've been talking about this for years and it's so nice seeing someone you love chase after their dreams."

A lump swells in my throat.

Well, damn. He's getting sentimental in his old age.

"Thanks, grandpa. That means a lot."

"But—" he adds.

I press my lips together, fighting the urge to smile.

"—I think there needs to be a lava lamp . . . or three." Arty winks and I shake my head laughing.

"Go sit over there with your friends, old man," I joke, jerking my head in the direction of his buddies. "I'll be over with your drinks."

After I bring my grandpa and his friends their coffees, I sit and chat with them for about an hour until I have to kick them out. The daycation van was impatiently waiting in front of Dark Side Brews and I knew they had to get back to the retirement home. I give my grandpa one last hug before I make sure they all safely get into the van and no walker is left behind.

The rest of the day goes by in a complete blur—new faces, unique drink orders, and finding a rhythm with the staff proves to be challenging yet rewarding. Needless to say, the grand opening of Dark Side Brews was a success and I couldn't be happier with how everything turned out. I hired great baristas who know exactly what they're doing.

They're quick and efficient, which is how these locals like it.

Despite all of my concerns, fears, and anxiety about opening the shop, today made me realize that life is too short not to take risks that can make a positive impact. Sometimes, what we desire most is on the other side of our greatest fears.

Chapter Ten

Finn

It's 7 p.m. and I have to meet Charlie at Freddie's in a half hour. Which means I'm pacing around my living room, rehearsing what I'm going to say to her.

Poor Frank's ears keep twitching back and forth from the couch, listening to all the different variations of my rehearsed explanations.

"Hey, you're probably wondering why I'm here. Well, you see, funny story. Ha. I'm a fucking dumbass." I abruptly stop in the middle of my living room, pinching the bridge of my nose and shaking my head at myself. I grab my jacket and keys, practically sprinting out of the house. I can't keep pacing around any longer or else I'll drive myself mad.

Freddie's is a pretty cool spot. It's a moody pub with rustic brick walls, vintage sports memorabilia, and mismatched tables. It looks like a cross between a high-end yard sale and your grandparent's basement—it's incredible. I find a spot near the back corner facing the door so I can spot Charlie when she walks in. Once I sit down, the server stops by and introduces herself as Jody. She looks to be mid-fifties with bleach blonde hair and a T-shirt so tight it's a miracle she's able to breathe.

"You're Donna's nephew, right? New in town?" she asks while smacking her gum.

Just the mention of my aunt is enough to put me on edge. "Yep. Just moved here recently," I reply. "I own the coffee shop a couple of blocks down. We just opened today, actually."

"Oh, wow!" She smacks her gum. Again. My irritation is already beginning to rise.

"Yeah, I'm happy to be here! It's a great town you guys have. You should stop by the shop for a coffee, on the house."

Her eyes widen with joy as soon as the words left my lips.

Why the fuck did I just say that? I blame that online marketing course I took a month ago for my loose lips.

"Well, aren't you a sweet thing? I'll have to take you up on that." She winks. As if I wasn't already on edge enough, I'm hoping she doesn't misconstrue my kind offer for something more.

"Well, Jody, my mom raised me right." I flash her a quick smile. "Do you think I could get a beer? Whatever's on tap is fine." Then again, I may need something a bit stronger if my nerves refuse to calm down.

"Sure thing, darlin'!" She hits me with another, more seductive wink this time.

Clearly, I fucked up. Again. If this is any indication of how this night will go, I'm in for a wild ride.

I'm fidgeting now with unease, and my heart is racing a

mile a minute. I look at the clock. It's 7:27 p.m.; she could walk in at any moment. My phone buzzes with a text.

This was a mistake. Earlier at the park, I should've told her it was me she was meeting tonight at Freddie's, not some random stranger. I take a few calming breaths to regulate my heartbeat. After what seems like an eternity, Jody brings my beer over, and I immediately take a large gulp of the cool, crisp liquid.

Just as I swallow, the door to the bar swings open and Charlie walks in. Her long, shiny, mahogany hair cascades over her shoulders, and she's wearing a chocolate brown wool coat that hits just above her ankles. Charlie's dark features pop with the warm glow of the bar surrounding her.

Simply striking.

She glances around, seemingly looking around for an unfamiliar face, and I, being the shameful idiot I am, keep my head down and refuse to make eye contact.

My heart hammers with each steady step of her boots, until they suddenly come to a halt. Out of the corner of my eye, she's standing directly in front of me. There's a light laugh that's followed by a teasing voice.

Sheepishly, I look up at her.

"I knew it," she says, a smirk spreading across her face as she shakes her head. "You little—" Her eyes trail up and down my long limbs. "—well, I guess *not so little,* scoundrel."

It's clear she's not angry in the slightest, and my chest deflates with relief. "I-I'm sorry, I should've told you it was me you were talking to when I saw you at the park earlier," I say, clenching and unclenching my hands—a nervous habit of mine. I fight the urge to anxiously run my hands through my hair, trying my best to play it cool.

Charlie clicks her tongue. "I deserved it, honestly." She gives me a nonchalant shrug. "Though it's good to know you can give as good as you get." She sits down across from me and a rush of excitement has now replaced the unease I felt earlier.

"It was a clever prank. I was curious how many more horror movie references you had up your sleeve," I say, taking another sip of my drink.

She slips off her heavy wool coat, revealing a soft, dark gray sweater that flows over her curves and highlights the warmth in her beautiful eyes. Charlie tosses her shiny, dark hair over her shoulder with a careful hand. "Not that many. I had to Google a few since I'm not a huge movie buff. Once I sent the first message, I knew I had to keep up with the theme."

I smile. "Oh, of course. I would've been disappointed if you changed topics or even movie genres."

"I had a brief moment of *Shit, is this guy going to call the cops on me?* And I was preparing a speech in my mind to say to the officers. I was calculating whether I had enough money available for bail. Then I was wondering whose phone number I knew off the top of my head for my one call. My brain was going down a very dangerous path on Saturday night." Her eyes widen as she shakes her head at the memory.

I tip my head back and laugh. "Wow. You would make a horrible criminal."

"Or"—she places her hands on the table—"and hear me out, would I make an excellent one? Because I think through all possible outcomes?"

I grimace and shake my head. "Nope. I think I read some-where that overthinkers make the worst criminals."

"I think you're lying about that."

"I most definitely am." I shoot her a playful wink.

We both pause our conversation and smile at each other. She looks down bashfully—a faint pink blush coloring her cheeks.

I barely know her, but I'm already captivated by her. I have a deep desire to draw out a smile so bright it lights up her doe eyes. I want to make her laugh with such intensity that her face flushes with uninhibited happiness.

In my defense, the night I met her, I felt like something shifted in my world. When I saw her, a flood of emotions tightened in my chest. I got the sense that my life was about to change, but I couldn't pinpoint why or how.

I'm about to ask Charlie a question when Jody comes over with her excellent timing and bursts our blissful bubble.

Damn woman and her gum smacking.

"Charlie girl! The usual?" she asks, her teeth chewing that gum within every inch of its life.

"Yep. You got it." Charlie's lips flatten into a thin line, looking displeased. Jody walks away, and before I have a chance to say anything, Charlie speaks up.

"Well, that's not annoying at all."

"What?"

"The gum smacking. Like, could she swallow it or some-thing? Spit it out? Chew gum normally? Don't chew gum at all?" Her brows pull together in disgust, and it's endearingly cute.

I chuckle. "Yeah, I noticed that too. It's a tad off-putting."

"You're just being polite." She raises an eyebrow at me.

Jody comes back with Charlie's drink—a Diet Coke—and

I make a mental note of that for later, then spins on her heel to leave, but not before Charlie grabs her attention.

"Hey, Jody?"

"Yes, sweetie?"

"Stop that." Charlie gives her a *you know what I'm talking about* look with a single cocked eyebrow and hands Jody a napkin.

"Yes, ma'am," she says, spitting her gum into a napkin and promptly leaving. My eyes practically bulge out of my head.

The ovaries on this woman sitting before me are impressive.

Charlie shakes her head in disbelief, plucks the menu from behind the napkin dispenser, and looks at it. Without looking up, she says, "I've told her so many times she has to stop smacking her gum. It's so rude."

Wow. I can't figure out if I should be turned on or scared of her.

"Wait." Charlie pauses, and her eyes widen as she looks up. "You're Mrs. Jenkins's nephew."

I swallow. "Uh, yes." I'm not sure I like where this is heading.

"How do you handle holidays with her? She's a bit . . . much. And very loud." Charlie freezes, covering her mouth with embarrassment. "Oh god, I'm sorry. Sometimes I don't have much of a filter and forget who I'm talking to."

A hearty laugh escapes from my chest. I lean over the table slightly, meeting her eyes. "No, you're putting it lightly. She is a lot. The only way to handle holidays and family gatherings is to first scope out the exits, and then you drink enough bourbon to make a cowboy cry."

A faint smile touches her lips. "Ahh. Well, that's one way

to handle her." Charlie looks around the bar briefly, and I can't take my eyes off her. Her rich brown eyes scan the room while she nervously bites the inside of her lip.

"So, how did this whole little setup come about?" I say, motioning my hands between us. "Wait, let me guess. Donna barged into your store, acting like it was some kind of life or death emergency and then dropped the bomb on you?"

"That is shockingly accurate."

"And then, you couldn't say no because she does that weird lip thing, right?"

Her eyes crinkle with a smile, and her jaw drops open. "Yes! It's really strange, right?"

"So strange. Growing up, my sister and I would steer clear whenever she went on one of her tirades." I shudder. "And just for the record, I told her multiple times I didn't need someone to show me around. I mean, Hemlock is just a single long street with a lot of trees. I can't get too lost."

Her head gently nods up and down, taking in every word I'm saying. She also keeps looking around the room as more and more people pour into the place, creating a much more crowded atmosphere.

I want nothing more than to keep talking to her, but I can sense that she's getting antsy and tensing up. She must not enjoy super crowded spaces.

With that observation, I clear my throat. "How do you feel about getting out of here and maybe going for a walk? I'm feeling a bit jittery."

Charlie's body relaxes as she says, "Yes. That would be great."

After I paid the bill, I led Charlie out of the bar by placing my hand on her back. Once she gets outside, she takes a deep breath, her shoulders dropping with relief.

"Thank you for suggesting we get out of there. It was getting too overwhelming for my liking."

For a few moments, we walk in silence underneath the starlit sky. The wet pavement reflects the twinkling lights that wrap around the trees lining Main Street. It's a calm night with just the sounds of the occasional car passing us by.

"So, do you have family in the area?" I ask, our arms casually bumping into one another.

She stops abruptly, and I immediately sense her discomfort. Instantly, I know that I've hit a sore spot, and I'm pissed Aunt Donna didn't mention more details about Charlie to me.

Gazing down at her, Charlie's lost in her thoughts. Not wanting to pressure her, I stand there patiently, waiting for her to speak. I want to give her as much time and space as she needs.

She sharply inhales before looking up at me with misty eyes. A heavy weight settles in my stomach, and I realize this is more than petty family drama.

"Charlie, we can skip this question if—"

She lifts her hand, interrupting me. "I have two siblings: a younger sister, Joey, and an older brother, Jack. I'm the middle child." The other shoe is about to drop, and my suspicions are confirmed as she goes on. "My parents died almost a year ago in a car accident around Christmas. I moved back here after they died to take over their shop and take care of Vera." She sniffles, dropping her chin to the ground.

My heart drops with an overwhelming sadness. The pain she and her siblings are going through is unimaginable.

She wipes a stray tear away from her eye, and I grab a tissue out of my pocket. Holding it out to her, she looks at me like I'm holding an alien. "Do you really think I'd give you a used tissue? It's clean, you little weirdo," I say with a half-smile. Her tear-streaked face lets out a faint laugh as she grabs the tissue and dabs the corners of her eyes.

My voice grows somber. "I'm sure you've heard this a million times—"

"I know. You're sorry for our loss." Her eyes fall to the ground. "It's all we've heard for months and months."

My heart is on the verge of shattering as I see her glossy eyes veiled with dark sadness. As I look at her, I notice her red-tipped, button nose and rosy cheeks, wanting nothing more than to scoop her up and tell her everything is going to be okay.

Even though I know that won't fix any of her pain.

I do have an idea that could ease some of the sadness, even just for a night.

"Charlie," I say softly. The beautiful, broken girl's eyes flicker to mine. "How do you feel about hot chocolate?"

"Is it topped with marshmallows?" she questions.

"Would it be considered hot chocolate if it wasn't?"

She hums in agreement. "Good point. But yes, I love hot chocolate."

"Great, I know of an excellent place."

Chapter Eleven

CHARLIE

I'VE NEVER BEEN one to turn down hot chocolate, so I follow Finn like a moth to a flame. Is it smart to follow a near stranger to an undisclosed location? Absolutely not.

Though, at this point, the man seems pretty harmless.

While we walk down Main Street, I take in the vintage lamp posts emitting a soft glow, reflecting on the damp pavement. It's a perfect autumn night here in Hemlock. As we walk, our fingers subtly brush up against one another—twice.

My chest flutters—twice.

Within two minutes, we find ourselves in front of a café called Dark Side Brews. I press my palm to my forehead. "That's right, the nephew with the coffee shop." I drop my arms to my sides, annoyed that I didn't piece these facts together.

He chuckles. "You would be the worst detective, you know that?"

"Got me there. I tend to be in my own little world most of the time," I say on an exhale.

Finn smiles down at me while taking his keys out. It's a soft, knowing smile that says, *I know this, and that's okay.* When he unlocks the door and switches the lights on, my eyes take in every intricate detail of his coffee shop.

This guy poured his heart and soul into this place, and it shows. From the vintage photos in wooden frames that line the walls to the whimsical trinkets and colorful mismatched furniture—it looks like a home away from home.

I take a seat on an oversized blue armchair, continuing to observe the space.

"Uh. Nope. You come up here with me, sweetheart."

His deep voice snaps me out of my thoughts, and I lock eyes with a smiling Finn. With two fingers, he gestures for me to join him by the shop's wooden counter.

Well, if my head wasn't fuzzy before, it sure is now. I brush off the nickname and get up from my comfortable spot on the chair.

"Where do you want me, then?" I ask, clearing my throat and anxiously running my hand through my hair.

Finn's behind the counter, grabbing ingredients for hot chocolate, when he nearly fumbles two mugs the moment those words left my mouth.

Whoops.

Without looking at me, he pats the counter next to him. "You can sit right here." He blushes, looks over his shoulder, and gives me a shy smile.

I hum with joking uncertainty. "Am I allowed to sit on the countertop?"

He glances at me over his shoulder once again. "Don't worry about it. I know the owner." My eyes roll in amusement, and he doesn't miss it. "Oh, come on. That was clever!" He points a spoon at me in a weak attempt to get me to agree with him.

As I laugh and remove my jacket, I've become a bit too flustered in his presence due to his bad flirting. I'm not used to guys giving me this kind of attention.

In the past, the men I dated were subpar at best. I always felt I was a "just enough" girlfriend. Just nice enough to make pleasantries with. Just pretty enough to look put together. Just smart enough to hold a conversation. I was simply "just enough" and nothing more.

When I could finally let my guard down and breathe, they always wanted more from me than I could give them. More touching, more vulnerability, more emotional connection, and more . . . love. I was "just enough" but yet never enough for them. I couldn't open up because, deep down, every relationship didn't feel right. It seemed that no guy could accept me for who I was, and I got tired of pretending to be someone I wasn't. Eventually, I wanted to take the pressure off of myself and gave up dating completely. Dating and finding someone to be vulnerable with are so fucking hard. To build that trust and safety with someone and feel comfortable enough to let your guard down was completely, incredibly daunting. And with failed date after failed date, I was too tired and discouraged to continue.

Before my parents died, my last relationship ended in a complete dumpster fire. I remember asking my mom if something was wrong with me.

My mom and I were sitting out on the back porch, it was the middle of summer and the sun was setting. The crickets were chirping, and the air was cool, but humid. We were both rocking on the patio swing, absorbing the last rays of the evening sun.

"Mom, don't get weirded out. Or make this a big deal . . . I need to be vulnerable with you," I say, letting out a deep sigh.

She laughs, shaking her head. Her chocolate brown curls are extra bouncy in the summer due to the humidity. Turning to me, she smiles. The smile lines around my mother's mouth are my favorite feature of hers. "Even when you were a kid, you always prepared us for when you were about to have feelings of any kind. It's always been one of your most endearing qualities. Now, what's the matter?" She pats my leg.

I glance into my mom's warm, caramel eyes. "Is there something wrong with me? I'm in my thirties without a stable relationship to show for it." I will not cry. I will not cry. This has been prying on my mind for years and I need to get it out.

She releases an appalled scoff. "First of all, the guys you've dated in the past had zero redeeming qualities. Your father and I thought it was impressive. Who doesn't have a single redeeming quality? Seriously, Charlotte. Even your dad said mosquitoes were more useful than the last guy you were dating," she says, shaking her head. I start to laugh and nod in agreement. "Secondly, you, sweet girl, only deserve the best. And if it takes until you're eighty years old to find the best, then so be it." A lump of emotion swells in my throat. I stare out into the backyard, watching the sun dip below the horizon, casting that hazy summer glow over the trees.

My mom gently turns my chin to face her. "When the right guy comes along, all those walls you have up will completely drop. Your heart will know before your brain does. You just have to trust your heart, okay? Promise you'll do that for me."

My eyes swell with those damn tears again, and I give her a tight-lipped smile. "Okay, I promise," I whisper.

She gently pushes my hair behind my back and kisses my temple. "It's all gonna be okay, sweet girl, I promise. One day, a day when you least expect it, the right man will stumble into your life and turn it upside down. He will see you for you. He will love you for you. He will want to be with you because you're you."

I shake the memory from my brain, shoving down the swell of emotion that bubbled to the surface. Begrudgingly, I walk behind the counter and hop up on it. Finn isn't looking at me directly, but he coyly smiles at my closeness to him. His glasses slip down his nose, and he pushes them up with the back of his wrist. I'm momentarily distracted by the way he casually rolls up the sleeves of his sweater, revealing toned and defined forearms. Watching the muscles flex as he moves has my heart fluttering.

Finn moves with such confidence—it's quite a turn on. My eyes are entranced by Finn's skillful hands making us drinks. Those long fingers move with fluidity, guided by the simple motions of muscle memory. His hands look strong enough to knock someone out in a dark alley, yet gentle enough to wipe away tears.

Shaking off my trance that has me ogling this poor guy's hands, I run my own hands down my thighs. While wiping my sweaty palms, I try to think of what I should say to him. "So, is this some secret family recipe? Are you going to have to kill me after I watch you make this?"

Concentrating on the task at hand, he doesn't look at me, but his deep laugh fills the room. "What is it with you and murder? Should I be concerned? Are you hiding something? Or someone?"

"Why do you think the plants in my shop are thriving? Human remains make for excellent fertilizer," I deadpan, giving him a shrug.

Finn stops what he's doing and turns his body towards me with a concerned expression on his face.

Oh, I fucked up.

I made things weird.

"What is wrong with you?" Finn says, shaking his head.

Yep. I made things really weird.

My body tenses with regret. The urge to bolt for the nearest exit is at the forefront of my mind.

"You sent me home with all those plants and didn't think to offer me that fertilizer? You're setting this Plant Daddy up to be a failure, Charlie," he says, shaking his head before going back to make the drinks.

This son of a . . . I blink a few times, trying to process what he said, before a bag of mini marshmallows is tossed in my direction.

"Open these up for me? I can't have you just being a pretty face. You gotta earn your keep around here, sweetheart," he teases.

Ignoring the increasing temperature spreading across my body, I open the bag, pop a few in my mouth, and anxiously eat the sugar pillows because what else is there to do.

"Hey, throw one of those to me." Finn opens his mouth and waits for me to throw a marshmallow in.

"Don't do that to me. I have bad aim." I wince.

Again, that sexy chuckle escapes from him. Casually, Finn strolls over to me, sticking his hands in the bag of marshmallows. With my hand still in the bag, our fingers gently touch, sending a shiver up my arm. He pulls a few out, popping them in his mouth before turning his focus back to the hot chocolates.

Once finished, he tops each mug with a hefty handful of marshmallows and hands one to me.

"Cheers," he says as we clink our mugs together. The first sip is heavenly—rich, smooth, and comforting. A hug in a mug that warms me down to my bones.

"I must say, Finn, this is much better than the powder hot chocolate mix I usually buy on sale. You did good." I take another sip, humming in appreciation.

He sets his mug down and gives me an incredulous look that makes me laugh.

Finn's eyes bore into mine. I could easily see myself getting swept away in his ocean-blue irises.

Overwhelmed by his gaze, I avert my eyes and stare into my mug. The energy between us is unlike anything I've experienced before. Even though I don't enjoy meeting new people, I somehow feel drawn to Finn. The way he carries himself, the warmth of his smile, and his kind eyes are the perfect combination to lure me in.

Jokingly, he scoffs. "If you think this is just 'good,' then wait till you have my specialty coffee drink. I've heard that it's 'really good.'"

It's clear he's amused by my word choice, but I refuse to stroke his ego. My compliments are a privilege that you must earn, and one drink isn't going to change that . . . regardless of the dopamine rush I get from each sip.

I let out a contemplative hum. "I hate to break it to you, Finn. I don't like coffee." He goes to speak, and I raise my hand to stop him. "No matter what you say or how you make your drinks, you can't change my mind."

He releases a sigh full of regret. "Well, Charlie, it's been nice. I've enjoyed the time we've shared together. The exit is that way." He nods his head toward the door with a crooked smile. "What do you drink in the morning to wake up if you don't like coffee?"

My face is devoid of emotion, and my tone is deadpan. "The tears of those who scorned me in the past. Obviously."

His piercing stare locks on mine. "Hmm. Makes sense. Things are slowly coming together now."

Finn absolutely thinks my plant fertilizer's secret ingredient is dead people.

He clears his throat. "Let's play a game." Finn rests his hip up against the counter, crossing his arms. I'm temporarily mesmerized by how his navy sweater tightens over his biceps.

Those arms. He may be a lean guy, but those arms have enough definition to show through his thin sweater and pique my interest.

"Uh. No. I don't like games," I blurt out, perhaps too quickly.

I do love games. Very much. But this man is making me feel things that I thought were in hibernation—putting me on high alert.

"Charlie, play along." His tone is stern yet playful.

Well, that gave me a weird tingle.

"Do I have to?"

He tilts his head, feigning annoyance."Yes, Charlie."

All it takes is him saying my name again in that voice, and I fold like a lawn chair. "Fine."

"I'll bring you a different coffee a couple of times a week. If you like any of them, I win." His lips part into a confident smile.

I raise one unimpressed eyebrow at him. "What the hell do

you win? And, Mr. Cocky, what if I don't like any of them? Because that's what's going to happen."

"Doubt it," he scoffs, uncrossing his arms. Finn picks up his mug and takes a tentative sip, like he's nervous. Licking his lips, his eyes dart quickly to the ground and then back at me. "Dropping off coffee and getting to know a pretty girl is already a prize. I'll enjoy the bragging rights."

There's a warmth and sincerity in his voice that's difficult to ignore. I quickly glance down at my mug. "Does that usually work? The whole flirting thing?"

"Not sure. It's my first time using the line. Is it working?"

When I look up to meet his eyes, I notice the tips of his ears are pink. Quiet lingers between us before Finn's voice fills the silence. "I'll give you free hot chocolate for as long as you want. That's what you win."

Nerves begin to settle in as self-doubt floats to the surface. Finn barely knows me. He sees surface-level Charlie—a nice-enough plant store girl. I worry that the more he gets to know me, the less he'll like me. At the same time, I'm looking at him and his hopeful face, and something inside tells me to go for it. Because if I said no to this man standing in front of me, it would feel like accidentally stepping on your dog's paw.

"You got a deal." I stick out my hand.

Finn's large hand grasps mine, and I swear my stomach plummets because of the way his long fingers wrap around my wrist. It's that whooshing sensation you get when you drive down a steep hill, or when you're on a rollercoaster.

My phone chimes with a text and I notice it's getting very late. Letting go of his hand, I hop off the counter. "Well, Finn, thank you for not being a random phone creep and making me a *really good* drink. But I have to get going. Vera needs to be let out before she disowns me for leaving her alone."

I'm waiting for him to scoff or groan with annoyance and convince me to stay longer. Instead, empathy flickers across his features.

"Next time, bring her," he says softly, with understanding eyes.

Next time?

What does that mean?

My cheeks are on fire. *He wants there to be a next time?*

Stunned, I reply, "That . . . uh . . . sounds good. Have a good night, Finn."

I need to get out of here fast before I ruin this moment.

"You too, Charlie." He flashes me a devastating smile.

I leave his coffee shop with that same whooshing sensation in my stomach again.

Chapter Twelve

CHARLIE

MY FAVORITE PART of the night has arrived.

The part of the night where I ruminate on my couch while listening to my dog snore.

All I can think about is Finn and his obnoxiously charming smile. Along with my abrupt exit, my brain is running in circles with questions. *Does he hate me now because I left too fast? What if he thinks I'm weird? Will he change his mind about me?*

Amidst the spiral in my mind, one sentence cuts through the anxious thoughts.

Next time, bring her.

He said that in such a low, rumbly tone that I think some parts of my brain stopped functioning. It's been so long, almost a year, since I've felt any kind of strong emotion at all.

Grief is like the weather. Sometimes, it's just this weird

fog that follows you around as you go about your day, and other times, it's a category five hurricane. All of your emotions are dulled yet heightened at the same time. Plus, when you add on the responsibility of looking after a store that keeps your parents' memory alive and a sappy dog, everything seems heavier.

There are two versions of me. The one that existed before experiencing a tragic loss and the one that exists now after experiencing said tragic loss.

Even though I'm the middle child, I've always been the one to keep an eye out for my siblings—even while we were growing up. My parents dubbed me "the responsible one" ever since I admitted to reading the terms and conditions on websites.

In my defense, you can never be too careful when your information is at risk of being collected and distributed to who-knows-where.

Now, since we're adult orphans, I feel like I've taken on the parental figure role for my brother and sister. For the last year, there has been a constant stream of calls, texts, and random shop visits from them about anything and everything. My sister once called me for advice on how to cook boxed macaroni and cheese.

Don't get me wrong, I love my siblings; I would help them commit semi-illegal crimes.

But sometimes, they exhaust me, and I would like a small break. Which brings my thoughts back to the floppy-haired Finn, as I absentmindedly pet Vera's head and stare at the ceiling. In the few encounters I've had with Finn, I feel as if he's softening something inside of me.

Which terrifies me.

I've never been described as "soft" in my life.

Abrasive? Yes.

Steely? Sure.

Cranky? Duh.

But why do I feel like part of me can just relax around him? It's almost as if my brain can power down for a bit and there's nothing left in the world to worry about.

Despite only knowing him for a little while, being in his presence has eased some of the mental and emotional burdens I carry. There's an unmistakable air about him that I can't quite put my finger on.

What an interesting effect he has on me.

"What am I actually doing with my life," I whisper to myself as I stroke Vera's soft, golden fur. Unsurprisingly, her response is a judgmental groan.

At least she's a dog who matches my energy.

"Vera, I'm a grown woman, lusting over a strange man like a teenager and talking to you—a dog. Don't you think that's a bit of a cause for concern?" I look down at her, and she just yawns, licking her lips before promptly setting her head down again on my thigh.

I finally decide to take my rumination station of a body to bed and continue to overthink everything in the comforting embrace of too many pillows and blankets.

Vera quietly follows me as I shuffle to my bedroom because she also knows my inability to say no. Every night, she stands at the bottom of the bed and places her head on the mattress with her huge, puppy dog eyes and gentle tail wags while huffing to get up.

And every night, I pat the bed and say, "Get up here, drama queen."

As I stroll into the room, I head toward the window to crack it for some breeze. I love this time of year—the changing colors, cool temperatures, and the crispness of fall just ignite a bit of happiness in me.

After changing into a baggy T-shirt and flannel pajama pants, I crawl under the covers and fluff a pillow behind me. Lately, I've had difficulty sleeping. My doctor said it's normal for sleep patterns to be disrupted with grief. Which is why I'm up reading until 3 a.m. and then consuming three Diet Cokes to get me through the next day.

With a heavy sigh, I turn over in bed, shut off the bedside lamp, and grab my paperback with its equipped book light and read until I drift off to sleep.

***

"HEY, HEY, MY LITTLE GROUCHY GREMLIN!" Marnie bellows from the front of the store.

Sighing, I rub my forehead. "Must you yell that every time? What if we had customers in here, and they heard you?"

I was deep in thought before being so rudely interrupted by Marnie. It's been a week since that night with Finn, and that's all I've been thinking about. I haven't heard from him or even seen him, and at first, I thought maybe he was ignoring me.

Earlier this week, I took Marnie's advice and paid more attention. The long lines coming out the door of the newly opened Dark Side Brews proves that Finn is busy. The man has been getting slammed with business ever since he opened. Especially because people in this town love their coffee.

Personally, I think they should be drinking more water. It

may even out their overzealousness. Their high energy is too much for Vera and me.

I'm at the front counter rescuing a snake plant that one of my customers left in rough shape. How they almost killed this plant is beyond me.

Marnie drifts towards me, ignoring my previous question and stopping at the counter, a puzzled expression settling on her face. "Why does that snake plant look like it's ready for the grave?"

"Because it is. Nick brought it in and told me to 'fix it.' No 'please,' no 'thank you.' Just 'fix it' and he walked out," I grumble, clipping away at the limp, unsalvageable leaves.

"How does someone even manage to kill one of these?" she says, flicking the plant. "It's virtually impossible."

I shrug. "The plant probably got tired of his bullshit. It probably couldn't breathe because his arrogance was taking up too much oxygen in his house."

Marnie snorts. "That's a good one, Grem."

"Oh wow. We're shortening that nickname now?" My eyes raise over the plant, pinning her with a humorous glare.

Marnie gives me a sly smirk and I can't help but shake my head. Turning my focus back on the plant, Marnie begins organizing a few things behind the counter.

"Oh my god. I forgot to ask! You met Jenkins's nephew, right?" she questions, stuffing some papers in folders that she'll most likely misplace.

I was hoping she would have forgotten about that. She was off visiting some family for the past week, so I haven't had a chance to speak much with her. Plus, Marnie has the memory of a goldfish. It's both endearing and enraging.

My shears drop to the counter with more force than I

anticipated. "How on earth do you remember that but can't remember to lock the front door of this place?"

She shrugs nonchalantly. "Who the hell would willingly steal plants?"

"You're fired," I deadpan.

Marnie checks her watch as she walks over to grab her apron. "It only took you thirty-two minutes into my shift to say that. That may be a record. Anyway, you have to tell me how it went!"

Leaning on the counter, I thread my fingers through my hair, resting my head in my hands. I sigh so deeply that I'm sure the next town could hear it.

Marnie starts chuckling. "No. Fucking. Way. Was it—"

I don't let her finish. "Yes, it fucking was."

"Well, this calls for a 'Closed' sign discussion." She walks over to the front door and flips the sign that now says we're closed. She only does this when she wants uninterrupted story time from me. Rare, but when I do have a story, it's usually pretty good. Marnie grabs a stool behind the counter and sits down with her face in her palms. She's looking at me like a child ready for their bedtime story.

I straighten up, setting my hands on my hips. "It was indeed *that* Finn. Or, as you know him, Gumby."

"What a small fucking world. Is he as crazy as his aunt? Does he also do that weird lip thing?"

"No, and no. He's shockingly normal and very nice." I debated telling her what happened after meeting him and how he made us hot chocolate. Knowing her, she'll make a huge deal out of it, and I'm not in the frame of mind to handle all of her Marnieness right now.

"Wow. So, he's the one that owns Dark Side Brews down the street? Sick name, by the way," she says with admiration.

"So what happens next? Are you going to hold up your end of the deal? You know what happened last time you told Jenkins you would do something and you didn't."

Oh, do I remember. The damn woman told the whole town, including my parents, that I was unreliable. Granted, I was only nineteen; of course I was unreliable. But in my defense, she wanted me to dig up FBI-level information on her second husband (or was it her third?). Thankfully, my parents put her in her place and told her I wasn't breaking any laws to gather the information she needed.

I look at Marnie, rolling my lips as I shrug with indifference. "He seems pretty nice and not pushy. Also, he seems to be on our team regarding Jenkins."

"Really? How so?"

"We discussed best practices for getting through her gatherings with your sanity intact, which included getting very drunk and knowing the exit routes." I chuckle.

"Oh, he sounds like my kind of guy!"

When there's a knock at the door, our heads snap to the front of the store. Due to the ridiculous number of plants here, you can't see anything from the counter except for a wall of green.

Marnie eyes the door. "Do they not read? Can't they see we're closed?" She begrudgingly walks to the door, unlocking it for the customer. There's a moment of silence, followed by hushed voices. Marnie's tone of voice is a bit higher and friendlier than usual.

She's also *giggling*. Which is wildly out of character for her.

Huh. Marnie's flirting.

Amidst the forest of plants, I spot Marnie with Finn trailing behind her. In his hand is a small to-go coffee cup. I can't help but feel a tad skeptical because I don't think she knows who he is. She's laying the charm on thick, between her fluttering eyelashes and lip biting.

My poker face fails when Finn and I lock eyes, and I try to suppress a smile. Marnie is in her own world, gazing up at Finn as if he's a gift to all women. I turn my back to compose myself. This whole flirtatious interaction goes on for about five minutes—five minutes too long, because now I'm getting secondhand embarrassment.

In those five minutes, Marnie has complimented his hair, his biceps (I make a mental note to sneak a peek later), his dark gray sweater vest, his eyes, and the list goes on. I have to give her credit: she's really putting it all out there and leaving no compliment stone unturned. Marnie has nothing to lose, and it's admirable.

Finally, Finn interrupts her using such a gentle, kind tone that my heart does that annoying fluttery thing again.

"I don't mean to interrupt, but I didn't catch your name. What was it again? My apologies if you told me and I didn't hear you," Finn says to Marnie.

What a fucking gentleman. His mother should be so proud.

Marnie's swoon can be felt throughout the entire store. She loves a polite, self-aware man.

"Oh my goodness, no worries! I'm Marnie. And you are?"

Who is this person and where the hell is Marnie? What did she add to her water bottle this morning? She's never flirty. I've seen her shoot daggers out of her eyes if a man so much as glances in her direction.

Finn laughs softly, a hint of amusement laced in his tone.

The bomb is about to drop.

"I'm Finn. And I'm here to bring Charlie this," he says. I hear him place the cup on the counter.

The heavy silence of realization smacks Marnie in the face. Feeling brave, I turn back around to them, and my friend looks at me like she's ready to disown me.

Arms crossed, hip popped, and one eyebrow raised—she's ready for battle. I cover my mouth with one hand and start laughing.

"Charlotte," Marnie says, using my full name, which means I'm in trouble.

"Yes?" I look at her with the best, innocent facial expression that I can muster up.

"Were you just going to let me go on and continue?"

"I mean, it did sound like you were enjoying yourself. Who am I to rob you of that kind of joy? That wouldn't make me a very good friend." I shrug innocently.

Marnie huffs. "I quit."

"No, you don't," I reply. "Now, stop talking and head to the back. You have inventory you need to take care of."

As she steps behind the counter, heading to the back, she faces me. "Fine. But this conversation isn't finished." Quickly, she glances around the store, takes a few steps closer, and leans close to my ear. "I don't know about you, but he's rocking that slutty little sweater vest. What a saucy little minx."

I shoot her a glance from the corner of my eye. "Get to work, or I'll fire you . . . again."

"I just quit three seconds ago!" Her chuckle fills the room as she takes off to the back, hopefully checking inventory and not social media. I really do need her to do some work.

I take a steadying breath and turn my gaze to Finn.

Resting my hands on my waist, I look up at him. "So, what brings you in today? Need a fourteenth plant?"

His face breaks into a smile, his eyes crinkling at the corners. Finn's charming personality matches his annoyingly charming face. Immediately, my heart beats faster in my chest with his simple smile. Completely forgetting how to form sentences, my mouth goes dry, and all that confidence I had earlier goes out the window.

I'm screwed.

Chapter Thirteen

Finn

"WELL, it's day one of Charlie's Coffee Journey, and I brought you your first drink," I say, nudging the cup towards her with my index finger.

"Oh. I thought you forgot about that." She seems taken aback, but I'm a man who never goes back on my word.

I tilt my head. "Charlie, there's absolutely no way I could forget about this."

Despite her poker face, that compliment had a definite impact on her. The pinkish hue on her cheeks says so.

I clear my throat. "Sorry it took so long, though. The shop has been extremely busy. This town *really* loves their coffee."

"How many times has Dan visited?"

My jaw drops. Dan comes in three times a day, at minimum. He's probably keeping me in business. "Are we talking about—"

"Yes. You know exactly who I'm talking about. I know,

you know. The dude must have a caffeine addiction," she says, her soft laugh echoing through the store. I swear my heart briefly stops beating in response to hearing her laugh.

I'm stunned. "Wow. Everyone really knows everything about everybody around here."

"Oh, I'm aware. I keep to myself and, against my will, I still know more than I'd like to," she says with a grimace.

I shake my head. I'm definitely not in the city anymore. "Well, you'll have to get me up to speed on the town's . . . unique residents."

A small smile touches her lips as she nods. "Sure. I can do that."

Charlie looks equally ready to garden or to go work on a wartime assembly line with her denim overalls and a red bandana wrapped in her hair. Her outfit gives her the appearance of a plant lady version of Rosie the Riveter.

I always did have a thing for her during my high school history class.

What can I say? Strong women make my knees weak.

Charlie eyes the cup like it has a contagious disease. "Do I have to drink this? Like, right now?"

"Yes. Drink up."

"With you here watching me?" Her eyes are wide with revulsion.

I dip my chin, raising my eyebrows at her. "Yes. I need to watch your facial expressions to see if you're lying."

She scoffs. "I have *never* lied a day in my life."

"THAT'S A LIE, FINN!"

We both startle and look towards the backroom where Marnie just called Charlie's bluff.

"DON'T LISTEN TO HER!" Marnie continues.

I cast a knowing smirk Charlie's way. "Busted."

Charlie mutters under her breath, "I need to reduce her hours."

"I thought she already quit?" I question.

Her head tilts with a hint of sass. "I fired her. There's a big difference."

"I thought you were reducing her hours . . ." I trail off.

"This is not the hill you want to die on today."

I let out a laugh, unable to contain my amusement. Her expression is indignant, and she's standing with one hand resting on her hip, looking like she's ready for an all out battle.

She's irresistibly charming.

Slowly, I nod my head, agreeing with her. Because that's what you do when you don't want to battle a woman who knows her way around a golf club.

Plus, I want to keep my kneecaps intact. I kind of like them.

Although fleeting, her expression softens briefly until she looks down. Deep brown eyes narrow with repulsion at the harmless coffee cup before her. You'd think she was about to swallow cough medicine. Carefully, she picks it up and the way her soft pink lips wrap around the edge of the cup hypnotizes me.

Just as I suspected, she scowls. "This is disgusting. I thought you were trying to convince me to like coffee, not hate it even more."

"I forgot to mention the first cup is the control. So, it's just a classic black coffee. It should get better from here." I shrug. "At least I hope so."

She lifts her chin to me. "Well, I don't have high hopes. You can have this back and get it out of here, thank you very much," she blurts out the last words in a single breath. Setting the cup back down and sliding it in my direction, she crosses her arms and lifts her chin in defiance.

This woman makes me laugh. She's cute, feisty, and keeps me on my toes.

I like it.

When I eye the cup, a grin tugs at my lips. "And what am I supposed to do with this? I made it for you."

Realization blankets her face as it dawns on her that I came here for her, and only her.

Her body slackens a bit. "Oh. When you put it like that, then I'll just take it. Maybe try to tolerate it." Her inhale is sharp as she nods. "You know, kind of like exposure therapy?" She grasps the cup and holds it close to her chest.

My eyes work hard not to focus on the cup settled between her breasts. Because I'm a gentleman, I steal a brief glance and file the mental image of her away for later.

I clear my throat, propping both hands up on the counter in front of me. "You're going to dump it down the sink as soon as I leave, aren't you?"

Her nod is curt. "Bingo."

A laugh rises out of my chest, and I shake my head. "Charlie, what am I going to do with you?"

The moment those words leave my mouth, a flush of pink blooms across her round cheeks. I swear, she must have no idea how beautiful she truly is.

Charlie reminds me of that cute girl next door that you'd have a crush on growing up. A special type of beauty radiates from her. It's more than just surface level, it's soul deep—a beauty you can feel from the inside out.

"Hopefully not subject me to any more terrible coffee, but that doesn't seem to be in my future if this cup is where we're starting." She grimaces, shaking the cup.

"Fine. Give it to me."

She hands the coffee over, and I take a sip.

Her forehead creases. "You just took a sip out of a near-stranger's cup. I could have the flu, or strep, or mono! Or another illness!"

My head tilts to the side as I raise my eyebrows at her. She's wrinkling her nose at me, glancing from the cup to my face.

"Charlie, do you have the flu, strep, or mono? Or another illness that you're so, *so* worried about?" There's noticeable humor in my tone, so she knows I'm only teasing her.

She swallows, thrusting her chin forward. "No, but—"

"Then I have nothing to worry about." I wink. "I have to get back to the shop before Frank takes over and makes everyone his minions. He can be a very persuasive pup." I shrug.

At the simple mention of Frank, Vera saunters over to me, her tail wagging with happiness. After a quick ear scratch, I give Vera one of Frank's treats from my pocket. I don't miss the way Charlie's eyes soften at this simple gesture.

As I spin on my heels to leave her store, I call out, "See you tomorrow! Same time, same place. Don't forget to put your game face on, champ!" Her sound of disapproval makes me smile and gives me the fuel I need to get through the day.

There's a full-blown grin on my face as I walk down the street back to Dark Side Brews. When I look ahead, I see that Frank is now patiently waiting outside for me as he receives ear scratches from strangers passing by. My walk begins to slow the closer I get to my dog.

He has a random, bright purple shoe that I suspect belongs to a small child in his mouth. It only took him two hours to steal something that's not his. Then again, he's probably got a collection of items hidden in some corner of the shop.

I stop in front of him, giving him my stern *I'm not fucking around* voice. "Frank, drop it." His ears perk up at the sound of my voice, and his nub of a tail begins to wag. "No, Frank, now is not the time to be happy to hear me. You stole a poor kid's shoe. Drop it."

Frank whimpers and reluctantly drops the small purple shoe to the ground. I search to see if there's anyone nearby who has a kid with a missing shoe. About two stores down, I notice a dad with a stroller and a small child with one bare foot.

Swiftly, I hurry down the street to catch up to him before he gets too far.

"Excuse me, sir? I think you dropped this." I smile, holding out the shoe.

Confusion is written all over his face until he looks down at his daughter in the stroller. "Oh, thanks, man. My wife would've killed me if I came back with another missing baby shoe. For some reason, this little one keeps kicking them off." He chuckles.

"Ah. Well, I can't blame her. Sometimes you just need to rock that sock life. Also, sorry that it's a little soggy. My dog was keeping it safe . . . in his mouth." I wince.

"No worries at all. Your dog was just helping to break them in," he jokes. "Thanks again, and thanks for saving me the extra twenty dollars for another pair of shoes."

I smile. "Anytime. Have a good one!"

Heading back to my shop, I begin venturing down the dangerous road of thinking about the future. When the dart landed on Hemlock, pointing me to where I'd be opening my new business, I was a bit worried about moving to a smaller town. When I moved out at eighteen for college, I'd only been drawn to bigger cities—basking in the busy atmosphere with so much to do and being surrounded by thousands of faces daily. I never saw the same person twice, which always kept things fun and interesting.

Until it didn't anymore.

Since I've moved around so much, it's always been easy to compare one city to the next. It struck me that I haven't compared Hemlock to any other city I've been to before. Maybe it's because it's still so new? Maybe it's because it has a unique quality?

Or maybe it's because of a mysterious brunette woman working a few doors down from me.

<hr>

AFTER FLIPPING the café's sign to "Closed" and locking up for the evening, I feel like I can finally take a breath again. Since opening, we've had a constant stream of customers, and it's tough to keep up with the demand.

My feet lazily shuffle to my back office. I rub my aching lower back, which is feeling the strain and fatigue from being on my feet all day. All I can think about is collapsing onto my soft, comfortable bed.

Originally, my idea was to work shorter days at the café and let the staff run the show. But getting to know the town and its interesting inhabitants has been a lot of fun and, time after time, I find myself having stayed far later than I planned. Today, I got caught up in a story from an older gentleman who told me he saw BigFoot in the Calapooya Mountains in the eighties. He was so animated while telling his story that my whole shop had paused to listen to him. With how engrossed everyone was, you'd think it was an open mic night.

Not even a month in and more ideas to expand the offerings of my coffee shop are simmering in the back of my mind. Maybe hosting events such as book clubs or even open mic nights? The passing thoughts about future possibilities have stopped me in my tracks.

I smile to myself because this is a *good* sign. This newfound hopefulness and optimism for what lies ahead is a feeling I want to hold close to my heart.

Trying not to get too far ahead of myself, I flick off all the lights in my shop, with getting home back on my mind. I've overstayed my welcome here to the point that I'm becoming borderline delusional with bone-deep fatigue. Briefly checking the clock, I notice it's 8 p.m. already.

Definitely way too late to be here, considering we closed a few hours ago.

I whistle for Frank as I grab my keys and head out the front of the store to lock up. As I step outside, a refreshing cool breeze sweeps over me. Frank's nose tips to the sky as he sniffs, the wind tousling his fur. After I double-check the locked door, we make our way to my car when the orange glow of a shop's light catches my eye.

My feet carry me a few steps closer down the street. Charlie's store appears to still be open. The warm light of A New Leaf reflects on the wet pavement outside, practically beckoning me to go in there and give her a visit.

I glance down at my dog, keeping my voice calm and even so he doesn't get too excited."Come on, Frank, let's go make a house call, shall we?" His nub of a tail wags, and he prances behind me with such joy that you think he'd stolen someone's wallet.

I could be wrong, but I think Frank may have a crush on Vera, the sweet, lazy-as-a-sloth golden retriever.

The breeze picks up a bit, making it an even chillier fall night. Buttoning up my jacket, Frank and I continue making our way down to A New Leaf. I can't help but soak in the quiet stillness of the town at night. The trees are lined with glowing twinkling lights, there are no cars on the road, and everything feels peaceful. You'd never guess that it was bustling with people just a few hours ago.

Upon arriving at Charlie's storefront, I gently tap on the window with my knuckle, patiently waiting for her to appear. Not seeing any hint of movement, I tap on the window again.

Still nothing.

Thinking she just forgot to turn the lights off, I pull out my phone to send her a quick message.

I'm looking down at my phone and typing out a text as Frank and I begin to walk away. We both stop when we hear the clicking of a door being unlocked. When I turn around, a modern-day Rosie the Riveter is ready for battle with her trusty 5-iron golf club clutched in one hand and a vining plant in the other.

Chapter Fourteen

CHARLIE

A LOUD YAWN breaks free from me as I look over at my phone and notice it's 8 p.m. Leaning back in my office chair, I look around; the backroom of A New Leaf is still filled to the brim with my parents' things. It's like a time capsule in this office —photos of my siblings on the wall, the first dollar bill they made, random posters of botanicals that have begun to yellow with age.

I love it. It feels like a hug from beyond the grave whenever I'm in this room. Sometimes, when I'm overwhelmed by the store's chaos, I'll flip the sign to "Closed" and sit here for a few minutes to allow myself to calm down.

My eyes blur with tears as I reflect on the last time I hugged my parents. It was a week before they passed. We were all together for a family dinner. On the outside, you'd assume I hated the silly weekly dinners. On the inside, I loved them.

My parents knew I loved them by the subtle glances they gave me at dinner and how my mom would always have my favorite dessert at the ready. Dinner was always chaotic, with Joey rambling on about her travels, my dad talking about his new propagated plants, Jack telling stories about his foolish employees, and my mom spilling the town gossip while Vera snored underneath the table.

Crazy how things can change so fast.

So fast that my head still can't wrap itself around their death almost a year later.

Vera's loud snore pulls me from my deep thoughts. I should get home and get some sleep. I know that the second my head hits that pillow my brain will decide it's time to kick into overdrive, causing me to toss and turn all night long until the sun peeks through the curtains.

With my lack of sleep, I'm starting to believe these dark purple circles under my eyes are taking up permanent residency.

Releasing a deep sigh, I gaze down at Vera, who remains curled up, completely sound asleep with her head resting on my foot. What many people don't mention about grief is that animals can experience it just as much.

A few months after my parents died, my siblings and I decided to go through some of their clothes. We made a donation pile on their basement floor and, once we were done, we saw Vera snuggling on top of a massive pile of their clothes.

As expected, we all started sobbing and decided to just leave the pile as is for her. Joey decided to sew a blanket out of some of their old shirts, which Vera adores so much that she'll even carry it with her around the house. A few times, she's been snuggled up with her blanket and in such a deep sleep that her tail wags. I imagine she's dreaming about playing fetch with my parents on a warm, sunny, summer day in a wide-open field.

Some people would say, "She's just a dog! She'll get over it!" To which I would reply they can kindly fuck off and that dogs, just like humans, experience grief. Every day, I do what I can to help ease her sadness a bit. Whether that's taking her to the store with me, feeding her part of my sandwich, or showering her in so much love that she'll want to run away from me.

Still looking at her peaceful face, I hear a soft knock at the store's front door. Vera looks so content that I don't want to move my foot. Hopefully, the knocking will go away. I wonder if someone thought the store was open since I left some of the lights on.

Another knock, with a bit more force, follows moments later.

Okay, this is annoying. Who is out this late? Everyone in this town has the early bird special and is in bed by 6 p.m.

I carefully extract my foot out from under Vera's head and she makes a faint little groan. Glancing over at my trusty 5-iron, I grab the club and pick up a potted plant on my way to the front door.

You never know when the club may not be enough and you'll need reinforcements.

Not that a plant will help at all, but it's better to be safe than sorry.

Once I'm near the door, I see someone turning to leave.

That someone is Finn.

I unlock the door, and he turns around and smiles, casually walking back to me with Frank by his side.

"You know, we have to stop meeting like this," he says, eyeing my golf club. "I really need to know the story behind the golf club. Why a 5-iron?" Then he glances at the plant in my other hand and points. "Were you going to chuck that at my head, too? Damn. I'll need you on my team if a war breaks out in this town."

I, unsuccessfully, fight a smile and roll my eyes at him. Without saying anything, I drop my club and use my hip to open the door wider. Finn's bright eyes sharpen with interest as they trace the curve of my hip. Clearing my throat in the hope of redirecting his gaze to my face, I motion for them to enter with a quick tilt of my head. A blush rises on his cheeks and up to the tip of his ears when he realizes his lack of subtlety. Adjusting his glasses that slipped down his nose, Finn whistles for his faithful pup, who enters the room first. When Finn follows, his hand touches my hip briefly as I stand in the doorway—even though there's more than enough room for him to get by.

My pulse picks up for a fraction of a second at the slight bit of contact.

It probably wasn't intentional, and I'm most likely overanalyzing the touch.

As he retreats to the back of the store, I can still feel the warm pressure of his hand on my hip. I swallow nervously, shifting my eyes to his back. My eyes linger on his incredibly tall frame, which makes his perfectly tailored peacoat look downright indecent on his body. Sensing my stare, Finn's deep blue eyes meet mine and he flashes me a devastating smirk over his shoulder.

A smirk that's paired with those obnoxiously attractive dimples.

My heart slowly hammers in my chest, and I realize that the brush of his strong hand on my hip was most *definitely* intentional.

There's a battle in my brain between being mildly annoyed and mildly turned on by that simple gesture. After steadying my breath, I finally shut the door behind me. The clicking of the lock echoes throughout the quiet store as I trail behind Finn.

The store lights create a warm, calming ambiance throughout the space. Bright lights give me a major headache, so whenever I'm here late, I turn down the lighting. With Finn here, it feels less calming and more . . . romantic.

Internally, I groan.

Vera strolls up to Frank and swishes her large tail. Frank senses her, and now his little nub of a tail is fluttering like a butterfly's wings. These two are soulmates who must've met in a past life.

I want to hate it, but it's really fucking cute.

Finn is standing at the front of the store with excellent posture, looking as tall and handsome as ever. Glancing around the shop with curious eyes, Finn focuses on a cactus. His hand inches slowly toward the plant.

"Seriously? Do not touch that. Are you five? You'll poke yourself," I scold.

He startles and puts his hands in his pockets.

Why are men idiots sometimes?

"You know, I'm starting to wonder if you're magnetized to my store since you keep popping in." I pull a stool from behind the counter and motion for him to sit.

"You're the one that had the light on. I just assumed that was your 'Finn Signal.'" He shrugs, plopping down on the seat. Those long legs stretch out below the counter so that his feet are now encroaching on my side.

I narrow my eyes. "Cute." I sit opposite him; my arms rest on the counter while my body subconsciously leans closer to him. With my feet firmly planted on the ground, Finn shifts so that his long legs surround mine.

He bites his lip, holding back a laugh. "My mom thinks so."

"At least someone does," I deadpan.

"Rude."

"You'll get over it."

With matching serious looks, our eyes lock. Unable to hold back, smiles break free on our faces. Our laughter carries through the store, creating a safe bubble surrounding us. In this moment, it feels like we are the only two people in existence.

Dammit. I think I like him.

He's charming, he has a cute dog, and he makes incredible hot chocolate. He's not smart with cacti, but I think I can overlook that.

With my arms folded, I gaze at him with suspicion. "Alright, let's address the elephant in the room. What the hell are you doing here so late?"

"What are *you* doing here so late?"

I lift one brow and tilt my chin up. "Don't answer my question with a question. That's the oldest trick in the book. We both know you can do better than that."

"Has anyone ever told you that you're kind of feisty? I didn't know anyone wearing overalls could have so much spice," he says, holding in a smile. He leans in even closer to me, enveloping me in his cologne. "I think I kind of like it," he whispers. When I roll my eyes, that smile of his breaks free, and I try my damndest not to let it affect me.

Unfortunately, it does.

Thank god the room is dim enough, or else he would see my face on fire.

I also think I'm sweating. Am I coming down with something? I must be sick because no man has ever gotten a rise out of me like this.

I'm shaking my head at myself. I cannot believe this guy —tall and a bit lanky, he probably watches the History Channel while organizing his sweater vests for fun. And yet, he's so endearingly charming that I can't help but experience that pesky flutter in my stomach whenever he speaks.

"Well, congratulations. It seems like you're the first to like the feisty, overalls-wearing girl." I laugh, self-deprecation evident in my voice.

He's watching me carefully now—borderline studying me —and it makes me squirm.

"I highly doubt that," he says, his voice low.

"Let's agree to disagree." I pause for a moment, gathering my thoughts. "So, you never answered my question. Why are you here so late?"

"I've never been the greatest sleeper."

I nod, knowing exactly what he means. "Ah. So you're a night owl."

He sits up a little straighter now. "You too, I presume?"

My chin dips, and a lump begins to form in my throat. "I used to be able to sleep well until . . . well, you know."

Still looking down at the counter, I grab a stray leaf and fidget with it between my fingers—giving me something to do while this heavy cloud of emotion hovers over us.

Finn's voice is filled with sorrow. "You don't have to say more. No explanation needed."

We sit in silence for a moment as I try to tear my focus away from the sadness that looms over me. While I'm thinking of ways to change the subject, Finn's warm hand reaches over and covers my hand that's incessantly fidgeting with the leaf. With soothing strokes, he rubs his thumb along the back of my hand. I can hear my pulse rising in my ears—louder than ever. Looking down at our joined hands, I can't help but notice how his completely envelopes mine, and my fidgeting stops.

Immediately, the overwhelming sadness storming inside of me begins to subside, giving me a chance to come up for air and breathe. Even though I'm not the biggest fan of being touched, feeling his hand against mine grounds me.

A temporary reprieve from my hectic mind.

What would a hug feel like if a simple touch of his hand makes me feel this way?

A kiss?

I swallow thickly, making sure my mind doesn't wander further than that at this moment.

When I finally gather the courage to glance up at him, his gaze is locked on me, with no plans of leaving. There's something unreadable brewing in Finn's eyes. It's not pity or sorrow. I can't tell exactly what his expression is. If I had to guess, he's thinking of ways to help me—comfort me. Like he senses what I'm feeling and what I need without me having to verbalize it.

"Come for a walk with me," he says.

I speak so quietly that I can barely hear myself as I simply say, "Okay."

Chapter Fifteen

FINN

I COULD TELL she was hurting. She didn't have to say anything. I could see it in her teary eyes, filled to the brim with grief. For me, a walk helps to clear my mind; it's almost like a temporary reset button. Sometimes, I can get so caught up in my own thoughts that it feels like I'm trapped in my mind, slowly suffocating from the inside out. Getting outside, especially at night, always has a way of making me breathe again.

Right now, Charlie needs to feel like she can breathe again.

Her voice was so small when she agreed to come on a walk with me that it took every bone in my body to not wrap my arms around her and hold her snug against my chest. Even though she doesn't seem like the hugging type, I could sense she needed one the second those painful memories surfaced.

I study her face and give her a small smile. "Go get your jacket, it's cold out there."

She sniffles and nods, disappearing into the store's backroom for her coat.

Charlie calls out, "Should we bring the dogs? I don't have a leash for Vera."

The dogs. I completely forgot about them. A quick glance next to me shows the two lovers curled up together.

"Let's take them back to my shop. There's less damage they can do there!" I shout back to her.

Charlie walks back out, and she has on her long, dark brown wool jacket that ends at her ankles. "Uhh. Like I said, I don't have Vera's leash, but—"

I stop her mid-sentence before her worried thought gets away from her. "Vera isn't going very far. Plus, you and I know she isn't the fastest dog, so it'll be easy to catch up to her if she makes a run for it."

She chuckles. Her eyes are still sad when she laughs, but I've never seen anything more beautiful. She adjusts her coat, flipping out her long dark hair that was tucked into the collar. "Alrighty. Let's head out?"

I take in the sight of Charlie for a brief moment, from her shiny dark hair and beautiful brown eyes down to her full hips and black boots. My heart beats an unusual rhythm at the mere thought of being close to her. Clearing my throat, I nod and lead her to walk ahead of me. Instinctually, my hand settles on her lower back, making her steps falter before regaining her stride.

I pretend not to notice her stumble because she'd most likely kick my kneecaps in. Though I can't help but feel the thrill coursing through my chest, knowing I have this kind of effect on her.

Once outside, I watch the dogs while she locks up her shop. As we make our way down the cobblestone sidewalk, I realize that ours are, in fact, the only two stores on Main Street with their lights on. Tonight, the deserted town belongs to us, with only the rustling trees in the wind keeping us company.

"Are you sure this is a good idea?" she asks, keeping a close eye on Vera.

I lower my head, intently listening to her words, not wanting to miss anything she says.

"You know, keeping them together . . . alone? In your new building?"

"Positive. Unless you're not ready to leave her alone with a boy? If that's the case, we can divide them into separate rooms." I peer down at her smiling. My fingers ache to brush those wind-blown strands of hair away from her face, wanting to see her more clearly.

"I don't want to corrupt Vera. Frank can be very persuasive," I joke.

"Oh, shut up. You're ridiculous."

"Ridiculously cute."

"Only according to your mother. As you've stated previously."

Laughter spills out of me. She definitely won this round, making me eat my words.

Whenever I'm near her, her presence is all-consuming. I unveil a new layer during every encounter I have with Charlie. Every conversation, every look, and every touch intensifies my desire to learn everything about her.

I keep glancing at her out of the corner of my eye just to make sure she hasn't run off. The more I do, the longer my gaze lingers on her. She licks her lips and my focus zeroes in on that small movement. All I can think about now is what she tastes like, the softness of her skin, and how her body would feel pressed against mine.

We continue to walk in silence before she gives me a double take.

"Uh. Finn? Your glasses are fogging up again."

A sheepish laugh escapes me. "I guess I'm also pretty hot, along with being cute." I remove my glasses, and try to discreetly clean off the fog with my sweater.

She groans. "You're actually the worst person I think I've ever met." Her voice is filled with playful humor. I am absolutely positive she doesn't feel that way about me, considering her cheeks have gone a deeper shade of pink.

"Lies. You met my aunt," I scoff, looking down at her.

A loud, genuine laugh from deep in her belly breaks free from her. If I thought she was beautiful before, she's jaw-droppingly gorgeous when she lets go like this. Looking so carefree and relaxed, I wish I had a camera to capture this moment so that I can replay it over and over. Instead, I make a mental note to figure out more ways to make her laugh like that again.

When we come up to my shop, I swiftly unlock the doors and usher the dogs in to let them roam free. Once I lock up, I turn to Charlie. "Ready to go?"

She nods, taking a step forward. The slick cement catches her boot at the right angle, causing her to lose her footing. I react reflexively, grabbing her before she tumbles to the ground.

"Whoa!" she pants, shaken by the slip.

"You okay?"

"Yeah. I think so." Her breath is coming out in quick huffs.

Without a second thought, I hold out my arm for her to grab onto while we walk. "Here, hold on to me. I don't want you falling."

A bashful smile flickers across her face before she links her arm in mine.

It feels good.

It feels right.

As we fall in step with one another, it settles over me that I have absolutely no idea where I'm going. My faux confidence is working overtime trying to impress this woman.

Since moving here, I've been to my coffee shop, the grocery store, and Charlie's plant store. End of list. I've been working so much that there hasn't been much time to explore. My smooth, confident side is trying its best to take the lead, though I'm mildly panicked about not knowing where to take Charlie.

"Tree!" she yells as I run face-first into a low-hanging tree branch.

I was so caught up in my thoughts that I ran into a fucking tree.

Embarrassed, I croak, "Can we pretend that didn't happen just now?" I rub my forehead from where the branch smacked me.

She looks puzzled. "Huh? What happened?"

Yep. I think I want to keep her.

As if she senses my nerves, Charlie speaks up, her fingers curling around my bicep tighter. "If we keep walking this way, we'll end up near a small bridge that'll take us to the board-walk on the beach."

"That sounds perfect. Are you warm enough, though? I have some gloves in my pocket you can use if your fingers get too cold." I reach for my pockets to give her my gloves, but her tightening grip on my arm stops me.

"I'm okay for right now, but thank you, though," she replies with a soft, appreciative tone.

I can't help but keep looking down at her as we walk. I'll probably run into another tree at some point if I can't take my eyes off of her.

With flushed cheeks, bright eyes, and a faint smile on her face, Charlie looks radiant.

Completely content and at ease.

Which is exactly what I set out to accomplish.

We make a turn to walk down a cobblestone road that's lined with vintage lamp posts. Strolling arm in arm, we fall into a comfortable silence. For many, this would be awkward, but for some reason, with Charlie, this peaceful silence is effortlessly comfortable.

Eager to learn more about her, I ask, "So, did you grow up here?"

Immediately, she stiffens beside me, and a faint laugh escapes from her lips. "You should know that I hate small talk."

I smile. Of course she hates small talk. There's amusement in my voice when I reply, "Well . . . how else am I supposed to get to know you? I have to start with the basics, right?"

She hums. "I don't know. Why do you want to get to know me?"

I scoff. "Uh. There's a cute girl who wears overalls and wards off threats with a golf club. Who wouldn't want to get to know her?"

"Really laying it on thick there with the 'cute' compliment, aren't you?"

"Time is of the essence, sweetheart. I'm not getting any

younger. Have you seen these grays forming?" I point to my temples, where my hair is light brown with soft streaks of gray beginning to appear from too many years of stress.

She gives me her classic eye roll. "Oh, Finn," she says on an exhale.

"Oh, Charlie," I echo.

Charlie peers up at me from the corner of her eyes and I mirror her action. Our matching smiles give way to more laughter on the late night walk.

Eventually, she gives in. "Fine. What do you want to know about me? I can assure you that I'm not that interesting."

"What's the wildest excuse you've given to leave a party or a social engagement early?"

"Oh, that's a good one." Her eyebrows raise, clearly impressed by my ability to avoid small talk using creative tactics. "I was forced to go to a party once in college because my roommate thought I needed 'the full college experience.' So I had my brother call me and tell me that my pet lizard died." A giggle rises from her. "I never had a pet lizard, but fake cried and everything to get out of there," she says with pride.

I was expecting a million possible replies, but that was not one of them. "You are so strange. Wasn't expecting that," I respond, chuckling at her story.

"I take that as a compliment, you know."

Stopping, I carefully grasp her upper arms, turning her to face me. Gazing intently into her large, brown eyes, a smile forms on my lips. "I'm two for two with the compliments tonight. Cute and strange. Just how I like 'em."

She drops her gaze, blushing at my words. Without thinking, I hold out my arm for her to take again. Her arm slips into mine, and we continue on our stroll.

During our walk, we take turns asking ridiculous and random questions. I discovered she enjoys throwing on a fresh pair of socks after a bad day, eating pancakes for dinner during a storm, and shopping at antique stores for Depression glass. She learned that I always shield the lines in the book below where I'm reading to prevent spoilers, I only do laundry on Wednesdays, and I have a playlist for every mood. The walk was a total success. Charlie seemed lighter and less weighed down by the heavy emotions from earlier.

We eventually make our way back to the coffee shop and grab both dogs. Because Frank and I are gentlemen, we walk Charlie and Vera to their car. Charlie had parked in the front of her store this time, right on Main Street.

Vera hops into the backseat of her car, and Charlie closes the door when she's settled.

Before getting into the driver's seat, Charlie turns to me. "This was nice."

"Yeah? Same time tomorrow?"

Her head shakes slightly. Quietly, she murmurs, "No . . ." before trailing off.

I wince. My chin lowers to my chest, and before I look up to speak, Charlie beats me to it.

Her feet shuffle over to me, and she touches my arm to get my attention. "No! Oh my god. Sorry, I didn't speak quickly enough, it happens often, and my siblings hate it," she confesses. "Anyway, I meant to say, 'No, I can't tomorrow since I'm getting dinner with them.' My sister Joey is finally back in town, so I'll be spending some time with her. How about Friday instead?" She blinks slowly, waiting for my reply.

"I would love that," I say, trying to keep my tone calm and even. Internally though? I'm absolutely ecstatic.

She nods. "Great. I'll see you soon, okay?" There's so much sincerity in her tone that it wraps around me in a comforting hold.

I take both of her hands in mine and give them a gentle squeeze. "Have a good night, Charlie. Text me when you get home."

Her cheeks bloom with that stunning shade of pink that I love. When our hands drop, she turns, hops in her car and drives off, waving at me as she leaves.

That night, I drift off to sleep, replaying the scenes of her carefree laugh with a smile on my face.

Chapter Sixteen

Charlie

As soon as I got home last night, I crawled into bed and passed out the second my head hit the pillow. What I like most about Finn is that he didn't pressure me to talk about things I wasn't comfortable with. He could sense if we were entering uncomfortable territory and he would quickly reroute the conversation.

Ever since I can remember, it's not been easy for me to open up to others. My therapist and I are working on that, but it's a painfully slow process. I've mainly been opening up to Marnie; she's been my lab rat for my "big feelings" moments. With her, I can safely blurt out my thoughts or emotions in peace.

The store is practically dead at this time of day, with me and a snoring Vera being the only ones here. A chime fills the store and, when I look up, a younger guy comes in with slumped shoulders; he can't be older than nineteen or twenty.

He hurries over to the counter, and I can't hide the confusion on my face as he approaches.

He pants, face red from exertion. "Are you Charlie?"

My eyes narrow. "Depends who's asking."

"He said you would say that. Here." He sets a small cup on the counter. "This is from the boss."

The squirrelly kid spins around and marches back outside. I blink, stunned by the interaction that just happened.

What the hell was that about? I grab the cup and inspect it. Sure enough, it came from Finn. On the cup, there's a message that says,

I'm feeling hopeful about this one, –Finn

And he drew a smiling flower on the cup's sleeve.

I feel myself grinning from ear to ear, thankful no one else is around to see me.

Finn must be slammed with customers today because, knowing him, he'd much prefer to hand deliver this cup. I take a sip, and it tastes like an elevated hot chocolate.

As much as I hate to admit it, this is delicious.

While part of me is glad he isn't here to see my poker face slip, another part of me wants to see him smile with pride after successfully finding a coffee I enjoy.

Maybe I won't tell him how much I like this cup.

Setting the paper cup on the counter in front of me, my attention returns to his friendly note on the cardboard coffee sleeve.

Anxiety simmers inside my chest when I think about falling for a guy like Finn. Suddenly, that anxiety morphs into sadness as I worry I may not be good enough for him. He'll probably end up disappointed, just like the rest of the guys I've dated. I've been burned so many times that I tend to shy away from dating completely—too afraid to let people in because of every failed relationship I've had.

When the excitement wore off in my last relationship, I thought it was safe to fully be myself. In the beginning, my ex and I would go on all the stereotypical dates: we'd try new restaurants, head to the movie theater, or get together with groups of people for a night out. As the relationship began to settle, I thought it was okay to let my guard down. I finally confessed that I didn't like going out because I've always been more of a homebody. But my ex loved being around people and needed it to feel alive.

He just couldn't understand why I wanted to stay home and decompress after a long day. When I pulled back from socializing, he continued to push forward. Eventually, he became distant and weirdly obsessive over his phone. So obsessive that he would get upset whenever I would casually ask who he was talking to so much. Days of unhappiness evolved into weeks, which turned into months. I was stuck in this continuous, tortuous loop of countless fights filled with hurtful words about my character.

Can't you smile more?

Why must you always have an attitude?

Do you think you could turn on the charm for one night?

You should really start acting more like this girl I work with— people love her.

I finally ended the relationship. There's only so many hits a woman can take before she's pushed over the edge. I knew I deserved better.

Even if that meant staying single.

Admittedly, I know the feelings that I'm never enough are irrational—not all men are the same. Annoyingly, sometimes those tiny voices deep in your mind can begin to scream so loud and are impossible to ignore. Those deep-seated insecurities try to claw their way to the surface, and I try my best to push them down for as long as I can. I can't handle these emotions right now.

It's an internal struggle because, while I like Finn and want to get to know him better, it takes me a while to warm up to someone.

A FEW HOURS pass by and the steady stream of customers poking around the store keeps me busy.

Off to the side, I hear my phone vibrate twice on the store's counter. Stepping over Vera, I look at my messages and see a text from Finn.

FINN

It's been two hours. Did that huge monster
of a plant in your shop swallow you whole?
I knew that monstrosity was out to get you .
. .

Anyway, I need you to rate the drink on a
scale of "good" to "really good." What will
it be?

Satisfactory. Maybe a B?

FINN

I'm just going to quit my job now. Maybe I
can join the circus since you're making me
feel like a clown.

Must you be so dramatic?

FINN

Only because you wound me, Charlotte.

> We're getting formal now, Griffin?

FINN

> I don't like that. I feel like I'm in trouble, but
> I've been a very good boy.

I feel my cheeks start to burn at the thought of him whispering those words in his gravelly tone. My fingers fly over the keyboard, typing a reply to steer this conversation into a less . . . intense direction.

> Please don't. You're making it weird now.

> Don't you have a job to do? Coffee to
> brew? Milk to steam?

FINN

> Yes, I'm multitasking.

> Maybe if you stopped multitasking, your
> skills would improve.

FINN

> OUCH. I'm going to take this as your way of
> flirting with me.

> Whatever helps.

FINN

> You're a tough one to please, Charlie.
> Lucky for you, I'm a tenacious gentleman.

> See you Friday.

> I'm not sure you can put "tenacious" and
> "gentleman" in the same sentence.

FINN

> I can, and I did. *Wink Emoji*

Setting my phone on the counter, I stare at his last

message—an emoji. How do you reply to an emoji? Do you send another one back?

Ugh. This is too much effort for me right now.

I set my phone down on the counter and begin to repot a few philodendrons that a couple of customers brought in. When I hear the store bell chime, I'm up to my elbows in potting soil.

"CHARLES!"

That could be one person, and one person only.

Josephine.

She and I see each other at most once a month, mainly because this woman is always on the move exploring new places. Her rich auburn hair, colorful clothes, and vibrant personality come barreling into my store and make their way to my workstation.

"Hey, Joseph. What brings your van into town? Did you run out of bell-bottoms?" I look up, wiping my hand on my apron.

As she claps her hands, her copious amount of rings and bracelets clink together. "Charles has jokes! You're just jealous that I can pull them off."

"Oh yes. So jealous," I deadpan.

Joey takes after our parents' flower child spirit. Even though she has a home nearby, she travels all over the country in her VW van, wearing 1970s clothes and jamming out to folk music.

"Did you forget it's our little dinner thingy?" she asks, bending down to pet Vera. Vera lets out a content groan when Joey begins scratching her belly.

Rounding the corner, Joey rises from the ground and launches herself at me—wrapping her arms around me in a way-too-tight hug.

I think I'm going to puke.

"You know I hate this," I croak out.

"Feel the love, sis. Just *feel* it." She squeezes even tighter, and I'm about as rigid as a statue. "Wow. You smell amazing." Her nose presses against my hair as she inhales deeply. I can feel each strand go up her nose, making me shudder in disgust.

I hate this.

A familiar chime echoes through the store once again, which could only mean—

"Char and Jojo!" Jack yells, his heavy work boots thumping on the floor as he makes his way over to us.

Stopping at the horrific sight of Joey hugging me, his eyes dart back and forth between us. "Uh oh. Why are you hugging Charlie? The last time everyone hugged her, and she allowed it, was when Mom and Dad died."

Accurate.

I'm not a big hugger. I tolerate it like I tolerate a root canal.

Jack, being the obnoxious asshole that he is, joins in on the hug.

This day has officially taken a turn for the worse. It's worth mentioning that both my siblings are taller than me. My brother is six foot four and my sister is five foot eleven. So not only do I have twice the amount of humans hugging me, but I'm being smothered by two tall bodies radiating an ungodly amount of heat and affection.

"Can everyone get the fuck off me? Please?" My voice is muffled because Joey has pressed me so hard against her chest that I'm sure the fringe of her coat will leave an imprint on my cheek.

"Say the magic words," she taunts.

"Yeah, we won't let go until you say it. You know how this ends, Char." I feel Jack's body shake with laughter.

I'm definitely writing them out of my will and adding the dog as the sole heir to my belongings.

"You're the best brother and sister I could ever ask for, and I love you *oh so* very much." My voice is saturated with sarcasm. "Happy? Now get off! I can't breathe between Jack's weird, musky cologne and your overpowering floral body spray."

"I don't appreciate the sarcasm, but I'll take it." Jack releases me before Joey pulls away as well.

We're standing in the middle of the store, and the few customers in the store give us the strangest looks.

"Don't worry about her!" Joey shouts to the customers, wrapping her arm around my shoulder. "Our sweet Charlotte just can't get enough of our love. Sometimes, she asks us for hugs at the most inconvenient times. Ain't that sweet?"

Jack is chuckling, offering zero help for my situation.

With puzzled expressions, the customers drop the plants they were holding and leave the store.

"You owe me for those." I turn to my sister.

Joey scoffs. "Whatever. Those people suck anyways." Joey hops up onto the counter, swinging her legs. "Are we cooking tonight at your place, or going out to eat? I'd prefer to stay in. Since we're staying in, what should we eat? I'm kinda feeling chicken. Let's do chicken. What should we have for a side? I'm thinking we should have a salad. Let's have a salad."

Jack and I exchange a glance while shaking our heads. Joey loves asking and answering her own questions.

Jack chimes in, smiling. "Chicken sounds good." He looks at Joey, knowing I already need a break from her. "How about you come to the grocery store with me? We'll head to Charlie's after."

"Sounds good to me. I'll close up in a few," I add.

Joey smiles. "Sweet. See ya then, Charles!"

After my siblings leave the store, I pull my phone out of my pocket and set a reminder in my phone to text Finn later. I was a little disappointed that it wasn't Finn himself walking into my store earlier with my drink. He has an air of charisma about him that leaves me wanting more whenever he isn't near.

And as I stood behind the counter, gazing out at my store, I couldn't ignore the fluttering feeling in my chest. The small, secret part of me that quietly accepts that my crush on Finn was starting to take root.

Chapter Seventeen

Finn

It's late and I'm ready to fall face first into my bed. Running your own business while employing two college student baristas is *exhausting*.

At thirty-five years old, I'm feeling the effects of being on my feet all day. My ankles make a mildly concerning crackle as I shuffle to the medicine cabinet for some ibuprofen. From across the bedroom, my phone chimes and my head whips in that direction. Who is texting me this late?

Frank's sound asleep, his soft snores filling the room. Hobbling over, I reach for my phone and see a text from Charlie.

CHARLIE

Don't forget to water those plants of yours.
Some of them are really finicky.

Shit. I'm supposed to water them? I thought they were in those innovative self-watering pots. What kind of plant store are you running?

CHARLIE

Griffin, please tell me you're joking.

Charlotte, of course, I am. I set reminders on my phone to check on them weekly. And if I have an issue with them, I know of a girl who could help . . .

CHARLIE

Eh. Don't be so sure of that.

Now that you know that I water responsibly, what are you and Vera up to?

CHARLIE

My brother and sister just left, so I'm finally able to decompress. Vera is snoring—out cold to the world. I'm reading a book.

Oh? What are you reading?

CHARLIE

No. Ask a different question.

Come on. Tell me!

CHARLIE

What are you and Frank doing?

Charlotte (I'm not sure what your middle and last name are, so let's pretend I'm using your full legal name), do not deflect by changing the subject. I see what you're doing.

CHARLIE

Charlotte Rose Thorne.

Wow. That's the most fitting name I've ever
heard of.

CHARLIE

Number one, rude. Number two, my
parents came up with it one night after
smoking too much weed at a music festival.
They wrote it on the back of a McDonald's
receipt so that they wouldn't forget it.

Oops. I lied. It wasn't weed. It was
shrooms. I texted my sister and had it fact-
checked.

I'm laughing hard enough that Frank wakes up. Of course,
the beautiful, grumpy girl with warm brown eyes has the most
interesting name, with a wild story attached to it.

Wow. So, if you had to identify with any
flower . . .

CHARLIE

Weigh your words carefully, Griffin (I also
don't know your last name).

West is my last name. *Winking Emoji*

CHARLIE

Weigh your words carefully, West.

I'm just saying. Albeit prickly and thorny,
the rose is thought to be one of the most
beautiful flowers in the world.

CHARLIE

Are you trying to flirt with me?

Is it working?

CHARLIE

Goodnight, Finn.

I smile. Slowly but surely, she's lowering her walls, one inch at a time. Being patient has always been one of my best qualities. With Charlie, I'll gladly take whatever is developing between us at whatever pace is most comfortable for her.

Knowing better than to push my luck, I send a simple goodnight message back to her.

> Goodnight, Charlie.

I'VE SPENT the entire week eagerly anticipating my walk with Charlie, and the day has finally arrived. Although the town is small, I haven't seen her around much, besides a quick sighting from afar at the park where she walks Vera during the day. Even then, I didn't want to disturb her—it looked like she was sitting on a bench, either deep in thought or decompressing.

Annoyingly, I haven't dropped off any new drinks to her since I haven't had a single breather at the café. We're one staff member short, which means I'm doing two people's jobs this week.

But today's morning rush of customers has slowly died down to the point that I can make a quick escape. After I prepare Charlie's drink, I look over at Joe, the scrawny barista, and tell him I'm running a quick errand. Careful not to spill her drink on my favorite sweater vest, I walk down the street until I find myself standing in front of A New Leaf.

When I open the door, Charlie's laughter fills the store and I see that she and a customer are deep in discussion. She has an air of approachability about her—something she doesn't often show to others.

She notices my staring and raises her brows, not breaking conversation with the customer. Finally acknowledging the tall dude loitering in the corner of her store, she lifts her hand in my direction, making a 'give me a minute' gesture. A few minutes later, the customer thanks Charlie and leaves the store.

She blows out a deep sigh when the customer can no longer be seen from the store windows. With one hand in my pocket, I stroll over to her, a bemused expression on my face.

"Did I just witness you laughing with a customer? And making small talk?" I joke.

Those big brown eyes give me their signature roll. "Oh, stop it. I can turn on the charm when needed. My social battery just depletes a little faster." She playfully slaps my bicep, and my heart momentarily skips in my chest.

"But you still hate it, right? Making pleasantries with innocent townsfolk?" I adjust my glasses, silently begging the universe for them not to fog up. A tingling sensation runs down my arm, a lingering reminder of her delicate touch.

Her tone is flat when she replies, "With every single fiber of my being, West. Every. Single. Fiber." She walks over to her laptop, types something, and then looks back to me. "Where've you been this whole week? I haven't seen you at all."

"Have you missed me that much?"

Scoffing, she replies, "Don't get ahead of yourself, Gumby. You're kind of hard to miss." One side of her mouth quirks up, and her fingers go back to typing at rapid fire on her computer.

I hum. "So that's your way of saying you miss me. Got it. I'm really starting to understand how to translate your 'Charlieisms.'"

The clicks on the keyboard abruptly stop and she looks up at me through her dark eyelashes. We don't break eye contact until we both begin to laugh.

"Here, I brought this for you," I say, setting the cup on the counter. I drew a small leaf smiling on the cardboard sleeve, and when she notices my excellent art skills (*that haven't progressed past the age of five*) she smirks.

"Cute." She brings the cup to her lips, taking a small sip. Her nose wrinkles in disgust.

Completely ignoring her facial expression, I'm entranced by the way her alluring lips wrap around the edge of the cup. They look soft, supple, and kissable. It's surprising how many illegal activities I'd be willing to commit just for the opportunity to kiss her once in this lifetime.

If I keep going down this path of thoughts, then my glasses *will* be fogging up again.

Clearing my throat, I watch her carefully. "So? What do you think?"

"Oh, it's disgusting," she replies matter-of-factly, placing the cup back down on the counter.

"Please, for the sake of my ego, tell me how you really feel." I grab the cup and take a sip, not missing the way her eyes drop to my lips. This is a good sign. I like this. Maybe my flirting is working after all. Her eyes drop down to my neck, tracing how my throat moves as I take another drink from the cup.

"Since I know you'll most likely dump it out, I'll take this back with me."

She looks slightly disappointed as her eyes dart to the coffee sleeve and the drawing on it. Picking up on subtle cues is the quality that I'm most proud to have. Right now, from my point of view, Charlie wants the drawing I created for her.

I attempt to hide my smile, take the sleeve off the cup, and nonchalantly say, "Do you have a trash can somewhere? I just want to toss this since I don't need it, and it keeps slipping." Hoping she catches on to what I'm trying to do, I hold the sleeve out for her to take.

Something flashes in her eyes, and her normally guarded eyes soften briefly for a moment.

"Yeah, I'll take it. Just hand it to me." She reaches out, taking the small piece of cardboard from me. As she does, our fingers brush against one another. She's soft and warm, and I want nothing more than to hold her hand.

Her eyes brighten when she looks down at the coffee sleeve, a small smile tugging at the corner of her lips.

"Well, Miss Thorne, I'll see you tonight?" I ask, hoping and praying to a higher power that she remembers our planned Friday-night walk.

She lifts her gaze to me, and a softness settles over her features. "You know where to find me," she says.

Chapter Eighteen

CHARLIE

KNOWING I would see Finn tonight, I may have put a little extra effort into how I look. Instead of overalls, I opted for straight jeans, brown boots, and a black turtleneck sweater. Glancing once more in the small mirror on the wall of my office, I attempt to smooth the barely tamed flyaways in my dark hair.

I don't always know when Finn will drop into my store with a coffee, so it's always a surprise when he does appear. And when he mentioned tonight, I was relieved he remembered because I want to spend more time with him.

Not that I would ever admit that aloud.

That pesky, nagging voice of self-doubt in my brain kept pinching me, and I tried to ignore it as best I could. Figuring he would bail on me, I tried not to get my hopes up. But the moment I heard those words, *"I'll see you tonight,"* my heart rate picked up alarmingly quickly as relief surged through me.

Earlier, Finn looked incredibly handsome when he strolled confidently into my store. His long, lean frame was enhanced by dark jeans, a white button-down shirt with the sleeves rolled up to his elbows, and a deep tan sweater vest. Pair the outfit with his wavy hair framing the tortoise-shell glasses perched on his straight nose and you have the ultimate hot nerd look.

Irritatingly enough, it makes my knees weak. I love a hot nerd.

Even though I try, I fail miserably at keeping my indecent thoughts at bay. On more than one occasion, I wanted to figure out what he was hiding under that sweater vest.

I'm just a horny girl standing in front of a hot, nerdy guy wanting to strip him down and drag him into my back office.

Finn has an air of calming charisma to him. He's confident, not cocky; persuasive, not pushy. 'Captivatingly charming' are the words that come to mind every time I see him. When you talk to him, he gives you his undivided attention. His head dips down ever so slightly, leaning in as he looks deep into your eyes—listening intently. You'd think he was preparing for a quiz on whatever you were saying.

For many, that would make them feel special. But for me? I just feel overwhelmed. I'm not used to someone, aside from Marnie or my family, actively seeking to spend time with me. In my past relationships, I felt as if they were spending time with me out of obligation. Almost like that's what they had to do because it's what was required to keep up appearances—not because they wanted to. My past self couldn't care less if I was wanted or not.

Right now, though, I'm having very different feelings because being wanted almost feels *too good.* I have to remind myself to tread carefully so I don't end up drowning.

Needing to clear my head and focus on work, I grab my apron, roll up my sleeves, and begin to water the plants around the shop. This is normally Marnie's job, but I need to do something about my overabundance of anxious energy. My stomach feels like it's full of a dozen hummingbirds, all ready to take flight.

"Hot damn, little mama! You look like a snack! No, wait. You look like a whole meal!" Marnie yells and scares the absolute shit out of me. Water spills to the floor, and all I can do is scowl at her.

She winces. "I'll go get a mop to clean that up . . . I forgot how jumpy you get when you're deep in thought. I should've known better once I saw your little gremlin brows creating that line that's right between—"

I put my hands up and cut her off. "Stop talking. Get the damn mop."

"Ma'am, yes, ma'am!" She salutes and heads to the back.

Marnie comes back out with the mop and starts to clean up the puddle of water around my feet. Out of the corner of my eye, I notice her pair of blue eyes looking at me through thick black lashes. Marnie is practically bursting at the seams to say something.

"Go ahead. Say it." I groan, setting the watering can on the table.

"Oh, thank god. What's the occasion? Do you have a hot date?"

"Finn and I are going on a walk tonight," I say to her, avoiding eye contact. I can feel my cheeks begin to flush at my admission. "Please, don't make a big deal out of it. You know how it makes me uncomfortable."

Marnie stops what she's doing, and her face softens. "I know, Charlie. As much as I want to heckle you, I respect you too much. I think it's a great idea. He seems like a really nice, genuine guy."

She's oddly mature about this, and it makes me uncomfortable when she acts like a responsible human.

Marnie continues. "Plus, I heard a little extra cardio before bed helps you sleep better at night." She shrugs and wiggles her eyebrows at me.

And there it is.

My jaw drops. "You were almost there. *Almost.* You just couldn't help yourself, could you? You couldn't have just stopped before you crossed into that territory."

"When there's an open door for a dirty joke to be had, you know I'll walk through it."

"Clearly."

"How long has it been?"

"How long has *what* been?"

Marnie tilts her head to the side. "Don't play coy with me. How long has it been since someone explored your gremlin cave?"

My eyes widen. "You repulse me." My phone starts ringing, putting an end to this conversation in record time. As I walk away to answer the phone, I call out over my shoulder, "Two years!"

Marnie screeches, "TWO WHOLE FUCKING YEARS? Does it even work anymore? I can't believe it—Oh, hi! Sorry I didn't see you come in! How can I help you today?"

My laugh is unladylike, and I can only imagine what the customer who just walked in is thinking.

As soon as the sun sets, my hands begin trembling with so many nerves. I've been dropping anything and everything I touch as I anxiously wait for Finn. Part of me starts to panic, wondering what we're going to talk about, or if he feels like this is an obligation and he's too nice to say so. I take a few steadying breaths and scratch Vera's head in the hope of soothing some of the anxiety that's consuming me.

My thoughts are interrupted by a soft knock. I lazily make my way over to the front of the store. When I get to the door, Finn stands in his long, wool peacoat with Frank by his side. I unlock it and give him a small smile, motioning for him to come in.

"Whoa. No golf club tonight?" he says. "I was hoping you'd whip out a sand wedge one of these days."

He steps inside the store, and we're standing so close to one another that we're nearly touching chests.

I cross my arms and roll my eyes. "One more sly comment, and I'm walking alone. You can stay and watch the dogs."

"You can't get rid of me that easily, sweetheart."

My heart jolts in my chest as I turn away from him to grab Vera. That damn nickname again throws me for a loop. "Do you want to keep the pups here? Or stick them in your shop?" I call out over my shoulder.

"Definitely mine. Frank has been acting out a little too much for my liking lately, and you may not have any plants when we get back if we leave them here."

"You should really keep your kid in check. He's going to be a bad influence on Vera."

"Charlie, I mean zero disrespect when I say this, but Vera didn't even bark that night Frank and I crashed in here. She wagged her tail like I was a long-lost friend. There's no way your dog is being influenced by my furry delinquent."

I contemplatively tilt my head to the side. "Valid point."

Slipping on my jacket, I untuck my hair from the collar, letting it fall down my back. Finn's gaze lingers on me, causing my posture to stiffen.

"What's wrong?" I ask, buttoning my jacket.

Finn rakes his fingers through his wavy hair, clearing his throat. "N-nothing. You just look really pretty." A flush blooms across his cheeks as he nervously swallows.

I can't remember the last time a man genuinely complimented me. A warmth floods through my body, and my heart beats a little faster, knowing his words will stick with me for days to come.

My head tilts to the side as I give him a gentle smile. "Thank you. You look very handsome tonight. I really like your sweater vest." My voice is barely above a whisper.

"Really?" He looks surprised—borderline shocked.

"I'm capable of giving compliments, you know." I laugh.

A deep chuckle escapes from him. "No, I was just shocked that you specifically pointed out the sweater vest. My sister gives me shit for it all the time."

"Well, I personally like the hot professor look."

Oh. Fuck.

That was a thought that didn't need to exit my brain. My gaze drops to the ground as I spin on my heel to clip on Vera's leash—hoping he misheard me and will ignore everything I said. The compliment from earlier is still bouncing around in my head, clouding my thoughts.

I'm kneeling with Vera, pretending to struggle to clip on her leash, when I hear his slow footsteps approaching me. He's so close now; I can see the creases in his jeans and the scuff marks on his brown boots. I quickly glance up at Finn and then back to my shaky fingers on Vera's collar.

Seemingly confused, he quirks a brow. "Hot professor?"

"Yeah. Sort of like a hot . . . nerd." I practically choke getting that last word out. Suddenly my mouth feels too dry.

A faint smile tugs at the corners of his lips, clearly amused by my embarrassing confession. "Miss Thorne, are you flirting with me?"

I silently pray that the ground miraculously decides to swallow me whole. How the hell do you respond to that? I could own it, which would make my therapist proud.

Still not looking at him, I continue to fidget with Vera's collar and make an attempt to change topics. "Hey, how are your plants doing, by the way?"

"Don't change the subject, Charlie."

Ugh. Slowly, I pull myself up, wiping my clammy palms on my jeans.

I guess I'm owning my subpar flirtatious ways today.

"Maybe," I say with false confidence.

He cocks his head to the side, a devious smile on that devastatingly handsome face. "Maybe, what?"

He takes another step closer to me and I'm certain he can see my heart ready to beat out of my chest. Swallowing nervously, I stare up into his deep blue eyes, which render me speechless. He's watching and waiting for me to speak, so I put my hands on my hips in a power stance, ready for this battle. "Maybe I was flirting . . . attempting to anyway."

His chuckle is deep and laced with satisfaction. Finn steps even closer, crowding me with his body. His head dips to the shell of my ear, and I'm overwhelmed by his woodsy cologne, which has traces of lavender and pine. I once read that lavender has a calming effect. Right now, I'm feeling anything but calm.

"Good. I like it." His warm breath caresses my ear, sending a shiver down my spine. Goosebumps rise on my heated skin, and suddenly wearing a turtleneck feels like a bad idea.

Backing up a few steps, he flashes me a smile, clearly pleased with himself for how flustered I am and for how I'm not putting up a fight about it.

"Are you ready to head out?" he asks, grabbing both Frank and Vera's leashes.

I'm trying to think of everything I can to tone down the arousal and desire that I feel pumping through my veins. My face feels hot, my neck is damp, and my damn turtleneck feels like it's choking me.

Unable to form any coherent sentences, I squeak out, "Sure."

My strength is no match for his charisma.

Chapter Nineteen

CHARLIE LOOKS BREATHTAKINGLY BEAUTIFUL. Earlier, I noticed she wasn't wearing her usual attire of overalls and sneakers—which I adore because they suit her so well. From the moment my foot stepped into her store, a million thoughts tumbled through my mind. One thing I wasn't prepared for: how to handle her returning the flirtatious banter I was sending her way. So of course I couldn't help but tease her a bit.

When I closed the distance between us, I could hear her breath hitch and felt her shiver. Her scent was an intoxicating mix of citrus and lilac, like a warm spring evening, and all I wanted to do was bury myself into her neck and inhale as if it were the last breath I'd ever take.

It took a lot of restraint not to just kiss her right then and there.

After getting the dogs settled in my shop, we venture out

into the crisp autumn air. Main Street is illuminated by the glow of the street lamps reflecting off the wet pavement. It rained earlier in the day, giving tonight's chill a little extra bite.

As we stroll down the sidewalk together, I break the silence by asking an off-the-wall question.

"If you could only eat three things for the rest of your life, what would they be?" I ask, glancing down at her.

Since she doesn't like small talk, I opt for random questions. Last night, I researched a handful of them, memorized the questions as best I could, and filed them away for this moment.

Her cheeks puff out as she exhales. "Let's see," she says, her brows pulling together as she thinks. "Funfetti cake, chocolate ice cream, and gummy bears."

Wow. My idea of making her a dinner that incorporates all of her favorite foods goes right out the window. This woman has the palate of a sugar-starved child.

I abruptly stop and look down at her. "You wouldn't survive off of all that. You'd get scurvy."

Turning to me, her chin tips up defiantly. "I could take a multivitamin!"

"Do you take one now?"

"No."

I tilt my head and raise one brow at her. "And what makes you think you'll start taking them during your Candyland feast?"

"I thought this was a judgment free zone?"

"No one said this was judgment free," I deadpan.

She playfully slaps my arm. "Asshole."

We both smile at each other and continue our walk. My

nose feels about two minutes away from falling off from the cold, but I don't dare tap out.

I'm not a quitter.

I'll stand out here all night in a swimsuit and freeze to death if it means I get to know more about Charlie.

"Do you think goldendoodles are programmed by the government?" she asks.

I turn my head away from her and try not to laugh. Where *the hell* did this question come from?

She continues. "Because if you think about it, they're hypoallergenic, so lots of families own them. And have you seen their eyes? They're oddly human-like, Finn. I swear they look like they're up to something."

"Charlie, what goes on in that mind of yours?" I say, as I tap the top of her head with my index finger.

"It's better if you don't know."

Nah. I think it's better if I do know. Her mind seems like an interesting place that I'm eager to explore.

"My neighbor has a goldendoodle. Actually, now that you mention it, his dog does look at me suspiciously. I'll keep an eye on him. Maybe the IRS found out I didn't file my taxes two years ago and is checking up on me." I shrug.

Her laugh is soft, and I look back down at her, noticing her cheeks are pink and eyes are bright. Comfortable silence stretches between us as we make our way to the small park in town.

"All right, I have to know. Why funfetti cake?"

Charlie's face drops, touched with a sad smile. "My mom used to make the best cakes. Every year for our birthdays, she'd make everyone's favorite cake. Jackson loves coconut, and Joey loves strawberry. Mine was funfetti." She sniffles, and I'm not sure whether it's from the cold or the distant memory. "The sprinkles make it taste better."

I feel my chest tighten. Not only did she lose her parents, she lost the familial traditions that brought endless happy memories. She sniffles again and I notice her eyes are glassy, with a single tear falling from the corner.

"Wait," I whisper. We both stop and I pull my hand out of my pocket, wiping away her lone tear with the pad of my thumb. It lingers there for a bit on her cool, smooth cheek. "It's the superior flavor. You have excellent taste."

Her eyes close, nodding in agreement. My hands unwillingly drop from her face as we continue our walk.

"When's your birthday?" I ask.

"November eleventh," she replies.

In this exact moment, I decide to take up baking as my next hobby. In a few short weeks, Charlie is going to have a funfetti cake waiting at her doorstep if it's the last thing I do.

"When's your birthday?" she questions. "Actually, how old are you?"

"Didn't anyone tell you it's impolite to ask someone's age?"

"Oh no. You're that old? Forty-seven? I always did have a thing for silver foxes."

I come to a sudden stop, swinging my body toward her. "Whoa. Shots fired. What did I ever do to you?"

She stands there, looking at me with a devious glint in her eye. Her head tips back, and she laughs. It's the kind of laugh that's infectious—a deep, genuine laugh that can't help but make people smile.

With a disbelieving shake of my head, I chuckle. "You're such a troublemaker."

Shrugging, she continues to walk ahead of me, leaving me

standing there with a goofy smile on my face. With my long stride, it takes no time for me to catch up with her.

"April tenth," I finally say. "And I'm thirty-five."

"Ooh. National Hug Your Dog Day! That's a good date," she says. "I'm thirty-four, by the way."

My face twists in confusion. "I have so many questions, mainly how you just randomly knew what national holiday falls on my birthday."

"I can't give all my secrets away, West. A lady has to have some mystery to her." She scoffs as if this is some universally agreed upon fact that I should know.

A hearty laugh escapes me. I've traveled all over the world and can confidently say I have never met anyone like her. Charlie is unique, captivating, and impossible to resist.

While we walk, I can't help but notice how our fingers brush every so often, making my heart beat a little faster with each innocent touch. It's happened enough times that I've realized she doesn't shy away from these brief touches. Occasionally, I'll see her glance down at our hands out of the corner of her eye, but she doesn't notice me looking.

I decide to make a bold move and hope she doesn't flee like a frightened deer. Our fingers brush again, but this time, I loop my pinky around her pinky. My heart is pounding so hard in my chest that it feels hard to breathe. I hear my racing pulse in my ears. The collar of my shirt feels suffocating, my neck is sweating, and, to top it all off, I can sense my glasses will fog up any minute now.

I'm *such* a fucking nerd.

Rather than pulling away, she responds by curling her pinky tighter around mine.

Sneaking another glance, I notice Charlie is acting cool, calm, and collected. You could even say she looks unfazed by what's happening. Meanwhile, my nervous system is misfiring at every corner, and my chest feels ready to burst at any moment.

"So," she begins, "why Hemlock? I know you said your aunt lives here, but I'm positive that's not why you came."

"I've moved around a lot. Before moving here, I was working in New York, in finance, specifically—"

She interrupts. "Ew, a finance bro?"

"Did you eat or drink something different tonight? You're on a whole new level. Don't get me wrong, I like my women like I like my cocktails—spicy. And you, Miss Thorne, have some spice in you tonight."

"What a cheesy line. Does that usually work? Probably not. Good thing you're cute." She mutters that last sentence and it's barely audible, but I hear it clearly. "Anyway, you were saying?" she inquires, looking straight ahead of her.

"I'm going to ignore the fact you called my line cheesy and only acknowledge that you called me cute." A smile gradually appears on her rosy-cheeked face. "So, as I was saying, I was working in finance and it was soul crushing. I woke up every day anxious and stressed about putting on a tie and heading to work. I knew that lifestyle wasn't going to be healthy in the long run. My family was getting concerned because every time we talked, I wasn't myself." My voice falls with sadness. "They kept saying, 'We miss the old Finn!' They were worried I was headed to a dark place. With therapy, I realized I couldn't keep living my life the way it was going."

Charlie takes a moment to absorb everything I just said.

It's quiet between us, the only noises coming from the crunching gravel underneath our boots and the rustling leaves caught in the autumn breeze.

She runs her free hand through her dark, shiny hair. "So, would you say moving to Hemlock is your third life crisis?"

"Bingo."

It's quiet again between us. I look up at the inky sky dotted with glittering stars. The cool breeze fans my face, which is now warm after walking her through my life story.

"Well, you're in good company. Because that makes two of us," she says, meeting my gaze and flashing me a playful wink.

The way I would drop to my knees for this woman.

It hits me that we're both in the throes of massive life changes in our thirties—navigating a messy new chapter in our lives, each starting over in some way.

"Look at us, two peas in a pod." I laugh softly.

"I'm not sure I'm ready to share a pod with you, but sure, you could say that." She giggles. "And you chose to move to Hemlock because . . . ?"

"Well, I wanted to move back to Oregon because it's home. Besides my sister, who lives in Hawaii, most of my immediate family lives in Eugene. I didn't want to be too close, though. I love them, but I need my space. So one night I threw a dart at a map of Oregon, and that's how I landed in Hemlock. As fate would have it, Aunt Donna also lives here. Strange how the universe works sometimes."

She gives an approving nod. "Strange, but I like that approach. Let fate handle it."

My gaze drops down to her as she looks up at me with her big doe eyes. "Yeah, fate," I say, nearly whispering.

We're slowly looping back to the coffee shop. As much as I don't want the night to end and would love to keep holding on to her pinky, I sense a bone-deep exhaustion in Charlie. She seems ready to head home to rest and recover.

"It's scary, isn't it? Starting over? Especially at this age when everyone around you seems to have everything figured out—big careers, families, and huge houses." Charlie sighs. "Yet, here we are, trying our best to keep going and not knowing what the fuck we're doing day in and day out. Every morning, I encourage myself just to try to make it through the day."

"It's terrifying." I nod in agreement. "I remember asking my mom once if the older you get, the more you know what you're doing."

"And what did she say?"

"Every day is a guessing game. You hope for the best, prepare for the worst, and assume it'll all work itself out in the end."

"I like your mom already. She seems like a smart woman," she concludes, her voice tender and quiet.

After a long and chilly walk, we approach my shop and grab the dogs. While we're making our way to our cars, I'm hit by an idea.

This idea may backfire. But, again, life's too short to be unhappy, so I'm hoping for the best.

"Charlie, Halloween is a couple of weeks away," I state.

Her face twists in disgust. "Yep, I'm fully aware. I hate Halloween. I'm too old and jumpy for that nonsense."

"You sound like you're eighty years old."

Her arms cross over her chest. "Well, Griffin, sometimes I feel like it. And by sometimes, I mean most of the time."

Now I'm the one who rolls my eyes in amusement. "All right, grandma. I was wondering if you and Vera wanted to pass out candy with me? Frank will be dressed up as a burglar."

"That's impressive. Solid choice on the costume for your kleptomaniac dog."

"Oh? That impressed you?" My eyebrows raise to my hairline.

"Don't get used to it."

I give her a wink. "Charlie, I have many, many other ways that I can impress you."

"Are you flirting right now?"

"Is it working?"

Her eyes are wide, her lips part, then close again.

"I think so, actually," she says, looking surprised with herself.

"Good, then I guess I'll just have to keep it up." I smirk, allowing my eyes to drop to her mouth and then slowly move back to her wide brown eyes. "On Halloween, I'll see you at my house? How about 6 p.m.? You don't need to bring anything. I just need you and Vera." I stop, realizing how that last sentence came out. My face heats. Hopefully, the cold masks the red flush spreading across my face and up to my ears.

It's too late, though, because Charlie cocks one eyebrow in my direction. "Me and Vera it is then."

As those last words linger with me, I watch Charlie spin on her heel and settle into her car. Frank is now whimpering because he misses Vera. And, just like her mom, Vera looks back at Frank with one last parting glance. I flash Charlie a smile and a wink.

Tonight was a good night.

Chapter Twenty

FINN

FOR THE LAST couple of weeks, I've visited Charlie at her store almost every day, dropping off a new drink and relishing the opportunity to find the right coffee for her. Our Friday night walks have continued as well, becoming a favorite part of our weekly routines and giving us both something to look forward to at the end of a long week.

The last few walks have lasted deep into the early hours of the next morning. On our most recent evening stroll, there was an extra chill in the air, courtesy of a late October temperature dip. I made a point to stop and lend her my scarf. Charlie hasn't yet returned the gloves that I lent her the previous week, so I may never see that scarf again. But knowing that she is holding on to them gives me a deep sense of satisfaction.

Night after night, we continue exchanging texts, asking each other the most random questions that come to mind, which has only deepened the bond that we've slowly been developing. Though it's barely been a month since we first met, I feel like I've known this woman for years.

With her, there's a sense of familiarity.

It doesn't feel like I'm getting to know her; it feels like I'm reconnecting with someone I've always known. Every word we share draws me closer and closer to the conclusion that we must have known each other in another life.

After a long day of work at Dark Side Brews, I've closed the shop early on this Saturday afternoon of Halloween weekend. I'll be spending tomorrow evening with Charlie and Vera, but today I'm scheduled for my biweekly grandson duties. Since moving back to Oregon, I've been visiting my grandpa a couple of times a month at his retirement home.

When I walk outside to my car, I glance down Main Street to see my pretty brunette setting out a sign in front of A New Leaf. Charlie looks deep in thought, with a cute scowl on her face. She glances up as if she senses me, so I smile and give her a quick wave. Her scowl deepens until she squints, recognizing that it's me who waved, rather than some weirdo. Relief washes over her, and a radiant smile overtakes her face.

That smile alone is enough to make my good day great.

I hop in the car and hit the road. The drive to my grandpa's retirement home takes me out of Hemlock on scenic winding roads through tall pine trees, shrouded by the calming and gloomy Oregon skies. After forty minutes, I arrive and park. As I walk into the grand entrance of the facility, I stop at the front desk to sign in and to say a quick hello to the receptionist.

"Art is in rare form today," the older blonde woman casually mentions.

"I mean, is he ever not in rare form? He didn't get written up again, did he?" I inquire.

"No, nothing that bad. Just the usual hustling of those damn mini liquor bottles. He's using them to bribe other residents, to bet with during the evening card games, all sorts of things . . . it never ends!" She shakes her head, exasperated. "I don't know where in the world he gets them from."

I freeze and try as hard as possible to not act suspicious. I have enough mini liquor bottles lining my coat pockets to open a small convenience store. I remind myself to walk extra carefully so that none of the bottles clank together.

Fuck. Does this mean I'm his accomplice?

I give her a curt nod and quickly say, "Well, let me know if you get any leads. Sorry he's being a hassle."

She waves me off. "No worries, Finn. Enjoy your time. Your grandpa should be out in the enclosed patio area."

The facility is nicer than my home: the main foyer has tall ceilings adorned with wood beams, a stone fireplace, huge windows that allow natural light to shine through, and cushiony furniture. The space epitomizes comfort, giving the feel of a real home rather than a sterile retirement facility.

I make my way out to the patio, which overlooks a crystal-blue lake surrounded by a forest of pine trees. The view is so spectacular that it could be easily mistaken for a painting.

But there seems to be another spectacular view from the patio—the scene unfolding in front of me.

My grandpa is seated at a fire pit, surrounded by three older women. The women are oohing and ahhing at one of my grandpa Arty's wild stories from back in the day. They must be enjoying the tale, as all three women break out into giggles simultaneously and one boldly pats her hand on Arty's upper thigh.

My grandpa has an endless supply of those old stories. Some I like. Some I wish I could delete from my memory.

Noticing me standing in the entryway, Arty looks up and stops. "Finn! How are you, son?"

The three women snap their heads around, shooting lethal stares in my direction.

This is fun. I didn't know that grandpa Arty and I would have an audience today.

"Hey, Grandpa. Sorry to interrupt. Is this a bad time?" I wring my hands together, uncomfortable and feeling as though I'm intruding.

He scoffs, waving me off. "Not at all. Pull up a chair!"

Pulling over an unoccupied chair from the adjacent fire pit, I'm unsure where to sit, since the ladies are fawning over my grandpa and do not seem eager to share. The smell of powdery, floral perfume invades my senses, making me sneeze uncontrollably.

"Bless you, son. Allergies again? Betty, do you mind scooting over? I'd like my boy to sit next to me." Arty flashes a wide smile.

Betty licks her cherry red lips and touches his knee before making room for me, while the other two women are twirling their hair and making heart eyes at my grandpa.

What *the actual fuck* did I walk into? Mom will have a field day when we have our regular debrief call.

Attempting to navigate this uncomfortable situation as best I can, I clear my throat. "So, Grandpa, care to introduce me to . . . the team?"

Arty slaps his knees with both hands. "Of course! How rude of me. This is Betty to your left, and Edith, and Florence. They are my *best* friends here." He winks.

He fucking winks.

I wish he hadn't emphasized the word "best". My thoughts are going in fifty different directions, trying to deduce what he might be implying.

Slowly, I take in all three women. "Nice to meet you all, I'm Finn."

They say hello in unison, and then they all resume their previous conversation. I nod back, still trying to process what's really happening here.

First of all, good for Arty for putting himself out there. Secondly, he could be more subtle about it. His constant eyebrow waggles, seductive winks, and flirtatious touching of the three women make me feel like I'm interrupting a private moment.

"Did you hear about the new girl, Angie? She just moved in down the hall from Marsha. I heard she murdered her last husband," Florence says. The other two women gasp, shaking their heads in disbelief.

"I believe it." Edith tsks. "When do you think Marsha will finally kick the bucket? I've been wanting her room for months!"

I'm so confused.

Betty speaks up. "Speaking of rooms, I heard that Agatha was caught coming out of Clarence's room late last night? She really gets around. Wait until Chester finds out."

Okay, wait, who the hell is Chester?

"Who is Chester?" I blurt out, trying to follow the conversation. I immediately regret my question.

Florence answers in rapid fire. "Chester is Agatha's second husband. She cheated on her previous husband, Fred, with Chester. Serves Fred right though, because Fred was caught sleeping with the nanny forty years ago. Agatha said she would never cheat on Chester, but, by the sounds of it, it seems like Agatha and Clarence were up to something yesterday." She pauses to take a breath. "Who knows, maybe they also decided to open up their relationship?"

I'm doing mental gymnastics, trying to keep track of all the people and relationships that the ladies have shared with me. I'm about as lost as Frank in a new room. My eyes are so wide that I forget how to blink. Should I really be listening to this right now? Next time, instead of showing up unannounced, I'll plan on giving Arty a quick call before I stop over. This is a lot to process, and I'm not even sure where to begin.

"Don't stare, son, it's not polite," Grandpa murmurs in my ear.

I shake off my stare and accept my fate. I'm stuck listening to retirement home gossip for the next couple of hours. Shrugging off my jacket, I finally relax a bit into the chair.

Grandpa notices that I'm settling in and places his hand on my knee. "I'm really glad you're back, Finn. It's nice to see you around here more. You seem lighter. Happier."

A soft smile touches my lips. "Me too, Grandpa. It's good to be back."

As Arty and his ladies drone on about who's having sex with whom, whether or not the resident of room thirty-two is a convicted murderer, and placing bets on who will kick the bucket next, I sit back and let my mind drift off to Charlie.

I can't stop thinking about our intertwined pinkies and how she didn't pull away. A flicker of hope and excitement ignites in my chest at the thought of Charlie slowly opening up to me.

I really, *really* like her.

By the time I get home, it's so late that the street lights have come on. The second I enter the front door, Frank's batlike hearing detects my arrival, and he comes wiggling at me like he hasn't seen me in years. More like he hasn't smelled me in years. Technically, he hasn't seen me at all.

"Hey, bud! Did you look after the house? Scare off any intruders with your charm?" I give him a good head scratch and his nub of a tail starts wagging at a mile a minute. I love this damn dog.

I let Frank outside and grab my phone from my back pocket. Leaning my hip against the kitchen counter, I fire off a quick text to Charlie. Waving at her from afar isn't enough to satisfy my Charlie-fix for the day.

> 6 p.m. tomorrow, Thorne. I'll text you my
> address.

A message dings back almost immediately, and I smile.

CHARLIE

> If I had an ounce of the confidence you do,
> I would be unstoppable.

> Is that a compliment?

CHARLIE

> No.

> That came out rude. Actually, I don't know if
> that's a compliment or not. Maybe it is? You
> can take it as one. That's fine.

I start to laugh. The woman comes in hot but cools off quickly.

I'm taking it as a compliment. So, thank you. That was so nice of you to say about me. Is this where I compliment you back?

CHARLIE

Please don't.

You sure?

CHARLIE

Positive.

You're a woman of many words.

CHARLIE

Thank you.

Most people wouldn't take that as a compliment.

CHARLIE

Yes, I know. But I took it as one.

I run my fingers through my hair and let out a soft laugh to myself. After the day I've had, this is the perfect way to end it. This lighthearted, easy, back-and-forth banter with Charlie somehow fills a part of me I didn't know was missing.

You're a strange one. But I like it.

A lot.

Also, don't forget a costume.

CHARLIE

I will most definitely forget a costume.

. . .

CHARLIE

Wait. Not like that!

I can get on board with no costume.

In fact, I encourage no costume. *Winky face*

CHARLIE

That is NOT what I meant.

You brought it up. I was just being a good friend and encouraging your great idea.

CHARLIE

Rolling eye emoji

Grinning down at my phone like a love-struck fool, I finally pull my attention away from our conversation. Frank comes speeding inside when I whistle out into the dark back-yard. The dog is more than ready for our nightly routine of lounging on the couch and listening to TV.

Grabbing my phone, I settle onto my couch with Frank snuggled next to me. Opening the notes app on my phone, I pick from a random list of questions I've saved to ask Charlie —readying myself for another night of off-the-wall questions.

What's something you think is true that no one else agrees with you on?

CHARLIE

Great question. How much time do you have? Because I have a list.

I've got all night.

Chapter Twenty-One

CHARLIE

HALLOWEEN IS the worst holiday of the year. Small children running around with their sugar-induced energy, wearing obnoxious costumes, and wreaking havoc everywhere they go. It's pure nightmare material. And don't get me started on those creepy, prepubescent teenagers wearing freaky masks, wielding faux weapons, and manically laughing as they terrorize people—hard pass.

Even though I hate Halloween, when Finn invited me over to his place, he radiated such optimism and hope that I couldn't say no. I like the gentle giant so much that I'm willing to be with him on the worst day of the year, even if it means being terrified of every trick-or-treater that comes to the door.

Does he look like he could protect me from the little sugar-high hellions in costumes? Yes.

Does he look like he could protect me from the scary teens with fake knives? Absolutely not.

Finn may be tall and lithe, but some of those teens have at least fifty pounds on him. Then again, maybe there's some muscle hiding under all those sweater vests.

Either way, I accepted his invite. And now I need a costume. *Ugh.*

My parents loved Halloween and would dress up every year. They would even dress up Vera as an aloe vera plant.

Cringy and cliché . . . and cute.

Because our town is so small, we close early for holidays, meaning I closed the shop about an hour ago and called Marnie to help me with my costume emergency. We're currently going through my closet and trying to figure out what in the world I should wear.

I've ended up in my own personal hell.

Marnie's currently lying on my bed with a snoring Vera. Meanwhile, I'm frantically rummaging through my closet. Clothes are strewn everywhere as I search for something that could be considered a costume.

"Do you have anything slutty?" Marnie asks with a mouth full of candy, piling the empty candy wrappers neatly on the corner of my bed.

"When have I ever been slutty?" I poke my head out of the closet, blowing a loose strand of hair out of my face.

"True. You do kind of dress like a grandma," she replies with her mouth still full.

"I'm ignoring that."

"But you're a cute grandma!"

I head back into the closet and yell, "That doesn't help!"

A pair of navy blue coveralls catches my eye. How I acquired these, I'll never know. I think maybe it was that time I drank too much tequila and thought it was a great idea to shop online for things I definitely didn't need.

I pull them off the hanger. "I have an idea!"

Marnie laughs, and I hear her mutter, "Oh, I can't wait to see this."

<hr>

AFTER CONSUMING TOO MUCH CANDY, talking about books, and relaxing on the couch, I decided that it's time to get ready for the evening. Looking in the mirror, my eyes roam over my reflection. I have my hair up, with a red bandana tied around my head, and the sleeves of my blue coveralls are rolled up. The coveralls are unbuttoned just enough to give the slightest hint of cleavage. Not enough to be indecent, but also enough to say, *"Hey, I can be kind of hot! Look at my boobs!"*

When I finally emerge from the bathroom, Marnie yells, "FUCK YES. You make a HOT Rosie the Riveter! I bet Finn's a history guy. This is totally his wet dream." Wiggling her eyebrows, Marnie gives me another slow look from top to bottom, really taking in my costume, and nods with approval. "Oh yeah, he's definitely going to want to peel that off of you with his teeth. Amazing job. You're doing the Lord's work for all the history nerds out there." She gives me an exaggerated salute.

How fitting.

"It's amazing how I still keep you around," I remark on an exhale.

"I know, right? Every day, I wonder if you'll ever get rid of me." She shrugs. "You can't get rid of me though. I'm such a delight."

"And humble," I mutter.

"Duh." She winks.

I have to leave for Finn's in about fifteen minutes, but he

lives in the next neighborhood over, so it's a quick walk. It's still light enough outside that we can make it to his place without too many pint-sized monsters scaring me half to death.

Before Marnie leaves, she crouches down to Vera and holds her face. "Be good for your sister, okay? And make sure she uses protection—"

I prop one hand on my hip and cock my head. "Is this a joke?" My tone is flat while Marnie snickers at my displeased face.

She covers Vera's ears, afraid her words will corrupt the poor dog.

"Two years without sex is two years too long. He's cute. You're hot. You've got great tits. Go for it. Climb that tall man like you're a koala and he's your favorite tree."

"You've overstayed your welcome. You can leave now." My voice is rushed as I motion for her to come to the front door.

"Fine, fine. I love you!" She walks out the door, heading to her car.

"I tolerate you!" I holler back, my way of saying I love her.

"Keep me updated, Rosie! I need to know if his flag is at full staff!" Marnie cackles as she gets into the driver's seat.

I whisper-shout to her, "Shut the fuck up! People can hear you!" I slam the front door shut, pretending she didn't just yell that out loud and hoping my neighbors didn't hear any of that.

Christ. That woman needs a muzzle or something.

After that joke, my cheeks are flaming hot.

If I can't handle a penis joke, how am I going to handle the real thing?

Maybe two years is two years too long.

VERA and I stroll over to Finn's place as the sun sets. The dark, moody, gray sky is the perfect backdrop for Halloween. A soft gust of wind blows a few leaves across the pavement, causing Vera to chase after them as we approach Finn's bungalow. His home is lightly decorated outside, with a skeleton holding a pumpkin and strands of orange fairy lights weaving around the stone pillars that frame his front door.

Taking a deep breath, Vera and I make our way up to his door. My hand goes to knock, but the door opens forcefully. Jolting back, my throat makes an embarrassing, squeaky yelp of surprise.

Worst. Holiday. Ever.

My hand flies to my chest as I close my eyes, trying to catch my breath. "You scared the shit out of me! Were you watching out your window for us?"

His deep voice surrounds me like the cool autumn breeze. "S-sorry. Frank and I are excited for company. No one's been here since we moved in." He pauses, and a deep chuckle emanates from his chest. "You can open your eyes, you know. There will be no more jump scares."

With my eyes sealed shut and hand clutching my chest, any hope of me playing "the unbothered girl" has gone right out the window.

I've never been an "unbothered" girl. I've always been very much "bothered."

Unclenching my hand from my chest, my eyes flutter open and connect with Finn's. He cracks an infectious wide smile, with dimples on full display. My stomach flutters as I stand nervously before him.

Finn's eyes roam over my body, taking in my Rosie the Riveter costume. He slowly nods as he bites his lip and quietly mutters, *"Nice"* under his breath.

Looking at him, the steady beat of my heart begins rapidly picking up its pace.

Mirroring his actions, I take in his entire costume, giving it a slow perusing from shoes to hair. Embarrassingly, my brain decides to start thinking about what's *under* his costume.

How the weight of his body would feel on top of me.

What his warm lips on my soft skin would feel like.

Whether he's gentle or dominant between the sheets.

Fucking Marnie. I blame her and that flag pole innuendo.

Standing on the porch, I'm on the precipice of being overwhelmed by these thoughts about Finn that are swirling around in my brain. I start feeling lightheaded, my skin is on fire, and my lungs are devoid of oxygen.

His smile drops, looking concerned. "Are you okay? You look a little flushed. Do you need some water? Here, come in." Finn waves for me to enter, which most definitely doesn't help my flustered state. Firmly placing his hand on my lower back, I can feel his assuring touch burning through my clothes as he ushers me over to sit on the couch.

"Don't move, I'm getting you water," he says, making his way to the kitchen. I hear Finn's sharp whistle for Frank, calling out to the pup. "Frank, go sit by Charlie and keep an eye on her." He pauses, realizing his mistake. His voice drops low as he says to his dog, "Sorry, bud, it's a figure of speech. Just keep a nose on her, okay?"

Watching Finn apologize to his dog, not wanting to offend him with his words, causes my smile to break free. Frank prances over to me and lies down on top of my feet. Practically anchoring my legs to the ground with his heavy weight. Looking around, I realize my dog is not beside me, making Frank a more loyal companion than Vera. I lean over the side of the couch to get a better view of the kitchen and notice Vera is in there with Finn, following his every move. She's watching him with such intensity that you'd think he was performing magic. Faint murmurs come from where Finn's standing, and I'm wondering who he's talking to when I realize it's Vera.

He's talking to Vera, and her big, blonde tail swishes with glee.

My mom always said that people who talk to their dogs as if they're human are trustworthy people, and I'd have to agree with that. I look down at Frank and smile, thinking about how lucky he is to have a good owner.

"What're you smiling about over there?" Finn approaches me on the couch, a gentle smile playing on his lips.

My head perks up. "Oh. Nothing. Just thought of some-thing my mom once told me."

He settles beside me, our knees brushing up against one another. "Oh yeah? What did she say?"

"People who talk to their dogs like they're humans are trustworthy."

"That's a very wise woman." Finn hands me the glass of water. "Did you eat today? I brought you something in case you didn't," he says, placing the granola bar in my other hand.

I look around his living room, which opens up to the kitchen. The lights are dimmed, and soft music fills the home. My eyes catch on a few familiar potted plants scattered around his space, which makes me smile. It's cozy, warm, and intimate.

Feeling more relaxed, my tense shoulders finally drop as I

settle into his plush couch. A sense of calm washes over me when I take in the dogs at my feet and Finn beside me with a concerned gaze as if he's afraid I'll break.

With a bit of courage, I shift my body toward his until our knees touch. Though I feel the warmth of his body against mine, I don't pull away.

"Thank you for all this. Sorry, I don't know what happened at the front door. It's either exhaustion, dehydration, or starvation—could be all three." I shrug.

Finn also seems more relaxed when a gentle smile tugs at his lips as he casually drapes his arm behind me on the couch. "Lucky for you, I have food if you're hungry, drinks if you're thirsty, and a guest bedroom if you need rest. Tell me what you need and what I can do to help."

Finn's voice is calm and reassuring. Similar to the feeling of being wrapped up in a blanket after a bad day. He's the ultimate gentleman. I need to call his mom to thank her for raising him right.

Finally, I'm taking a good look at Finn's costume, and I'm having a tough time figuring out what he is. He's dressed in a brown robe with a hood, paired with a long tan shirt, tan pants, and a brown belt wrapped around his waist.

Taking a sip of water, I eye him suspiciously. "What exactly are you supposed to be? That old guy from the Lord of the Rings?"

Finn's eyes widen in shock. The look on his face is an interesting battle between being offended and disappointed.

"First, that's Gandalf. Second, I'm a Jedi, *Charlotte*. How could you not know that?"

I nearly choke and spit my water back into my glass, trying not to laugh. "Is that some geeky *Star Trek* thing?"

Now, he gets up and paces around the living room. I'm

trying to hold in my laughter. Finn is an endearing, full-blown geek. Much to my surprise, this makes me like him even more.

He stops pacing and clears his throat. "It's *Star Wars*, not *Star Trek*," he says, placing his large hands on his narrow hips. Finn's stare is so intense that a laugh threatens to escape me.

"Cool," I remark, innocently shrugging my shoulders.

"Cool? Just 'cool,' Charlie?" Exasperation lacing his voice.

Watching him get all worked up about this is only adding to my amusement. I continue to flaunt my naïvety to see how close to the edge I can push him.

"Do you go to those little nerd gatherings?" I set my glass on the table and lower my hand to give Frank a head scratch. He makes a little whimper of approval, probably because his dad is losing his shit right now and not paying any attention to him.

"Conventions?"

I give him an innocent smile. "Oh, there's a formal name for the gathering? How cute."

"What are you doing tomorrow?" His hands are still settled on his hips, as his eyes narrow and cheeks flush from either embarrassment or frustration.

"Well, I have work, obviously, followed by my afternoon cry session, and then I plan to head home. Why do you ask?"

Slowly, Finn walks over and sits on the coffee table directly in front of me. His legs cage mine as he places both of his hands on either side of the couch cushion I'm sitting on. Finn is very much crowding my personal space. If this were anyone else, I'd probably punch them. But because it's Finn, I find myself practically leaning in closer to him. We're so close that I can smell his clean aftershave.

"We're having a movie date tomorrow." He leans in even closer. "You're getting a lesson in the finer points of the *Star Wars* saga." Finn's mouth is so close to mine that I can almost taste his mint toothpaste when he speaks.

"What if I don't want a lesson?" I murmur. The energy between us has shifted, now charged with attraction and desire.

Finn inhales as he grasps a strand of my dark hair between his two fingers. My silky hair is twirling around and around those long, deft fingers of his. His eyes are transfixed on my strands of hair while my eyes are transfixed on him.

My chest feels like it's about to implode with how close we're sitting—our breaths mingling mere inches apart.

Finn's gaze snaps to mine. Eyes so dark, they look navy blue, bore directly into mine.

"Charlie, rest assured, you'll want this lesson. I can almost guarantee it."

He lets out a dark chuckle. The implication hiding beneath his words does not go unnoticed.

Warmth spreads straight down my spine, my body runs hot, and arousal settles in my core. A deep, aching need to be touched. My breathing comes out sharp and ragged as Finn's demeanor changes. Strong hands move from the couch and grip my thighs, the heat burning right through the heavy fabric of my coveralls. He studies his hand placement, giving my thighs a gentle squeeze.

Finn lets out a deep, satisfied groan that only adds to the dampness forming between my legs. I'm practically at Finn's mercy right now. He could bend me to his will and I would thank him for it.

That's how intoxicated I am by him.

He leans in closer, looking down at my lips. I can feel his fast, shallow breath on my lips. My tongue darts out to lick my bottom lip, drawing his gaze to the motion, only urging him to close the space between us faster.

Our lips are now a hair apart—

"TRICK OR TREAT!"

We jolt apart at the sound of the doorbell ringing and our maniac dogs barking. I roll my lips, biting back a laugh.

Finn drops his head, muttering a curse under his breath. He hastily gets up, grabs the bowl with annoyance, and passes out candy to the spawns standing at his door.

Chapter Twenty-Two

Those little fuckers.

I got cockblocked by overgrown teenagers dressed as Mario Kart characters. Not exactly cockblocked, but kissblocked. I open the door with a little more force than necessary, throw the miniature candy bars into Mario and Luigi's pillow cases, and shut the door. When I turn back to the couch, Charlie is now sitting on the floor, petting Frank and Vera. Contentment consumes her features. With a gentle smile curling on her lips and a soft twinkle in her eye—she looks absolutely perfect in my home.

It's a beautiful sight.

Stepping towards her, I open my mouth to compliment her costume, but another group of trick-or-treaters is at my doorstep, practically banging down my door. I drop my head, feeling irritation flare in my chest.

These damn kids are ruining my night.

After passing out candy to the cast of Sesame Street—Big Bird and Elmo, specifically—I spin toward Charlie and stroll over to where she's seated on the living room floor. Crouching down, I sit next to her and the two dogs, who are both belly up with wagging tails.

From this angle, I can see down the neckline of her costume. One of the buttons must've accidentally popped open, and I completely lose my train of thought at the sight of her soft cleavage. Seeing the swell of her full breasts causes me to lose all focus. Every time I've been around Charlie, she hasn't worn anything that dipped this low. I feel myself harden beneath the zipper of my pants—the fabric pressing uncomfortably against my growing erection at the sight of her breasts covered in nude lace.

My one-track brain is having difficulty concentrating on anything else except for the beautiful sight before me. I'm like a man stuck in the Victorian Era who just saw a woman's ankle for the first time.

She clears her throat, looking up at me like I got caught. Which I did. Heat burns from my chest to my neck and finally arrives at my cheeks. Charlie tries hard to hide a smile while I quickly look away, wishing the embarrassment would soon disappear.

"S-sorry," I wince, my voice sheepish. "That was creepy and weird and I'm sorry. If you want to leave because you're uncomfortable—"

Please don't leave early.

"How do they look?" She intercepts my ramble quicker than the speed of light.

My pulse is thumping loudly in my ears, my dick is achingly hard, and I feel like a creep gawking at her cleavage like that. When I meet her eyes, she pins me with a stare. Her expression is neutral and unreadable.

I swallow hard. "Th-they look g-good." The sweat on the back of my neck is practically dripping down my shirt.

Wow. Smooth, Finn. I've been transported back to my bumbling sixteen-year-old self again. I'm really knocking this whole "charming" thing out of the park.

Charlie's face hasn't changed. She gives a slow, pensive nod and her eyes lock on mine.

I definitely fucked up.

A few seconds of her intense glare pass before she suddenly breaks into a fit of giggles. "Oh my god, you should see your face! I've never seen a person's face turn that red before!"

I'm too stunned to speak. This woman's poker face is unmatched. I breathe out a long exhale and drop my head. She's still laughing, and the dogs think something is very wrong. Frank is all over Charlie, practically crawling in her lap, and Vera is licking my face to get my attention.

I turn my head to Charlie. Her smile is so big that her kind brown eyes are creasing at the corners. As always, her classic smile proves to be infectious, and I feel my own lips curling up at the ends.

"I thought you were going to punch me!" I say, laughing. I swipe my hand across my damp forehead. "I felt like such a fucking creep."

"Listen, I'm only handy with a golf club. The last time I tried to throw a punch, I broke two knuckles." She shrugs.

I throw a bemused look her way. "We'll need to discuss that incident at a later date, because I'm sure there's a good story there." She nods in agreement. "Remind me to help you work on your self-defense skills. I can teach you how to throw a few punches without injuring yourself too badly." I give her hand a quick squeeze, but don't move it away.

Any chance I get to touch Charlie, I take it and run. At least until she pushes me away. Which she hasn't so far. She rolls her eyes with a light laugh. When she looks down at our joined hands, I notice her chewing on her inner lip, worry etched on her face. With my thumb and index finger, I gently tip her chin to meet my gaze.

"Hey," I say gently. "What's on your mind?"

She opens her mouth, ready to speak, before we hear another loud banging at the door with more trick-or-treaters.

These little twerps.

My hand drops from her chin, and I groan in annoyance. Begrudgingly, I get off the floor and grab the candy bowl, charging to my front door. "I'm shutting off this fucking porch light, I've had enough of these hellions interrupting—" I open the door with agitated force, though I don't dare finish my sentence. Instead, I freeze, my eyes taking in the scene before me, carefully weighing my next words.

A man, who easily has seventy-five pounds of muscle on me and looks like he belongs in a motorcycle club, raises a single, displeased eyebrow at me. I look down and see that he's holding his daughter's hand, who's wearing a sparkly pink princess costume.

Clearing my throat, I put on a cheery voice. "Wow! Beautiful costume. You know what? Tonight's your lucky night. Here, you can take all of the candy." I pour everything from the bowl into her pumpkin pail, and Mr. Clean's tattooed, Harley-riding cousin nods in approval. "You guys have a great night. Hope to see you around the neighborhood!"

I hope I never see them again.

Stepping back inside my house, I lock the door and

turn the porch light off. Charlie is now sitting on the couch with both dogs, fighting a smile at the sight of my exasperation. Heading back to the couch, I whistle for Frank to move over so I can sit next to Charlie. The damn dog doesn't move an inch, and Charlie's shoulders shake with laughter.

"You're loving this, aren't you?" I say, moving to sit in the chair across from the couch. I pull my glasses off my face, set them on the coffee table, and rub my eyes. A laugh bubbles out of me.

"This is not how I expected tonight to go." Sighing, I run my hands through my hair.

"I don't know about you, but I'm having a fun time," she says with a fit of delicate laughter.

"Yeah?"

"Of course. Seeing you get flustered is much more entertaining than reading one of my romance books."

My head whips in her direction. Even though I can barely see her without my glasses, I don't miss the pink stains on her cheeks when she realizes her admission.

"Ahh. So you read romance. Any recommendations?" I pry. As I put my glasses back on, I lean forward in the chair. My elbows rest on my knees, and I cradle my face in one hand, patiently waiting for her to tell me *anything* about her reading habits.

"No," she says, her voice flat.

"Oh, come on. I'm looking to get back into the genre. Maybe I want to learn a new thing or two?"

"Hold up. *Back into the genre*? What does that mean?"

This revelation will put me into an early grave.

Sighing, I anxiously adjust my glasses before I look up at her. "Aunt Donna convinced me to join her book club when I was seventeen. I have three boxes of historical romance books in my attic."

"Three boxes?"

"Three boxes," I echo.

She looks off into the distance, nodding thoughtfully. "I could see you with long, flowing hair and your chest on full display, ripping a bodice."

I slump back in my chair, groaning. "This is embarrassing."

Charlie laughs. "If you want updated recommendations, go look up the bestsellers. You don't need to know my favorites to learn more." She shakes her head, laughing.

Leaning forward again, I fix my gaze on hers. "See, sweetheart, that's where you're wrong." Charlie's eyebrows knit together in confusion, tilting her head to the side as she does. "I want to know your favorites so I can learn what you like," my voice is hushed and rough. Charlie's eyes widen in surprise while the flush on her face deepens in color. My mind wanders to an entirely different place.

Does she blush when she comes? If a little flirting gets her blushing this quickly, I can only imagine the shade of red her pretty cheeks turn as she moans my name, writhing beneath me in my tangled bedsheets.

We sit there looking intensely at one another for what feels like an eternity. The tension in the room has turned into something palpable enough that the dogs have hopped off the couch and disappeared elsewhere in the house. I can see the wheels in Charlie's mind turning over and over again. Trying to work out what just happened and what could happen between us.

It's driving me crazy that I can't read her thoughts.

She clears her throat. "Let's go for a walk, yeah?" Charlie

briskly stands up, grabbing both our jackets and handing me mine before she puts hers on.

As we walk out into the cold, damp darkness outside, I don't say anything. The night is calm, and the sky is clear, dotted with bright stars. Our walk is silent for the first five minutes, and I can't help but think I royally fucked this up and flirted too close to the sun.

I glance down at her. "Hey, about earlier—"

An amused smile washes over her. "Don't," she says. "I liked it."

She whispers the last part, intentionally not meeting my eyes. It's adorable how shy she gets around me sometimes. Each time she does, my heart thrums with excitement.

We keep walking until we end up in a clearing at the edge of my neighborhood. Lush, tall pine trees surround the grassy field, and a small stream runs through it. The sounds of the stream soothe my racing brain. She said not to apologize, but I can't help but feel that something in the air is off with us.

I can't pinpoint it, but there's just *something*.

The mood has changed.

We feel different.

"Fuck it," I hear her say, pulling me from my thoughts.

My eyes flicker over to her. "Huh? Fuck what?"

"This."

The next thing I know, she grabs me by the lapels of my jacket, pulls me down to her level, and kisses me senseless.

I'm stunned.

Her lips are soft and warm, and the kiss is so careful and tender that it takes my breath away. She pulls away and we lock eyes. I'm still stunned, unable to form any words. My face must be twisted in confusion, because panic quickly settles over hers.

"Oh, dear god. I misread the situation." She lets go of my jacket and starts backing up. Her panic-stricken face morphs into regret and defeat.

Charlie turns to leave, walking away from me at a speedy pace.

Finally, my brain catches up after trying to process our kiss. All I feel is relief, desire, and lust rapidly burning a path through my veins. In a rush, I catch up to Charlie. Closing the distance between us, my arm wraps around her waist, spinning her to face me.

"Get back here." My voice is gruff as I draw her closer to me. "I wasn't done yet."

With one hand around her waist and the other cupping her jaw, it's my turn to press my lips against hers. Our kiss is gentle but desperate. Demanding but intimate.

I remove my arm from her waist and deepen the kiss by cupping her face in both of my hands, carefully tilting her head back. Her hands reach for my coat again, gripping the lapels tightly, like she's afraid she may drift away. As she lets out a soft, satisfied whimper, I instinctively pull her closer against me.

Our bodies meld together, enveloped in a kiss so intense and passionate that it overwhelms all of my senses. From the scent of her citrus shampoo and the taste of watermelon candy on her lips to her lush curves pressing into my body and the sweet sounds she's making—I'm completely and utterly consumed by this woman.

There's no chance in hell I'm letting this one get away from me.

Chapter Twenty-Three

CHARLIE

MY HOLD on Finn's jacket is so tight that my fingers begin to ache down to the bone. Never in my life have I ever grown the ovaries to make a move like this on a guy. Stretched to its limit, something inside me snapped tonight.

My therapist is definitely going to be hearing about this next week. She'll be so proud.

Bringing my thoughts back to the moment, Finn's grasp on my face is firm. His strong, warm hands envelop my cheeks, cradling them completely. When our lips part, a brief silence hangs in the air between us. We stand, staring at each other breathlessly, on the cold, dark street. A gust of wind blows, sending an unruly strand of hair across my face, and Finn gently tucks it behind my ear before resting his hands on my cheeks again.

"I've been wanting to do that since the moment I first saw you," he says as his thumbs caress the soft skin of my cheeks.

I chuckle. "Lies. No one wants to kiss the 5-iron-wielding maniac."

"I don't know about that. You had a strong grip on that club . . . it was kind of a turn on." A playful smirk flashes across his face, and I can't help but mirror his smile.

A sudden shiver runs through me, and I'm unable to tell if it's from the cold or from the kiss with Finn. Being the observant man that he is, Finn reaches for his scarf. Still warm from his body, he carefully wraps it around my neck. Warmth and his scent slowly seep into my skin, wrapping me in comfort. It takes every cell in my body to not just stand here and inhale him for the rest of the night.

"There," he says, removing my hair trapped under the back of his scarf. His fingers graze the back of my neck, lingering for a few moments. Goosebumps, not from the cold, erupt over my body. "Better?"

I give a gentle nod. "Yes, thanks."

Finn smiles down at me while tucking another strand of escaped hair behind my ears. Once again, his hands cradle my face as he places a tender kiss on my forehead.

My heart nearly stops in my chest. The air leaves my lungs, and I begin to feel dizzy. No one, and I mean absolutely no one, that I ever dated had given me a simple forehead kiss. Even though it was a small gesture, it carried immense meaning for me.

When Finn planted his soft lips just below my hairline, a wave of reassurance and adoration washed over me. Two feelings that I have never felt before in any of my previous romantic relationships. I want to hang onto this feeling—hold it close to my chest and never let it slip through my fingers.

"Let's get back to my place, okay?" Finn whispers, noticing my sudden change in demeanor.

I sniffle from the cold and nod in agreement. Before turning to walk in the direction of his house, he laces his fingers in mine.

Here we are, just two people stumbling through life, both starting over. We hold our warm hands together on a cold night, finding comfort in one another.

Throughout the entire walk back to Finn's home, we walk in easy silence. The air between us is comfortable, free of any awkwardness. One of the things I like most about Finn is that he doesn't have the urge to fill the silence with conversation. He's completely okay with the quiet.

Periodically, I look up at him, and find that he has a shy smile on his face while looking ahead, which makes me smile in return.

We're just two giddy fools with crushes on one another.

As we slowly approach his cozy bungalow, I can't help but reflect on how at ease I feel with Finn. After the year I've had, my lungs feel like they can finally take a nice, full, deep breath. I'd bet my life savings that if I curled up on his couch right now, I'd fall into the deepest, most restful sleep.

Worries and insomnia be gone.

Finn unlocks the door and both dogs start barking, worried that an intruder is here to steal all their toys. The second that they realize it's us, Vera practically jumps into Finn's arms, and Frank wiggles around at my feet, frantically circling my legs and looking for attention. Finn and I face each other, laughing at how these dogs are clinging to the opposite owners.

"So, I guess Vera is staying with you tonight?" I joke.

Finn chuckles. "Yeah, and I'll pick Frank up tomorrow at your place?"

"Solid plan." I giggle. "We should get going since it's getting late, and we both work tomorrow."

Awareness sinks into me. I don't want to leave. In fact, I'm sad that I have to head back home. Usually, I'm champing at the bit and making excuses to leave early.

Not now, though. Now, I wish I could stay.

"You walked here, right? Let me drive you home." A look of concern flickers over his face.

Not one to turn down a ride home, I nod, letting him lead Vera and I to his car.

The drive was short, as we live only a few streets apart. When he pulls up to my house, Finn gets out of the car, grabs Vera's leash, and walks us to my front door. His hand finds mine like it has a gravitational pull—our fingers intertwining effortlessly and naturally. This whole gentlemanly act he puts on makes my knees wobbly and my heart all fluttery.

Then again, maybe it's not an act. It sure doesn't feel like one. Perhaps it's just who Finn is—a truly good, earnest man, down to his very soul. Not a single disingenuous bone in his body.

As the three of us slowly approach the door, my treacherous mind does what it knows best—overthink. Internally, I begin to panic. Do we kiss goodnight? Do I ask him inside? If I ask him inside, does he expect sex? That wouldn't be a bad thing. Though I'm quite tired and a little hungry, which won't make me great company.

"Hey, where did you go just then?" He's looking at me with his head tilted. His low voice snaps me from my thoughts and grounds me in reality.

"Hmm? What do you mean?"

Did he just read my mind? No. That's not possible.

"You just looked like your mind was somewhere else for a moment." His eyes flicker between mine, searching for any hint of what my thoughts might have been.

Finn is incredibly observant. At times, it feels like he's inside my head, knowing every thought that passes through. More than once, he knew what I needed before I even realized it myself. Those moments are when I feel the most grateful for him. It's often hard for me to express what I want or need, so for someone to take the lead? Perfection.

"I, uh . . . it's nothing." I smile timidly, feeling my cheeks redden with embarrassment.

"You sure? You can tell me." His gentle, comforting voice makes me want to blurt out every thought that is bouncing around in my head.

For a moment, I think about doing just that. Then, reality dumps on me like a bucket of ice water, and I decide there's no way in hell I'm inviting him inside, only to turn him down for sex because I needed a sandwich rather than some dick.

Shaking my head, I gaze down at our joined hands, with Vera sitting between us. Half of her weight is on my foot, and the other half is on Finn's. Her large puppy dog eyes swing back and forth between us, begging for one of us to make a move to go inside. If I didn't know better, I'd say Vera is playing matchmaker.

Knowing her, though? I think she just wants to go to sleep.

"I'm sure," I reply with a warm smile. "We should get inside. It's late." I stop, and Finn's eyebrows raise. Realizing my error, I blurt out an anxious stream of clarifications. "When I said 'we,' I meant Vera and I. Not like *you and I*. Not that I don't want to invite you in, because I had an incredible night . . . and I hope you did, too. Actually, I didn't even want to leave! It's just . . . I'm a bit hungry, and I don't want to be too forward. Though you can come in if you like. But also, no pressure. I also don't know if I have any snacks you'd enjoy. . . . I have a lot of sweets and I get the feeling that you're more of a salty-over-sweet person. But—"

Mid-ramble, Finn interrupts me by placing a soft kiss on my lips. Thankfully, this stops me from spilling all of my deepest secrets on my too-small porch. When Finn pulls away, his lips hover over mine for a brief second. His deep blue, empathetic eyes bore into mine, speaking a silent message saying, *You don't have to explain yourself. I understand.* Before he steps away from me, he cups my face with one hand, stroking my cheek with his thumb as he does, and places another kiss on my forehead.

I'm such a fucking goner.

"Get some sleep, sweetheart. I'll see you tomorrow." He smiles down at me, rendering me speechless.

Finn patiently waits for Vera and I to get inside and lock the door. When he hears the lock click into place, he walks to his car and drives off.

A million thoughts are swirling around in my mind, but the one that stays at the forefront is how much I enjoy spending time with Finn. It's an indescribable feeling in the best way possible because I've always preferred being alone to being surrounded by people.

With Finn, that's changed. I crave his company more than I crave my solitude.

Whenever he's around, my heart thrums, I feel breathless, and there's an overwhelming sense of happiness inside me.

A surge of relief shoots through me, enough to make my eyes burn with unshed tears. With everything that's happened over the past year, I didn't know if I could feel happiness and peace again. Blinking back my tears, I'm relieved to know that I'm not broken; I can still feel happiness, I can still laugh, and I can still enjoy life, despite my grief.

It only took a charmingly persistent guy to chip away at my walls, take me by the hand, and help show me the way.

Chapter Twenty-Four

Charlie

MONDAY MORNING ARRIVED quicker than I anticipated. It was a downright battle dragging Vera and myself into the store today, as neither of us had any interest in leaving the bed.

As I begin to open up the store, I let out a huge yawn and rub my tired eyes. The crisp November air sends a chill through me. Bright sunlight pours through the shop's large windows; definitely too bright for me. Groaning, I draw the shades down for some relief.

Why am I practically a zombie this morning?

Because I stayed up too late, staring at the ceiling and thinking about the kiss that Finn and I shared.

That, and Vera was snoring so damn loudly.

The memory of our kiss still lingers on my lips. I can't help but let my mind wander back to the moment when I firmly pressed my lips against his and every small detail that followed.

The sudden sharp inhale of his breath as I clutched his jacket, drawing him closer to me.

The way his strong arms felt wrapped around my waist, pulling me to him with desire.

The warmth of his hands, which kept a firm hold on me, pressing me tighter against his body.

Memories of last night begin to dissipate as anxiety slowly creeps in. I wonder if I'll see Finn today and whether he's suddenly regretting last night. Maybe after a restful night, he just wants to be friends and only friends. Nothing more.

My stomach plummets at the thought of seeing him with another girl. Especially in this small town. Groaning, I drop my head into my hands. Whenever my mind spirals like this, constantly second-guessing myself, it drives me insane. I never used to be like this—until my parents died. It's impressive how much grief can affect your brain. Even though I'm working on my spiraling thoughts in therapy, sometimes my mind does whatever it wants.

Vera senses my unease and settles her head on my thigh, which I instinctively begin to stroke. The heavy weight of her little head, paired with her soft fur beneath my fingertips, slowly brings me back to reality. Since I inherited Vera, it amazes me how much less anxious I become whenever I'm around her.

After a few deep breaths and some Vera therapy, I feel a bit better.

My eyes pause on a pile of mail sitting on the counter and I reach over to grab the stack. While shuffling through the stack of letters, my hands freeze on an obnoxiously colored flyer.

"Fuck," I groan.

In my hand is a flyer for the Hemlock Harvest Festival. I

completely blanked on this insufferable event that my parents adored. This will be the first year I'll be partaking in the event since their passing.

And I have no clue what in the world I'm doing. All I know about this event is that it has hundreds of jovial people and an abundance of small town camaraderie.

My personal hell.

Panic spins into anger, and anxiousness rises in my chest again. Tears well in my eyes, and my skin suddenly feels clammy with worry. I don't know what I'm doing.

The worst part? My parents aren't alive to tell me how they managed the event. Anger now turns to guilt for not asking more questions about their business so I could be more prepared.

That's the funny thing about death. Sometimes, it happens so fast that no one can prepare you.

At all.

Day in and day out, you live with three statements that will forever haunt you. *I would've done this*, *I could've done that*, and *I should've done this*.

A loud knock on the door pulls me from my thoughts—a well-timed welcome distraction from this emotion-filled moment. I wipe my nose and dry the tears under my eyes as I open the door for Marnie.

Before I get the door fully open, she barges in, grabs me by the shoulders, and looks at me dead in the eye.

"What's wrong? You're not okay. Don't fucking lie to me because I know your lying face. Did you eat? Do you need water? Did your blood sugar drop again? Where's Vera? You need her, even though you say you don't. Here, sit down." She hastily drags me across the store, plopping me down on a stool behind the counter. "Drink some water from my bottle.

Don't be weird about it because I know you don't like sharing glasses or straws. I don't have cooties, you freak."

Rolling my eyes, I grab her bottle and take a few sips of the cold water, which, admittedly, does help a bit.

"I got the stupid flier about the stupid Harvest Festival." I exhale.

"I've always hated that damn festival. It really brings the crazies out, you know? What's got you so upset about it? Let's talk about your favorite thing." Her hands come together, fingers moving like a villain plotting an ambush. "*Feelings.*"

I take another gulp of water, huffing out a sad laugh. "I panicked because I've never done this before. I'm angry because my parents are dead and can't help me. I feel guilty because I didn't ask them more questions. And I'm sad because I'm doing this alone."

She nods and hums, taking in everything I told her. "Want me to perform some black magic? Get the Ouija board out? Maybe we can talk to the dead?" I point an annoyed glare at her. "Too soon? I'll reel it in." She winces. Marnie's gaze softens before continuing. "Okay, first off, you're not doing this alone. You have me. I can figure this shit out in a week, tops. Secondly, *do not* feel guilty about things that are out of your control. You didn't know you'd have this huge traumatic life event happen, and there was no way you could've prepared for that. Personally, I think you're doing great. And I know you loathe when people say this, but your parents would be so proud of you. You need to cut yourself some fucking slack."

She wraps one arm around my shoulder and pulls me in close for a hug. I exhale, feeling some of the emotional weight lift off my chest and shoulders.

"I'm surprised you're letting me hug you this long," Marnie says with disbelief.

"Me too," I muffle into her shoulder. "Honestly, it's impressive how good you are at—"

"Talking you off the ledge? Yeah. I've had a lot of practice." She laughs.

In the midst of our hug-fest, we hear the bell chime. Glancing down at my phone to check the time, it looks like we're officially open, and I officially have to get my shit together. Usually, we don't get customers first thing when the store opens. They tend to filter in later in the morning or early afternoon.

Marnie goes to welcome the customer as I quickly glance at myself to make sure there's no mascara running down my face. Pulling my hair up with a clip, I notice my eyes look sad today. What a change from how happy I felt last night.

Funny how emotions can change so quickly.

"Well, well, well. If it isn't the hot professor," I hear Marnie say up near the front of the store.

"I wore this sweater vest just for you, Marnie," a familiar, deep voice replies in amusement.

"You know I love a good, slutty sweater vest," Marnie replies.

Oh god. It's Finn. Finn is here. And I've been crying. For a brief moment, I contemplate sneaking out the back. It's too late, though, because I hear them both talking, voices getting louder as they approach me. I take the tissue out of my pocket and wipe my nose.

This morning, I was worried he wasn't going to show up today. Now, I'm worried he'll run for the hills after seeing my ugly crying face. It's too early for him to see me as a snotty, teary mess. Because nothing says *Wanna make out again?* like wiping your runny nose and gazing longingly through red, swollen eyes.

They both come to an abrupt stop in front of the counter where I'm sitting, still drinking out of Marnie's skull-patterned water bottle and sniffling. My puffy eyes go wide when I see them staring down at me. Marnie bites back a smile and Finn looks like someone stole his dog. I slowly blink at them as my lips are frozen around the straw of Marnie's water bottle.

Marnie speaks first, breaking the thick tension in the room. Her voice is almost a whisper as she says, "And here we have a rare sighting of a beautiful mammal with shining locks of deep chestnut hair. She usually expels tears in her cave but has decided to venture out into the forest for a change of scenery. Speak low. Don't make sudden movements so as to not scare her."

She's lost her ever-loving mind—acting like I'm a rare creature in an Animal Planet documentary.

Leave it to Marnie to make jokes about your tears in the most light-hearted way. We all stare at her before breaking out in a fit of laughter. She sends a knowing wink my way. A wink that says, *We got this, don't worry about a thing.*

"I come bearing gifts," Finn says. "A drink for Ms. Thorne," he says, handing me a to-go cup. "And a black coffee for Ms. Morticia Addams." He hands a cup to Marnie.

Marnie opens the lid of the cup and sniffs it. "How did you know I take my coffee black?"

Finn tilts his head to the side and sighs. "Come on. Black clothes, black hair, black tattoos—it doesn't take a genius to figure that out, Marnie. I'm sure you also tell the barista, 'I take my coffee like my soul—black,' right?"

Marnie clutches her heart, her voice filled with dramatic

flair. "You are so dreamy. I hate it." Marnie heads to the back, yelling, "Thanks, Professor!"

Now it's only Finn and I as I'm sitting here with sore eyes, a runny nose, and a coffee that I have a fifty-fifty chance of hating. Finn walks around the corner of the counter and kneels down on the floor next to where I'm sitting. He's looking up at me and places his large hand on my knee. Embarrassingly enough, I sniffle. Again.

"Now's a good time to tell you I brought you a hot chocolate today, not a coffee." He gives my knee a gentle, comforting squeeze. "So what's going on, sweetheart?"

I shrug, rolling my lips so I don't start crying again. "You know, the usual. Dead parents, running a store I know nothing about, and that stupid Harvest Festival." My shoulders drop, blowing out a huge exhale.

"Oh, I saw that too. I have no idea what to do with that. Is it mandatory?"

"Unfortunately."

He looks off into the distance and shakes his head. "What a weird town."

"Big time," I say, forcing a smile. "This is my first year running my own station at the festival. I have no idea what I'm doing."

Finn looks at me with softened eyes filled with empathy. "Well, you're in good company, because this city boy has no clue what he's doing either." With the pad of his thumb, Finn wipes away a rogue tear that just fell from my eye. "What are the chances we can get our tents next to each other? You know, so we can be each other's support system?"

"Zero chance. Your aunt runs a strict ship when it comes to the festival."

His eyes widen. "Donna is in charge of all that?"

"Oh yeah. I've heard the horror stories from my parents." An exaggerated shiver rolls through me as I recall some of the things they had said about her.

He sits there, pondering for a second. "She gets back this week. I'll fix this." Finn pats my leg before he lifts himself off the ground. "I have to get back to the shop since we're short-staffed today. Seriously, don't stress about the silly festival. I'll take care of it."

He gives me a quick kiss on my temple before walking out the door, brimming with swoonworthy confidence. My eyebrows raise as he leaves, and I glance over at Marnie, who's hiding behind a big, indoor palm plant, giving me a huge grin and a thumbs-up.

The moment Finn steps out the door, Marnie rushes over to me so fast she runs into the counter and knocks a plant over.

"What was *that*?" she asks, eyes wide and tongue practically hanging out.

"We kissed," I blurt out, covering my mouth with my hands.

Marnie's eyes bug out of her head and she squeals. She may look like a modern-day Morticia Addams, but she sure doesn't act like one.

"How was it? Was it just a kiss? A full-blown make out sesh? Did you break your neck trying to kiss him? He's so fucking tall. Was he wearing the slutty tan sweater vest? Or the dark blue one? Come on, spill!"

On an exhale, I say, "Pull up a stool."

I tell Marnie everything. From the moment I got to his house up until the word vomiting on my porch. Her face is frozen in shock and I'm not entirely sure whether it's good shock or bad shock. A customer calls over to us, asking for help, and Marnie doesn't budge. I carefully get up and make my way around her as she sits, still unmoving.

I help the customer pick out a low-light houseplant, give her some fertilizer for free, send her on her way, and return to find Marnie in the same spot—still frozen and not making any sounds. Now, I start to get nervous as I walk up beside her.

"Uh. Are you okay?" I look at her with concern, wondering if I broke her.

"I'm racking my brain trying to find another moment in my life where I was as proud of someone as I am of you right now. I can't. I feel like a mom whose child passed their driver's test. No. I feel like a mom whose child graduated college. With a doctorate. At the top of their class. And had perfect attendance," she says.

Huh. Okay, so this is a *good* shock. Marnie slowly turns her head to me, her face lighting up with an idea. I jump back a little, unsure of what will escape from her mouth next.

"Remember that wedding everyone in Hemlock got invited to on New Year's Eve?" She looks at me, and I can sense the wheels turning in her mind.

My eyebrows pull together. Where is she going with this? "Uh. Yes. The one that I'm still trying to get out of. How easy is it to break a foot?"

Slowly, Marnie shakes her head. "You should ask Finn to go with you."

"Absolutely-fucking-not.   Are-you-out-of-your-damn-mind? Don't answer that, actually. You're too self-aware for your own good." I start to anxiously pace around the store, finding any and every excuse to completely ignore this conversation.

"I'm just sayin'. This could be good for you, you know? You seem lighter. Less grouchy . . . which I didn't think was possible. Maybe just a good ole fashioned dicking is what the doctor ordered?" she asks.

My eyes widen and my cheeks get hot. This girl is going to give me a coronary with her wild remarks.

A customer gasps from behind us and we both turn around. They're clearly aghast by what they heard Marnie say.

"Sorry about her. She has this condition where she gets a dopamine rush by making people uncomfortable. We've been to see many specialists, and they just haven't found a cure yet." I shrug. "They did brain scans and everything. Everyone is stumped."

A horrified look spreads across the customer's face.

Yep. She won't be coming back anytime soon. If I had a dollar for every time I lost a customer due to one of Marnie's "Marnie-isms," I would have enough money to put a down payment on a nice SUV.

I spin, looking back at my obnoxious friend. "You've got to stop doing that."

"Never," she replies, a devilish grin lighting up her face.

Chapter Twenty-Five

Finn

Charlie's legs bracket mine as she straddles me on my couch. Her delicate fingers are frantically pulling at the buttons on my shirt, fumbling her way down to get them undone. My hands trail up under her shirt, gripping her waist in a possessive hold as I press her down onto my aching cock. I can feel the heat from her pussy as she grinds down against me, letting out the sexiest moan as she desperately chases her pleasure. Her nails scrape down my bare chest, eliciting a deep, satisfied groan from me. My body feels like it's on fire and it can only be quenched by the woman on top of me.

Hazy with lust, I grab her hair at the nape of her neck, dragging her down to my lips for a desperate, passionate kiss. With wandering lips, I plant soft kisses on her smooth skin from her jaw to her collarbone. My lips find their way to that heavenly spot between her full breasts, gently nibbling, then sucking on the delicate flesh. Her breathless pants are only driving me crazier. It's taking every ounce of restraint not to strip her bare and finally sink into her. Kissing my way back up to her lips, I continue guiding her hips back and forth against my throbbing cock, hoping it'll provide some relief for both of us.

Our foreheads are pressed against one another as she pants, "Don't stop. Please."

"You feel incredible, Charlie." I crush my lips against hers like a man starved. The demanding kiss is sloppy and frantic —a tangled mess of tongues and teeth. Before I can flip her over onto her back, she starts kissing up my jaw.

Which then turns into her . . . licking the side of my face?

Then something cold and wet digs into my ear.

What the . . . ?

Jolting up in bed, I dazedly look over at Frank's guilty face. Blinking a few times, I make a weak attempt to shake off my drowsiness, still enamored with my lust-filled dream. When I turn to grab my glasses, I realize that my head is pounding, I can't breathe out of my nose, and my throat is killing me. To top it all off, my dick is so hard that it's physically painful.

Fantastic combination.

As the confusion lifts, it becomes clear that I must've caught the cold going around town. Which led to the hottest fever dream of my life.

No pun intended.

I turn over in bed, my shirt damp with sweat and sticking to me uncomfortably as I grab my phone. I feel like absolute shit. There's no way I can work today. I'm a walking, talking Petri dish. My fingers type out a quick text to the barista that is working today, asking him to put up a sign that says we'll be closed. While I'm still semi-aware of what's happening, I make a reminder on my phone to hire more staff. I didn't foresee that Dark Side Brews would be as successful as it has turned out to be. Mentally kicking myself, I should've prepared for this situation and hired a few more people. In my defense, I thought I had an iron-clad immune system. Sadly, judging by the war raging in my head and the fire trickling down my throat, I was wrong.

Once I get a reply from my barista telling me the sign is up and everything has been taken care of, I promptly go back to sleep, hoping to pick up where my dream with Charlie left off.

A LOUD BANGING on my front door wakes me up from a deep sleep.

What time is it? What day is it? What year am I in?

Groggily, I roll out of bed and barely stop myself from falling head first to the floor. The banging on my door isn't making my headache any better, and I'm about three seconds from losing my cool on whoever is busting down my door.

When I descend the stairs, a chill runs through me despite my fever. With my vision blurring and head pounding, I grab the handrail because I feel dizzy. Before I open the door, I pause and rub my eyes.

Fuck. I forgot my glasses.

More obnoxious, head-shattering noises come from the opposite side of my door. Whoever is on the other side needs to calm down. You'd think a stampede of elephants is trying to break it down. Taking a deep breath, I whip open the door and croak out, "What the actual fuck is wrong—"

"Wow. You look like absolute shit," a feminine voice says.

Looking down and squinting my eyes at the short figure, I vaguely guess who it could be. But I also just had a sex fever dream about said person. At this point, I don't trust my brain anymore. It's too much of an unreliable narrator for my liking.

"Let me in," her voice commands, sharp and insistent.

Without waiting for permission, she ducks under my arm that's holding the door open, and strolls breezily into my house like she owns the place.

Frank's nails click on the wooden floor, and her voice is bright when he barks for her attention. "Hey, bud! Here, let's get you outside, and then I'll feed you."

Groaning, I make my way towards the kitchen and slump onto the chair at my kitchen island. Without my glasses, everything looks like misshapen blobs of color.

Charlie's ruffling through the large paper bags she brought with her, putting away what I assume are groceries as if I'm not even here. "Where are your glasses?"

"Why are you here?" I groan, my throat feeling like I lit it on fire.

"How about, '*Thanks, Charlie, for taking care of me after I contracted the Hemlock plague!*'" She mocks, still putting groceries away. "No problem, Finn. Super happy to help," she replies to her own statement.

Maybe it's the cold or my relentless crush on her, but Charlie's cute when she's snarky.

Charlie opens my pantry door, looking for Frank's kibble. Grabbing a cup of his food, she drops it in his dish.

"Especially since the whole fucking town won't shut up about your coffee shop being closed for the day, and I need a reprieve from all the chatter and complaining," she mumbles the last part quietly to herself.

Leaning my elbow on the counter, I rest my forehead on my palm. "I feel like shit."

"Well, you look like shit. Did you take anything? I brought some Tylenol to bring your fever down, if you have one." She shakes the bottle, the sound of the pills rattling around causing me to wince.

Oh, I have a fever alright. Pushing the thought of Charlie straddling me out of my congested brain, I try to think about anything and everything except my dream. The thin material of my pajama pants leaves little to the imagination, so I need to *really* focus on anything else.

"No. I didn't take anything. Not yet, at least. I texted my barista to close the café for the day and then fell asleep." I swallow, my mouth dryer than a desert.

She sighs and, I assume, rolls her eyes, grumbling, "*Men.*"

Charlie walks closer to me and places her cool palm on my forehead. I close my eyes, leaning into her touch because it feels like heaven against my flushed skin.

"Jesus, Finn. You're burning up." She sighs. "Alright, here's the plan for the day: take some Tylenol and then get in a cool shower because your clothes are damp and you smell gross. I'll quickly change your sheets and will throw the contaminated ones in the wash." Her nose wrinkles at that in such an adorable way that my brain momentarily buffers. "After that, get your ass back in bed and don't move. Sound good?"

All I can do is nod. Mainly because I'm so overwhelmed by everything that's happening right now that my brain isn't processing as fast as I would like it to. Charlie places two Tylenol in my palm and hands me a glass of orange juice to wash it down. I hear the sliding door to the backyard glide open and Frank trots inside towards his food bowl.

"Thank you," I say after taking the medicine. "I'm going upstairs now to shower. Yell if you need anything."

She whips her head around to me. "I don't need a thing. If *you* need anything, just give me a call. My ringer is on. For the love of all that is holy, please don't yell."

Before I leave, I look in her direction. "Thanks again for stopping by with everything. I can lock the door on the way out if you want me to walk you to the door."

Her exasperated sigh fills the room. "I'm not leaving you alone, you big germ. Go shower, get back in bed, and when you wake up, I'll be here with mediocre soup and saltines ready for you."

I'll be here.

Warmth spreads throughout my whole body, wrapping around me in a comforting embrace at her words. Even though my head feels like it's underwater, I know for a fact it isn't the fever making me feel this way.

WHEN MY EYES PEEL OPEN, the room is pitch black, and moonlight casting a few streaks of silver light on the walls. As I lay there, staring up at the ceiling, I can't help but think about the wildest dream I had. Charlie was here, in my home, putting away groceries and caring for Frank like he was her own. Turning on my side to grab my phone off the nightstand, I see a glass of water, two Tylenol, and a threatening note that says, '*Dearest Finn, don't be a man-child. Take these, or else,*' stuck to the glass.

Definitely not a dream. With my heart hammering in my chest, a few worrying thoughts cross my mind. *Did I put the toilet seat down? Did I leave the house a mess? Is my under-*

wear out for the world to see? I'm positive a few pairs of dirty socks are lying around, since Frank is obsessed with stealing those. I pride myself on keeping a clean and tidy home, but sometimes life gets in the way, and things fall by the wayside.

I fumble for my glasses on the nightstand and slide them onto my face. After rolling out of bed, I swallow the medicine that was left for me and make my way downstairs. Glancing at my phone, I realize I've slept all day long, and it's already well into the evening. The stairs creak as I slowly descend; a low noise comes from the television, and the lights are dimmed low. When I peer over at the couch, my knees go weak at the endearing sight before me.

Charlie is curled up on her side with a blanket tucked under her chin, and Frank is nestled between her and the couch with his head propped up on her hip. They're both sound asleep, looking perfect and peaceful. Frank is in such a deep sleep that his fluffy nub of a tail is wagging inter-mittently.

It's starting to get late and, as much as I don't want to wake Charlie up, I know she has a store to run and a dog to care for. Carefully, I brush her hair back off her face and trace a knuckle along her cheek, hoping that's enough to wake her up.

The last thing I want to do is scare her because, if I do, there's a 90 percent chance she'll punch me in the balls.

Her eyes flutter open, inhaling a deep breath after her restful nap. "Wow. Sorry about that." She laughs. "I didn't mean to pass out on your couch." Rubbing her eyes, she yawns and reaches down to give Frank's head a loving scratch.

I smile down at her. She looks so good on my couch, wrapped in my blanket, with my dog. It just looks so . . . right.

"Don't worry about it. You can sleep here longer if you'd like, but I know you have to get home to Vera."

As her tired eyes look up at me, her features soften with relaxation. She looks rested and happy. A part of me feels like she needed a bit of rest, and I'm elated that she chose my couch to sleep on.

"Yeah, you're right. Marnie was able to take care of Vera for a few hours and then, I assume, dropped her off at my place." She groggily gets off the couch and runs a hand through her long hair. With a quick glance toward the kitchen and then back at me, she mentions, "There's mediocre soup on the stove—enough for a few days. Make sure you eat it. And keep up with the medicine, got it?" She points a joking finger at me, a small smile curving on her lips.

I give her a quick salute. "Ma'am, yes, ma'am."

That gets a big smile from her as she walks to the foyer to grab her coat. Spinning towards me, she adds, "Oh, one more thing. Frank has been fed, walked, and let out. He should be good for the night and shouldn't bug you too much. Just focus on getting better . . . the town will riot if you aren't back soon." Charlie flashes me an earnest smile before opening the door to leave.

I know I shouldn't ask and ruin the moment, but before she leaves, the words fall out of me before I can stop them. "Why? Why did you do all of this? Don't get me wrong, I'm so thankful because I was a shell of a human a hours ago and couldn't tell you my name. But you didn't have to interrupt your day for me."

Spinning quickly on her heel, she looks up at me, tilting her head. A look of bewilderment clouds her features before they soften again. "Because I show up for the people I care about, Finn. That's how I was raised, and that's how I live my life. Regardless of how big or small someone's troubles are, I'll always show up and help make their lives a fraction easier." She pauses, then flashes me a mischievous smirk. "Even if it means I'll get sick within the next twenty-four to seventy-two hours."

I stand motionless in front of her, processing everything she just said. The woman with captivating eyes and a heart too big for her own good has rendered me speechless. If I wasn't a human germ, I'd kiss her right here, right now.

For the first time in a long, long time, I feel a deep sense of home, comfort, and belonging. I've found solace in the woman standing before me. Of all the places I've lived, no one has ever cared for me like this. The way she barged in here with determination, not worrying about feeling intrusive or getting sick, makes my chest swell with happiness.

Charlie breaks me out of my trance as she wishes me goodnight and reminds me to get some rest. Standing in the foyer, I'm lost in thought, reflecting on everything that happened today as the low hum of her car's engine fills the silence.

It could be the fever, but I can't ignore that feeling of warmth permeating through my entire body once again.

After all these years, I'm starting to believe that this is where I'm finally meant to be.

Chapter Twenty-Six

After being sick for a couple of days, my body feels completely wrung out, but I'm thankfully on the mend. Following the departure of Charlie's caretaking services, which deserve five stars across the board, I sent her a text to make sure she didn't catch what I had. Thankfully, she told me that she felt fine and that her immune system must be resilient after being exposed to "the human Petri dish" all day.

She's a feisty one.

And I can't get enough.

Sitting at the edge of my shop's long countertop, I'm leafing through resumes for additional staff when a rush of cool air and the chime of a bell fill the space.

"Oh, WOW! I love what you've done with the building!" Aunt Donna bursts through the door with enough force that every patron in my shop takes notice. I tilt my head to the side and raise my eyebrows, giving her my *What the hell are you actually doing?* look. She shimmies up to the register and stares at the chalkboard menu on the wall.

Getting up, I stand behind the counter with my hands at my side, patiently waiting for whatever eccentricity is to come. I love her because she's family, but I still stand by the idea that she could benefit from less caffeine and more social awareness.

"Hey, Aunt D, how was the trip? Will you be having the usual?" I force a smile. Alarmed by Charlie's distress about the Harvest Festival, I've made it my personal mission to take some of the burden off of her. The only obstacle in my way is Donna and her approval of Charlie and I sharing a booth at the festival. She's very set in her ways. Donna loves to say no with a smile on her face and a loving pat on the shoulder. From years of experience, I've learned that, in order to get what you want, you have to lay it on thick.

"Oh, it was lovely! Steve and I had the most wonderful time." Her smile is wide as she drones on about her trip.

Feigning an interested expression, I make her favorite (albeit annoyingly complex) drink and slide it across the counter to her while she talks. Rounding the corner of the countertop, I pull up a chair next to her.

I nervously run a hand through my hair as I turn to her. When she pauses for breath in the midst of a story about her attempt to smuggle an exotic plant in her luggage, I take the opportunity to interrupt her. "Aunt D, I wanted to talk to you about something." The words cautiously escape my lips.

"Yes, Finny? What is it?"

I hate that fucking nickname.

"The Harvest Festival is right around the corner. It'll be a first for me and I'm just not totally comfortable being alone at my own booth." *I'm totally comfortable being alone at my own booth, but my life would be significantly enhanced if an overalls-wearing brunette is by my side.* "So, I was wondering . . . since Charlie did such a great job showing me around Hemlock—which, thank you for setting that up, by the way—is it possible that she and I could share a booth? You know, just so she can help show me the ropes."

Her speculative eyes narrow and I'm really hoping she can't smell my bullshit. My demeanor stays calm and unassuming as she considers my proposition.

"You know, Finn, we've never done that before. Each business always has its own booth. The festival has been set up the same way for the last decade, and I don't like to—"

Stopping her mid-sentence, I put my hand on hers. "Yes, I totally understand. I was hoping this could be a one-time exception. Just so I can get my bearings at the festival. I'm a little nervous, you know? With me being new in town and all . . ." I flash Donna a pleading smile, hoping that she remembers that I'm her second favorite member of the family.

Despite how loud the coffee shop is, Donna's disapproving silence is louder.

Sighing heavily, I level her with a serious look. "If you do this for me, I'll slip you an extra hundred bucks in your Christmas card this year."

"Deal," she says finally.

Do not look too happy. Do not look too happy.

I breathe a sigh of relief, grasping both of her hands in mine. "Thank you so much. You're my favorite aunt."

She's not.

Her hand goes up to pat my cheek. "Of course. I just want you to be comfortable. It's so nice to have you planting roots here." She takes a sip of coffee. "Plus, the extra cash doesn't hurt."

A smile spreads over my face as I release her hands and glance down at the floor, willing myself to not smile in front of her. Little does she know there's one person in particular who knows a thing or two about planting roots—someone I wouldn't mind growing roots with someday.

***

It's the night before the Harvest Festival and I'm working tirelessly in my office trying to finish the last-minute preparations. I check my watch and see that it's almost time to meet Charlie for our Friday night walk when I hear a gentle knock on the shop door. My body reacts in anticipation, knowing exactly who it is. Shamelessly, I haven't been able to get Charlie's lips out of my mind.

Or the feeling of her body pressed against mine, her soft curves in my hands.

Or hearing her soft moans when I went back to kiss her again.

Not to mention seeing how her cheeks flushed and pupils dilated when we pulled away to look at each other, completely breathless.

Our kiss was unlike anything I've ever experienced before. It was magnetic. Utterly intoxicating. Every one of my senses was overwhelmed by her presence.

At that moment, the world went quiet around us and Charlie, wrapped in my arms, felt heavenly.

Between that kiss and my sexual fever dream, I haven't been able to stop thinking about her, her incredible body, and how good I'd make her feel if she ever allowed me the privilege.

I wonder how she would react if I hauled her to my back

office and we made out like two sexually deprived adults? There's a battle brewing between my two brains—one wants to take her and make her forget her name, while the other yearns to uncover every tiny detail there is to know about her. However, my cock seems to be winning this battle, as I daydream about dragging her into my office by those fucking overalls, pulling her curvy body snug against mine, and claiming her. I can picture her on my desk, knees parted with my name escaping her lips on a breathy moan as I pull aside her—

The knock on the door grows louder and more impatient, causing me to startle. My jeans are painfully tight as I shake my head to tear myself away from my fantasy. I take a moment to compose myself before I really scare Charlie away. My face is flushed with desire as I try to get my mind back in the headspace for innocent conversation and maybe a casual kiss with her tonight. Even though the thoughts lurking in the shadows of my mind are anything but innocent or casual.

Rushing out from the back office to the front door, I find Charlie standing there with her cheeks glowing, nose kissed with pink, and eyes sparkling warmly when she sees me.

God. She's so beautiful.

She gives a small wave, and I hear her muffled voice say, "Hurry up! It's cold out here!"

Unlocking the door, she and Vera rush inside. Frank hears the commotion and makes a speedy beeline for Vera. A few squeaks and tail wags later, they're off doing whatever they do, completely out of sight of their parents.

"The temperature really dropped. I'm freezing my ass off," she says, wrapping her coat around her tighter for warmth. "I knew it was silly to wear a skirt today," she mutters under her breath, looking down at her outfit.

Charlie gazes up at me and abruptly stops, tilting her head. Her face twists with concern. "Are you feeling okay? You look a little flushed. Are you still sick? Here, crouch down." She waves at me to lower myself down to her level. "Let me feel your forehead. I don't think your cheeks should be this red. I thought your fever broke a few days ago?"

Little does she know that the reason I'm flushed is because I was thinking about fucking her in my office.

I crouch down, refusing to make eye contact with her because if I so much as glance into her dark eyes, we'll be in the back christening the desk. I'm at an awkward angle, with my legs bent and back hunched over, so she can touch my cheeks and forehead. Her coat falls open, and underneath, she's wearing a burgundy cardigan with a few of the buttons undone.

Fuck. Me.

I can see right down her sweater to the lacy black bra that she's wearing. My eyes trace the outline of her stunning curves. Every bit of my restraint is needed to keep my composure at the sight of her soft breasts that are barely contained by her bra. Hands down, this woman has the most immaculate cleavage I've ever seen. I silently thank the universe for the good karma that it has bestowed on me this evening— this is worth every good deed.

I take a deep breath to steady myself, but her intoxicating scent isn't helping my barely contained composure. Sure, I was turned on before she arrived, but now I'm so aroused that I'm aching.

Still crouching and still inches away from Charlie, I close my eyes in a weak attempt to redirect my thoughts to reduce even an ounce of tightness in my jeans.

Alright, let me think . . .

Coffee? Would love to lick it off of her.

Not helping.

The weather? It's getting colder. Sharing body heat with her naked, tight against me sounds incredible.

This is pointless.

When I look up at her, our eyes connect instantly.

"Whoa. Okay. Your face looks even more flushed. Also, your pupils are slightly dilated, which I'm sure isn't a good combination with the fever." Her voice is laced with concern. "How about we get you sitting down, okay? Do you want to sit out here or in the office?"

That fucking office, my lust filled brain, and my hard cock will be the death of me tonight. I don't say anything, which probably concerns Charlie even more. Without a word, Charlie takes the initiative, grabs my arm, and guides me to the back office.

As soon as we step inside the room, she turns on the desk lamp and forces me to sit in the armchair nestled in the corner of my office. Frantically, she begins shuffling things around in her purse. "I think I have some Tylenol in my bag—"

I gently grab her wrist to stop her, and her breath catches at the sudden, unexpected contact. My eyes are fixed on my hand, gently encircling her delicate wrist. Softly, I run my thumb back and forth on her smooth skin, completely hypnotized by the motion. Her breathing falters briefly before I pull my eyes up to her. Charlie's gaze is fixated on the spot where we're touching.

Still smoothing my thumb back and forth on the tender flesh, I rasp, "Do you have any fucking idea how beautiful you are?"

It's the first thing I've said to her since she stepped inside here. We are almost at eye level, with me sitting and her standing. She doesn't say anything, but I see her nervously swallow.

The delicate column of her throat moves ever so slightly. "Charlie, did you hear me?"

Her eyelashes flutter as she nods. "Yes," she says, her voice barely a whisper.

My resolve is depleted. I'm so intoxicated by this woman.

I circle my arm around her waist, pulling her between my parted legs. She looks at me with intensity as my hands slide underneath her jacket, touching the soft fabric of that teasing sweater. The air in the room feels so thick that I can barely take a full breath. I know she feels it, too, because her breaths come out in sharp, shaky pants.

With one hand anchored on her waist, my other cradles her cheek. My thumb caresses her warm skin as our eyes lock on each other.

Her face is flushed, but not from the cold. Charlie licks her pink lips before whispering, "You're going to kiss me now, aren't you?"

My eyes dart back and forth between hers before I finally murmur, "Yeah, Charlie. I'm going to kiss you now."

The hand cupping her cheek now weaves into her silky hair. Pulling her down to me, I capture her lips with a slow, thorough kiss that'll leave us both gasping for air.

My tongue dips ever so slightly between the seam of her lips. When she parts her lips, allowing me to enter, Charlie moans softly into the kiss. Her fingers clutch onto my hair at the base of my neck, evoking a deep groan from me. Our kiss takes a desperate and demanding turn when she settles herself onto my lap, her body pressing against mine. A perfect fit. Despite her being physically on top of me, I need her closer. I need more. Pushing her heavy wool coat off her shoulders, it falls to the ground with a soft thud.

Much better.

My hands roam eagerly under her sweater, feeling her skin burning up with need. She moans at my touch, causing me to press her even closer to me. I tighten my arms around her, bringing her body flush against mine, and she melts into me. We're devouring each other like it's the last thing we'll ever do. An intense longing fills the air of this cramped office space. A frantic combination of hands touching everywhere, lips pressing together with intensity, and an overwhelming desire to be close to one another.

My lips stay tightly pressed to hers as I undo three more buttons on her sweater, revealing her flushed, heaving chest. The sweater falls open and off her shoulders—my fingers ache to touch every part of her. Moving my hands upwards, I gently trace the soft curve of her jaw with my fingertips before gliding them down to her chest. My hand lightly settles over her wildly beating heart.

Our lips still haven't broken apart, but I'm dying to lick my way down the newly exposed skin I've uncovered. Forcing myself to break away from her lips, my mouth trails down the soft column of her neck. I nuzzle my face into her silky skin and breathe her in like I need air. With force, her hands clutch my shoulders as she grinds herself against my throbbing cock, letting out a soft whimper as she does.

Something inside me snaps.

I pull away, panting. She looks beautifully disheveled and aroused. As I look into her large, alluring eyes, I push a stray strand of hair out of her flushed face.

"On the desk. Now."

Chapter Twenty-Seven

"On the desk. Now." His voice, deep and gruff, echoes in my mind—unlike anything I'd heard from him before. This night has, undoubtedly, taken an interesting turn.

"Wh-what?" Words tumble out of my mouth as I look down at him from my position on his lap. I'm slightly out of breath, my lips are sore from kissing, and my cheeks tingle from his stubble.

There's a whirlwind of emotions and sensations flowing through my veins. An overwhelming rush that leaves me feeling equally delirious and intensely alive. One moment, I think Finn is sick; the next moment, he's telling me to sit on top of his desk, readying himself to do unspeakable things to my body.

As I sit here, his eyes drink me in with intensity, roaming over every inch of my body with a hunger that makes my pulse quicken. Finn takes his large hand, cups the side of my face, and runs his thumb down my bottom lip. The touch sends shivers down my spine as I lean into his body. Intense blue eyes are fixed on my lips, a penetrating gaze that ignites a deep ache in my core.

"Lift up your skirt and sit on the desk." His tone is laced with dominance.

Slowly, I get off his lap and make my way over to his desk. Spinning around, I prop myself up and sit on it with my feet barely touching the floor. My heart is racing as his eyes burn into me. Finn looks . . . hungry. His watchful eyes rake over the entirety of my body, from my boots to the sweater hanging off of my bare shoulders.

He stands and slowly stalks towards me with careful, methodical movements. Dark blue eyes study mine as he places his hands on either side of me, gripping the edge of the desk. His tall frame cages me in, with an intense desire radiating off of him.

"Tell me you want this," he pleads, his breath hot on my lips. All I can do is nod. My whole body feels like a live wire, ready to spark at any moment.

"A nod won't suffice. I need your words, Charlie."

I'm seeing a whole new side to Finn. Confidence is radiating off of him. He's a man who knows what he wants, and I'm ready to give it to him.

"Yes," I breathe, unable to hold back any longer. "I want this."

"Good," he says. Finn stands to his full height, removes his glasses, and sets them aside. My heart is pounding against my ribs as if it could escape my chest. Before I can register what's about to happen, Finn drops to his knees right in front of me.

Holy. Shit.

His hands slide up my legs at a tortuously slow pace, gently pushing them apart. Finn's intense stare locks onto mine as he lifts one eyebrow, wordlessly instructing me to hold my skirt up by pushing the chiffon fabric in my hand. My hands tremble with anticipation and excitement.

"You still doing okay?" he asks.

"Yes," I whisper.

"Good. I need you to do two things for me," he asserts, not asking a question.

I swallow thickly and nod. Every cell in my body aches for this man to touch me.

"One. Lift up your hips," he asserts. Warmth floods my body as I lift my hips off the desk, and his fingers hook into my panties, pulling them down my legs.

Once they're off, sweet, nerdy Finn makes my jaw drop.

He takes the discarded lace fabric and casually puts it into his back pocket.

"Two. Relax," he whispers, tenderly stroking the inside of my thighs while looking at me with intense blue eyes. A warm flush works its way from my neck to my cheeks at the sight of him before me. His hands splay over my thighs, fingertips digging into my skin, and eyes wild with desire.

When my ass touches the bare wood of his desk, I realize how exposed I am. I'm leaning back on my elbows, skirt hiked up around my waist, and no panties with my thighs parted. Nerves creep under my skin as I try to force the anxious thoughts out of my mind.

I'll be damned if a little insecurity stands in the way of me and a man on his knees.

Finn must have felt me tense up because he pauses for a moment. "Charlie, I need you to know how beautiful you are. I can tell your mind is racing, but I'm going to take care of you. If at any point you aren't comfortable or want me to stop, just let me know." He presses a soft kiss on my inner thigh, and his words wash away my anxious thoughts. Finn takes my legs and hooks them around his neck as he lowers his head to my core.

Teasing me, he starts planting soft kisses on the delicate skin of my inner thighs, causing a shudder to run through me. Finn continues to tantalize me, lazily trailing his tongue against my heated flesh before lightly grazing the sensitive skin of my pussy. It's a barely there touch, but enough to make me squirm for more. A dark chuckle escapes him, and I sense he's enjoying keeping me on the edge. When his tongue makes one long stroke from my wet entrance to my clit, my back arches off the desk at the sensation, as I let out a soft moan.

Holy. Fuck. This man knows what he's doing.

I can feel the vibration of Finn's moan as he tastes me. It's obvious he's savoring this moment as much as I am. His enthusiasm turns me on even more.

My head tips back and I feel every muscle in my body loosen under his skilled mouth. Each stroke of his tongue sends sparks through my body. Instinctively, my hips press forward for more, but I pull back, worrying about seeming too forward.

Finn grips my legs, pulling me right against his mouth. Looking up between my legs with a sly smile, he says, "Use me. Take what you need, sweetheart."

Those words. His mouth. My head spins with an intoxicating and euphoric dizziness while my body becomes overheated by lust.

His tongue moves in expert swipes over my pussy before pulling my clit into his mouth, gently sucking. The sensation makes me cry out, my voice echoing off the walls of his office. As he sucks and licks, he slides one finger into me, and I let out a desperate whimper. I drop from my elbows, my back connecting with the hard surface of his desk. The combination is almost too much for me to handle—but I only crave more. I'm at his mercy. He's working my body with expert precision. Every worry and fear I previously had has completely vanished. Finn continues to taste me with precision and passion, and I'm unable to think about anything else except him between my legs.

As I whimper and moan beneath his mouth, he makes his own satisfied groans—enjoying every second of the pleasure he's pulling from my body. Hearing his noises only pushes me closer to the edge of my orgasm. I tighten my legs around Finn's head, feeling the roughness of his stubble against the inside of my thighs as I press myself closer to him.

He chuckles against me. "That's my girl. Get there for me."

Finn slides another finger into me as he goes back to sucking my clit. Two fingers curl inside me, and I cry out again, covering my mouth with my arm to muffle the noise.

Finn takes his free hand and pulls my arm away from my face. "Absolutely not. I need to hear what I'm doing to you." His voice is rough, and his eyes are filled with determination. When he dips his head back down, my needy body rocks against his face. My pants become frantic as I grind myself against him, desperately chasing my release.

The waves of my orgasm begin to flow through me. I grip the soft strands of his thick hair, pressing myself harder against him as my body shudders. Finn doesn't stop; he continues licking and sucking every last drop of pleasure out of me.

Still lying on Finn's desk, I'm breathless as he pulls away, smoothing my skirt down my legs. When I finally come down from my high, my body feels weightless. All the tension that I've been holding onto for months has almost dissipated.

After a moment of silence, I feel like I may be able to form a coherent sentence. I sit up and look at him wide-eyed. "Holy shit. You've known how to do that the whole time we've known each other? What the fuck? You've been holding out on me!"

Finn's head tips back as he lets out a loud laugh. His cheeks pink slightly at the compliment- it's cute how bashful he is. "Stick with me, and you can get that anytime you want." He winks, grabbing his glasses off the table and setting them back on his face.

There's an offer I can't refuse.

Before I can reply, Finn closes the distance between us in a single stride. His eyes study me, tracing every intricate detail of my features as if he's committing them to memory. I look away, feeling vulnerable under the intensity of his gaze. His hand cradles the side of my face, his thumb affectionately stroking my cheek.

The room is so still and quiet. The only sounds are our hushed breaths echoing softly.

Shakily exhaling, I lift my gaze to meet his and give him a smile. Finn responds with a gentle smile of his own before pressing his lips to my forehead.

It's a tender, intimate moment.

A moment that makes me feel safe. A moment that makes me feel desired.

Unfortunately, the moment ends too soon because we hear a crash. By the sound of it, it seems our dogs have also been getting into mischief.

Chapter Twenty-Eight

MY BRAIN IS in a haze this morning. Last night, what was supposed to be an innocent walk turned into something far from innocent. The old Charlie would've been mortified at what had happened, but, honestly, I haven't felt this relaxed in months. It's as if my brain was reset to its factory setting, especially after Finn said *please, use me.*

Who am I to not give the man what he wants?

Finn, being the gentleman that he is, helped me pull myself together by smoothing out my wild hair and fastening the buttons on my sweater last night before he followed me home—something he's been doing quite regularly. Patiently, he waited for Vera and me to enter the house before he drove off. We didn't speak much after our . . . *moment*, mainly because I was too tired to string two words together. When I got home and fell into bed, I slept like the dead.

Finn's commanding voice, skilled mouth, and deft touch

refuse to leave my thoughts after igniting every nerve ending in my body last night. I shift on my stool, already feeling myself getting aroused again, and it hasn't even been a full twenty-four hours since what went down last night. Or, more specifically, *who* went down last night.

"What the hell kind of look is that on your face?" a snarky voice bellows out, causing me to jolt and almost fall off my stool.

My face flushes, caught thinking indecent thoughts about my night with Finn. Luckily, it's just Marnie. We're at the store earlier than usual to prepare for the Harvest Festival later today.

Lord, help us all, because this will be an experience that no one wants to endure.

Marnie is carrying a gigantic cardboard box of plants that we plan on selling today at a discounted price. These plants aren't our bestsellers in the store. Upon further research, I've discovered that these plants can be a nightmare to take care of and require filtered water, not tap water. I drink water from the tap, and I haven't wilted . . . *yet*. I'm hoping some amateur plant enthusiasts will take on these high-maintenance weeds as a passion project. Either way, they hopefully won't be my problem anymore.

She sets the huge box on the counter with a grunt, wiping her hands on her jeans. "You know, I told you to start using retinol to help those grump lines of yours." She points to her forehead. "I can see you haven't taken my advice, Charlotte." She clicks her tongue, raising one dark eyebrow at me.

I tilt my head at her, simultaneously amused and baffled by her honesty. "Please, Marnie, tell me how you really feel."

"Well, now that you opened that door—"

Funnily enough, the store door bursts open with force, and

Finn walks in looking like a hot professor on his day off. His long legs are clad in dark denim, matched with a black cardigan sweater, a t-shirt underneath, and a long charcoal gray wool coat. His hair is extra disheveled today from the breeze outside, but he pulls it off effortlessly.

As he strides into the store, his coat breezes behind him, which is so inexplicably attractive. Frank comes running in, cutting Finn off, and skitters across the floor. The tapping of Vera's nails on the wooden floor comes from behind me as she stretches after a restful nap and spots Frank. The moment they recognize each other, the dogs start wiggling and begin to play. Eventually, they'll tire of us and scurry off into another part of the store where they can be alone.

I still haven't figured out where they hide when they're together.

"That's so fucking cute." Marnie sighs, looking down at the dogs, who are now squeaking with excitement upon seeing one another.

"I know," I reply. "It's so annoying."

"Right? Like it's annoyingly cute. They're just so happy . . . and here we are dealing with these assholes," she says, hitting the box of plants.

A deep sigh escapes from me. "If someone doesn't take these, I'm throwing them off a bridge. If I have to filter water one more time, I'll lose it," I groan.

My head shakes, peering down into the box of sad, high-maintenance souls. I really do hate these plants. Pothos? Easy. Philodendrons? No brainer. Succulents? Simple. Calatheas? They're the devil incarnate. Marnie and I are still relatively new to plants, but it didn't take long for us to learn that these are absolute nightmares to care for.

Finn casually saunters up to the counter with a shit-eating

grin on his face and three cups of coffee. Marnie quickly glances back-and-forth between us a few times, trying her hardest to decode why the vibe in the room changed all of a sudden.

I didn't tell her about last night, mainly because she would make a huge deal out of it. Like, throw me a party kind of deal.

Hard pass.

"Okay . . . now, why do *you* look like *that*, Finn?" Marnie asks with narrow eyes.

"No reason, Morticia. Here, take your coffee." He hands her a cup, and Marnie tentatively takes it. Her eyes are still narrowing at him, unsuccessfully trying to decipher his thoughts, which frustrates her since she can read just about anyone. I can see her brain working overtime to get inside of his head.

Finn glances over at me and cocks an eyebrow. My face is emotionless as I look at him—refusing to crack under his gaze. Despite his composed demeanor, his eyes are telling a different story. They're saying *I know what you taste like and how you sound when you come against my tongue.*

Call it stubborn, but there's no way he's getting the upper hand this early in the day. I'm a pro at staying emotionless. Plus, I love to win.

"And a coffee for the woman who may turn me to stone with that look." He slides the cup across the counter with a single finger, biting back a laugh.

"Right? I keep telling her to start using retinol. Those little grumpy gremlin wrinkles are asking for Botox in the near future." Marnie shrugs, sipping her coffee and burning her tongue in the process. "Christ! That's so fucking hot."

My gaze moves slowly over to her. "Karma. That's called

karma. Leave my wrinkles alone. I happen to like them." My voice comes out a little higher than expected, which takes all of us by surprise.

"I happen to like them, too." Finn joins in, nodding in agreement and taking a sip of his coffee. Marnie and I look over at him with our heads tilted to the side. Finn shrugs when he adds, "What? I just wanted to feel included."

Marnie shakes her head. "What a sweet boy you are. You're a momma's boy, right?"

"And you're the daughter of the Dark Lord, correct?" Finn quips back.

An approving smile takes over Marnie's face. She looks over at me, pointing a single, sharp-tipped finger painted in black in Finn's direction. "I like this one. You should keep him," she whispers.

"Morticia, I'm quite literally standing right next to you and can hear everything you say," Finn remarks. "But, to your point, I'm also trying to get her to keep me." He makes eye contact with me as he takes another slow sip of his drink.

Marnie looks over at Finn and smirks. "You know about the golf club, right?" she questions.

He chuckles. "Very well acquainted with it, yes."

With an approving nod, she asserts, "Good. Don't fuck this up. I know a lot of people in high places."

"Well, lucky for me, *technically* I'm in a high place because. You know . . . because I'm tall," he quips back.

Marnie and I groan, rolling our eyes at his remark.

I mean, it's true. *He is* in a high place due to his height advantage.

Marnie turns abruptly and strides towards the backroom, gathering the necessary supplies to set up for the Harvest Festival.

For a brief moment, Finn and I stand in silence, sipping our drinks, enjoying the peacefulness of the quiet store. I open my mouth, about to ask why he isn't back at his shop setting up for the event, when Marnie comes barreling in from the back of the store. She halts when she notices that Finn has not moved from his spot.

"Hold up. Don't you have to set up your own tent or something? Why are you here?" she questions.

"Ahh. I forgot to tell you two." He looks at Marnie and I. "We're sharing a booth today." A proud smirk that radiates victory spreads over his face.

My jaw drops while Marnie's eyebrows hit her hairline. Unsure how he convinced his unyielding aunt, I decide it's better if I don't ask questions.

Ever since I got the flyer in the mail, I've been dreading the Harvest Festival. There have been several sleepless nights of tossing and turning in bed, my brain wracked with worries about the event. Feelings of guilt and sadness keep me awake for longer than I would like to admit. My parents loved the festival and I should've paid more attention when they were running A New Leaf's booth. Maybe even offer to help for a year or two.

But that time has come and gone.

I can't rewrite the past, but I can certainly shape the future.

I can only hope that wherever my parents are, they're looking down (or up) at me, proud that I am carrying on their legacy, stepping outside of my comfort zone, and moving forward with my life.

Because when you lose someone, you never move on. You simply learn to move forward with the memories that you've gathered with them and tuck those memories snug inside your heart for safekeeping.

Even though it's painful, it has to be done.

As I reflect, hopefulness and optimism wrap around my chest.

Maybe today won't be so bad after all.

Chapter Twenty-Nine

FINN

MY FEET ARE FIRMLY PLANTED in front of the counter of A New Leaf while I'm looking at two very surprised women. My eyes bounce back and forth between them as they both look at me like I've grown a second head.

"What?" I ask. "I thought this was a good thing?"

"Do you even know what you're supposed to be doing at the festival, or are you just winging it?" There's a hint of suspicion in Charlie's voice. Her narrowed eyes are burning a hole right through me.

"Nope. Which is why I thought we could all figure this out together." I shrug.

Marnie nods. "I love this. The Harvest Festival virgins pourin' brews and sellin'—" She pauses, biting her lip while she thinks for a second. "I actually can't find anything plant related to rhyme with 'brews.' Sorry." She winces. "Either way, let's make this festival our bitch."

Charlie and I lock eyes. She shakes her head and rolls her eyes at Marnie's antics. Honestly, these two couldn't be more opposite if they tried. It's like watching a sketch comedy show whenever they interact. Charlie's endearing grouchiness complements Marnie's exuberance perfectly.

I enthusiastically clap and rub my hands together. "Are we ready to roast some beans and sell some greens?"

Marnie scoffs, shaking her head. "Of course you had a pun lined up."

Charlie tilts her head and laughs. "Honestly, that was pretty good. Give credit where credit is due."

I feel myself grinning like I've won an award for impressing Charlie. Deep down, I'm hoping that this is a sign of good things to come.

WE'RE SLAMMED. The festival has been going on for hours and our tent is a hit. Marnie's lively personality draws in the customers, while Charlie stays in the background and ensures that the operation runs smoothly.

I glance over at Charlie. She's deep in thought, reorganizing the plants so that the display doesn't get too chaotic. You can tell she puts all of her heart and soul into her store, even if the workload drags her down. I'm sure she's feeling a lot of emotions today, considering her parents used to do this every year. Knowing the girl behind the mask, she just wants to make her parents proud.

There's a deep ache in my chest when I look over at her, but it's not sorrow or sympathy. I just wish I could take her pain and worries away, even if only for a moment.

Her concentration breaks and she looks up at me, flashing

me a small smile. One dimple makes an appearance before a customer pulls her away.

How that woman knows so much about plants, I'll never know.

"Oh fuck," I hear Marnie say.

I look in the direction of Marnie's glare, and Aunt Donna comes waltzing in like she owns the place. She doesn't look happy. At all.

I exhale, my body slumping as I let out a long, heavy sigh. "Christ. Okay, let me handle this," I say to the girls.

They both nod and go about their business. I tap my barista on the shoulder and tell him I'll be right back. Rounding the corner of the tent, I block Aunt Donna from going any further.

"Hey, Aunt D. How's it going?" I ask, pretending to be cheerful.

"Griffin, you're taking business away from everyone else! All the patrons are flocking to this tent only." Her face is going red. *Oh boy.* "This is not how the Harvest Festival is handled. Each business should get equal attention."

I actually cannot stand this woman sometimes. The statements she makes are silly and make no sense. This is her trying to pull rank, and I'm not in the mood for it today.

"Aunt D, you know I love you, but you should be happy that our area of the festival is bringing in so many people. I've already heard from other customers that they'll return next year. We're not taking anything away. If anything, we're bringing more attention to Hemlock," I say a silent prayer, hoping that the single undergraduate business class I took is enough to convince her to go away.

She nods, eyeing me suspiciously. "Fine," she huffs, walking away.

Thanksgiving is going to be fun this year. I can feel it.

I spin on my heel and head back to my station when I notice Charlie is gone. Marnie and my barista seem to be fine without me, so I decide to go and search for her. Dodging festivalgoers, my feet carry me back onto Main Street and into A New Leaf, but still Charlie is nowhere to be found. Maybe she's in the back office? Making my way towards the back, I hear an unmistakable sniffle. Behind the counter, Charlie's on the ground with Frank and Vera—tears streaming down her face as she pets both dogs. Vera's head is settled in her lap while Frank is snuggled so tight against her side that it looks like Charlie and my dog are now one being.

She doesn't notice me until I calmly crouch down in front of her. The dogs don't move from her side, knowing instinctively that their comfort is needed. Charlie looks up at me, giving me a sad smile that pierces right through my heart. Her big brown eyes are rimmed with red, tears pouring out of them. Reaching into my pocket, I pull out a tissue and offer it to her.

Grief won. Today got to be too much for her.

She eyes me suspiciously, and I tilt my head. "It's clean, you little weirdo," I say.

She hiccups at my words—well, it's a cross between a hiccup and a laugh. Either way, it's adorably *her*. Our fingers brush when she takes the tissue out of my hand. The tips of her fingers are cold, and I'm sure sitting on this cement floor isn't helping. I take off my jacket and wrap it around her shoulders as she dries her tears.

"It hits you out of nowhere, you know?" She sniffles, wiping at the corners of her eyes. "One moment I'm fine, the next I'm thrown back into that nightmare of a day." Her chin dips, her shoulders shake as she cries.

I know she needs to let it out and feel everything, so I stay quiet, allowing her to process every emotion.

"And all these fucking 'firsts' . . . I hate it." She shakes her head, her nose twitching as she sniffles again. "First, this Harvest Festival. Then, my stupid birthday. My first birthday without them. God, knowing I'll never get another cake from my mom or never hear my dad sing his horrific rendition of 'Happy Birthday' just guts me. It's stupid." More heavy sobs escape from her. "I hate that I can't call them. After they died, it took three months for me to stop pulling out my phone to give them a call." Vera snuggles deeper into Charlie's lap like she's trying to hug the grief right out of her. "I want them to be proud of me, you know?"

Despite intending to wait patiently for Charlie to finish her thoughts, I have to intervene before the darkness pulls her fully under. I scoot closer to Charlie and grab both of her hands in mine.

My voice is firm but gentle. "It's not stupid. Not at all. Nothing about grief is stupid. Everything that you're feeling is completely valid. Grief comes in waves, and all you have to do is stay afloat until the wave recedes. From an outsider's perspective? You're doing a kickass job treading water."

I wish I could sit next to her, but both of these damn dogs are looking at me like *one wrong step buddy and you're dead.*

"Thanks." Her voice is sad and soft. "I'm sure this is not what you signed up for."

With confusion, my eyebrows pull together. "Huh? What do you mean?"

She inhales sharply, trying to keep herself from falling apart. "A grieving girl, sobbing on the floor of her dead parents' store while you're acting as a substitute therapist." Her shoulders sag, and she rests her chin in her hand. Charlie looks utterly spent with exhaustion. "I totally understand if you want to end things here and now."

I can't help but laugh. "Sorry, I know it's not funny. I shouldn't laugh, but—" I nudge Frank out of the way. He groans, clearly annoyed with me, but I'm sitting next to her now, and Frank can go steal someone's wallet for all I care. "You think *this* will make me want to leave you alone? Sweetheart, I think you're underestimating how much I like you."

She looks up and hopefulness fills her eyes. I wrap my arm around her, pulling her close to me. Sighing from emotional exhaustion, she places her head on my shoulder. I kiss the top of her head, burying my nose in her hair. She smells of oranges and freshly fallen rain—a scent as warm and comforting as staying indoors on a stormy evening.

"So *that's why* you don't leave me alone?" Her voice is soft.

A playful laugh escapes from my chest. "Yes, Charlie. That's why I don't leave you alone. It's because I like you. *All of you* . . . plus, I've never met someone who pulls off overalls as well as you do. You're a babe. Especially when you wear those green ones." I pause and do a dramatic full-body shiver before I continue. "They make me feel some type of way, you know? I can't explain it," I express, hoping to make her smile for a brief moment.

Charlie lifts her head and playfully slaps my shoulder. "What am I going to do with you?"

I casually shrug. "Hopefully, a lot." I wink.

"You're taking advantage of me when I'm all teary and snotty—trying to flirt with me when I'm at my weakest." She wipes her eyes again, this time smiling at me. It's not a sad smile; it's a smile of relief.

Relief that someone was here when she needed them, but was too proud to ask for help.

Relief that someone was able to help carry the weight of some of her emotions, if only for a quick moment in time.

"Is the flirting working?" I question.

She rolls her eyes, looking away from me. "Obviously."

I can't tell whether there's an undertone of sarcasm or not. For the sake of my own ego, I choose to believe she was being serious. We've been here for a while, and I'm positive Marnie will perform some kind of witch magic if we're not back at the tent soon.

Plus, sitting on this floor is absolutely killing my back. Sometimes I forget that I'm not in my twenties anymore, and this is one of those moments. Charlie gets up with ease, dusting off the back of her pants with her hands.

I can't help but take a quick peek.

"Stop looking at my ass, Griffin."

Does this woman have eyes on the back of her head?

Charlie turns around and offers a hand to help me get up off the ground.

"Okay, I'm old, but not that old," I tell her, not needing any help to get up.

"I heard you groan when you moved over to me, grandpa. Take my hand." Her voice is stern and confident. It's kind of a turn on. My hand reaches out to her, and her soft fingers wrap around mine, trying to pull me up. While Charlie may *think* she's helping me up, my ulterior motive was to simply find another reason to touch her.

When I stand up fully, I give Frank a passing glance.

Wait. What the hell does he have in his mouth?

"Frank! Drop it!" I yell, horrified by what I see.

"What does he . . . OH MY GOD, FRANK, DROP IT!"

Charlie is now yelling. Which is shocking because I've never heard her voice go any higher than her typical speaking voice. My treacherous brain thinks about her screaming my name—

Her shriek breaks me from my ill-timed, inappropriate thoughts.

"Finn! Grab Frank! He's got a kitten in his mouth!"

This is a new record for Frank. Shockingly, he's never kidnapped someone else's pet before.

Charlie's able to quickly grab Frank by his hips, who's parading around the store like a proud new parent showing off his newborn.

This dog is going to put me into an early grave. I can just feel it.

Slowly, I walk up to Frank, his little nub of tail wagging in a frenzy. Crouching down, I carefully remove the kitten from his mouth.

"Huh." I'm examining this small, black cat with huge green eyes staring directly into my soul. "Like father, like son. Seems like we both like pussy."

Charlie's mouth pops open, her eyebrows raising slowly. "Your dog stole a living, breathing animal that someone is probably looking for. And your very first thought is to make a vagina joke?"

"Seemed like the right thing to do," I say, standing up. "Do we know who this belongs to?" The little kitten is small enough to fit in the palm of my hand. He meows softly, and Frank's head tilts at the sound. "You're a menace to society, Franklin."

Frank lays down and whimpers, knowing that he fucked up.

Charlie rubs her hands down her face and then back up,

placing her fingers on her temple. "I'm getting a migraine from all of this," she mutters under her breath.

"Come on, let's go see if we can find his owner. If not, we just became parents." A huge grin springs across my face. I glance over at Charlie, and her expression immediately makes me burst into uncontrollable laughter. Her head tilts to the side, her eyes fill with confusion, and her mouth twists like she ate something sour.

"Did you pass biology in high school? Because that's not how reproduction works," she states.

I make my way to the front of the store with the kitten nestled against my chest. Noticing Charlie isn't following me, I look at her over my shoulder.

"Come on, sweetheart, I need you to be a hands-on parent with me. Our child needs you during this difficult and confusing time in his life." I give her a wink.

For all I know, this cat could have an owner. But seeing her squirm about us adopting this cat together is giving me immense joy. She rolls her eyes again and groans. I can't help but chuckle as I hear her reluctant feet scuff against the floor.

"Fine," she replies. "But I won't like it."

She walks up next to me and stops. She and the kitten are now at eye level, and the kitten gives her a quiet meow. Charlie defrosts ever so slightly when she hears his tiny voice.

Bending down, I give her another quick kiss on the top of her head. "I wouldn't expect anything less."

Chapter Thirty

THANKFULLY, the kitten has a loving home, and we were able to drop him off safely with his owners. There's no way in hell I'm becoming the mom to another animal . . . except possibly Frank, the klepto pup.

Slumping back onto my couch, I kick my feet up on the coffee table and wrap a soft blanket around Vera and I. After yesterday's festival, I decided to close the store today. I desperately need a mental health day to recover.

Vera and I are on the couch eating vanilla ice cream and watching rich housewives in a faraway city fight over rich people things. My brain isn't registering what's on the TV because my mind is elsewhere—specifically, on yesterday's breakdown.

What no one tells you about grief is how the smallest reminder of a lost loved one could set you off at a moment's notice.

For me, it was the bustling crowds of the festival on a sunny morning in the fall.

For Jack, it's the scent of plywood being sanded down on a rainy afternoon.

For Joey, it's the taste of blueberries on a warm spring morning.

Any of these tiny moments can send you into a spiral. A spiral that leaves you on the floor alone in a puddle of tears with the only person who can pull you out of that deep place —yourself.

It pains me to admit it, but I was thankful that Finn saw me. For so long, I've kept my emotions tightly locked inside of me. I built up an impenetrable wall to keep myself safe. But in the end, all it took was one memory.

A single passing moment that caused all of my walls to crumble.

Strawberries. It was the strawberries that derailed me from a plant-selling machine to a puddle of tears laying on the floor. I saw a customer come up to our tent with three cartons of strawberries. They were my mom's favorite fruit. Every single summer growing up, she would buy them by the bushel and make every kind of strawberry dessert imaginable. When I saw that customer with strawberries, I got a tight, constricting feeling in my chest. My vision turned foggy, and I knew I had to get out before it was too late.

The moment I entered the store, I collapsed into a heap of tears and anxiety. The pain in my chest was indescribable. It felt like my heart was shattering over and over again. No matter what I did, I couldn't stop the pain from consuming me.

As goofy as I think they are, the dogs immediately knew something was wrong and rushed over to me. When I heard the creak of the store door open, I knew it was Finn. I tried to be silent, but my sniffles betrayed me.

This guy, who probably should've looked the other way, sat beside me on the cold, hard ground, handing me tissues and trying to make me smile, if only for a quick moment.

Pushing the memory of yesterday's breakdown aside, I finish my ice cream and give Vera the leftover remnants in the carton. I prefer strawberry ice cream, but Vera loves vanilla. So I always buy vanilla to share with her. My mom and dad are most definitely rolling in their urns at the fact that I base my ice cream purchases off of Vera's preferences rather than my own. This is my first experience being a full-time dog owner, so every day is a new adventure and a learning experience.

I give Vera's soft, fluffy ears a good scratch as she continues to lick the practically empty ice cream carton.

"You have good life with me. Don't you forget it."

Although she doesn't talk back, it doesn't stop me from talking to her. I'm still scratching Vera's ear when I hear a soft knock at the door. Getting up off of the couch with a groan, I quickly shut off the TV because I refuse to admit to anyone what trashy shows I watch. Quietly, I walk over to the door and peer out of the peephole.

Finn.

What is he doing here so late?

I open the door more forcefully than needed, and he jolts back.

"Uh. Is everything okay?" I question.

He smirks down at me. "You opened that door like you were a woman on a mission. I should be asking if *you* are okay. Where's your golf club, by the way?"

His head casually dips inside my house in search of my 5-

iron. When he doesn't find it, he turns back to me. Those cute dimples and those perfect white teeth are staring back at me with an amused gleam in his eye. I know he's joking, but the weapon is safely secured in the closet.

Suddenly insecure about how I abruptly opened the door, I clear my throat and make up a lie. "I thought you were a salesperson. They've come around here twice already today." I shrug.

Finn's eyes narrow, clearly detecting my lie, but he's too polite to say anything. "Right. Well, I've come to give you this." He hands me my wallet. "I noticed your store was closed today and figured you'd need this. Frank stole it . . . obviously."

Finn tucks his hands in his pockets, rocking back on his heels. It's obvious his dog's sticky paws embarrass him.

I chuckle, my hand goes up to scratch my forehead.

Oh no.

I forgot to take my forehead wrinkle patch off. I smack my hand over my forehead in a panic, feeling my face go hot.

Finn's laughing now. "I was wondering if you knew that was on your forehead. What is that, by the way?"

My head drops in embarrassment. "They're for my . . . forehead wrinkles. Eyebrow wrinkles. As you know, it's a whole thing. Marnie gave these to me. Can we forget that this happened?" I manage to say all that without taking a breath—the words stream together in one very long sentence.

He nods his head, smirking. "Not to correct you, but I think Marnie called them '*grumpy gremlin wrinkles.*'"

I'm writing Marnie out of my will. Definitely calling my lawyer tomorrow.

Finn rocks back and forth on his heels again. "So . . . what are you up to tonight?"

I feel too defeated and exhausted to deliver a clever quip. I know exactly what he wants, so I open the door wider and motion for him to come in. Granted, I may be oblivious to social cues, but Finn is as subtle as a firework.

"I thought you'd never ask," he says. Finn breezes inside and takes his shoes off before joining Vera on the couch, where he immediately proceeds to rub her belly. Vera is so happy to see Finn, her tail makes thumping noises against the couch cushions.

For someone who has never been inside my house, he sure knows how to make himself comfortable.

"Please. Go ahead and make yourself comfortable," I say with a wry smile.

"Already did, sweetheart." He looks back at me and winks. I hate the way that wink makes me feel. It's a panty-dropping wink. One where he could have his way with me, and I would happily thank him for it.

I shake my head, amused, and let out a sigh. "I'll be right back. I need to take this thing off my forehead." I shuffle quietly in my frog slippers over to the small bathroom, where I immediately set about removing the anti-wrinkle patch from my forehead. After peeling it off, I'm convinced it took at least two layers of skin off with it.

When I take a good glance at myself in the mirror, I shake my head.

I'm a sight to behold.

The outfit of the night consists of green pajama pants with a gray sweatshirt that says *"Lookin' Sharp"* with a prickly cactus on the front. My hair is in a claw clip with my baby hairs sticking out in every direction.

I am the epitome of sex appeal.

I don't see any point in fixing how I look right now. Finn

has officially seen me at my worst, on so many levels. Some flyaway hairs and a wrinkle patch won't keep him from relaxing on my couch, apparently.

When I emerge into the living room, I wish I could capture the moment before me and hold on to it forever. He doesn't see me right away, but Finn is cradling Vera's face. Both are staring deep into each other's eyes. I catch Finn quietly murmuring, "*Are you being good for your sister? You take care of her when I'm not around, okay? We'll trade shifts. When I'm here, you can take a break. But when I'm not there, I need you to take the lead. Deal?*" With tenderness, he places a kiss on her forehead.

Is that what Finn feels like he's doing? Taking care of me? I mean, sure, he brings me coffee with a side of his signature charm, and we go for walks where I feel freer than I usually do.

It hits me then.

Finn is taking care of me in small ways. So small that it's easy for them to go unnoticed by anyone but me. Granted, I still hate coffee with a burning passion, but it does seem like he comes in every day just to check in on me. It's comforting to know that someone cares enough about me to make sure I'm doing okay. The way he cares for me with these simple acts goes above and beyond anything I could have imagined.

My slippers scuff across the wooden floors, and both human and dog perk up at the sight of me.

"Am I interrupting?" I softly laugh. "You two look deep in conversation."

Finn clears his throat, and his tone turns serious. "Yes, Charlotte. Vera and I have a strong bond and have developed many top-secret mutual agreements. It's very serious business, you wouldn't understand."

I nod, biting back a smile. "Gotcha. Okay. I won't pry, out of respect."

"I deeply appreciate your understanding. Now, please, sit down. Preferably next to me."

A boyish smile tugs at the corner of his lips as he pats the open spot on the couch next to him. Still biting back my smile, I roll my eyes, walk over, and sit down. I turn my body to face him, and I swear he's even more handsome in the warm, glowing light of my living room, with my dog on his lap.

He looks at me, studying my face as if it holds the answers to every question he has about me. Usually, I'd be self-conscious about my hair, clothes, and lack of makeup. But with Finn, it feels like all of that doesn't matter. It's as if he truly sees me for who I am—unafraid to smash my walls down to get to a part of me that no one has reached before.

"So," he begins, "I can't help but notice you don't have many plants in here. Actually, I think I have more plants in my house than you do in yours." Finn glances around my living room. "You have two plants. Two. And that one in the corner looks fake. Woman, explain yourself." He cocks one eyebrow at me, looking devastatingly handsome.

"Before my parents passed away, I was horrible at keeping stuff alive." I pause. "Wait, that came out so wrong."

Finn's expression turns appalled. "Jesus, Charlie. Did I just become an accessory to a crime?"

I hit him with a pillow. "You're the absolute worst, you know that?" A fit of laughter bubbles out of me.

"Yeah, but I got you to laugh. Worth it." He flashes me a smile that makes my stomach flip.

"Anyway, when I lived in the city, I tried to take care of a plant here and there. No surprise, they died. All of them. Even air plants. It was impressive. An ex of mine thought it was a good idea to get me a goldfish. I'm sure you can guess what happened next."

"Whoa. Hold up. You had a fish? What was its name?"

I swallow. "Fish."

He gives me a look of disbelief, and I sheepishly shrug my shoulders.

Finn takes off his glasses and pinches the bridge of his nose. He then looks up to the ceiling, thinking deeply. I can see millions of questions running through his mind. I set my arm on the back of the couch and rest my head in my hand, waiting for him to unleash it all.

Finn slides his glasses back on, his eyes peering over the frames as he looks intently at me. "Okay, okay. If you kill everything, how do you keep Vera alive? She looks pretty happy and well-fed," he says, giving Vera more scratches.

A heavy sigh escapes my nose.

"Uh oh. I have to buckle up for this story." He laughs.

Sighing, I thoughtfully nod. "So, Joey travels too much and can't handle a dog. Jack was worried about leaving Vera at home for too long because he works long hours. So, Vera was left with me. But Joey and Jack love Vera, and they were very concerned for her well-being, knowing she'd be staying with me."

Finn runs his hands through his hair as he impatiently waits for me to finish the story. His blue eyes are bright with anticipation, giving me his undivided attention.

I continue. "Jack took three months to train Vera to bring her food bowl to me whenever she got hungry. Now, whenever Vera needs food, she will pick up her bowl and set it at my feet. It was a weird doggy boot camp." My hand covers my mouth. Just thinking back to that time in our lives still makes me giggle.

Finn is silent for a moment too long. A moment just long enough to make me wonder if this was the final tipping point that will cause him to run out that door as fast as he can. I stop laughing and begin to fidget with the hem of my sweatshirt.

Finn doesn't run from me, though. Instead, a deep, rumbly laugh bellows out of him. He's wiping his eyes because tears are falling from laughing so hard.

"That is the funniest thing I've heard in a long time." He gasps. "And the fact your brother and sister were both in on it? Training Vera? Charlie. Wow. Okay, remind me to never trust you to watch Frank."

"Honestly, that's the smartest choice you can make. I wouldn't trust me either." I sigh, gazing down at Vera on Finn's lap.

He stops laughing and pauses briefly. "Wait. How do you know so much about plants, then?"

My head rears back in mock offense. "Google. Duh. Do you not see my computer out on the counter? I never leave home without it. I have about fifty tabs open at any given time with random information about soil, pruning, lighting, pests—you name it." His jaw is practically on the floor, and I can't help but laugh again. "I leaned into the 'fake it until I make it' plan because I have no idea what I'm doing with those things," I say, nodding toward the single, real plant that I own.

Finn's piercing eyes study me. His tongue darts out, tracing his lower lip before disappearing back into his mouth. The gesture is more erotic than it should be.

"Charlie, I do believe I like you even more now."

Chapter Thirty-One

We're both sitting on the couch in my dim living room and it all feels incredibly intimate. Finn's lounging on one side, his feet resting on the coffee table like we do this every night. Finn had been cuddling with Vera until she decided to put herself to bed because it's so late. Anyone else might think that this all adds up to the idyllic romantic evening. But, unfortunately for Finn, I resemble a swamp creature, with my hair looking very troll chic. Fortunately for me, Finn is incredibly handsome and put together, as usual, wearing an emerald green sweater, inky blue jeans, and accessorized with a gold vintage watch. Finn's hair is model worthy with perfect, shiny curls at the nape of his neck.

I let out a deep sigh. My moose pajamas and sweatshirt aren't even on the same playing field. I think there's a rip at the hem somewhere on the left leg and my sweatshirt is tattered at the neck.

Finn slings his arm on the back of the couch. "Why the big sigh?"

"It's late, after what I presume was a long day at work for you, and you look really good. Like really good. How do you dress so nice?" I, not so subtly, try to tame a little bit of my crazy hair by smoothing it down. "I look like a swamp creature right now . . . and I'm sure I have leftover pimple cream on my face somewhere." I look back up at him and tip my head to the side. My eyes are drawn to him, feeling the urge to trace every inch of his body.

His big, ocean blue eyes are full of kindness as they gaze down at me through his glasses. A smattering of pale freckles dot across his nose and cheeks. My eyes sweep down from his defined jaw, wandering down to his long torso and even longer legs. Eventually, my gaze locks on to his hands—my pulse rising at the memory of them gripping my thighs, making me feel delicate and desired as his fingers pressed into my skin.

I would commit unspeakable acts just to have his hands on me again.

Finn's dimples make an appearance as he notices that I'm checking him out.

I'm not ashamed. He's a good-looking guy and I enjoy looking at pretty things.

I set my chin in my hand and smile. I'm not sure whether it's because I'm extra relaxed from the day off, or seeing Finn so comfortable in my house, but I feel lighter, more relaxed. When I'm around him, the tension in my body always subsides and my mind clears. It's a feeling I wish I could bottle up and carry with me wherever I go.

"Are you done checking me out?" He smirks, breaking my thoughts.

"Maybe. Maybe not," I quip. "Does it bother you?"

After these last few moments of looking at him, my skin suddenly feels on fire, with a low pulse simmering between my legs. The vibe in the room has seemingly shifted. What was once relaxed has now become thick with tension and anticipation.

"Not in the slightest. Come here." Finn leans forward and wraps one strong arm around my waist, pulling me closer to him. He presses a soft kiss to the spot below my ear, causing goosebumps to ripple across my skin.

"You smell incredible," he hums against my skin.

Words fail me as I feel myself become overcome with need.

It's been too long since I've felt desired by someone. My breath catches in my throat when his warm lips find mine. At first, the kiss is gentle and tender—a classic Finn kiss. It's his way of testing the waters, seeing if I want more and allowing me to set the pace.

I want *a lot* more.

In fact, I want all of it and then some. I'm greedy and desperate and I'm not ashamed to admit it.

He pulls away, resting his forehead on mine, looking deep into my eyes. His pupils are wide with longing. A silent understanding passes between us, both knowing exactly where this night will lead.

The feeling of yearning has become so intense that it's consuming me from the inside out. Becoming impatient, I grip his face with both hands and kiss him hard and with desperation. The combination of feeling his five o'clock shadow, his soft lips, and his woodsy cologne are enough to turn me feral. He groans at the contact of our lips colliding and gets the hint that I need more.

His large hands snake their way up under my sweatshirt, brushing against my soft stomach. As his fingers slowly trace over my curves, he hums in approval of what he finds.

Pulling away from our kiss, he pants, "No bra?"

"Shut. Up. You're ruining the moment with your commentary."

I grab his sweater and pull him towards me. He chuckles just before our lips devour each other again. His hands confidently explore my body, palming my breast and gently pinching my nipple. A desperate moan escapes from my lips.

"Take this fucking sweatshirt off," he says against my mouth.

"Take it off yourself," I challenge.

Finn pulls away, and his eyes connect with mine. Pure, hungry lust is written all over his face. I watch as his careful self-control begins to slowly unravel before my eyes. We're both staring at each other, completely breathless, with flushed cheeks and swollen lips.

I can't seem to tear my eyes away from this uninhibited side of Finn.

He closes his eyes and thickly swallows, composing himself before he speaks. "Sweetheart, I'm a patient man. But my patience is beginning to wear thin with you looking at me like that." One of his hands cups my cheek as his thumb slowly moves back and forth. "I need your words. Tell me what you want and I'll give it to you. Anything, Charlie. Anything at all." His words are a plea laced with desperation.

My body feels like it's vibrating, overwhelmed by the rush of emotions I'm feeling.

One thing is for certain, though, I know exactly what I want.

"I want you," I whisper. "Please, just—" I pause, and my eyelids flutter close. "I just need you. Right now."

He nods, tucking a strand of hair behind my ears, and then gives me a soft kiss filled with adoration. "Bedroom. Now," his voice hovers over my lips. "I can't wait to take my time with you."

My body trembles with excitement at his words and promises. The tension in the air is so thick I can barely breathe. Once we make it up to my room, we find Vera sleeping peacefully in the bed.

"Vera," Finn bellows, his voice low and gravelly. "Off. Now."

Okay, *wow*.

That sent a shiver straight down my spine and directly to my clit.

Where the hell did that authoritative voice come from? How can I hear more of it?

Vera groans and hops off the bed, giving us a major side eye in the process. When Vera is no longer in the room, Finn shuts the door and locks it. I furrow my brows and tilt my head at him.

"Nothing will interrupt what's about to happen. Especially not the dog." He takes three big strides to me and grabs my face in his large palms, kissing me possessively.

Finn backs me up slowly to the bed. As soon as the back of my knees hit the edge, I fall backwards, and his body is on top of mine. Our bodies clash in a frenzy of gasping breaths, teeth, and tongues. I slip my hands under his sweater, feeling his warm skin beneath my fingertips. When my nails graze his bare skin, scratching lightly, he moans into my mouth and then playfully nips my bottom lip.

I'm deliriously aroused.

With one swift movement, Finn's hands grip the bottom of my sweatshirt, tugging it over my head.

"Fucking stunning." He lets out a deep groan before pressing his lips against mine in a passionate kiss.

My body aches to feel his warm skin pressed against mine. As my fingers inch towards the hem of his sweater, Finn stands up swiftly, pulling it over his head and revealing his lean body. Even though Finn isn't overly muscular, his height and defined features make him the most handsome man I've ever seen.

Tossing his sweater off to the side, he undoes his belt with a swift flick of the wrist. After unbuttoning the top button of his jeans, they slide low on his narrow hips, giving me a glimpse of his black boxer briefs.

Without breaking eye contact, Finn grabs the waist of my pajamas and hastily yanks them down my legs. I make a noise that's halfway between a laugh and a yelp.

When he goes to toss them aside, he clicks his tongue. "First, no bra and now no panties? Charlie, what are you doing to me?"

I lean up on my elbows, cocking my head to the side. "You're ruining the moment with your commentary again." I chuckle, raising one brow.

Now, fully exposed to this man, Finn looks down at my naked body, taking in every single inch of me with his hungry eyes. He's standing at the edge of the bed, biting his fist and shaking his head.

"Fuck," he groans, his voice thick with desire. Finn doesn't say another word as his eyes trace every curve and dip of my bare skin.

"Oh no. What?" I say, keeping my voice even and controlled.

He shakes out of a trance. "Huh?"

"You're staring and not saying anything. Usually, when you see a naked woman for the first time, there's a little more enthusiasm and less—"

He kneels on the bed, grabs my chin and lifts it to meet his gaze. "Charlie, stop talking."

"But—"

One finger covers my lips so they don't move. My eyes widen as his face turns serious.

"You're so fucking striking that I was momentarily speechless." He breathes, slowly dropping his finger from my lips. Finn rests his forehead against mine, our eyes lock onto one another. The intensity of this moment has my chest heaving and my skin buzzing with lust.

Finn hovers over me, his warm breath caressing my face as he rests his forearm beside my head for balance. The warmth radiating off his skin only intensifies my already overheating body.

His hand makes a trail starting at my thigh, gliding up to my hip, dipping down to my waist, and finally to my full breast. He gives it a gentle squeeze before brushing his thumb over my nipple. The sensation makes me shiver. Finn softly chuckles, and he continues to trace the curves of my body with his deft fingers. When his hand makes its way to the base of my throat, carefully holding my neck, he feels my fluttering pulse.

"Your heart is racing," he whispers.

I swallow thickly, unsure of what to say. Right now, I'm so overwhelmed by his touch that I feel like I'm gasping for air.

Finn's large hand moves away from my neck to my collarbone, gently holding me at the back of my neck. He's breathing so heavily that I can feel him trembling. Every wall of his restraint is begging to crumble.

Finn takes a deep breath, as if he can't get enough oxygen to fill his lungs. "My god, woman. Have you seen yourself? I'm going to be dreaming about this body every night until I'm six feet under, sweetheart."

With those parting words, Finn stands up, grabs my legs and pulls my body to the edge of the bed. I yelp, taken aback by how he handles me with such fervor.

I'm loving every fucking moment of it.

He slowly walks over to the bedside table and takes his glasses off, setting them down. When he walks back over to me, he's looking at me like I'm his prey. Before I can register what he's doing, he sinks to his knees, never breaking eye contact.

"Why'd you take your glasses off?" I question.

"This is serious business, sweetheart. I'm a gentleman, meaning ladies always come first."

I don't even have time to reply before he takes one, achingly slow swipe of his tongue from my wet entrance to my clit. A full-body shudder travels through me from the top of my head down to my toes.

"Fuck, that felt good," I pant.

"Good. Just relax and turn that pretty little brain off while I taste you."

My mind is short-circuiting seeing this side of Finn.

Finn's strong arms are around my legs, holding me tightly to him. Softly, he leaves a trail of kisses along my inner thighs. Each brush of his lips on my sensitive skin makes me shiver with desire. I can feel myself getting more and more aroused as he teases me with his featherlight touches.

Finally, his mouth covers my clit, applying the perfect

amount of pressure as he sucks and licks with expert precision. My body responds eagerly to him, writhing underneath
his grasp.

As I'm thinking it can't get better, Finn releases one of my
legs and pushes two fingers deep inside me, curling them in a
beckoning motion. I gasp uncontrollably, my hands tangled in
his hair, gently tugging the strands. An appreciative groan
rumbles out of him, the vibrations only intensifying my
pleasure.

Heavy pressure rapidly builds within me. I'm on the verge
of falling off the edge and into the depths of my orgasm. My
body is squirming under Finn's mouth, with one hand in his
hair and the other clutching my bedsheet.

Involuntarily, my back arches off the bed and my eyes
flutter close as I surrender to the overwhelming pleasure. Finn
doesn't stop, though. His tongue continues to work my pussy
at a slower pace. Allowing me to savor every moment,
drawing out my orgasm to new heights.

A fucking gentleman indeed.

Chapter Thirty-Two

FINN

WATCHING Charlie come completely undone on my tongue is an image that will live within me for the rest of my life. I've never seen anything so beautiful, so sexy as her coming.

Deep down, I know I've jumped off of the edge without a hope of returning. The woman lying in front of me, with a flushed face, disheveled hair, and a smile on her face has ruined me for anyone else. After tonight, I won't be able to get enough of her.

Lifting myself up off my knees, my eyes rake over her body, splayed out on top of the rumpled bedding. Her full breasts with pink nipples, lush thighs, and flushed skin are on full display. I've never seen anything so strikingly gorgeous in my life. Charlie's chest is heaving, and there's a sparkle in her eye, and a blissful smile makes the single dimple on her left cheek appear.

I make my way onto the bed and slide next to her. We're

both on our sides when I grip her face, kissing her deeply as she tangles her fingers in my hair. I groan at the feeling of her nails lightly scraping the nape of my neck. Charlie then removes her hand, trails her nails down my stomach, and traces the waistline of my boxer briefs. My heart races as a shiver runs straight down my spine at the feel of her touch, branding my skin.

Delicate fingers slip teasingly under the elastic, softly stroking the area just above my stiff cock. I'm so hard it's painful but, as much as I want relief, I want this moment to last as long as possible. Her hand grips me as she begins to stroke me achingly slowly. I groan into her mouth and can feel her smiling into our kiss.

Our bodies are tangled with one another as we lie on the bed, exploring each other, taking our time learning what the other likes. Neither of us wants to rush this moment, but we are equally becoming impatient.

The room fills with heavy breaths, quiet moans, and whispered words. Charlie pulls her hand away from my cock, fingers caressing up my chest, and places her palm over my rapidly beating heart. Breaking our kiss, I gaze down at her glassy brown eyes and swollen pink lips. I place my hand over hers and we both look down at our intertwined hands, consumed by the intense desire to be touched by one another.

Charlie slowly rakes her warm eyes up to mine. Gently, her body leans into me, her face so close to mine that I can feel her hot breath on my lips. "Grab a condom."

At this moment, those are the three most beautiful words strung together in the most perfect sentence. Reaching into my back pocket, I grab a condom out of my wallet before standing up and taking off the rest of my clothes. Charlie's leaning back on her elbows in the bed, her generous curves and soft skin on full display. Grabbing a pillow, I place it under her hips so she's angled just right. Confusion washes over her face. It appears she's never been with a guy who's done that for her.

Fucking amateurs.

I smirk. "Just trust me." Giving her a wink, I quickly put the condom on and kneel on the bed between her legs. "Are you ready for me, sweetheart?"

"Yes. Please," she pants.

"I like it when you beg."

"Oh fuck off and fuck me already." She gives me a sexy smile, and I can't help but laugh.

I start slow by running the head of my cock against her wet entrance, sliding up and down, and adding pressure against her clit. Her body shudders, so I do it once more before I just barely push the head of my cock into her entrance. Watching her face, her eyes flutter closed, and a soft moan escapes from her parted lips, I continue to slide in until she's filled by my length. Once I'm buried deep inside her, a groan rumbles low in my chest as I slowly begin gliding in and out of her.

She's warm and tight.

And all for me.

When I increase the pace, her head tips back, obscuring my view of her pretty face.

That won't work. I need to see those big eyes and flushed cheeks with each thrust.

"Eyes on me, sweetheart. I want to see your face when my cock is deep inside of you," I command.

As our bodies move in perfect rhythm, our eyes lock on to each other with intensity. Her lust-filled eyes make my heart beat erratically in my chest, only fueling my desire for this breathtaking woman.

My hands glide up and down her smooth legs, reveling in the feel of her hot skin beneath my touch. I can't get enough of Charlie. Even though I'm inside of her, I still want more.

I lean forward, covering her body with mine, savoring the warmth radiating from her skin as she writhes below me with each thrust. My lips find hers with a hungry kiss and, when I pull back, our noses barely touch. Our breaths mingle together, hot with passion and want. With one arm braced on the bed next to her face, my other hand intertwines with her fingers above her head, and we get lost in each other's eyes; an overwhelming sense of vulnerability and connection only heightening my ever-growing feelings for her.

Her legs wrap around my waist, pulling me deeper into her, and we both moan together at the heightened feeling. I bury my face into her neck as I quicken my pace, my boding sinking deeper into her.

"Fuck, it's so good," she breathes.

"I know, sweetheart. I know," I say, low in her ear.

Charlie's breathy moans are growing more desperate as my arousal intensifies.

Unlacing our fingers, I trail my hand down her trembling body. My fingertips brush over her hardened nipple, evoking a desperate whimper out of Charlie. When my fingers slide down to the apex of her thighs, I take two fingers and gently circle her clit, her body shuddering beneath my touch.

I *love* the way she responds to me.

Adding a little more pressure, Charlie cries out my name. Her nails bite into my biceps, holding onto me as her pleasure increasingly builds. My release is on the brink, and I feel myself about to tip over the edge. Her soft, sexy moans fill the air, her eyes glaze over with pleasure, and her face flushes with desire, creating a perfect storm.

But I need one more thing from her.

"I'm right there, Charlie. I need you to come for me again. Think you can do that for me?" My breath comes out ragged as I fight not to come before she does.

"I . . . I don't know. It's too much," she whimpers.

I chuckle and lower my mouth to her ear as I whisper, "Close your eyes and just focus on what you're feeling, okay? Don't think, just feel, sweetheart. Feel everything I'm giving to you in this moment." I give her earlobe a small nibble and she gasps. "You can handle this. I know you can."

I feel her pussy flutter around my cock, her body starting to tremble. My fingers are still massaging her clit when I feel Charlie's body tense and her breathing stutter. Her fingers now dig into the skin on my back as she grips me close to her. Her eyes flutter shut, and a moan escapes her lips as her orgasm consumes her.

"That's my girl," I murmur in her ear.

With a final thrust, my whole body shudders as my cock pulses inside of her. My eyes fall shut as intense pleasure courses through my body, hot and fast, leaving me breathless and panting. Our bodies are slick with a sheen of sweat as Charlie tightens her hold on me while I come down from my release.

Rolling off to the side, I lie next to her on the bed and pull her towards my chest, tucking her head under my chin.

"Well, that was something," she says, out of breath.

Laying on the bed, staring up at the ceiling, we both break out in laughter. Charlie nuzzles closer into my chest with a content sigh. But as much as I would love to stay here, I desperately want to chug a glass of water and get Charlie a washcloth to help clean her up.

"Before we get too comfortable, I'm going to get us cleaned up. Stay here," I say before pressing a kiss on the top of her head.

Once I walk into her bathroom, I dispose of the condom, hydrate, and dampen a washcloth. Making my way back to her bed, I see Charlie's eyelids are getting heavy.

"Here, let me clean you up, sweetheart. Then I'll settle you into bed before I head out," I whisper.

"Can't you stay?" Her voice is quiet with a whisper of vulnerability.

I'm stunned. She wants me to stay with her? Is she sure?

"You sure you want me to stay?"

She becomes more alert now. "Unless you have somewhere else to be, get your ass in bed and hold me, dammit. Don't make me ask again."

Assertive. I like it.

Looking down at her, I shake my head and smirk. She is such a spitfire, even when she's exhausted. Before I get into bed, I clean her up and bring her a glass of water. When I step into her room, she's already sound asleep. Setting the glass on her bedside table, I make sure her phone is plugged in and charging. I walk over to the opposite side of the bed, pull back the sage green covers and crawl under the soft sheets.

It's been a long, *long* time since I've spent the night with a woman.

Do I give her space?

She did tell me to hold her. Maybe she changed her mind?

As if she could sense my thoughts, Charlie lazily takes my arm and drapes it over her side. I cuddle up closer to her with her back to my front. My nose is buried in her hair as I drift off, inhaling her citrus scent and listening to her soft breathing.

SUNLIGHT BLAZING through the window wakes me up the next morning.

Holy shit. When was the last time I slept that well? I open my eyes, completely groggy and disoriented, having zero idea where I am.

Where are my glasses? Why is my arm numb? How come Frank didn't wake me up? A stir next to me shakes me back to reality, and then it hits me.

I'm in Charlie's bed.

Internally, I'm giving myself a fist bump. Externally, my body is fully aware of the naked woman tucked into me.

"It's too early. Put it away, Finn," she mumbles into her pillow. Suddenly, she jolts, realizing I'm in bed with her. She abruptly turns to face me, eyes wide and confused. "You stayed."

I look at her, utterly perplexed. "I stayed."

"Why?" Her eyes narrow, as if I'm up to something.

Running my hand through my hair, I start to chuckle. "Uh, because you asked me to last night and there was no way in hell I was turning down that offer."

Her speculative eyes are drilling a hole into my soul. "Why?"

My head tilts. This whole interaction is leaving me very confused. Does she not know how incredible I think she is? Or that any man would be lucky to fall into bed and spend the night with her? Or how I desperately hope she reciprocates my feelings because she's ruined me for everyone else?

Before I can reply, her eyes zero-in on the small tattoo on my inner bicep. She looks up at me and arches a single brow.

"Huh. You have tattoos? Wow." She gives me an approving nod.

"A couple." I smirk. "This one is the Rebel Alliance symbol." I pause, noticing her confused look. "That's Star Wars." I pull the cover back, revealing the one on my upper thigh.

One drunken night in college, my buddies and I thought it was a good idea to get tattoos. Now, a sleeping Snoopy is permanently branded on me.

She rolls her lips, biting back a smile. "Such a nerd. And how did I not notice the Snoopy thigh tattoo?"

"I don't know, Charlie. You seemed a bit preoccupied last night." I grin.

A hint of amusement crosses her face and I can sense her mustering a clever remark.

So, I beat her to it.

For extra dramatic flair, I clear my throat. "Look, just because I look like I watch the Discovery Channel every night doesn't mean that I'm a complete nerd."

"Wait, do you?"

"Do I what?"

"Watch the Discovery Channel every night."

"I plead the fifth." I pause, then quickly change the subject. Grabbing my phone, I hold it up to her. "Would you look at the time? We should probably get going. Can we stop by my place before we head downtown? I need to get Frank. He's probably taken over the house already . . . also after I drop you off, I'll grab you some breakfast super fast. Sound okay to you?"

Her eyes soften. "We?" she says that single word so softly

I can barely hear it over the chirping birds outside her window.

I reach my hand out to cup her soft cheek. "Yeah, Charlie. *We*." My thumb gently strokes her soft skin, feeling her cheeks plump as she smiles faintly.

"We should probably get ready then. I bet the lovely people of this town are *ecstatic* that you aren't at your café right now to serve them coffee." She grimaces, sarcasm evident in her voice.

Yikes. I definitely forgot about that part. I'll make a mental note to myself to not check my shop's Yelp reviews in case there's a pissed off customer. Sucking in a breath, I nervously run my hands through my hair. "Fuck. Okay. Good point. Mind if I use your shower?"

"Yeah, go for it. You'll smell like oranges though since I don't have any other kind of shampoo." She shrugs.

I breathe out a laugh. "What a hardship that is." My tone is sarcastic, which gets another smile from her. I stare at her for a beat longer until she shoos me out of bed to go get myself cleaned up.

Chapter Thirty-Three

CHARLIE

I'M SO LATE.

It's been hours since the store opened, and I have about fifteen missed calls from Marnie. Stumbling into the store in a frenzy with Vera by my side, Marnie glances up from the counter and gives me *the look*. Her *You were clearly up to something and didn't tell me and, for that, I'll make your life a living hell for the next seven hours* look.

I'm not making eye contact with her because you don't look directly at Medusa or you'll turn to stone. Stealthily, I make my way to the back office when a body appears in the doorway, blocking my way.

"So, Charlotte. How was your night? Hmm?" She has her arms crossed over her chest.

Does she know? She couldn't know. Could she? How could she know? Panic must be written all over my face because she laughs villainously.

"How was it?" she inquires.

I swallow thickly. "How was what?"

"Don't be coy. It's not a good look on you."

I slap my hands to my side. "How the fuck do you know?" The pitch of my voice jumps to a new high while she laughs even harder.

"Well, funny story, actually. I stole your phone while you weren't looking one day and turned on your location since sometimes you like to go AWOL."

My jaw drops. I'm not sure if I should be impressed by her hacking skills or furious due to the invasion of privacy.

Marnie continues, despite my bewildered expression. "When I saw you weren't here, I checked your location and saw you were home. I assumed you were exhausted since you often don't sleep well. Being the lovely and generous friend that I am, I decided to get some coffee for myself and a tasty little treat for you. Figuring you had a tough night and needed something to turn your grouchy little frown upside down. But, I didn't anticipate that our beloved, small town coffee shop would also be closed. After that, I connected the dots. Decided that you didn't need a treat to make you smile since . . . well, by the looks of you right now, I'm sure you got a *very special* treat last night."

The way this woman's mind works is downright terrifying. At the same time, it's impressive. How could you be angry at someone with this level of detective skills? You can't.

Finding my voice, I squeak out, "Have you thought about a career with the FBI?"

Marnie waves her hands at me, brushing me off. "Nah. This is only an extracurricular activity. Now. You need to tell me everything, and I mean everything. Did hot professor Finn give you a lesson? Did he have to reprimand you for bad behavior? Please say yes. What *is* under his slutty sweater vest?" She looks at me with hopeful eyes and clasped hands, her stream of consciousness making my head spin.

I let out a deep sigh, making my way to the front of the store to put the closed sign up. Before I get there, the man of the hour walks in. And, as if this situation couldn't get any more awkward, Finn walks up towards the counter, acting as though everything's normal. My stomach's a queasy pit of anxiety because Marnie has a wicked gleam in her eye, and her mouth is curved up on one side.

"Well, good morning, Griffin! You look well-rested this morning. Sleep well last night?" Marnie beams.

Finn looks utterly confused, and I would simply like to die —potentially pay my parents an early visit.

"Hey, Morticia," Finn says slowly. "I brought you your usual and something new for Charlie." He hands me a drink and a pastry.

Marnie waggles her eyebrows. "Yeah, I bet you brought something new for Charlie. You little devil, you." She clicks her tongue, giving him a mischievous grin.

You've got to be fucking kidding me.

Finn's eyes dart right to me, and I lift my hands in defense. "I said nothing! Marnie is part witch," I say quickly. "Thanks for bringing us coffee. How's the shop this morn-ing?" I ask, trying my damndest to change the subject.

"Did you thank him last night, too?" Marnie says, egging us on.

Oh my fucking god.

I'm going to kill her.

"MARNIE!" Finn and I both yell in unison. I cover my face in my hands, shielding myself from mortification while

Finn takes off his glasses, pinching the bridge of his nose. True to form, Marnie takes off to the backroom, cackling like the shit disturber she is.

———

After the horrifying encounter earlier, the rest of the day went by without too many more comments from my teasing best friend. Although I lost count of how many times Marnie called me a "Little Gremlin Minx."

Breathing a sigh of relief, I sit back in my office chair and slump down. It's late. Very late. It's almost midnight and I'm still at the shop. My heart feels incredibly heavy because, in about ten minutes, it'll be my birthday.

My first birthday without my parents. My first birthday without my dad singing "Happy Birthday" off-key. My first birthday without my favorite funfetti cake.

The wave of grief is about to come crashing ashore any second now.

Vera senses the impending doom and practically crawls into my lap.

"You're not a lap dog anymore," I groan. But Vera doesn't care that she's borderline-crushing me. All she cares about is giving me the love I need at this tough moment. My hand absentmindedly strokes her fur as I watch the seconds go by with a chest full of anxiety.

The clock strikes midnight, and the tears that I so desperately tried to suck back into my eyes are now falling freely on top of Vera's head. She begins to lick my face, catching any stray tears with her floppy tongue.

"Okay. Okay. Enough. I don't need a bath right now." I sniffle as Vera keeps licking my face, and I let out a giggle.

Our moment is interrupted by a soft tapping at the store door. Vera gives out one loud bark, which is shocking, considering she normally only ever groans. Lifting Vera off of me, I grab my trusty golf club and make my way over to the front of the store.

Slowly approaching the door, I see it's Finn and Frank. He smiles when he sees me and looks at the golf club.

"Again? Don't you know by now that it's always me?" His voice is muffled by the glass door, and I roll my eyes.

Unlocking the door, I usher them inside. "What are you doing here at midnight? Is everything okay?" I look up at him, then glance down at the box in his hand. My brows furrow as my eyes trace back to him again.

"Happy birthday, Charlie." Finn opens the box to reveal a funfetti cake.

My birthday cake.

The cake I never thought would be made again for my birthday.

Uncontrollable tears begin streaming down my face.

"Oh no. Oh god. I'm so sorry. Did I fuck up? I fucked up. Dammit," he says. "Charlie, I'm so sorry. I just thought—"

I interrupt him, shaking my head. "These aren't *Finn messed up* tears." My voice cracks. The weight of grief that was crushing my chest moments ago has now been replaced with a comforting warmth and a deep appreciation for the man standing before me. Clearing my throat, I look back up at him. "Thank you. So much," I whisper, my voice trembling with overwhelming emotion. My heart feels so full that I'm surprised it hasn't burst.

He knew I needed this. Knew I needed *him*.

I wipe my eyes with my sleeve and sniffle when Finn digs

into his coat pocket, once again, pulling out a tissue. And, once again, I eye him suspiciously.

He tilts his head, giving me a tender smile. "It's clean, you little weirdo."

I huff out a laugh at his term of endearment. Taking the tissue, I dab the corners of my eyes as I motion for him to follow me to the front counter. "Did you bring—"

"Forks? Of course I did. I'm not some kind of animal . . . that is . . . unless you want me to be?" he replies.

I turn around, looking at him wide-eyed.

"Too soon?" Finn grimaces. "Yeah, probably too soon," he murmurs under his breath while looking at the ground.

He's nervous tonight, and honestly, it's quite cute. The tips of his ears are tinged with pink, and his hand is anxiously running through his wavy hair. Yet, he still finds a way to make flirty little remarks that get a rise out of me—even though that rise is usually an eye roll and a shake of my head. An incredibly unladylike snort escapes, and I cover my mouth in embarrassment.

"You snort when you laugh? How did I never notice that?" he bellows with excitement. "Damn. You keep getting better, don't you?"

Finn places the cake on the counter, takes off his long wool jacket, and pulls out a stool. As he sits down, Finn removes his glasses and carefully wipes them off with the hem of his navy blue sweater vest. Trusting that Finn won't be able to notice without his glasses on, I take the opportunity to admire his handsome features. The way his hair effortlessly falls across his forehead, how his eyes crinkle at the corners every time he smiles, and the charming dimples on his cheeks all come together to make him irresistible.

It's my birthday after all. I deserve to ogle a guy who looks like he stepped out of my nerdy professor fantasy.

"Whatcha thinking about over there? You're looking a little flushed, sweetheart." Finn's voice shocks me out of my thoughts. His eyes, which look larger and more blue without the shield of his glasses, bore directly into me.

Clearing my throat, I pull a stool out and sit across from him. Finn opens the box, removes the cake, and sets it between us. Pulling out two forks, he hands me one and gives me a devastating smile. My heart is about to flutter right out of my chest.

I have never felt like this before about anyone.

This feels different. It feels good.

"Cheers," he says when we clink our two forks together. "Birthday girl first." He winks.

Hesitantly, I sink my fork into one side and take a bite.

Once again, I feel my eyes begin to mist over. I'm transported back to the memory of every birthday with a funfetti cake. Finn did good—no, Finn did *great*. Swallowing the bite, I look up at him and give him a soft, approving smile. His shoulders sag in relief as he takes a bite. We sit there quietly, eating cake, and simply enjoying being near one another.

Finn's the first to break the silence. "If it's too difficult, you don't have to tell me, but I would love to hear about your parents. I mean, they must've been pretty kickass if they raised three kids—especially one that I'm particularly fond of —and ran this incredible store."

His eyes dart around the shop, taking everything in, from the plants hanging off the ceiling to the tables filled with tiny succulents and huge tropical floor plants, and to the lush, green vines crawling over every available countertop.

For the second time tonight, warmth and appreciation for

Finn settle in my heart. No one really asks me about my parents anymore, which stings in a way that only people who have lost someone can understand. It's as though once they're gone, people don't feel the need to bring that person up again. I get happy when someone asks me about my parents, because I love sharing stories about them.

In a way, sharing their stories makes me feel like they're still here.

A smile tugs at the corner of my mouth, recalling memories of my parents. "They were pretty amazing. They had free spirit souls. My mom and dad were high school sweethearts and got married as soon as they graduated."

Finn's eyes bulge. "Wow. That's incredible."

I nod. "Both of them were a great example of what true love looks like. Sure, they fought like every couple does, but it never lasted more than twenty minutes, at which point my dad would always crack a joke to make my mom laugh." I set my fork down and anxiously fidget with a random piece of receipt paper. "They taught my siblings and me to be strong and independent, but also to be empathetic and loving at the same time. They emphasized the importance of being unique and authentic. And taught us how crucial it is to embrace ourselves—flaws and all, because that's what makes us special. Because that's what sets us apart in this world." His warm hand encloses mine to stop me from fidgeting, and I look up at Finn with tears pooling in my eyes.

Since my mom and dad died, I've recognized the importance of all the lessons they ingrained in my siblings and in me. There's a fire in my belly to carry on their legacy through their store, because this is all I have left of them. For me, it's physical proof that they actually existed. It's proof that they were once here. In some weird, witchy way, I hope they see me here. Every day I come into this store, I try to apply the values and morals they instilled in me to keep their memory alive. The people of this town loved them—truly, wholeheartedly, deeply loved them. And for good reason.

I glance up at Finn, and he stares at me with so much intensity and genuine interest that I can't stop myself from talking more about them. It feels so good getting all of this off of my chest.

So I continue. "The people of Hemlock loved them. They were the type of people who would drop off food at your doorstep if you were sick, compliment a stranger if they noticed they looked sad, and volunteer at the community center with what little free time they had. At one point, my parents took in three stray cats and four goldfish because a friend two towns over was moving out of state. My dad hated cats." I huff out a laugh as I wipe a fallen tear from my eye.

Finn starts to chuckle. "Wow. They sound like amazing people. And they raised three people with the same integrity and kindness they had, which is exceptionally admirable." He pauses for a moment to collect his thoughts. "We need more people like that in this world."

I solemnly nod. "Yeah." My quiet voice cracks. "They were taken too soon. They died a week before Christmas last year. A car accident. A reckless driver ran a red light and then—"

Finn's hand tightens on mine as I choke back a sob.

"Charlie. Don't. You don't have to continue." His words are tinged with sorrow. Finn looks at me knowingly while stroking my hand. Unspoken words of comfort and safety pass between us as we sit across from each other. His hand around mine pulls me back to the present and away from that horrific day.

"Charlie, we have to finish this whole cake before tomorrow. You know that, right? It's the birthday rule. You have to eat your whole cake on your birthday." He shrugs, breaking the tension.

Instead of replying, I take my fork and dig into the cake, grabbing a big bite. I might as well eat up since nothing temporarily cures sadness like a sugar high. The tension in my shoulders eases, and I feel infinitely lighter. Smiling as I chew the colorful cake, a thought hits me. For the first time in a long, long time, I feel safe—emotionally, physically, and mentally. All thanks to the long-limbed man with piercing sapphire eyes sitting across from me.

Brick by brick, Finn was demolishing my walls—crumbling them into unrecognizable dust. Although some bricks took more effort to knock down than others, Finn wasn't intimidated by the challenge.

In fact, he knocked them down with a smile on his face.

Chapter Thirty-Four

Finn

I hate baking.

Cooking? Easy.

Baking? It took me seven attempts to make a semi-edible cake and, even then, I had to call my dad for help. Every time Frank heard me open the flour container, he'd hide under the table.

Even my dog was concerned about my baking skills.

The evening walk where Charlie told me about her funfetti cake birthday tradition will forever be etched into my memory. How her face fell when she told me the story made my heart shatter into pieces. At first, I wasn't sure if baking her a cake was even a good idea; I didn't know if it would be too painful for her. Deciding to risk it, I spent a whole week baking test cakes until 2 a.m. to get it perfect for her. And by perfect, I mean semi-edible. Could I have bought one? Sure. But with Charlie, I strongly suspect that the sentimental act of

someone making a homemade cake is so much more important than the actual cake itself. Watching her now, eating all
the sprinkles off of the top layer of the cake, makes those late
nights and a sink full of dirty dishes completely worth it.

"So . . ." Charlie's looking down at her fork, weighing her
words carefully. A pale flush appears on her full cheeks.
"When are you making me dinner? Unless, of course, this is
dinner?" She still hasn't made eye contact with me, which I
find so utterly adorable that I can't help but smirk.

"First, you consider cake dinner?"

"All the time, actually." She shrugs.

Interesting. I'll make another mental note of that.

"What are you doing Friday night?" I ask.

Charlie sits up and sucks a breath through her teeth.
"Yikes. You see, I have this Friday ritual with this really tall
guy. We walk and talk at night."

Biting back a smile, I look at her and tilt my head. "Hmm.
Is he hot, at least? If not, you should ditch him and let me
make you dinner." I go back for another bite of cake. Damn. I
didn't do a half-bad job on this cake.

"He's okay looking. You're much cuter." She sighs.
"Yeah, I think I'll ditch him."

"This is the cringiest conversation I think we've ever
had." I laugh.

Her giggle fills the quiet room. "The worst. I tried to be
flirty and failed. Flirty doesn't fit me." She inhales, shaking
her head at herself. "My exes would get upset that I wouldn't
flirt with them. They would say, 'You're making it too difficult for me to figure out if you actually like me or not.' It was
always a pain point for me."

Bunch of fuckers.

I shake my head and scoff. "Amateurs. The seasoned

professionals know the best women are the ones you have to work for. Like coming into their plant store multiple times a week just to drop off drinks they despise when they explicitly told you they hate coffee . . . for example." Clearing my throat, I glance up at Charlie. "I'm not speaking from experience or anything."

Her arms are crossed as her chocolate eyes assess me with a slight smirk on her face. She rolls her eyes at me, her signature move that I can't get enough of. It's her way of saying, *You annoy the shit out of me, but I think you're cute and charismatic, so I'll tolerate it.*

"You know that every time you roll your eyes, it only makes me want you more, right?"

Her cheeks turn pink as she bites back a smile for a brief moment. "You have such weird turn ons." She laughs, shaking her head. "All right, fine, Friday it is. Your place or mine?"

"Mine. I have no idea where all the stuff is in your kitchen, and I don't want to make an ass out of myself the first time I'm trying to impress you."

Her gaze softens when she reaches to hold my hand. My hand feels so large in comparison to hers, as if I'm holding something so fragile, and I don't want to shatter it. "Finn, you've impressed me in more ways than I think you realize. I don't think you could screw anything up, even if you tried. Trust me."

Hearing those words come out of her envelops me with relief. My shoulders relax as I replay her words in my mind again. For weeks, I've been trying my damndest to show her that I can be someone she can rely on. Tonight, I finally got a sliver of confirmation that what I've been doing just might be working. Even though the future is unknown for us, it won't stop me from proving to her that I can be someone she can depend on no matter what.

I can't help it, I'm falling for this girl in a way that I've never felt before. There's this need inside of me to protect, take care of, and shield her from anything that could harm her.

"Um. I have another question," she says, shaking me out of my thoughts.

"Of course. What's up?"

She's fidgeting with her fork and rolling her lips. "No. Never mind. It's dumb." Charlie takes a big bite of cake and chews it thoughtfully.

I cock my head. "Absolutely not. Spit it out, Thorne." She stops chewing and looks at me. "No, not the cake, you little weirdo. Spit out what you were going to say," I say in amusement.

Still chewing, she makes a dramatic swallow and then sighs. "On New Year's Eve. . .there's this wedding—"

Hell. Yes.

I'm trying to contain my excitement, keeping my face neutral yet attentive. If she says what I think she's going to say, I will have to work hard not to run around the store like a champion who just won their first gold medal.

"—we did all the greenery arrangements and I got invited to it and I can bring a plus one."

My head moves up and down slowly and thoughtfully. Charlie's eyeing me, hoping I get the gist of what she's saying.

"A plus one? That's nice. Are you taking Marnie?" I ask. My fork digs into the cake for another bite. I'm trying to act as calm as possible.

"Well. No. I was wondering . . ."

I swallow my bite, looking at her with a smile, wanting to explode with excitement. "Yes?"

Her cheeks go crimson as she drops her head in her hands. "Ugh. You're going to make me formally ask you, aren't you?"

My smile breaks, and a chuckle releases from me. "Oh yeah, sweetheart. You aren't getting off easy this time."

Needless to say, I'm enjoying every second of this. It's cute how nervous she's getting for someone who, I'm sure, hates weddings.

And plus ones.

And socializing in general, now that I come to think about it.

I hear her mutter *fuck* under her breath.

"I mean, I'm not sure if fucking was part of your plan, but I won't say no." I shrug just as she looks up at me. Her head tilts back, and she laughs. It's one of those full-on belly laughs that is infectious to anyone in a five-mile radius.

Her smile beams at me. "Okay, that was clever. I'll give you that. Fine, you win." She pauses before speaking again, her doe eyes gazing into mine. "Finn, will you please be my plus one at the wedding?"

"Yes, of course," I say.

"That was the most painful thing I've had to do in a while," she says.

I suck in a breath. "Watching you struggle to get those words out, it did look tough. I'm proud of you. I'd give it maybe a seven out of ten? An eight if I'm feeling generous. That seems fair."

"Rude." She laughs before taking another bite of cake.

"Yeah, but you like me," I quip.

"Now, now, don't get too ahead of yourself there." She points her fork at me and winks.

Being with Charlie is as easy as breathing. We don't feel the need to impress one another or hide our true selves. We talk without worry or fear of judgment.

In the quiet of the night, it's just us, sharing our flaws and strengths in equal measure while admiring one another for all that we've endured in our lifetimes.

THE WEEK GOES by in a complete blur. With the Thanksgiving holiday around the corner, Dark Side Brews has seen a significant increase in customers. I've never been so tired, nor have I ever taken so much ibuprofen.

It's Friday, which means I finally get to make dinner for Charlie. Yesterday, when I dropped off a hot chocolate, I asked her if she had any aversions or food allergies that I should know about. The last thing I need is to send her to the hospital because of a peanut allergy I wasn't privy to. I close up the shop early, sending the baristas home so I can head to the grocery store and grab a few last-minute items for tonight. With Frank by my side, we lock up and make the short walk down the block to A New Leaf. Frank, of course, bolts down the sidewalk ahead of me and runs head-first into Charlie's store sign. There's a loud crash, and I jog up to my derpy dog as I frantically try to fix the sign.

"What the hell!" Charlie comes sprinting out the front door. "Oh. It's just you two." She breathes a sigh of relief.

I look up at her. "Frank got a little excited and decided to make a break for it," I sheepishly shrug my shoulders, slightly embarrassed by my dog.

"Have you gotten his hearing checked?" she questions.

Charlie's eyes follow me as I rise to my feet. I went from looking up into her eyes to looking down into her eyes . . . and her shirt. She's wearing a green checked flannel today with the perfect number of buttons left undone. Damn, I love being tall.

She clears her throat. "I have eyes, you know." She arches one brow at me.

I feel a rush of warmth rise to my cheeks. Yes, I've seen her naked. Yes, I've felt every inch of her body.

But I still get embarrassed every time she catches me checking her out. "Uh. Yes. Hearing? The dog. Right."

She shakes her head and clicks her tongue. "Men are such simple creatures. Give them an inch of cleavage, and they start short-circuiting," she mutters under her breath.

Running my hand through my hair, I finally compose myself. "Yes. He's been checked twice, and the vet says he has selective hearing." I give her a quick shrug.

"I can see that." She gives Frank a scratch on his head before tucking her hands into the pockets of her apron. "Well, I better get back in there. Want me to be at your place by seven?"

"Actually, I was wondering if I could drop Frank off with you for a couple of hours? I'll come by and pick him up. I have a few errands to run—"

"So now you're using me for dog-sitting services? Low blow, Griffin." She shakes her head.

"I. Uh. No. Sorry, that's not—" I panic—full on panic as I feel a bead of sweat trickle down the back of my neck.

Her face goes from serious to amused in less than a second. "You have got to relax. I was kidding. I would love to have him here." She crouches down and gives Frank's face a big squeeze.

He's loving the attention. He needs a positive female role model in his life, and I'm happy Charlie is filling that void for him. Lucky dog.

"Oh, and don't worry about picking him up. I'll take Frank home with me and will drive both dogs over when I see you tonight," she reassures me as she rises from the sidewalk.

"Are you trying to steal my dog, Miss Thorne?" I say, taking a step forward. We are so close that I can practically feel her breasts brush up against my chest.

Her brows knit together, and that cute vertical wrinkle appears. I really hope Marnie was joking about Charlie getting Botox because I love the way her brows furrow.

"Unless you trained Frank to drop his bowl off in front of me when he's hungry, then no. Your chaotic dog is coming back to you tonight."

Fuck. I just remembered something.

Taking off my glasses, I pinch the bridge of my nose. "I forgot to mention that Frank stole a couple of your plants and dropped them off in front of my shop."

Slipping my glasses on, I look down at Charlie, who's looking at Frank.

Charlie drops to the ground again and carefully holds Frank's furry face. "You. Little. Thief. You stole that money tree? Didn't you?" She pauses, sighing. "I get it. Those do look like oversized sticks." She rises up from kneeling by Frank and smoothes down her apron. "As much as I would love to stay out here and talk, I have to get back inside. There's one pissed-off customer saying that my plant gave all of her plants fungus gnats. I don't even know what those are, so I need to do some quick research and pretend to be an expert." Her rosy cheeks puff out as she exhales a large breath.

I snicker, imagining the hundreds of tabs that must be open on her laptop, all trying to get to the root of the plant problem. *No pun intended.*

"You got it. See you at seven, sweetheart," I say, smiling at her. She starts to head back into the store when I yell, "Wait! You forgot something."

Confusion washes over her face as I walk back to her. The moment I reach her, I take my index finger, wrap it around one of her overall straps, and pull her body against mine. My lips gently claim hers in a soft kiss, and I feel her body relaxing against mine.

"Okay. That's all," I murmur against her plush lips before stepping away.

Her flushed face wordlessly nods, and I smile down at her.

Before I turn to head back down the street to my car, I wait for her and Frank to get safely inside the store. It's a routine at this point. Any time before I leave, I have to make sure Charlie is safely inside, wherever she is, for her own safety and for my own peace of mind.

My heart swells in my chest as she gently leads Frank into her store. She looks down at him, whispering soft words to the blind pup, who is loving all of the attention.

It's impossible not to fall head over heels for this girl.

Chapter Thirty-Five

VERA AND FRANK are so in love that I'm not sure if I should be envious of their relationship or disgusted by it. I'm just about to close the store and the lovebirds are still cocooned into one another, snoring peacefully as they have been all afternoon. I can't tell where one dog ends and the other begins —that's how close they are.

Pulling my eyes away from the giant fluff ball, I shuffle my exhausted, aching body to the front of the store to lock up for the night. Glancing outside, large water droplets pelt against the pavement. A small thrill runs through me because it looks like we're in store for another rainy night in Hemlock.

So many people love sunshine and bright cloudless skies. I, however, love stormy weather. It's so peaceful and calming. Plus, there's no better feeling than being stuck inside on a dark, rainy night while wearing your comfiest and coziest pajamas.

I speed-clean the store, getting everything prepped for opening tomorrow. As I'm wiping down the counters, a realization crashes into me at full force.

Is this an official date with Finn? What am I supposed to wear? Should I go home and shower?

I swiftly type out a message to Finn, hoping for some clarity.

What should I wear tonight?

FINN

Is this a trick question?

No. A totally reasonable question.

FINN

Well, if I had my way . . . *winky face*

Sweatpants and parka it is. See you soon!

FINN

Whatever you're most comfortable in is
perfect.

Also, whatever you think would look best
on my bedroom floor . . .

Oh god. What am I going to do with you?

FINN

Hopefully, a lot of things.

If you know what I mean.

I can feel your eyes rolling from here.

Goodbye.

Setting my phone down, I run my hands through my long hair and tie it up in a clip. With a deep exhale, I take one last look around the store to make sure I didn't miss anything. Wrapping both leashes around my wrist, I hustle the dogs out of the store's back entrance. We all sprint to my car, hoping to avoid getting too wet from the chilly rain. Pulling out onto the dark, damp, empty Main Street, the three of us head home to get ready for the night.

ONCE WE ALL get home safely and into the warmth of my house, I take a quick shower so I won't smell like dirt and foliage. Since my hair will probably get wet again from the downpour outside, I just leave it to air dry. But I do add a little bit of makeup to my face so I don't look like a brain-starved zombie. I throw on an oversized charcoal gray cardigan over my soft blue flannel. Then I slip into my most comfortable black jeans and sexiest green rain boots to finish off the outfit.

"Well, this is the best I can do. He's seen me with a wrinkle patch on my face, and I still got laid," I say to myself as I walk downstairs and whistle for the dogs. "Dogs! Let's go for a ride!" Both dogs come skittering to the front door, ready to head out with their tails wagging and tongues out.

Out of nowhere, I get the jitters. Intrusive thoughts start clouding my mind—*What if I'm not good enough for him?* It's funny how failed relationships can alter your perception of yourself. Logically, I know that my exes were assholes. Irrationally, my brain tells me it was my fault that the relationships failed, and that something must be wrong with me—that I have to change who I am to be loved.

I try to block out the negative thoughts during the quick

car ride over to Finn's house. As soon as we pull up, he's already got the door to his home open, waiting for us with an umbrella. I turn off the car, and suddenly Finn is right next to me with his umbrella in tow. My expression of surprise must be clear as day, because he looks at me and starts laughing.

When I open the car door, he says, "I couldn't let you get wet before our first date. That's being saved for after *dinner*." He looks at me with a mischievous smile and winks.

My eyes snap to him. "Really? Now, of all times, you whip out an inappropriate joke?"

He winces. "Sorry, sorry. It was good, though, right? Kinda fits the weather theme?" I shake my head at him. Still laughing at his terrible joke, he says, "Take the umbrella and get inside. I'll grab the dogs."

I don't question him as I head towards his house, and he follows me with the dogs in tow. Once I step inside, I slide my boots off at the front door and take in my surroundings.

His place has the same warm lighting as it did on Halloween, and his living room has such a cozy and romantic atmosphere that I immediately feel relaxed. Soft music is playing throughout his home while the smell of roasted chicken surrounds me. Deep within my bones, I can feel that this is going to be a good date.

Which is such an unusual feeling for me. I always think the worst is going to happen and I like to have time to prepare for it. I'm a passive pessimist to my core.

"Holy shit! It's getting worse out there." Finn opens the door behind me as a blast of cold, damp air sweeps over me. Both dogs come in, shaking off the rainwater, looking like two drowned rats.

"They won't smell good tonight," I say, looking down at them.

"Absolutely not," Finn replies. "How about all four of us head to the kitchen and not stand in this cramped entryway . . . Not that I don't like being in cramped spaces with you." He winks teasingly.

Feeling a smile tugging at my mouth, I roll my eyes and make my way to his kitchen.

I like that we have a fun back-and-forth. He'll say a cheeky remark with a wink, and I reply with an eye roll. He doesn't find it annoying. He doesn't tell me to stop rolling my eyes—he accepts and enjoys my personality.

More than anything, I think he likes it.

I abruptly stop when my feet hit the threshold of the kitchen, soaking in all of his hard work for tonight's dinner. Finn's kitchen is beautiful. Off-white cabinets with iron hardware surround stainless steel appliances, and the butcher block kitchen island is what dreams are made of. The rich wood countertop pairs exceptionally well with the Edison bulb chandelier above.

"Oof!" Finn runs into me, almost knocking me over. My back is pressed to his front as he wraps an arm around me, steadying me. "Listen, I will take every opportunity to touch you, but I also don't want any casualties tonight." He chuckles, quickly kissing my temple before releasing me to open the refrigerator. "Can I get you anything to drink? Water? Wine?"

Why does it always feel weird when someone asks you what you want to drink? "Uhh." I awkwardly walk over to the kitchen island and pull out a chair.

"Diet Coke?" He cocks a brow, glancing at me over his shoulder.

"That. I will have that. How did you know?" I ask, slightly confused.

"Sweetheart, whenever I visit you, I always see a Diet

Coke can . . . or three hiding away somewhere on your shop's counter." He flashes me a grin. "I'm a very observant man, if you haven't noticed."

Oh, I've noticed, all right.

"Do you want it in a can or in a glass with some ice?" he asks me.

"The can. The tin can adds flavor."

Finn pops the top on a can and slides it across the counter to me with a wide smile, his dimples on full display. "Such a little weirdo," he murmurs.

I lift the can to my mouth, about to take a sip. "Yeah. But you like it."

In a quick move, he spins around and leans back against the counter. Folding his arms across his chest, Finn fixes his intense gaze on me through his tortoise-shell glasses. The admiration swimming in his eyes when he looks at me makes me feel like the most special person in the world.

"I do. I like it a lot, Charlie." His voice is gentle and reassuring.

It's at this moment that I understand—Finn accepts me. Finn likes me for who I am. We've only known each other for a couple of months, but I've spent more time with him than with anyone else since moving back to Hemlock.

Except for Marnie. She's my fifth appendage at this point.

Finn turns, his back is now to me as he cooks something on the stove, humming a soft tune as he does. A towel is thrown over his shoulder, a sight which has no reason to be as hot as it is. This is also giving me the perfect view of Finn's ass. Which is a great one. I've never been an ass girl, but here I am, objectifying this man as if it's an Olympic sport.

"You're quiet over there, Charlie. You checkin' out my

ass?" He casts a quick glance over his shoulder with a devilish smirk.

I mean, I might as well own up to it. "Do you have a secret glute routine?" I take another sip of Diet Coke.

His back is still turned to me while his stare is fixated on the stove. "Ha! Yeah. It's called lifting an Australian Shepherd every morning and night on and off the bed. He's fallen one too many times. Now I just lift him so he doesn't injure himself. My arms and ass reap the benefits, I suppose." Finn shakes his head, a small laugh escaping from him and causing his shoulders to shake.

I think my heart just liquified in my chest. As if I'm not falling for him already, his incredible dog parenting skills may have sealed the deal.

"Alright," he says, turning around to face me and rubbing his hands. "Are you ready to try the most mediocre meal you'll ever eat?" His eyes sparkle with amusement.

A surprised laugh escapes from me. "I'm sure it'll be amazing. I mean, it smells amazing. Plus, I'm sure it'll be better than what I usually scrounge up for dinner."

A puzzled expression flashes on his face. "What do you usually eat for dinner?"

"Well, I've been eating grilled cheese for the last"—I check the calendar app on my phone—"three weeks?"

His face drops with mild disappointment. "Woman." He shakes his head. "Okay, if you don't get food poisoning tonight and if you don't absolutely loathe my cooking, I'm making you dinner more often." He pauses, putting his hands on his hips as my eyes widen. "And no, this doesn't mean you have to eat dinner *with* me. I'll just drop it off for you." He shrugs, turning away from me as he pulls the chicken out of the oven.

"Uh. Why would you just drop dinner off and not stay?" I question.

He doesn't look at me as he's preparing our plates. "Because, Charlie, sometimes you get peopled out—from my understanding, at least."

"How . . . how do you know that?"

He turns to me, setting a perfectly plated meal of chicken, potatoes, and green beans in front of me.

"Like I said, I'm an observant guy. I notice a lot of things about you." He gives me another one of his devastating winks, paired with a playful smile. I'm stunned but in a good way, because this reaffirms that Finn accepts me and all my little eccentricities.

Finn pulls a chair out to sit across from me at the kitchen island. We both look at each other in silence for a brief moment, a smile tugging at our lips. The kind of smile that says so much without saying a single word. The type of smile where you could read each other's thoughts.

Tonight, it's safe to assume that we're both feeling grateful that a clumsy, blind dog ran into my store at the most inopportune time and brought us together.

Chapter Thirty-Six

FINN

CHARLIE WAS PRACTICALLY silent throughout dinner, which put me on high alert. Countless questions raced through my mind because I was hoping we could talk more. After dinner, Charlie insists on helping me clean up, despite me telling her to sit back and relax. We're standing at my kitchen sink, side by side, shoulders touching like it's second nature for us, and a thought passes through my mind: I could definitely get used to this. A life where we have dinner together every night, watch mindless TV, and complain about the dogs snoring too loudly. That is the life I want—a life I never imagined myself having. Because, after all these years of drifting and floating from one destination to the next, I've always felt unsettled. And now, with her by my side, I finally feel something inside my chest settle.

Maybe home isn't a place. Maybe home is wherever your person is.

And maybe, just maybe, Charlie is my person.

My heart constricts in my chest with excitement and worry. For over a decade, I've felt directionless. Now, after only a few months in Hemlock, I find myself wanting to plant roots here. When I moved back to Oregon, I figured I'd start small with a coffee shop and eventually open a larger location in Portland. But now? I just want to be anywhere Charlie is. Since meeting the woman standing next to me, I can say with the utmost certainty that I haven't felt alone. Not once.

Elbow deep in dish soap bubbles at the sink, I glance down at Charlie, who is staring out the kitchen window as she dries the roasting pan. Her gaze is distant, with her mind elsewhere.

I wonder what she's thinking about? Seeing her soft face and unfocused eyes brings me back to reality as my own worries begin to settle inside my mind. Does she feel what I feel? Can she sense the connection we have? Or is she thinking that this is a one-and-done thing?

I'm falling hard for her, and the last thing I want to do is scare her off, but I've got to know what's going on in her mind.

Scrubbing a pot anxiously, I keep my eyes on the bubbles in the sink.

"So . . . whatcha thinking about over there?" I glance over at her, my voice shaking. I'm worried that she doesn't feel the same way. Worried she'll think that I'll eventually drift away from her.

But I know, deep in my soul, that nothing could be further from the truth.

Still drying the pan, a deep sigh breaks free from her lips. "Do you think all birds go south in the winter? Or do you think a few species go into something akin to hibernation?

The temperature has really dropped." Her gaze hasn't moved from the window, looking outside like she's entranced by the darkness.

The pot I'm washing slips from my grip and splashes into the sink, spraying us both with soapy water. I erupt in laughter, and Charlie looks at me like I've lost my mind.

"Do you know how deep in thought you looked? I was worried about—" I shake my head. "Never mind. I definitely didn't expect that to be what you were thinking about."

"What?" Her brows knit together, looking at me, perplexed. "Do you not worry about our bird friends? How thoughtless of you." She clicks her tongue, smirking at me. Spinning on her heel, she turns to set the dry pan on the counter and then proceeds to soak up the water splatters on the kitchen counter with the towel. "Uh, you said you were worried? About what?"

Picking up another dish, I scrub it slowly, taking the time to figure out how to respond to her question. My head tells me to change the topic, but my heart yells at me to be truthful with her. The dish slips out of my trembling hands, splashing water on both of us . . . again.

"Whoa!" She wipes her forehead with a towel. "Are you okay?" Her hand finds my bicep, giving it a gentle, reassuring squeeze.

"Sorry. I'm sorry. I'm just—" I anxiously rub my wet hand through my hair, which was a dumb move because now I have bubbles in my hair. Turning to her, I rest my hip on the sink, drying my hands off. I'm so nervous, you'd think I've never spoken to a woman before. "I . . . Do you . . . You feel this between us, right? Like, I'm not imagining things?" Heat from my chest reaches to the tips of my ears. I shyly look down and then back up at her.

I can't believe I'm about to ask this.

"Do you like me?" Burning heat shoots from my chest to my cheeks.

I should've written her a note that says, *Check yes or no if you like me because I like you, and there are perks to dating me!*

When those big brown eyes soften, and a gentle smile appears on her face, I feel my head go fuzzy and my heart rate speed up. Charlie reaches toward my forehead, pushing a stray lock of wet hair away from my face, and cups my cheek with her soft hand.

She sighs. "Finn, of course, I like you. How could anyone not like you?"

Nuzzling my cheek into her hand, I close my eyes. "Yes. But . . . that's not what I—"

"I know what you meant." There's a lightness in her tone of voice. Almost borderline amusement. "Finn, I am, as you know, the worst with words. Which I'm trying to be better about. It's a frequent topic of conversation with my therapist."

My eyes snap open with surprise. "You talk to your therapist about me?"

Dropping her hand from my face, she chuckles and leans against the counter, mimicking my pose. "Oh yeah. You're a hot topic every week. She loves hearing about the adventures of Charlie and Finn." She pauses. "Those are her words, not mine, by the way."

"I figured. We can workshop the title at a later date."

"But, as I was saying, yes, I like you. Yes, I like spending time with you—"

My shoulders drop. "But you like spending time alone more—"

She places a delicate finger over my lips, stopping me

from speaking. "Yes, I like being alone, with my own company," she says, before taking a deep breath. The pause she takes before continuing is taking ten years off of my life and giving me an extra twenty gray hairs. "But, even more so, I find myself wanting to be alone *with you*. And only you. Maybe both dogs in small doses. Mostly just you, though." Her finger drops from my lips. Turning away from me, she grabs a towel and starts drying another dish. "Just don't make a big deal out of it or anything, okay?" There's a playfulness in her voice, matching her cheeky grin. She looks up at me out of the corner of her eye, giving me a reassuring wink.

Clearing my throat, my mock-serious tone does little to hide my excitement. "Yes. Of course. No big deal at all. None. Nada."

She gives me her signature eye roll, accompanied by a soft laugh. My chest squeezes.

Yes, I could definitely get used to a life like this, with her by my side.

After the dishes are done, we settle down on the couch in my living room. Charlie's lounging in one corner while I'm on the opposite end. Her legs are stretched out, draped over mine like this is our normal nightly routine. My palm runs slowly up and down her leg as we talk about anything and everything.

"You know what I hate?" she blurts out.

"Knowing you, probably a lot of things," I joke, and she throws a pillow at my head. "I deserved that," I add, adjusting my now very crooked glasses.

"You did. But also, yes, you're right, there are many things I hate. But lately, I *despise* dress shopping."

Smirking, I decide to test my luck again. "For the wedding? Or is there another guy you're trying to impress?"

Charlie sits up but, before she can grab the other pillow, I quickly snatch it and throw it across the room. Nodding thoughtfully, I murmur, "Weapons of choice are golf clubs and pillows. Noted. I'll keep that info tucked away."

Her head tips back in laughter as she leans back on the couch. Dark hair splays across the cushion, and Charlie has never looked more beautiful. Completely relaxed and at ease, she is utterly breathtaking.

"Sorry, sorry. Dress shopping. Do you want me to help?" I ask her, still casually rubbing my palm up and down her leg.

"Ugh. No. I hate going in-store to shop. So, I ordered a bunch online. I found one that's acceptable. Now I have to return the rest and I just can't find the time." She sighs.

"Want me to return them for you?"

"Huh?" She sits up again, giving me a questioning stare.

"Let me return them for you." I shrug. "I have to run a few errands anyway. I don't mind making an extra stop."

Her large eyes look at me in disbelief. "O-okay. Yeah, that would be great. Thank you," she says before flopping back down on the couch. "You don't have to do that for me, though."

I take off my glasses, setting them on the table. I'm tired of sitting beside her and ache to be closer. When I move to drape my body over her, she laughs softly and opens her legs, letting me comfortably settle in between them.

"Charlie, I want to do it. Okay?"

"Okay," she whispers.

Charlie's soothing hands thread through my hair while my head lies on her chest. The steady beating of her heart could lull me to sleep. If I were to die right now, this is how I would want to go. I groan into her chest, directly between her full breasts, wanting to live and breathe in this moment forever.

"You good down there?" she asks playfully.

"I've literally never been better," I muffle into her flannel shirt. When I lift my head to look at her, she gives me an adoring smile. "Actually, I can think of something that would make this better."

"Oh? What's that?"

"Oh, I think you know." I arch a flirtatious brow as I slowly begin to unbutton her flannel. My cock begins to harden as I slowly reveal more of her smooth skin and lace bra with each button I undo.

Confusion washes over her face. "Uh, no. Actually, I don't. What would make this better?"

I shoot her an incredulous look. "Charlie, you're actually killing my game here." She's still looking at me, utterly confused. I drop my head and exhale before looking up at her again. "Christ, woman. Get upstairs, take your clothes off, and get in my bed."

"Sorry! I'm not good with subtlety!" She laughs.

"Obviously," I retort. "We'll have to work on these subtle cues. I'm trying to be smooth, you know."

With both hands, Charlie grasps my face, and her deep eyes stare directly into my soul. "You don't need to try to be sexy. You already are."

This woman.

She says she's not good with words but always knows the right thing to say at the right time. Every word she says has intent and genuineness behind it. Charlie speaks with purpose. She won't tell you what you want to hear. She tells you what you need to hear at that exact moment.

Before I get off of her, I capture her lips with mine, kissing her deep and slow. My hand grasps the side of her neck before my tongue dips inside her mouth, eliciting a soft moan from her. Her parted legs wrap around my hips tightly as she pulls me down even closer to her. The slow kiss turns passionate and feverish. Hands grab at one another's clothes, teeth nibble on each other's lips, and breathless moans consume us.

"Upstairs," I rasp. "Now." Her chest is heaving while her cheeks are flushed with lust. She simply nods, licking her tenderly swollen lips.

By the time we've tumbled onto my bed, our clothes are strewn all over the house, and we're a tangled mess of limbs. Our lips are hungrily searching for flushed skin while our frantic hands are pulling each other's warm bodies closer. Shared breaths quivering with desire are the only sounds echoing in the quiet, dim room. I pull back from her and Charlie whimpers at the loss of contact.

"One second, sweetheart," I say before I drop to my knees before her. "I have to make sure you're ready for me first." With a single swipe of my tongue up her center, she cries out, gripping my hair and pushing my face into her more.

I love it when she takes control like this. Nothing makes me harder than this woman getting what she wants.

I keep working her with my tongue, occasionally sucking her clit before inserting two fingers into her and curling them, reaching for that perfect spot that makes her legs buckle.

"Fuck. That feels so good," she pants, grinding herself into me with unabashed fervor.

"Take everything you need, Charlie. Use me," I urge, my voice thick with desire.

Charlie's moans fill the air as she reaches her peak. I can feel her release building inside of her as she writhes against my mouth. She uses me until she comes undone on my tongue in a shuddering release. Now, all I can think about is how desperate I am to be inside her.

I grab a condom from the nightstand, using my teeth to tear open the package and slide it on. Kneeling above her, I trap Charlie beneath me with my arms on either side of her head. My eyes fall to the rapid rise and fall of her flushed chest as she revels in the aftermath of her orgasm.

Lost in her beauty, I look down at her, taking in Charlie's pink cheeks, bright eyes, and upturned lips.

I absolutely adore this woman.

Claiming her lips in a possessive kiss, I gently take her plump bottom lip between my teeth. "You ready for me, sweetheart?"

Those big brown eyes look into mine with a desired plea. "Please."

All it takes is that one word and I sink into her. Her legs instinctively wrap around me, my cock pulsing inside her. Charlie's breathy moan fills the room as I drop my head to the crook of her neck, groaning at the feel of how warm and soft she is beneath me.

Buried deep inside her, my thrusts start out slowly but Charlie grabs my hips, encouraging me to quicken my pace. We're suspended in this dreamlike moment with feverish kisses, moans of pleasure, and soft whispers of encouragement. *Don't stop. You feel too good. Your body was made for me. You're perfect.*

As her legs lock tighter around my hips, she pulls my body in closer. The heat of our bodies only intensifies the desperate need we're both feeling. My muscles flex as my cock slides deeper inside of her, savoring every sensation. I glide my hand down to brush my fingers over her swollen clit, rubbing soft circles. Charlie's back arches off the bed, and her lips part and cheeks flush in anticipation.

She's almost there.

I can feel her pussy clenching around my cock, pulsing with desire as she moans. My fingers never leave her clit as her body shudders, letting the pleasure consume her as she falls apart. A surge of heat shoots down my spine, my body trembling as we move in perfect rhythm. I bury my face into her neck, reveling in the way she feels.

Every sense is heightened to new extremes. Her wet heat, soft body, and whimpers overwhelm me in the most intoxicating, alluring way. My lips press up against that tender spot behind her ear with force, breathing in her skin like I need it to survive.

With her name on my lips, I come harder than ever before, leaving me breathless.

I will *never* be able to get enough of this woman.

Chapter Thirty-Seven

CHARLIE

IN THE WEEKS since dinner at Finn's, I've been at his place almost every night. We walk the dogs, eat dinner, and sometimes watch a movie or read. There's an easy stillness between us when we're together. We'll casually glance at each other every so often and give the other a soft smile that says so much without having to say anything at all.

This new routine with Finn brings me a sense of comfort that I haven't felt in a very long time. When I'm with Finn, it feels like my brain can power down for just a moment—I can finally breathe easily again. The weight of the world no longer causes that crushing, aching feeling in my chest.

"Excuse me, ma'am?" a voice asks. "I have a question about this pothos . . ."

Jolted from my thoughts, I apologize profusely to the customer and answer her question, then give her a ten percent discount on her pothos purchase for having to endure my daydreaming on the job. With December's arrival comes a new wave of people bustling around the shops of Hemlock. The holiday crowds are by far the busiest and the most stressful, with everyone rushing to find unique local gifts for their loved ones. Though this is supposed to be the most wonderful time of the year—a dark, heavy feeling lurks on the horizon.

The first anniversary of my parent's death.

A delicate hand touches my shoulder, shaking me from my reflections. I have got to get it together today, or I won't last through this holiday season if I keep zoning out like this.

"You okay, lil' Gremlin?" Marnie questions, her warm blue eyes softening.

"Yeah." My voice is tinged with sorrow. "My mind just feels weighed down." I rub my hands down my face, paying special attention to my sleepy, unfocused eyes. A tension headache is looming. I can feel it.

The bell above the door chimes, and I groan. It's not even noon, and I need this day to be over like yesterday.

Marnie peers toward the front of the store, her eyes narrowing and then relaxing with recognition. "I got this, Grem. Head to the back and take a breather," she says with a salute.

My slumped shoulders and heavy heart drag me back to the office, but before I can sit down, I hear Marnie and Finn whispering.

When did Finn come into the store?

"Got it. Yeah. Okay. Jesus, you're scary," Finn whispers.

Marnie threatens, "You fuck this up, I'll end you. I'll burn every last one of your slutty little sweater vests. Got it, West?"

Fearing for his life, Finn replies, "You could've just ended with 'you'll end me.' What did the sweater vests ever do to you?"

Do I have the energy to deal with this right now? Definitely not. Am I going out there anyway because I'm nosey? Duh.

My clogs scuff the floor as I slowly approach the front counter. Marnie's pointing a finger at Finn, and Finn looks like he's seen a ghost. They both freeze with wide eyes when they see me.

"I have many questions, but I'm not sure I want the answers," I say with skepticism.

Marnie's blue eyes narrow at me. "How much did you hear?"

My eyes go wide. "You threatened the slutty sweater vests."

"I won't apologize for that."

"It would be out of character if you did."

Finn interjects, "Can we talk about why my sweater vests are slutty? I kind of like this topic."

"No," Marnie and I say simultaneously, our eyes narrowing at Finn's devilish smirk.

He gives a quick nod. "Noted."

A few customers begin filtering into the store, and Marnie walks over to help them, leaving Finn and I alone.

"Here you go," he says, handing me what I assume is a hot chocolate. "Oh. I brought these, too." Finn pulls out a small bag of mini marshmallows from his coat pocket. "You know, in case the ones that I already added in aren't enough." He winks.

It's a mystery how he does it, but sometimes he just knows what I need, when I need it. Like the time he returned my packages or stopped by my house to walk Vera when I was too tired. Sometimes, he'll even leave little notes with funny drawings taped to my front door. It's like he has a sixth sense for my emotions.

"How did you know I was needing this?'

A shy smile creeps across his lips. "I had a hunch." He shifts his weight on his feet, tucking his hands in his pockets. "I—uh, I wanted to ask you something. Twice a month, I visit my grandpa, and I was wondering if you'd like to come with me this time? We can make a whole day of it, get out of Hemlock for a bit." The tips of his ears are beginning to turn pink, which only happens when he becomes shy or unsure.

"I ask for one thing and that's what you propose?" Marnie yells from the front of the store, clearly eavesdropping. She stomps up to the both of us with a huge palm plant in her arms, shaking her head in disbelief.

Finn shrugs, pinning me with a warm smile. He's responding to Marnie, but his eyes are focused on mine.

"I'd like her to meet my grandpa. He's a fun guy, and I looked up to him growing up. I think he'd get a kick out of Charlie." Finn's bashful tone pairs perfectly with the cute blush on his cheeks. How can anyone say no to that? He's so genuine with his ask. If I said no, it would be like taking a toy away from a child.

Visiting Finn's grandpa will most likely be painfully awkward. And I'll probably need an escape plan. But I'm doing this because it'll make Finn happy, and that's important to me.

"Of course." I smile. "I'm not sure that I'll be the best company, but I can try to turn on the charm."

His brows pinch together as he tilts his head. "Charlie, I don't want you to 'turn on' anything. I want him to meet you for exactly who you are. Not some watered-down version of you just to please other people."

I blink a few times, completely taken aback by what he just said.

Speechless, my eyes dart over to Marnie; her eyes are wide and lips are slightly parted with shock. She knows all about my struggles in past relationships. She's heard all the conversations, all the guys who said, *"Can't you be a little more personable, just for one night? I need you to not be so standoffish, you're embarrassing me."*

Then there's Finn, who's asking me for nothing more than to be myself. Marnie gives me a quick, approving wink as she walks back to the office with the oversized palm in her arms.

Staring at Finn, I quickly nod, swallowing down the obnoxious lump of emotion in my throat. "Yes, I can do that."

Those dimples appear when he smiles down at me. "Perfect. We'll talk more about the details tonight. I should get going before Frank starts wreaking havoc at the café. He already stole a bunch of bananas earlier."

Before Finn leaves, I call out to him. "Also, did Marnie tell you to bring this?" I shake the cup of hot chocolate.

Stopping in his tracks, Finn faces me. "How could you say such a thing, Charlotte?" he says just a tad too loud. His hand clutches at his chest in mock offense, then he winces as he realizes that other customers are watching his dramatic performance. Finn takes a few steps until we're face to face again. "That's all me. She just gave me the idea to get you out of town for a day. Which, I hate to admit, is a good one." He pauses briefly, studying me for a moment. The moment feels intimate as Finn tucks a fallen strand of hair from my clip behind my ear. I lightly shiver at his touch as his thumb gently grazes my cheek. "Sometimes I just get a feeling that you need something. Whether it's hot chocolate, a random errand, to walk Vera–you get the idea. A small thing to make you smile or to make your day a little easier. I might not always get it right, but I'll try my best to figure it out."

Okay, so he does have a weird sixth sense. Strange. But I like it.

"I really appreciate it, you know. I might not always say it, but I really do," I whisper.

"I know, sweetheart." Finn places a heartfelt kiss on my forehead, and my eyes fall shut, relishing in his comforting touch. "I'll see you tonight, okay? Text me if you need anything."

Emotions overwhelm me, which he can see written all over my face. Right now, my feelings are out of control; my brain feels like a jumbled word search, where you can't find any words no matter how hard you try.

So I do the next best thing.

I stand up on my tiptoes, pull the lapels of his jacket down to me, and press my lips to his before he leaves to head back to the coffee shop.

<hr>

"Your grandpa is in a throuple?" My voice screeches like a frightened owl. It's safe to say that my jaw is firmly planted on the floor of Finn's SUV. Finn is caught between laughing and cringing as we drive out of town to see his grandpa.

"I'm not really sure it's a 'throuple' per se, because I think there's more than three people in the relationship. Not sure what the right label is. I don't ask questions. Mainly because I don't want to know anything about"—he takes his hand off the steering wheel and waves it in front of him—"all of that. You know?"

My cheeks puff as I exhale. "Fair enough. I wouldn't ask

questions either." I turn my face away from Finn to look at the deep green forest passing us by. We decided to take the scenic route to his grandpa's retirement home, which is a little out of the way, but the drive is beautiful.

After another thirty minutes on the road, Finn turns into the entrance outside of the facility and my eyes practically bulge out of my head. This place is nice. *Very* nice. At first glance, you'd think it was a five-star hotel. I'm envious that his grandpa gets to live in a place like this.

When we get out of the car, I put my hands in my jacket pockets for warmth. Finn takes notice and flashes me a confused expression.

"Give me that," he says, taking my hand out of my pocket and intertwining our fingers together. "Much better. My hand was getting cold, and it needed yours."

A smile spreads across my face as I shake my head in amusement at Finn's cheesy charm.

Finn gives a quick smile to the people working at the reception desk, and they tell him where we can find his grandpa and his . . . ladies. We continue down the hall, up a wide staircase, and enter a beautiful lounge room that is decorated from top to bottom for Christmas. My jaw, once again, plummets to the floor at the scene before me. Sure enough, an older gentleman is seated in a large armchair, surrounded by three older ladies. One lady's hand is gently rubbing the man's thigh and occasionally sneaking dangerously close to an area that is not appropriate for the public.

What the fuck did I get myself into?

As we approach them, I grab Finn's arm with my other hand, my fingers digging into his coat. I keep my shocked eyes glued to the scene before me.

"You owe me your life, Griffin," I whisper out of the

corner of my mouth. "Your entire fucking life. I want my name on your life insurance policy pronto. Got it?"

"Are you planning on killing me or something?"

My head slowly turns to him, pinning him with a threatening glare.

"Give me a week to get my affairs in order and then kill me. Okay?" He jokes, squeezing my hand and dragging me against my will over to the group.

"Can you believe Glenda? That snake. I know she cheated at Bingo. I'm so tired of her playing the dead husband card. For fuck's sake, we all have dead spouses! Ain't nothing shocking," says one gray-haired lady.

"Speaking of shocking, I heard Agatha got caught stealing Glen's Viagra and trying to sell it to that sweet Canadian couple on the second floor," says another gray-haired lady.

I'm in hell. Who did I wrong in a past life to end up here?

Again, I slowly turn to Finn and give him a death stare. He just mouths, "I'm sorry!"

Sorry isn't good enough. Sorry won't save him.

"Finn!" his grandpa Arty yells with excitement. "Oh! You brought a friend! Who is this?"

Finn blushes. "This is . . . uh." He looks down at me with his panic-stricken face. "T-this is my—uh . . ."

Ugh. This is painful to watch. My secondhand embarrassment can only take so much.

"Girlfriend," I blurt out. "I'm his girlfriend. Charlie." I reach out my hand to shake his.

"Nonsense, beautiful girl! We hug around here. C'mere!" Internally, I groan. *Not a damn hug.* At least I know where Finn gets his charm.

Reluctantly, I hug Arty, trying my damndest not to be stiff-as-a-board during the embrace. When I cast a glance at the three old birds, I see that they're all giving me a death glare.

I've entered the Twilight Zone.

Once Arty releases me from his vice-like grip, I look down at the three ladies who want my head on a platter during the early bird special and I blurt out, "Don't worry, ladies, I'm taken." I hike a thumb over my shoulder, gesturing at Finn. "Arty is all yours!"

It's all incredibly awkward, and I'm doubling down on the discomfort by making things weirder. Finn's snickering behind me, and I'm ready to hitchhike home.

This is why Marnie never lets me out in public.

Chapter Thirty-Eight

CHARLIE

I SURVIVED. It was a long, painfully uncomfortable day, but at least I survived.

Finn's grandpa was a character. Shockingly, I can see why he has three girlfriends—not that I would ever admit that to Finn. The ladies gave me "hot" relationship advice to keep my man happy (their words, not mine). It was about as awkward as anyone could imagine.

I'm not sure I can ever look at whipped cream or Jell-o in the same way again.

The drive back was quiet, mainly because I needed to decompress after such an eventful social interaction. Every so often, Finn glanced over at me, gave me a small smile and squeezed my hand, which he had been holding for the entire drive. By the time we pulled into Finn's driveway, it was completely dark outside.

We walk in silence as we approach his front porch and,

when he unlocks the door, two very happy and excited dogs are there to greet us.

Finn drops his keys, phone, and wallet on the entryway table before heading towards the back of the house to let the dogs outside. I'm taking off my shoes and setting my purse down when I see a text message pop up on his phone.

UNKNOWN NUMBER

Hey! I had an amazing time last night. Can we do it again tomorrow? I really want to see you again.

Nausea and panic sit heavy in my stomach. The blood drains from my face as I feel the anxiety creep up from my toes all the way to the back of my neck.

I said I was his *girlfriend* at the retirement home in front of his grandpa. How foolish of me.

Old feelings from my past relationships resurface. My heart feels heavy in my chest, torn between the hurt of the past and the optimism for a better future. The hurtful, damaging comments from years ago still hold a relentless grip on my self-esteem—pulling me into a well of uncertainty and causing me to doubt myself once again.

I let out a dejected sigh.

Of course, I was falling for Finn.

I allowed myself the grace to lower my guard around him, letting Finn demolish all those barriers that I took years to build for protection. I'm not even angry, I'm just disappointed. There's a deep sense of self-inflicted failure sitting heavy in my heart.

With one last glance at the glowing screen, I succumb to my self-destructive behavior, hoping the words will somehow change.

Slipping my feet back into my boots and grabbing my purse, I begin to call out for Vera when Finn slips out of the kitchen and walks to me with the dogs running after him.

"Hey, do you want me to order—oh my god, what's wrong? Are you okay? Did you get hurt?" He comes up to me and grabs my upper arms, trying to get me to look at him. Disappointment and sadness must be etched into every feature of my face, because Finn's looking at me like I'm about to break.

I can't look at him. I feel completely humiliated.

The need for space and fresh air is overwhelming; it feels as if I'm being suffocated with an ambush of emotions from the inside out.

"I have to go," I whisper. Drawing in a deep breath, I collect myself before calling out for Vera again.

True to form, she doesn't listen to me. A simple tilt of her head and an ear twitch are all I get. I'm experiencing so many levels of mortification right now, and I'm about to leave without the damn dog.

"Charlie, no, you don't. What's wrong? You were okay a few minutes ago. Now you're pale and you look panicked. Talk to me."

I make the mistake of quickly looking at him. Concern clouds his handsome features as he searches my heartbroken face for answers.

A humorless laugh escapes me as I shake my head at the situation when his phone lights up *again*.

Finn does a double-take at his phone on the wooden table. "What the hell?" He grabs the device, unlocks it, and rolls his eyes in disgust. "Fucking Dan," he mumbles under his breath.

Dan? Creepy coffee-loving, inappropriate grabbing, Dan?

Then, that blue-eyed gaze is back on me with a sense of

understanding. "I'm assuming you saw these, right?" He takes his phone and shows me the screen.

I sheepishly nod.

"I see." He pauses, a slight smirk tugging at his lips. "I need to come clean because this is definitely not what it looks like."

Here we go. If he says, *We can still be friends!* after he breaks off whatever this thing we have going on is, I'll steal his damn dog.

I'll steal his dog and open up a coffee shop across the street from him out of spite. Feminine rage has officially made its appearance.

Finally, after what feels like a decade long pause, he continues what he was saying. "Lately, I've been getting a lot of weird texts. I think Dan up the street sold my number because I wouldn't give him three extra shots of espresso five days in a row because his girlfriend threatened me if I did. She told me she was going to chop my . . ."—he pauses, shuddering— "You know what? I'm not getting into that." With a light laugh, he shakes his head. "As I was saying, in retaliation, I think he sold my phone number somewhere, and I've been getting these fucking spam messages a few times a day. See?" He shows me his phone screen with a few other messages with similar wording, all with no replies. "It's one of those dumb wrong number scams. I delete and block them. I'm still plotting how to get back at Dan for this." He swipes the message and deletes it. "I think I'll strictly give him decaf from now on. What an asshole."

I drop my head, my shoulders shaking from laughter at the absurdity of the situation. Finn starts chuckling too as we both stand in the cramped entryway.

Finn gently grasps my chin and tips it up to meet his gaze.

"By the way, my password is one-nine-six-two—the year my mom was born. I have nothing to hide from you. Nothing at all, sweetheart."

The amount of anxiety that swept over me in the past twelve hours is enough to last me for an entire year. Coming down from the anxiety rush, I feel my body start to relax with a wave of relief, now that the day is over and now that this little hiccup was shown to be nothing more than a silly misunderstanding. Naturally, I feel my eyes burn with unshed tears because I'm exhausted from everything—today, last week, this whole fucking year. I'm just *exhausted.*

Finn's hands carefully rest on either side of my neck, thumbs tenderly caressing my cheeks. He dips his head, forcing my tear-filled eyes to look at him. The pads of his thumbs smooth across my skin, wiping away any stray tears that have fallen. Finn doesn't pry into why I'm crying. He somehow knows intuitively and comforts me, regardless of the reason.

I begin explaining anyway. "I feel so stupid. This was a dumb thing to get upset over. I'm a grown woman standing here trying not to spiral and crying over the silliest thing. I'm so exhausted from everything."

His brows furrow. "Charlie, stop. Don't minimize your feelings like that. You've had a tough fucking year. Plus, this time of the year is even tougher for you. And this?" He releases one hand on me to grab his phone and shakes it. "You got anxious. It's my job to ease your worries and fears, no matter how large or small they may seem. If it's important to you, it's important to me. Simple as that."

"It's not your job." I sniffle, looking deep into his blue eyes.

"Well, that's too bad. I want it to be my job." He smiles.

"Don't be afraid to share every part of yourself with me. *You're safe with me.*" The way he emphasizes those last words feels as though he's draping an emotional safety blanket over me, providing the comfort and security I need. The earnestness in his voice makes it nearly impossible to fight with him. He speaks with such sincerity and conviction that I have no reason to doubt him.

Finn's comforting hands gently cradle my face. My eyes fall closed as I easily sink into this feeling of safety and comfort. His voice is soft and low as he tries to bring lightness to the situation.

"I mean, why would I be talking to other girls if you're my girlfriend? You said so back at the retirement home." That mischievous smirk of his makes an appearance that makes my knees go wobbly.

I sniffle. "You're going to take advantage of my vulnerability and bring that up right now? I was mortified!"

"Oh, it showed. It was adorable how you stepped in when I faltered. I always knew you could help me fight my battles, partner." He winks. "I'm really loving this team dynamic. Soon we'll start finishing each other's sentences. When do you think we'll turn into that couple that matches their outfits? I give it maybe another three months."

"Oh fuck off," I say with a laugh, as I sniffle and wipe the tears from my eyes with my sleeve.

Finn, as usual, pulls a tissue out of his pocket and hands it to me. And I, as usual, look at him skeptically.

"It's not used, my little weirdo." A soft smile plays on his lips, making my heart beat a little faster. "Now, take off your shoes and coat and sit with me on the couch."

I do as he says and pad over to the couch. Finn's already sitting with his long legs stretched out, and when I go to sit next to him, he pulls me onto his lap, enveloping me in a warm embrace.

"You said sit *with me*. Not sit *on me*," I say, wriggling around to get comfortable. "Your bony knees are digging into my ass."

"I want you close. Sue me." As if just now registering what I said, he remarks, "And my knees are not that bony. Also, you can relax against me. I feel like I have a mannequin sitting on my lap."

I eye him skeptically before rolling my eyes. "I don't sit on people's laps. I'm not a 'lap sitter.'"

"Well, that's a shame because you are one now." Reluctantly, I relax my body as much as I can into his. "There, that's not so bad, is it?" I can hear the humor in Finn's voice.

"Sleep with one eye open tonight, Griffin."

"You've got it, *girlfriend*."

I let out a loud groan while his body shakes with laughter. I'm never going to live that one down.

For a moment, we sit in comfortable silence, which feels as natural as breathing. Inevitably, my turbulent mind decides that it is ready to ruin the peacefulness. A million thoughts are racing through my mind and, in an attempt to better communicate my feelings, I blurt out what I'm thinking to Finn.

"What if you're disappointed by me? What if you find parts of me that you absolutely cannot deal with? What if I'm not enough for you?" I hate that my voice is so unsteady.

Finn's long fingers glide through my hair, sweeping it off my neck with a gentle touch. He then moves his hand down to my back, expertly rubbing soothing circles that feel incredible after my near anxiety attack from earlier.

Finn looks at the ceiling with a contemplative look and a heavy sigh. "Murder."

My voice doesn't hold back from shock. "What?"

"I'm going to murder all those assholes you've dated for putting those awful thoughts in your head." His voice is determined, and his eyes are calculating.

I shift in his lap to face him better, wrapping my arms around his neck.

"I need to pause the big emotional conversation for a moment," I tell him, as I try to figure out how to say what I want to say next without offending him. "Finn, no offense, but I'm not sure a gentle soul like yourself is capable of murder. What, are you going to use the Force to kill them or wave around that lightsaber on your bookshelf?"

"Should we find out?"

"No." I shake my head, sighing. "Of course I would end up with a huge nerd."

"A hot nerd," he corrects me. "Back to the bigger topic at hand. Charlie, you're everything I've ever hoped for, and more. Hell, I'm not even sure I deserve someone like you." His arms pull me closer to him, my head resting in the crook of his neck. Feelings of warmth and security flow over me again like a protective shield.

"I don't think that's true," I say on an exhale. "I'm sure you can find someone who has their shit together and won't keep stealing your pocket tissues for their random crying outbursts."

At that, I can feel him laughing against my cheek. All of my tense muscles begin to relax. Finn's warm body holds me tight, his woodsy cologne surrounds me, and he speaks reassuring words to ease my anxieties. My body feels like it's wrapped up in a secure little cocoon where I can finally *just rest*.

A moment of silence stretches between us before Finn

says, "Just like that night when we first met. I see you." His hand is running soothing strokes up and down my arm.

"What do you mean?"

"I see the person you show your friends. I see the person you show your family . . . and I see the person you try to hide from the world." He pauses, his voice dropping to an almost whisper. "I see *you*, Charlie. In every form. And I want to be with you because you're *you* and no one else."

That renders me speechless and Finn takes notice. He gives me a tender, loving kiss on the top of my head before shifting me over fully onto the couch. One hand goes up to cup my cheek as he gazes into my eyes. "Here's the plan. I'll order us food. You go find some sweatpants, and then I want to see you on the couch with the dogs. Okay?"

Still speechless, I nod in agreement as Finn places a chaste kiss on my lips before striding off into the kitchen to order dinner.

Once he's out of sight, prickles begin to form in my nose as my eyes water. Finn's words take me right back to that late summer evening with my mom on the back porch. Chills run up and down my body and my heart beats frantically in my chest.

My mom was right.

My heart knew before my brain.

Finn stumbled into my life at the most unexpected time. And Finn accepts me for who I am.

Being with Finn is daunting and terrifying, but simultaneously captivating and invigorating. It feels akin to jumping off a cliff and into the ocean. Scary at first, but once you land safely in the water, you're hit with an all-consuming rush of relief and excitement because you tackled your fears with relentless courage.

The scared introvert in me wants to run away. However, the rest of me wants to keep going. I want to keep pushing myself because, if I don't, I'll always wonder *What could have been?* with Finn. I want to discover what can happen if I don't close myself off.

Deep in my soul, I need to know what happens if I open my heart to him. Because being with Finn makes me feel wanted. He makes me feel *loved.* And if all this eventually implodes, then at least I can say forty years from now that I know what true, unconditional, insurmountable love feels like.

The kind of love where a single look is enough to read your mind.

The kind of love where simply holding hands can calm even the worst of your fears.

The kind of love where you can authentically be yourself without fear of judgment.

It's the kind of love that only happens once in a lifetime.

Because, of course, I'm falling in love with Finn.

Chapter Thirty-Nine

Finn

I'm in love with Charlie. If I'm honest with myself—I fell in love with her weeks ago. I've been in love with her ever since she came over to tend to me when I was bedridden with the Hemlock plague. At the time, I thought it was just the fever talking, especially with those wild dreams I was having. But now, I know that was when I fell head over heels in love with the pretty, brunette, plant girl.

I roll over in bed and reach for my glasses on the nightstand. Sunlight has already started to peek through the blinds, which means that it's time to get up and get moving. Frank is still snoring on the bed, and I physically have to pick him up and set him on the ground to get his day started. We're both dazed and confused with exhaustion. I'm sure he and I could sleep all day if we wanted to.

Once we make our way into the kitchen, I open the door and Frank runs outside into the backyard. While he's sniffing around, I grab his breakfast and refill his water bowl. After I set it down, I turn to the kitchen island and sift through my mountain of unopened mail. Checking the time on the microwave, I realize Frank's been out a little longer than usual, so I open the sliding door and whistle for him into the crisp morning air.

Nothing.

I whistle again.

Still nothing.

Typically, Frank is all too ready to eat breakfast and will run so fast that he ends up head butting me in the shins trying to find his way inside.

I whistle once more and that's when I begin to panic.

My bare feet hit the cold, wet grass as my head whips around looking for him. A heavy, sinking feeling drops in my stomach when I run over and see the side gate is open. I run out the gate and into the front yard, looking up and down the street, whistling for Frank.

I don't see him anywhere.

Fuck.

Terror rips through me as my mind jumps to every worst-case scenario. For a blind dog, the world can be a frightening place. My mission is to ensure Frank's life is as comfortable and happy as possible. There's an added layer of guilt settling over me, especially since every night I take his collar off for bed to make him more comfortable.

The collar that has an AirTag on it so that, if he does go missing, I can find him.

But I forgot to put his collar on this morning before he went outside.

Tears burn behind my eyes as fear crashes into me with relentless force.

There's no way I'm able to track Frank.

I run inside my house and grab my phone, dialing the number of the first person on my mind.

"Finn? Is everything okay?" Charlie says, after picking up on the first ring. She must sense something is off, judging by her greeting.

"Frank got out. I don't know where he is. He doesn't have his collar on," I choke out. I'm running my hands through my hair, tugging at the strands in frustration as I pace around the kitchen.

Without an ounce of hesitation, Charlie replies, "I'll be right there. Give me two minutes."

Sure enough, exactly two minutes later, Charlie is banging on my front door. I open it in a haste and she stands before me with messy hair and still wearing her pajama pants. A look of determination is written all over her face and, in true Charlie fashion, she takes charge.

"Get your shoes on. We're finding your dog. I'll be in my car." Charlie turns, stepping off my porch, and hustles over to her vehicle.

The moment I get in her car, before I even put my seatbelt on, she's already backing out of the driveway, tires screeching beneath us.

"Do you have any idea where he could've gone?" she questions, her eyes darting around in between the homes on my street.

I attempt to swallow the lump in my throat. "None. He's never gotten out before. I am fucking terrified, Charlie." I roll down the window and start whistling. Frank's recall isn't great, but he does respond to my whistling more than to the sound of his own name.

When we pull up to a stop sign, Charlie settles her hand

on my knee. "Hey, look at me." My gaze locks on her and she gives me a reassuring smile as she squeezes my knee. "We're finding Frank if it's the last thing we do. Got it?"

My mind is too frazzled for words right now, so I just give her a quick nod before she pulls onto the next street.

For the next twenty minutes, I whistle so much that my lips feel as though they're about to fall off. With no luck finding Frank in the neighborhood, we decide our next stop is Main Street. There was a good chance that he could be wandering into random stores, looking for food scraps, belly rubs, or trinkets to burgle.

All are plausible options that have happened with this pup many times before.

Charlie parks on the street and we both get out of her car. Before I begin walking, I take a few calming breaths to steady my panic. My body feels hot and jittery with anxiety. I'm positive that my heart rate is dangerously high. Charlie comes up to my side and notices my trembling hands.

"Hey, look at me." She steps in front of me, gets on her tiptoes, and cups my face in her palms. Her soft hands feel cool on my hot skin and my eyes flutter close. "We'll find him. I know it's easy to jump to the worst possible scenario, but I need you to hold on to the little sliver of hope that I know is inside of you."

Again, tears threaten to fall. "I just . . . I do everything I can to make sure he's safe. I don't move the furniture around. I scent mark everything, use sound cues he actually acknowl-edges, and keep a steady routine." I shake my head, angry with myself and with my carelessness.

"Finn." Charlie's voice is calm and soothing as her thumbs stroke my cheeks. "You're a better dog parent than anyone I know—" Her words trail off as we both hear laughter from some place farther down the street.

"He's soooo cute!"

"Can I feed him, grandpa?"

"His ears are so fluffy! Can we keep him?"

We both widen our eyes in surprise as our gazes lock. Without thinking, we break apart from one another and sprint toward the voices.

There, in the small park off of Main Street, surrounded by a group of happy people, is Frank. He spins around in circles wagging his nub of a tail, charming the morning parkgoers with his cuteness and earning pieces of their breakfast as rewards.

Every ounce of fear dissipates from my body. I can finally take a deep breath. My chest no longer feels as though it's being crushed by the weight of anxiety and fear. Charlie and I look at one another and smile as we race up to the crowd. As we run, I let out a whistle to get his attention. The crowd turns to us while Frank's ears perk up. The scene unfolding in front of everyone could be straight out of a movie: my goofy dog runs straight into my arms.

I sit down on the ground, ignoring the wet grass and mud soaking through my pajama pants. Frank wiggles with excitement. He's making little squeaks of happiness as I try to hold him close to my chest, but he's too excited to stay still. A few tears fall from eyes onto his soft fur.

"Dude, you can't scare me like that! I was so worried about you!" I sniffle, then bury my face in his neck.

I found him.

No.

We found him.

With Frank happily snuggled in my lap, I glance up to see

Charlie awkwardly talking to the group of people, explaining the situation in seemingly great detail. It makes me chuckle, because she looks so uncomfortable in front of an audience.

Charlie's unyielding strength, calm demeanor, and determination were critical in our search for Frank. If it wasn't for her, I wouldn't have found him as quickly. While I was panicking and struggling to focus, she remained composed. With every reassuring word she spoke to me, a flicker of hope ignited in my chest. Despite the chaos in my mind, deep down, I knew that we would find Frank together.

I've never admired anyone as much as I admire Charlie.

I notice Charlie walking over to us with a relieved smile on her face. She immediately crouches down and gives Frank some ear scratches.

"My man, you cannot give us a scare like that this early in the day. If you do get out next time, can you wait until the afternoon? My bones ache too much to go running around so early in the morning," she says to him, as if he can understand every word she's saying. "Come on, bud. Let's get you home."

THE DRIVE back to my house is short. Charlie pulls into my driveway and turns the car off, letting out a deep sigh. Both of us are silent for a few moments, letting our pulses settle down.

"Who needs caffeine in the morning when you have a lost dog fiasco to kick up the adrenaline?" She laughs, shaking her head in disbelief.

"I've never felt fear like that in my life." I sigh, taking off my glasses and rubbing my eyes.

Frank is panting in the backseat as Charlie and I sit in comfortable silence. Both of us need a quick moment to decompress from the morning's chaos. I feel guilty about needing her help in my search for Frank.

But I needed her and she dropped everything to help me.

A few ideas start bouncing around in my head. Maybe I can take her on a nice relaxing date? Just the two of us. No dogs.

Maybe I can convince Marnie to even babysit the pups? It's a long shot. And she may cast a spell on me. But I'm willing to risk it.

Slipping my glasses back on, I turn toward Charlie. "I was wondering, do you want to see a movie tomorrow? Maybe get some dinner?" I question, looking into her tired eyes.

Charlie's mood shifts. Her face drops and her eyes are suddenly misty with sadness. "I'm sorry, I can't." Her voice is thick with grief. "Tomorrow is the anniversary of my parent's death. My siblings and I are planning a small gathering at the store." A quiet beat passes as Charlie collects her thoughts. "I would really love it if you could join us, though."

A sadness weighs heavily on my chest thinking about the pain this beautiful girl must be feeling. As I look into her sad brown eyes, misty with unshed tears, a million thoughts storm into my mind. I want to wrap her tight in my arms and never let her go—protect her from anything and everything that could harm her. Take every ounce of her pain away.

If she calls, I'll come.

Just like she did for me.

I want nothing more than to be a source of safety and comfort that she can always rely on.

Just like she is for me.

"I'll be there, sweetheart."

Chapter Forty

THE MINUTE HAND on the clock ticks forward, marking the exact moment all our lives changed a year ago. Joey is sitting on top of the store counter, Jack is leaning against it with his arms crossed, and I'm sitting on a stool, resting my chin on my hand. Our eyes are laser-focused on the old-fashioned clock sitting on top of a small cabinet behind the counter, right next to an old picture of my parents from when they first opened the store.

Anyone who has ever lost someone they loved can confirm that the first year without them is the most difficult. It's a rocky ride of trying new traditions, creating new memories, and navigating a new life without them. All the while, you're carrying a deep, heavy sadness that sits in your chest like a rock, trying to make it from one day to the next, hoping that tomorrow will be the day when the weight begins to lift.

On the first anniversary of our parents' death, we all

decided to gather at their store, play a few of their favorite board games, eat their favorite foods, and reminisce about them. Marnie and Finn are joining us soon, but they wanted to give us some privacy first.

"Well, we did it," Jack says to Joey and I. He lays a comforting hand on my shoulder and says, "Mom and Dad would be so, so proud of you. You know that, right? A year ago, you didn't know the first thing about the store, but you've been kicking ass."

I look up at him as he wipes away his tears on his blue flannel. Usually, I hate it when people say, "*Your parents would be so proud!*" But coming from Jack, those words mean the world.

Sniffling, I nod. "Yeah." I swallow a lump of emotion lodged in my throat. Words fail me because this has been such a transformative year for all of us. In my head, I replay the sad, painful phone calls at 2 a.m. with Jack when he was having nightmares, or the moments of holding Joey on her bedroom floor as she sobs so hard that she can barely breathe.

Then there was me. Dealing with my grief with only myself to lean on because my siblings needed me to be their rock. They needed stability and saw that in me.

I didn't plan on becoming the pillar of strength for my brother or sister.

It just happened over time.

Many nights, I would sit on the floor with Vera, all alone, and cry until I passed out with her as my pillow. That poor dog had crunchy, tear-stained fur for about six months.

I could never resent my siblings for relying on me for strength and comfort. At the end of the day, all we have is each other. If one of us falls, we catch them and pick them back up.

Joey hops off the counter and walks over to Jack, giving him a hug. The three of us, with glassy, red-rimmed eyes, side by side, look over at the photo of our smiling parents in a loving embrace. Standing there, we each make a silent promise to continue living a life that they would be proud of.

Even though we aren't the same people we were a year ago, I like to think that we've all changed in positive ways. Because with grief comes transformation. Before, we were carefree and fearless. Now, we're careful and fearful. We've transformed into wiser, stronger versions of ourselves. The shattered parts of us that died with our parents that night have now regenerated into something entirely different.

Those pieces that burned hot and fast in the inferno of grief will eventually regrow. It may take days, months or even years, but eventually, those pieces will sprout new growth. Pieces that can help aid you along in this winding journey. Pieces that give you an unyielding strength to weather any storm that you may endure.

A sense of understanding comes with the hurt and pain of grief. Sometimes, a person's story finishes even though yours is still continuing.

And that's okay.

It's okay they're not there for your entire story. What's important are the countless memories you've shared with them that are now nestled between the chapters. Those memories will forever be dog-eared, like well-worn pages within a cherished book, patiently waiting for you to flip back and reread them over and over again.

The three of us stand in silence, with sniffles being the only noise in the room. Jack's arms are crossed as he walks around, taking in all the lush greenery of the plants. Joey is wiping her eyes, holding the photo of our parents close to her chest. And I'm still sitting on the stool, breathing a sigh of relief. We made it through the first year.

All of us.

We're all caught up in our own thoughts until the door flies open and two rambunctious dogs barrel inside. Our heads turn to see Finn and Marnie holding a stack of pizzas.

Jack gets down on Frank and Vera's level and is immediately drawn to Frank. "Who's this handsome guy?" he asks, giving the pup a thorough ear scratching.

"Oh. My name's Finn."

I'm not sure I can roll my eyes any harder at his lame attempt at a joke.

"You meant the dog . . . that's Frank." Finn quickly recovers. Marnie snorts from behind him.

I close my eyes, pinching the bridge of my nose. Thankfully Jack, being a father himself, understands Finn's bad dad joke and chuckles.

Jack walks over to Finn, and they do the classic bro handshake, shaking hands and slapping each other on the back. "Is this the guy you've been talking about nonstop?"

Oh, that fucker.

I'm going to kill my brother. We all know what he's saying isn't true. He's just trying to tease me after I taught Lucy when it's appropriate to use swear words at school.

Sure, I've casually mentioned to my siblings a couple of times that Finn and I are dating. But they love to make a big deal out of things. Especially if they know it'll make me squirm.

Finn looks over at me with a mischievous glint in his eye. I shake my head from side to side and run my thumb horizontally along my neck in a threat, giving him a clear message that if he so much as dips a pinky toe into Jack's joke then he will not see another sunrise.

Joey walks over to Finn and introduces herself. She walks around him in a circle with her arms crossed, giving him a thorough head-to-toe examination. "Yup. This one will definitely work. He'll keep the Thorne bloodline strong," Joey remarks with a devilish glint in her eyes.

"Yeah, Finn definitely has good genes. He'll make strong Thorne offspring. Tall. Nice hair. High tolerance for surly behavior." Jack slowly glances at me, raising a single dark eyebrow. "Good job, Char." He *winks*. Ugh.

Their strange comments about preserving our family's bloodline fill me with embarrassment. Sometimes I wish I was an only child.

Inhaling deeply, I run my hands down my face in exasperation. Finn has a shit-eating grin on his face, and it's obvious that my siblings already like him. Otherwise, they wouldn't joke around like that.

As much as I hate to admit it, they're good judges of characters, and this is a good sign.

They share a few brief words and laughs before we all sit down at the table that I set up inside the store. Finn and I are sitting next to each other, Jack is at the head of the table, and Marnie and Joey are side-by-side. I glance under the table, seeing Frank and Vera curled up together and spotting something in Frank's mouth that is most definitely not his.

"I think this is yours," I say to Jack, handing over his now damp, wool beanie.

A look of pure disbelief is written all over Jack's face. "How the . . . the dog can't see."

Finn winces. "He's got a strong sense of smell. That's not even the worst thing he's stolen."

"Do I even want to know the worst thing he stole?" Jack questions.

"To avoid implicating you as an accomplice, I think it's best that I keep it between Frank and myself," he replies in a sheepish tone.

Everyone at the table laughs. Jack nudges my knee under the table and shoots me another approving wink. Unlike my brother, my sister takes a less subtle approach. I glance over at Joey. She waggles her eyebrows and gives a quick thumbs up, followed by her feigning a swoon.

Out of the corner of my eye, I sneak a glance at Finn. He's looking down, fixated on the cards of the game we're playing. Knowing Finn, I'm certain he saw Joey's reaction because he's smirking, and the tips of his ears are flushed red.

After we finish the last board game, laughter and friendly banter fill the air of my parent's store. This is exactly what they would want—to fill a mournful day with beautiful memories. With a satisfied sigh, I crack open a few cold beers and pass them around the table.

Long, lush green vines hang from the ceiling, trailing down all around us, while the warm glow of the store's lights wraps us in a cozy atmosphere. Sitting back, I absorb the scene in front of me. Conversation flows easily between everyone. Marnie's laughing at a wild travel story that Joey is sharing, Finn and Jack are talking about the terrible aim of stormtroopers, and Vera is lovingly licking Frank's nose.

As much as I would never admit it aloud, it's nice to have my favorite people all together—sharing laughs, swapping stories, and enjoying each other's company. What was supposed to be a sad day has turned into a beautiful memory. One that I will cherish for the rest of my life. I'm so thankful to be surrounded by a group of people who care about me so much.

Right now, being fully immersed in the present, I'm deeply proud of how far I've come in a year. I now look at the future with optimism and hope. Healing isn't a linear journey, but if I can battle a painful storm like grief, then I know I'm strong enough to handle anything.

———

A FEW HOURS pass and the conversation naturally begins to dwindle. Marnie and my siblings begin packing up to head out for the night.

"So, Finn, got any holiday plans?"

Finn perks up. "I'm visiting my parents for Christmas. My sister, nephew, and brother-in-law are coming to visit too."

Joey gives a contemplative hum. "Huh. I wish I had parents," she says nonchalantly, stifling a laugh.

"*Josephine Iris!*" My brother and I scold her in unison. My jaw nearly hits the ground. Leave it to my sister and her dark humor. I shake my head, staring at her unblinking.

This girl loves to say the most inappropriate things at the most inappropriate times just to get a rise out of people. It's clear why she and Marnie get along so well. They both enable one another.

"Jesus Christ," Jack mutters under his breath. Closing his eyes and pinching the bridge of his nose, Jack lets out a heavy sigh. He turns, looking at Finn with a sincere expression. "Finn, I'm so sorry. I think she inhaled too much glue as a child."

Deciding I've had enough, I force everyone except Finn to

leave. "Alright, everyone out! You've overstayed your welcome!" I assert, shooing them out with my hands.

We say our goodbyes and everyone finally leaves. When I lock the door, I turn and slump against it, completely exhausted from the long, emotional day. Now that I don't have to put on a brave face for my siblings, I can finally let my guard down. Tears well in my eyes, because even though we filled today with good memories, the past still stings. Lingering above me like a heavy cloud.

I wish my parents could've met Finn. They would've adored him.

"I'm sorry I subjected you to all of this tonight." I sniffle. "I know it's a lot, and I promise—"

Finn steps towards me, dipping his head down to meet my eyes. He respectfully interrupts me. "Charlie, stop apologizing. I know what you're going through is painful, so let me be there for you, okay? You want to cry? I'll bring you an endless supply of tissues. You want to scream? I'll buy myself noise-canceling headphones. You want to share stories about your parents? I'll cancel everything just to listen to you speak. It's okay. You can lean on me. *Let me be that person for you.*"

I lift my head to look at Finn. "Thank you for being you," I whisper.

Death is a bitter pill to swallow. But it's important to remind ourselves that parts of them still live within us every day. We find their presence at the most unexpected times in the most unexpected ways. It's their way of letting us know they're still with us.

Even if they're not physically here.

Whether it's their favorite song randomly playing when you least expect it.

The shiver of a cool breeze driving on a wide-open road during a long drive.

Or the company of a charismatic stranger and his blind dog who strolled into their beloved store on a cold, dark night.

A stranger that turned their daughter's world upside down in just a few short months.

Finn pulls me into his arms, and I melt into his embrace, pressing my cheek against his warm chest, comforted by the steady rise and fall of his breathing. With his arms snug around me, he rests his chin on the top of my head. I nestle even closer to him, feeling his strong hold pull me in tighter against his body. The warmth and security emanating from him envelops me in peacefulness. It's as if my mind and heart can finally take a deep breath after a long, tiresome year. His kiss quiets a million racing thoughts, his hugs dull the pain of the past, and his smile makes me feel beautiful from the inside out.

Finn is truly, wholeheartedly, the most special person in my life.

He's irreplaceable in every way.

Chapter Forty-One

CHARLIE

CHRISTMAS FLEW by in an absolute blur. Jack, Joey, Lucy, Vera, and I spent Christmas together at my parents' house. Even though Jack is still renovating the house, he was able to finish the living room just in time so that we could all celebrate there.

Jack takes after my dad. Quiet, yet thoughtful.

Joey left yesterday, headed back on the road ready to explore whatever her next destination is. My sister wanted to stay with me for the remainder of the holidays, but I forced her to leave. I love her so much, but she always hugs me like she'll never see me again.

She takes after my mom—a tender-hearted free spirit.

It's New Year's Eve and I'm frantically making the final adjustments to my outfit before we head downstairs to the wedding reception. We decided to book a room at the hotel that is hosting the reception, because a night away sounded like a magical way to spend New Year's Eve. The room we got in the hotel is beautiful: large floor to ceiling windows, plush white bedding, and even a fireplace. It was so cozy and romantic that I was tempted to skip the reception and spend the evening curled up with Finn, watching a movie and ordering room service.

I shudder at the thought of having to mingle with all those people downstairs at the reception.

Cheerful, mingling people are among the top five things I detest the most in this world.

Followed by slow walkers. But that's a story for another day.

I've locked myself in the bathroom to get ready because, even though Finn has seen me in various stages of disarray, he does not need to see me struggle with a strapless bra. Dresses and my body do not get along well. Thankfully, I found one that I didn't hate too much. It's a floor-length gown in navy blue, with a plunging neckline and long billowy sleeves adorned with vintage gold buttons. The chiffon material flows all around me, revealing a slit that hits my thigh. My hair is styled in loose waves and pinned to one side to complete the look.

Between the deep neckline and high slit in my dress, this was all the sex appeal I could muster.

Taking a final glance in the large bathroom mirror, I mutter to myself, "This'll do." I smooth my hands down the front of my dress, feeling the soft, silky fabric beneath my fingertips. I have to admit, I think I look pretty good tonight, which puts a smile on my face.

When I look in the mirror, I see a different woman staring back at me compared to a year ago. Over the last year, I've been through a lot. So much so that I'd often not recognize the woman staring back at me in the mirror. But now? I finally see *myself* again, after so long. I see the new and improved version of me.

A woman who, despite having been through hell and back, has persevered.

A woman who was strong enough to endure every painful obstacle that came her way and kept her head held high the entire time.

A woman who has dealt with a constant stream of insecurities, who always doubted herself, but now knows her worth.

I see a woman turning over a new leaf.

Even though it's taken me thirty-something years to get here, this version of myself is the one I feel most comfortable in and the one I'm most proud of.

When I look in the mirror, I can confidently say that I love the woman I've become.

"What is taking so long in there? Does the tub drain lead to Narnia or something?" Finn hollers from outside the door. "Oh, shit. Is there a window in there? Did you make a break for it?" he says the last words in a barely audible whisper. I shake my head, softly laughing at his commentary.

I walk out of the bathroom and look down at my watch, mentally calculating the most acceptable and appropriate time to leave the reception without it being rude.

"Okay, here's the plan. It's six p.m. now. We can say our hellos, eat dinner, watch the first dance, and then steal some cake to go. We'll be back here . . . by eight-thirty, give or take a few minutes. Sound good?" When I look up from my watch, Finn is staring at me. His lips are parted, his eyes taking in my body, and a blush is beginning to form on his cheeks.

Finn's eyes sparkle with admiration and satisfaction behind his glasses.

"What?" I question. "Do I look funny?"

I'm fishing for compliments.

Finn takes a slow, tentative step toward me and reaches for my hands. His long fingers thread through mine as he continues looking me up and down.

"You look absolutely stunning, Charlie." Finn's voice is laced with adoration as a slow smile spreads across his face.

My whole body feels like it's been covered by a warm blanket, and I can't help but smile up at him. "Thank you. You don't look half bad."

"Are you kidding me? I look incredible. This suit was custom made because the store didn't carry my inseam." He laughs. "It's a tough life being *Gumby*, you know."

I give an amused eye roll, and he responds with his charming wink that never fails to make my heart race.

"When does the reception start?" he asks.

"Uhh. Right now, actually."

I walk across the room to grab my purse on the couch when I feel the heat of Finn's body close behind me. His hand delicately trails over my arm as his lips caress the shell of my ear. A shiver courses through my body.

"Sweetheart, I don't think I can keep my hands off of you for the whole night," he murmurs, as his fingers trace a line from my collarbone to between my breasts. He lets out a groan of approval when he slips his hand under the fabric of my dress, brushing his fingers over my peaked nipple. Giving my breast a gentle squeeze, Finn's lips gently make their way down the side of my neck. My eyes flutter close as his hands continue to explore my body, intensifying the pressure building between my thighs.

I hate being late.

But I also hate being horny in a public setting. "Fine." My voice comes out in a flustered huff. "Don't wrinkle my dress, though."

"The dress is coming off. I need to see all of you, Charlie." Finn stands behind me, his fingertips brushing the base of my neck as he sweeps my hair to one side, exposing the sensitive skin. He places a soft, lingering kiss on my neck, causing goosebumps to erupt over my body. The warmth from his breath fans over my skin, sending a shiver down my spine. I can't help but lean into his touch.

Slowly, Finn pulls down the zipper of my dress, catching it before it hits the floor. I step out of the dress, left only wearing my bra and panties.

Usually, I'd feel exposed standing here in nothing more than my underwear, but Finn makes me feel beautiful regardless of whether I'm in dirty overalls or completely naked.

His desire for me is all-consuming. He cherishes every part of me—flaws and imperfections included.

Finn hangs my dress up, so it doesn't wrinkle, and I turn to see him unknotting his tie and unbuttoning his crisp white shirt. His lustful gaze burns into me and I match it with equal intensity. With slow, deliberate movements, Finn removes the rest of his clothes.

A spark ignites deep in my chest at the sight of him standing before me in nothing but a snug pair of black boxer briefs, clinging tightly to his thighs, his tattoo in full view. My heart beats fast with anticipation when Finn walks over to me. I take in the sight of him before me. The dim light casts the most delicious shadows over him, highlighting every angle of his lean body.

Finn's hand goes up to cup my jaw and he smiles down at

me before placing a kiss on my forehead. Then he starts exploring my body with tender reverence. With a delicate touch, his fingers trace every curve with the utmost appreciation and adoration.

Beginning at the nape of my neck, Finn places featherlight kisses along my skin. As his lips reach my breasts, he unclasps my bra and lets it fall to the ground, leaving me on display for him.

Another groan of approval escapes from Finn's mouth. "*Fuck.* You are so stunning."

I'll never get tired of hearing him say that.

Eagerly, Finn drops to his knees before me, his lips and tongue tracing the curves of my body. His tongue swirls around my sensitive nipples before pulling one into his mouth. Finn gently nibbles on the tender flesh and my back bows at the rush of pleasure flowing through me.

His mouth moves lower, and I feel myself getting more aroused in anticipation of what's to come. Finn's lips skim over my stomach and just above the elastic of my panties. His fingers dip below the waistband, running them painfully slowly back and forth against my heated skin. I let out an impatient whimper as he breathes out a dark chuckle. After teasing me, he finally hooks his thumbs into my panties and pulls them down.

The intense ache between my thighs is all consuming. I feel like I'm on the brink of imploding. He's so close that I can feel every hot exhale of his breath against my pussy. All of my thoughts are overtaken by the intense need for Finn's touch to soothe the burning desire within me.

"I love how your body responds to me, sweetheart," he says, admiring how aroused I am.

I feel unsteady in the best way possible, having to lean my

body against the wall beside the couch. There's only a few minutes between now and when my knees will surely buckle. His large hands skim over the back of my calves and up behind my knee before lifting one leg and hooking it over his shoulder. Finn presses soft, open mouth kisses on the sensitive skin between my thighs. A gentle nip from his teeth sends an unexpected shiver through me. Arousal floods through my body as Finn's tortuous lips and tongue continue to tease me. Once again, I let out a frustrated whimper and Finn's low chuckle vibrates against me, relishing in my impatience.

Finally, he uses his thumbs to spread me as this tongue takes one long swipe from my wet entrance to my clit. I cry out in relief. Threading my fingers through his soft, wavy hair, I pull him closer to me and rock against him. He hums in approval as his tongue thoroughly works me.

My breaths come out sharp and fast with every stroke of his tongue. The throbbing ache in my core becomes almost unbearable. Every nerve in my body is on fire, begging for release.

I'm thankful for Finn's firm grip on my quivering body because when he seals his lips around my clit and sucks, I feel myself about to collapse. I press my head back against the wall, letting out a satisfied moan.

As Finn works my body, my eyes snap shut, and my grip tightens on his hair. I rock my hips eagerly against his mouth, desperately chasing my orgasm.

"Don't stop. I'm almost there," I gasp.

I feel Finn groan with satisfaction against me, which ulti-mately sends me over the edge. He slows his pace, savoring every moment as my limbs tremble beneath his touch. Finn takes his time, drawing out my orgasm and wringing every ounce of pleasure out of me.

Pulling back, he stands to his full height, looking down at me with pure lust.

"We're not done yet," he says hungrily. Finn leads me to the front of the couch, spins me around, and has me kneel on the cushions with my back towards him.

I'm staring outside through the large window behind the couch, admiring the beautiful view of the dark night sky and mountains in the distance. I hear the crinkle of a condom wrapper before feeling the heat of Finn's body behind me. He takes my hair and wraps it around his fist. Gently tipping my head up to his face, he claims my lips with a soul consuming kiss. When he pulls away, his intense gaze peers deep into mine.

"Please," I whimper. "I need you."

An appreciative groan escapes from deep in his chest. He swipes the head of his cock through my arousal, pressing it against my clit a few times, causing me to shudder. With one hand on my hip, Finn eases himself all the way into me and lets out a guttural moan. Once his pelvis is flushed against me, I know I've taken all of him.

My fingers grip tightly onto the back of the sofa, desperate for something to hold onto as the overwhelming feeling of him deep inside me takes over. I arch my back, letting out a pleasured moan. Every inch of my body tingles, longing to be consumed by this man for the rest of my life.

I can feel his body trembling as he bends to nuzzle into my neck. "Fuck. You feel incredible," he rasps. "You're it for me, Charlie."

Those words give me a euphoric high. *You're it for me.*

The feel of his body moving against mine makes my head spin with pure bliss. As he thrusts into me, his hands glide down the curve of my spine. Each affectionate touch of his fingertips ignites a trail of fire on my skin.

Our erratic breaths fill the room, both of us completely entangled in this moment of pure lust. Finn quickens his pace, each thrust more eager than the last. As if we aren't already close enough, he pulls me back, pressing my back into the front of his body. The heat of our bodies now melding together as one.

One hand roams over my curves before gently squeezing my breast, while his other hand settles between my legs. With two fingers, Finn begins circling my clit. The wave of pleasure makes my head tip back on his shoulder.

"Fuck," I whimper, my eyes fluttering shut. The sensation is almost too much, too overwhelming.

I'm addicted to it, though, because I'm completely lost in Finn.

I feel like I'm drowning in pleasure, desire—and *love*.

His head dips down near my face. "Look at me." His voice is deep and gruff in my ear.

So I do.

I turn my head to meet his ocean-blue gaze. He gives me a sexy smirk and then kisses me senseless, completely taking my breath away.

That kiss sends me over the edge as I come completely undone and cry out his name louder than I anticipated.

"That's my girl. Let everyone know who's making you feel this way," he rasps in my ear.

It's only moments before I feel Finn pulsing inside me, with his own release taking over his body.

Both our chests are heaving, and our bodies are seconds away from going limp.

I'm about to pull away before Finn grabs me tightly

against him. He nuzzles against me, still panting. "I'm never letting you go, Charlie. Never."

My lungs feel completely devoid of air, my head is in the clouds, and I'm blissfully happy.

I truly, deeply, and wholeheartedly love this man with every cell in my body.

And I'm never letting him go, either.

Chapter Forty-Two

Finn

We missed dinner completely but were able to catch the cake cutting. There was no way that I could sit through the entire night with Charlie looking so stunning. The moment she stepped out of the bathroom in that dark navy blue gown, it took every bit of restraint in my body not to rip the dress right off of her. I wanted nothing more than to spend the rest of the night in our hotel room with her naked and my head between her thighs. I am hoping we can skip out on the reception early and sneak upstairs for round two.

Both of us are standing near the back of the venue, watching the newlyweds' first dance. I look down at Charlie as she watches the couple twirl around under the twinkling lights. There's a faint smile playing at the corner of her lips. To anyone else, they wouldn't think anything of it.

To me? I know she's happy.

Charlie does a double-take when she catches me staring at her.

"For the love of god, could you stop looking at my boobs for like five minutes? People are going to start thinking you're a creep," she says in a jokingly irritated tone.

"One: I can't help it. They're looking right at me, and they're incredible. Second: You're right, I'll reel it in." I lock eyes with her, sneak one more glance at her spectacular breasts, and bite my lip.

She groans. "Ugh. Griffin! Down boy." She playfully slaps my arm, tipping her head back as she laughs loudly.

Standing beside her, she looks utterly effervescent. There's a lightness to her tonight. Her clear eyes, rosy cheeks, and beaming smile make my heart beat faster.

I *love* this woman.

I started falling head over heels for her the moment she threatened to break my kneecaps that first night I met her.

Meeting Charlie that night was like having the most incredible dream, where you can remember every detail in vivid color. The kind of dream that makes you want to fall back asleep as soon as you wake up just so that you can pick up where you left off. Except Charlie wasn't a dream.

She was here.

She was real.

She was mine.

When I saw her for the first time, golf club in hand and ready for battle, my soul said, *That's the one. Go get her. Proceed with caution, but go get her.*

I glance down at her again, admiring her beauty as I trace her features with my eyes.

Utterly breathtaking.

Once the newlyweds finish their dance, the DJ requests

that all the couples in the room join the bride and groom on the dance floor.

I grab Charlie's hand. "Come dance with me."

Horror washes over her face. "I don't dance. In fact, I don't know how to dance."

Pretending to nod in an agreement, I look at her. "Today's your lucky day, then." Her shoulders drop with relief, thinking she was able to escape this dance.

Oh how wrong she is.

"I do know how to dance. Now, follow me. I know I have long strides and you're a slow walker. Keep up," I joke.

Reluctantly, she follows me over to the crowded dance floor. I curl my arm around her waist, and my hand clutches hers as we begin to sway to the slow, melodic music. Unsure at first, she keeps looking down at our feet, worried she'll step on my toes.

We stop momentarily. My thumb and forefinger grasp her chin, tilting her head up so she's forced to look at me. "Eyes up here, Charlie. I've got you," I softly assure her. "Just follow my lead."

With those encouraging words, I feel her begin to relax in my arms. A quiet moment passes between us where we both sway with the melody, enjoying the warm embrace of our entwined bodies.

I pull our joined hands close to my heart and place a soft kiss on her knuckles. She looks up at me with those big brown eyes, giving me the opportunity to give her a lingering kiss on the forehead. Charlie breathes a content sigh, resting her head on my chest as we continue to dance.

Every moment we've shared, from the first night we met until now on this dance floor, has been laced with a sense of familiarity. Like this is how it's supposed to be—the two of us, side by side, standing together against anything and every-thing. As if our souls were connected in past lives, only to find each other again in this one. It's a feeling that surfaces so infrequently that when you have it in your grasp, you must never let it go.

Because everything that has happened in our lives—from shitty relationships to soul-sucking jobs, catastrophic life fail-ures, crushing grief, and everything in between—has led us to one another. Those moments, whether good or bad, have shaped us into who we are today. Five years ago, if Charlie and I met, we probably wouldn't have been ready for each other.

But our paths crossed at the exact time when we needed each other the most.

A time when we were both figuring out our new lives.

A moment when we needed someone to stand by our side, as we navigated the unexpected twists and turns that come with a third life crisis.

We both had whole lives before meeting one another. Though now, it's hard to imagine my life before I met her. My life that is now filled with crazy dog shenanigans, late-night walks, and hot chocolate dates with extra marshmallows.

A life that I wouldn't want to spend with anyone else. Because the cute brunette who wears oversized overalls and her lazy dog companion are the ones that I want to spend my days and nights with.

The wave of these intense realizations and emotions starts to overwhelm me. Swiftly, I pull Charlie closer against me and hold her tighter, worried that she'll drift away if I let her go. Burying my nose into her hair, I inhale her citrus scent.

I need to tell her how I feel. These feelings can't stay

bottled up inside of me. Is it poor taste to declare your love for someone at someone else's wedding?

Probably.

Fuck it. I don't care.

Charlie must have sensed that something is off because she looks up at me with a worried look in her eyes. "Everything okay?"

"Yeah," I whisper. "Can we get out of here? Go somewhere quiet?"

Her eyes widen with relief. "I thought you'd never ask."

WE WERE able to sneak onto the hotel's rooftop, where the commotion of the loud wedding was quieted to a muffled roar. It's almost midnight, which means it's nearly the New Year. Below us, the party is getting louder and rowdier by the minute.

The deep, inky blue sky stretches above us, dotted with twinkling bright stars. A cold, crisp breeze swirls around us, prompting Charlie to pull her jacket tighter for warmth.

Out of habit, I take my scarf off and drape it around her neck. Looking up at me, she smiles with her cold, pinked-tipped nose and rosy cheeks. We both turn, gazing out into the dense forest and towering mountains before us, which are coated in a blanket of darkness. A few fireworks begin to appear in the distance, signaling that the New Year is nearly upon us.

Quiet hangs between us as we stand next to one another, the sides of our bodies pressed close together.

Ten.

In the distance, I hear the crowd below us begin the countdown.

Nine.

Charlie begins talking.

Eight.

Her eyes sparkle when she describes the new rare plants she purchased from out of state.

Seven.

The corners of her eye crinkle with happiness as she reminisces about the way Marnie yelled at a customer yesterday for accidentally stepping on Vera's tail.

Six.

Her cheeks are touched with pink as she mentions a new book she picked up at the store with a questionable storyline.

Five.

As the gentle breeze tousles her dark hair around her face, I think to myself: I could listen to this incredible woman talk for hours.

Four.

She smells like oranges, and all I can think about is telling her that I love her.

Three

I want to start off this New Year right, and those need to be the very first words that she hears.

Two.

She deserves it. She deserves everything and more.

One.

I can't imagine my life without Charlie, because she makes everything more beautiful in my world.

The crowd below screams *"Happy New Year,"* and fireworks light up the sky. I look over at the woman who has forever changed my life.

"I love you," I tell her, sounding completely out of breath.

My nervous heart beats hard and fast in my chest. As the night wore on, my mind swirled with so many emotions and thoughts. She needs to know that I deeply and profoundly love all her beauties and flaws equally. Nothing she can say or do will change how I feel about her.

She stops mid-sentence—eyes wide, pink lips parted, and chest heaving. For a brief moment, I panic, afraid I misinterpreted our relationship over these last few months.

Her eyes go glassy, and she gives me an adoring smile that quenches all of my fears.

"I love you too, Finn."

With those five words, I grab her face and kiss her. Just like our first kiss, she grabs the lapels of my coat and pulls me closer to her.

Over the last few months, we have found a home in each other's hearts. It doesn't matter where we go, so long as we go together.

With a New Year and a new life together on the horizon, Charlie and I stand with our warm hands intertwined, looking at one another with the utmost love and appreciation.

With a shared smile, we make a silent promise to turn over a new leaf.

Together.

Epilogue

Five years later.

Finn

Standing in the doorway of A New Leaf, I'm admiring the view of my wife with a cute frown on her face and our two-year-old son beaming up at her with unconditional love in his eyes.

Charlie's eyebrows are pinched together as she clips away at the plant in front of her, handing our son Hayden the vines that they'll propagate together later. Her long hair is pulled up, with a few stray pieces framing her face, and she's wearing my favorite green overalls. Our son is dressed like me, complete with a blue sweater vest and messy light brown hair.

They're the cutest duo this town has seen in decades.

And I'm not just saying that.

A few months ago, they were featured in the local newspaper, *The Hemlocker*, and won an award for 'Town's Cutest Duo.'

Charlie hated the recognition.

I loved it, obviously.

I keep the article proudly framed in my office, not only because it puts a smile on my face, but also because it never fails to elicit an eye roll from Charlie.

Just like she was on the night I met her five years ago, Charlie is still the most beautiful woman I've ever seen.

Also, still the grumpiest. But that's ok, it's a turn on.

Every morning, when I roll over in our bed and see her with disheveled hair and rumpled pajamas, my heart beats just as fast as it did the night when I first laid eyes on her all those years ago.

I walk up to the front counter, where Charlie is hard at work and Hayden is playfully kicking his legs, giggling. Below the counter, our cat, Skywalker, is cuddling with Vera and Frank.

Funnily enough, Skywalker adopted us the day after our wedding. Much like myself, the black cat kept roaming into Charlie's store day after day. Eventually, he decided to stay forever.

Kind of like how I met Charlie.

Swiftly, I grab Charlie by the waist, pull her in close, and dip her back while I gently press my lips to hers.

A kiss in public.

She hates kissing in public, but I always try to sneak one in here and there because I can't resist her.

Momentarily, she melts into the kiss before realizing she is indeed in public. Then she makes a noise in protest as I bring her upright.

"You could've dropped me!"

I tilt my head to the side. Still holding her by the waist, I look down into her deep brown eyes.

"Sweetheart, you should know by now that I'll always catch you when you fall." I pause. "Literally and figuratively, of course. But it's a fair concern. You do have the balance of a newborn deer." I wince.

Her eyes widen. She steps over to Hayden and covers his ears. "You're the absolute worst," she teases, a playful smile tugging at her lips. "You're not wrong, though," she admits.

Today, Hemlock is hosting another festival. This time, Hayden and I are in charge of charming the townspeople.

"Come on, little H. Let's get out there and enchant the pants off of everyone. We'll sell so much coffee with our matching sweater vests."

He pouts, and his wavy, light brown hair wildly sways as he shakes his head in protest.

This little guy has been hanging around his mom too much, and it makes me laugh. He looks like me but acts like her, and I wouldn't want it any other way.

Covering Hayden's ears, I whisper to Charlie, "You should have no doubt in your mind that this is your child."

She rolls her eyes at me. Again, it's still a turn on after all these years. "My sister was legitimately almost switched at birth! Can you blame me for being paranoid?"

I tip my head back and forth, agreeing with her. That is her sibling's favorite story to share at family dinners.

Lifting Hayden up into my arms, he giggles, enjoying being so high up. Another perk of being ridiculously tall.

As I walk back to the front of the store, I turn around to look at my wife once more before we head to the festival. I've never admired someone so much in my life. One day, I hope our son inherits her strength, courage, and resilience.

Charlie notices me staring. "What's wrong?" Her eyebrows knit together in concern.

I smile warmly back at her. "Nothing. I just love you, my little weirdo."

Her face breaks into a smile. "I love you too, Gumby."

Acknowledgments

First, I need to give a massive shout-out to my husband for being the best support I could ever ask for. It was a tough road (with lots of tears and doubts!), but you were there every step of the way. Thank you for listening to my worries and wild ideas in the middle of the night.

To my dog Kira, you provided no help, but the side-eye stares were appreciated because they made me laugh.

Thank you to my friends and family, who were there for me every time I doubted myself and wanted to give up—only to talk me off the ledge and keep going. Thank you for answering the late-night panic text messages, listening to me rant about writer's block, reading snippets, and bouncing ideas off of. And thank you for wanting to tell everyone about my book.

To my amazing friends and beta readers, Ada, Brooke, Kat, Lisa, and Wren—there would probably not be a book if it weren't for you all! I couldn't have asked for a more supportive group to help me along this journey. The outpouring of love I've received from all of you has really kept me going.

To my undergrad advisor, Dr. Neal, I'm including you here so you don't revoke my degree. Thank you for teaching me everything I know about writing.

To my mom because if I didn't specifically mention her, I'd be written out of her will. Love ya.

Finally, to my dad. It's been a little over two years since your passing. Although you're not here with me anymore, it doesn't feel right not to include you. I can't tell you how many times I've repeated many of your classic phrases in my mind to keep me going. If it weren't for you, I wouldn't be chasing this dream I didn't even know I had in the first place. So, thank you. I'll see you when I see you.

About the Author

Samm Wilde is a romance author who weaves words into worlds filled with humor and heart.

When she isn't obsessing over word count, second-guessing plot points, or anxiously deciding between synonyms—you can find her lying on the ground with her dog or eating emotional support cake.

Samm writes to remind us all that love, even with all its imperfect quirks, is a feeling worth embracing.

Find her on Instagram @AuthorSammWilde and SammWilde.com